The Love Habit

The
Love Habit

The Sexual Confessions of an
Older Woman

Anne Cumming

PENGUIN·BOOKS

Penguin Books Ltd, Harmondsworth,
Middlesex, England
Penguin Books, 625 Madison Avenue,
New York, New York 10022, U.S.A.
Penguin Books Australia Ltd, Ringwood,
Victoria, Australia
Penguin Books Canada Limited, 2801 John Street,
Markham, Ontario, Canada L3R 1B4
Penguin Books (N.Z.) Ltd, 182–190 Wairau Road,
Auckland 10, New Zealand

First published in the United States of America by
The Bobbs-Merrill Company, Inc., 1978
Published in Penguin Books 1980

LIBRARY OF CONGRESS CATALOGING IN PUBLICATION DATA
Cumming, Anne.
The love habit.
Reprint of the 1978 ed. published by Bobbs-Merrill,
Indianapolis.
1. Cumming, Anne.   2. England—Biography.
3. Middle-aged women—Sexual behavior.
I. Title.
[CT3150.C85A34   1980] 301.41'76'330924[B] 79-20931
ISBN 0 14 00.5331 X

Printed in the United States of America by
Offset Paperback Mfrs., Inc., Dallas, Pennsylvania
Set in CRT Janson

The quotation by Alex Comfort is taken from *A Good Age* by
Alex Comfort, copyright © Mitchell Beazley Publishers, Ltd, 1976.
Used by permission of Crown Publishers, Inc.

To my daughters,
for my grandchildren's education

With acknowledgments to the women in my life:
The anonymous girl friend who suggested it;
Natalia Murray who encouraged it;
Helen Brann who fostered it;
Gertrude Buckman who helped edit it;
and Diane Giddis who discovered it for America.

Let's also never forget the boys themselves
who inspired it.
God bless them all!

✌ Contents

∽ Author's Note

As my friend William Burroughs once said, "Sex becomes a habit, the most difficult of them all to kick." Within the general habit are minor habits, which range from the harmless repetition of favorite pleasures to more dangerous and extreme practices.

Many of my friends have asked me why my lovers are so young, so I have begun to ask myself the same question. I think the answer is habit, and as with many habits I fell into it by mistake. I enjoyed it, and so I continued it. It seems to me harmless, and often beneficial to both parties. It is a little sad, because the end is in sight from the very beginning. There is a built-in obsolescence. I have sometimes asked myself, Is it worth it? Perhaps the young men themselves should answer this. I myself regret nothing and no one. Anyway, readers can judge for themselves. I have tried not to hide anything from them, or from myself.

A. C.

The first step in preserving your sexuality, which for many people is deeply important in preserving their personhood, is to realize that sexuality can be, and normally is, lifelong in both sexes. Sex is a highly undangerous activity. Stopping it unwillingly is far more dangerous to health than a little exertion.

Alex Comfort

The whole point of Camp is playful, anti-serious. More precisely, Camp involves a new, more complex relation to "the serious." One can be serious about the frivolous, frivolous about the serious.

Susan Sontag

The Love Habit

1 ∞ I Couldn't Live Without Them

On December 14, 1966, I decided to give up sex. The occasion was my fiftieth birthday, and I made a public announcement to the hundred and one guests gathered in the Roman apartment of my second ex-husband, who was generously giving me a birthday party.

"I think it's undignified for a grandmother to have lovers," I announced. "I'm giving the whole thing up."

"I seem to remember her saying the same thing at our silver wedding anniversary last year," said my first ex-husband, who was in Rome for Christmas. We usually all spent Christmas together— husbands, lovers, children, wives—an extended family Christmas, so to speak.

I denied Robert's words. "I was only cutting down last year. Thinning them out a bit. I had two grandchildren then; now I have three. It's time I sat back in an armchair knitting."

As if on cue the doorbell rang, and the hundred-and-second guest arrived late, plump and puffing

17

slightly—a dear friend, tremendously witty and slightly malicious.

"What could I give a woman who has everything," he said, "except a little more of what she likes best?"

He pushed forward a young man of transcendental beauty. As Mart Crowley had not yet written *The Boys in the Band*, the gesture was highly original.

"What a pity I've just given up sex," I said sadly. "I can't even unwrap him!"

The young man stepped forward and kissed me formally on both cheeks. "Happy birthday!" he said. "I've never been turned down so charmingly, and by such a beautiful woman. The disappointment is all mine."

"You don't know what you're missing, Anne," said my plump friend. "He has the most beautiful body in Italy."

"Well, I'll just hold him in my arms, then. If my ex-husbands don't mind, I'll have the first dance with him."

Someone put on a record, and the party really got underway; but I did not unwrap the young man that night.

We had a cozy family Christmas around my large oval dining table, and I dressed the tree with the all-silver balls left over from the silver wedding party of the previous year. That had been a lovely party. I had seen no reason not to celebrate a silver wedding to a man so dear to me, even if we had been divorced for the last eighteen years.

When the family had all departed, I took down the tinsel and felt a bit bored. I had several lovers in Rome, and quite a few elsewhere whom I visited from time to time—like my fisherman in St. Tropez or a skiing instructor in St. Anton. I called them my "away" matches, to distinguish them from those I played on home ground.

My local lovers had all phoned me after the party to ask if my announcement had been serious.

"Yes," I replied. "We're all just good friends now. Come around for tea, but don't expect the sympathy!"

By the New Year it was becoming difficult to stick to my resolution to stay at home knitting quietly. Chastity was not one of my habits. Adventure is engraved on my heart. I am an explorer of humankind.

On New Year's Eve I went to a party at the new home of my plump friend and met my unwrapped birthday present again. He had a new line in opening gambits. He insisted on taking me home early because he needed to get away from somebody else at the party. As I like going to bed early, I had no objection. We stole a bottle of champagne from our host and went back to my apartment. My birthday present unwrapped himself in my bedroom. Well . . . perhaps I did begin the process by unzipping his fly—but what better way can you begin the year than in bed with a beautiful young man?

Over the previous thirty years I had enjoyed two marriages and a dozen serious love affairs—but what had it brought me? Thirty years of heartbreak. Had the enjoyment ever outweighed the suffering?

At fifty I was tired of love. I no longer wanted a permanent relationship; friendships and a career were enough. Sex could be casual. My emotional security was within myself. I would never again have to rely on another person to provide it.

Around the middle of February my plump friend rang me up.

"How's the birthday present wearing?" he asked.

"It's worn out," I replied.

"Why? What happened?"

"Nothing unusual. My mother brought me up to believe that a real lady never accepts presents from gentlemen unless they are perishable and can be shared with others—like flowers or chocolates. The young man *was* perishable, like all great beauties, and wanted to be shared by a wider public—so I let him go."

"Are you heartbroken?"

"Not at all. It's rather a relief not to have to compete!"

My old lovers got the news that I was now in circulation again and came back on the part-time basis I preferred. Sometimes I let them overlap, and sometimes I stuck to one for a limited engagement. My love-style fitted my life-style, and both were carefully dovetailed into my professional life.

For twenty years I had been working in public relations, mainly for the Italian cinema. Now I was just off to Tuscany for some location shooting and would not be back till Easter.

Conversation on a terrace in Rome. Easter. 1967.

"Mother, I wish you'd have one lover at a time," my elder daughter Fiona said. "It's so confusing for the children. How am I going to explain it to them?"

My grandchildren were in the bathroom sailing paper boats in the bidet, oblivious to social and sexual problems, I should have thought. My immediate lovers were temporarily out of sight. The Third Secretary was at the Ministry for Foreign Affairs, Rudi was at the opera designing sets for *Aïda*, and my long-distance truck driver was halfway down Calabria on his way to Sicily. Bruno was in Paris photographing the collections, and Paolo was at the university in Naples.

We had all foregathered for Easter in my Rome apartment near the Spanish Steps. Fiona had flown out from England with her children, aged three and four, and Vanessa and her Sicilian husband had come in from the country with Matthew, aged one, who was busily crawling about the bathroom floor, trying to imitate his cousins.

"Darlings, I really can't run my sex life to suit my grandchildren!" I protested.

I turned from watering my geraniums to look at my daughters, who were sitting in deck chairs drinking iced tea. They were tall and distinguished, their long legs stretched out, their feet neatly crossed.

"This is the swinging sixties," I went on. "What have we all been fighting for? My mother campaigned for 'free love' in Bloomsbury back in the thirties, and *my* generation has been sleeping around uninhibitedly ever since then so that *your* generation could shout from the rooftops about a sexual revolution." I paused for breath. "Now you expect me to sit back and behave like a Victorian virgin!"

"Not exactly, mummy," Vanessa interposed. "But couldn't you cut out the younger men and settle down with a nice man your own age?"

"What is my age? I feel contemporary with everyone."

"You're fifty, mother," Fiona said coolly.

"But I don't appeal to older men, dear. Either they're too tired, or they're afraid to move out of their existing marriages, or they're running after young girls like you," I replied as I continued to water the geraniums.

"What about Rudi?" Vanessa persisted, referring to my hardy perennial, who still tormented me but no longer slept with me.

"Good God! I'd rather go back to your father!"

"That might not be a bad idea," interjected Fiona. "Why don't you?"

"Your father can't cook; neither can your stepfather. I made a great mistake with my husbands. I should have locked them in the kitchen instead of taking them into the bedroom, which only leads to overpopulation and heartbreak."

My daughters laughed. At least they have a sense of humor, I thought. If I've done nothing else in life, I've put two beautiful girls into the world with long legs and a sense of humor.

"Mother, do be serious for a moment," Fiona begged. "And sit down. You're overwatering those things. Give some to the oleanders if you must walk around with that hose."

I transferred my attention to the oleanders, which had been a birthday present from my second ex-husband, Charles, and his new wife, who conveniently lived around the corner. Ex-husbands are so handy. Mine were also generous. It's very important to choose your ex-husbands well.

I went back to the subject at hand. "Marriage and domesticity should have nothing to do with sex," I said. "Sex should be kept for lovers, and lovers for sex. The bees have it right. Marriage is a nice domestic job for people who like that sort of thing. A lot of men are very good at washing dishes, and even more of them are wonderful cooks. Encourage them, I say; lock them in the kitchen!"

My Sicilian son-in-law, who never lifts a finger in the house, smiled but said nothing. I continued my argument, waving the hose around as I warmed to my subject.

"Men should be kept off the streets, out of Parliament, and away from all those offices in which they've made such an economic mess of the world. Let them bake cakes and look after the children— then there might be fewer juvenile delinquents. I'm not so sure that women are good at bringing up children. Let's turn the world upside down and start again."

I was splashing the water around in my excitement, and Fiona leaped up and turned off the hose.

"Sit down and relax, mother. Be your age!"

"That's exactly what I *am* being. It's an age of

complete independence at last. I'm free to live anywhere, with anybody. I can travel all over the
world. Why should I want to settle down?"

"You're right," said Vanessa. "But at least stick
to one young man at a time. Why do you have to
have so many?"

"I never eliminate. It's unnecessary and unkind.
I just add."

I went over and sat beside my daughters and my
charming, lazy Sicilian son-in-law. My English
son-in-law, a hard-working boy, had not been able
to take a holiday at all. I stretched out my own
long legs and considered the situation. Which of
my young men could I do without?

My big, tough truck driver, Pietro, to whom my
daughters particularly objected, was so useful at
fixing things around the house and mending the
car. When not in bed or being useful, he sat quietly
in the corner reading *La Gazetta dello Sport*, or
went home to his wife. He was a furniture mover
who had picked me up one day when my car had
broken down. He had taken me home in his truck
and helped me get over Rudi, the last of my living-
in lovers, who had broken my heart in so many
places when he left me.

Then there was my Third Secretary, a nice
plump young man from the Foreign Ministry, perfect for diplomatic occasions, who got all my
permits and licenses and wrote my letters for me.

Then there was Paolo, my Roman Spring, so-
called because he had been picked up on the Spanish
Steps one fine spring day. He was a law student who
solved all those daily problems like how many

weeks' holiday you owed the maid, and whether you should pay your taxes or not. He was quietly efficient in bed and out.

Bruno, my little bearded photographer, kept all the family records, in black and white or color, from christenings to weddings to passport photos. No doubt he'd be there at my death, photographing my funeral. In the meantime, he filled all the gaps in my love life. He had a Casanova complex and could fit more women into a week than most men can into a lifetime. You could telephone Bruno and say, "I'm lonely and depressed," and he'd understand the situation at once. He'd put off the Signora A and Miss B, and after a quick telephone conversation with the Princess C, he'd pop in before meeting Madame D—and I really mean pop in. A quick pop in and out with Bruno and you needed no other stimulants. It was much cheaper than drink or drugs and much better for the health.

How could I live without any of my young men? They had become a habit, and I was useful to *them* too. I was always there when they had nobody else. As one of my friends (or was it an enemy?) put it, "You're the oldest and most distinguished call girl in the business, Anne."

I dispensed tea and sympathy, affection and serenity to my young men—sexual relief without sexual complications. Younger women were sometimes hard to come by, they cost money, and they kept getting pregnant. It was also unlikely that they would have such comfortable apartments of their own.

My daughter repeated her previous question: "Why do you have to have so many young men, mother?"

"There's safety in numbers," I replied. "If you settle down with one lover you risk getting married again."

"What's wrong with marriage?" both daughters exclaimed at once.

"At your age it seems divine, I know. You're longing to try out all those recipes in the Sunday papers. You *like* changing the baby's diapers. At my age all that's a drag. If I marry again, it's going to be to a nice rich old homosexual, a cooking queen who'll look after me and share my young men. We'll hang silver 'His' and 'Hers' labels around their necks."

"Mother, you're impossible!"

There were piercing screams from the bathroom, where the children were playing, followed by thuds and raised voices.

"Your grandchildren are killing each other," my Sicilian son-in-law announced calmly, speaking for the first time. "I wish they'd do it more quietly, though—they're disturbing my thoughts."

He lay back indolently in his chaise longue and helped himself to another glass of iced tea while we three women got up hastily and went indoors to the scene of battle. The children were fine, but the bathroom was completely flooded.

We spent Easter Sunday that year at Vanessa's farm in the Alban Hills outside Rome. I organized an Easter egg hunt for the children in the long grass of her orchard, and then we went indoors for the traditional Italian meal of roast spring lamb followed by a cake shaped like a dove.

"Is it the Dove of Peace or the Holy Ghost?" Fiona asked her sister.

"I don't know," Vanessa replied. "Although I had to study the catechism to marry into the Catholic church, they didn't tell me that one."

In spite of the fact that her husband was a Communist, they had married in church. It is one of those strange Italian anomalies that good Communists often go to mass on Sundays.

I went back to Rome alone, leaving my two girls and their little families together in the country. I was quite relieved. I had grown to love living alone; I nearly didn't even answer the telephone that was ringing as I got home. It seemed like an invasion of my privacy.

It rang insistently. The caller had to be someone who knew my habits, the size of the apartment, and my reluctance to answer telephones. It was probably one of my part-time lovers—but which one?

"Hello, Anne. Where have you been all day?"

"Attending to family duties."

"Feel like a little love?"

"I always feel like a little love—that's my trouble."

"It's not your trouble, Anne; it's your strength. It's what keeps you young."

"Come on over, then. I was beginning to feel my age."

I replaced the receiver, and for a moment I

couldn't remember which of my young lovers was coming to see me. The wonderful thing was that it didn't matter.

Later, as I went to open the door, I realized how lucky I was. At fifty years old I had got my life into a pleasant pattern of working and playing, based on discipline and balance, with a dash of madness. My work in public relations for big film companies fitted in perfectly with my way of life. It too required discipline and balance, and the movies themselves provided the dash of madness. I was never bored. Boredom is a killer—and I liked to live.

My bell was ringing furiously—a joyous, youthful ring.

"Darling," the young man said as he came through the door and his strong young arms went around me. "We've only got time for a quick one. Do you mind? I've got to leave for Milan in half an hour, and I just wanted to *feel* you before I left."

"Of course I don't mind! I'm glad you want to feel me. Feeling is friendship. Copulation is communication. I *want* to be wanted—that's what sex is all about."

We walked across the hall and into the sitting room, where he took me into his arms again and kissed me lightly. At first his tongue fluttered around the tip of mine, and then it pushed hard into my mouth.

"I'm sorry we haven't more time," he said when he came up for air.

"It's the strength of the desire that matters," I replied. "Not the length of time."

We went into the bedroom, but we did not fully undress. When we had finished, I smiled.

"Never underestimate the value of the five-minute fuck," I said.

Diary entry. Cannes. Film Festival. May 10, 1967. High noon.

I arrived in Cannes yesterday. The sun is shining on the Croisette, but it's windy and the palm trees look dusty. I'm here because an Italian film I have been working on is one of the entries, and I've been delegated to get it as much publicity as possible. I've spent all this morning queuing up to get the pass that will give me entry to all the private viewings. This year we have been divided up into sections: producers, distributors, journalists, and, last but not least, the star performers, known in the Festival offices as "les artistes." These are not only actors but also directors, designers, and others not involved in selling films but very involved in selling themselves. Cannes is a combination of big business and a Mediterranean slave market.

It looks like rain, but then the weather is usually bad for the Film Festival. In the old days this was important, when glamorous exposure was all, and starlets wore mink bikinis on the beach, but soon found that it didn't help them get contracts—only pneumonia. Now actors stay away unless actually brought here to launch the film in which they are starring; otherwise, to be seen at Cannes is to be seen not working. The Cannes Film Festival is a big business operation, with producers looking for distributors, not directors looking for actors. Only the crowds along the Croisette and outside the cinemas are looking for actors. I shall go out and join them and try and find Rudi.

In 1955, when I separated from my second husband and went to live in Rome, I met Rudi for the first time. He was sitting in the corner of a little trattoria frequented by artists and writers, where we all sat at communal tables and got to know each other. No one seemed to get to know Rudi. He always sat alone, shy but beautiful. I sometimes sat with him and found him to be full of charm and intelligence and an unexpected sense of humor. He was Austrian, but had studied in Rome at the Accademia di Arte Drammatica and was now a talented young designer. He never arrived at the restaurant with anybody, never left with anybody.

"Are you anti-sexual or just anti-social?" I asked him one day. "Do you have a mysterious mistress or a secret male lover? Are you gay or straight or untouched by human hand?"

"Perhaps I'm just waiting for the right hand," he said, avoiding the issue; but he smiled as he said it.

I had no time to pursue the matter further, because two gentlemen at the next table were drawing lots for me. I knew them both slightly, and I hoped the one in the red sweater would win. He did. I had met him during a period when I was sleeping around with anyone who asked me in an attempt to forget my departed second husband. The red sweater claimed me and bore me off for coffee in the Piazza del Popolo. As I left the restaurant, I said to Rudi, "I hope you recognize 'the right hand' when you see it. I myself find trial and error the best method."

"I wish I had your courage," he said.

"It pays to be bold," I called from the doorway, and vanished into the night.

It was some time before I went back to the little trattoria again. The red-sweater affair lasted two weeks. It did not help me to forget my husband any more than all the other sweaters had. Then one rainy night I went back to the little trattoria. I was crying into my soup when Rudi came into the restaurant.

"I've never seen you unhappy before," he said. "It makes you more approachable."

He drew a rose on the paper tablecloth, tore it off, and put it into my hand. "To cheer you up," he said. When we had finished eating, I invited him home for coffee. I was surprised when he accepted.

Neither of us had an umbrella, and, as it was still raining, we ran all the way to my apartment. We arrived breathless and soaking wet.

"You'll have to take off your clothes and let me dry them in front of the electric fire," I told him. "Get into bed and keep warm."

He was very shy, but he did what I told him. Then I stripped and got in beside him. It was some time before I could get him out of his underpants, but it was all right in the end. They came off, it came up, I got on top, and Rudi stayed with me for five years.

"I didn't know women took the initiative," he commented at the time. "It makes it easier."

Rudi admitted that he was a repressed homosexual, but we were blissfully happy both in bed and out, so it didn't seem to matter. It was a problem we never discussed again, because happiness knows no problems. He became a well-known designer in films and the theater, and I went into public relations and became a publicist for the Italian cinema. My languages and my stage training helped considerably, and I was good at my job.

Unfortunately, Rudi and I seldom worked on the same movie, and we began to be separated for long periods. One day I came home from two months' location shooting and found that someone else had taken the initiative with Rudi as I had once done. It was another man. He and Rudi went off to live in America, and my heart was broken once again. However, Rudi's work brought him regularly back to Europe, and on every visit he tried to move back in with me. At first I couldn't resist, and I let him do so; then finally I decided to break the spell. From then on, I insisted on separate rooms and separate lovers. Now at Cannes we even had separate hotels, and so I couldn't find him even when I wanted him.

Conversation on the terrace of the Carlton Hotel in Cannes. Noon. May 12, 1967.

"Rudi, darling, I couldn't find you anywhere! I've been looking for you for twenty-four hours!"

"Where else would I be but here, Anne? Anybody who is somebody is on the terrace of the Carlton before lunch."

"Conceited bastard! Just because you've designed the sets and costumes for the film likely to

win the award doesn't mean that *I* have to come
looking for *you*. *You* should have been looking for
me. The man looks for the woman."

"Our roles have always been reversed, darling.
It's too late to change now."

We looked around us at the neighboring tables.
They were mainly occupied by middle-aged, pot-
bellied Californians in Hawaiian shirts. A few
smooth European operators were wearing well-cut
navy blue blazers with gold buttons and were ush-
ering in their attendant ladies with careful hairdos
and snazzy Pucci-Gucci resort wear. The Vuitton
handbag had not yet arrived.

"It's what the Chinese would call The Year of
the Hawaiian Shirt," I commented. "Now who do
you think that beautiful young black man is? An
Ethiopian prince?"

"Probably a New York hustler."

Rudi and I had sat at café tables all over the
world and played the game of guessing who and
what our neighbors were. We never tired of it.
Here it was almost too easy. The name of the game
was movie-making and -breaking. It was a moneyed
gathering of the clans, affluent but not elegant.
Only a few local Frenchwomen in simple slacks
and with sea-bleached, wind-blown hair looked
really chic. The others just looked rich.

"Now I wonder who *she* is?" I asked, referring to
a tall, thin, flat-chested girl who was drifting down
the central aisle between tables in an expensive
hippie outfit.

"The Titless Wonder," Rudi replied. "Andy
Warhol will discover her."

We fell silent for a bit. One thing about being

with old lovers is that you don't have to talk to them all the time.

"Look at that," Rudi said suddenly. "What a tasty morsel!"

I followed Rudi's predatory gaze. A beautiful child was pushing his way through the crowd, a boy of about sixteen. His golden hair was untidy, his face was tanned, and he had a beautiful little bottom encased in the tightest, most worn jeans on the Croisette, and there was nothing of the cinema about him. He looked as if he had just been sailing with some young friends and had swum ashore.

"He's divine," I said. "But hands off, Rudi. I don't want you arrested for corruption of minors."

"Fortunately, I don't usually like the very young. But this one has something special. You can tell he hasn't just come out of a suitcase like everyone else here. He's probably a local. I wonder who he is and where he comes from?"

Still playing the game of guessing who people were and what they did, we watched the young man's progress through the crowded tables. The boy reached a table fairly near us and stood talking to a middle-aged man who was already sitting down. The man looked up at the boy, and I recognized him, although I hadn't seen him for nearly thirty years.

"Good God!" I said. "It's Aurélien."

"Who's Aurélien?" Rudi asked. "The boy?"

"No. The man he's talking to. The first real lover of my life. He took my virginity on a park bench under the Tour Eiffel when I was studying French in Paris before the war. God, how old he looks! He can't be much older than I am. Rudi, do I look as old as that?"

But Rudi wasn't listening to me. He was watching the boy, who was now sitting down beside Aurélien and talking animatedly with French gestures. Occasionally he ran his hand through his wild blond curls in a useless attempt to tidy them.

"Do you think he's for you or for me?" Rudi insisted.

"Who? Aurélien?"

"No, the boy, you idiot!"

"Oh, I hadn't thought. What would I do with a teen-ager? I'm fifty years old, Rudi. He could be my grandson."

"And Aurélien could be your husband. Why didn't you marry him?"

"I went back to England in the middle of our affair. My mother was dying of cancer, and she needed me. Aurélien and I wrote to each other for a time, and then war broke out and we lost touch. France was cut off from England during the war—remember?"

"Didn't you try to find him again after the war?"

"Vaguely—but I was married to Robert by then. On a trip to Paris I once called at Aurélien's old lodgings, but they only remembered that he came from somewhere in Provence. It was all too difficult. I thought he might even have been killed."

I sat looking across at Aurélien. He was now a middle-aged Frenchman, gray-haired, prosperous, slightly professorial, but with enough of his old charm left for me to have easily recognized him.

He had been a handsome law student, so now he was presumably a successful lawyer.

"Why don't you go over and speak to him?" Rudi was asking.

"I don't know. It all seems so far away ... like another person's life or a figment of my imagination. Perhaps I shouldn't intrude."

"Nonsense. Go on. Get over there. Ask them to join us."

So I went back thirty years—only a few yards away.

Diary entry continued. Cannes. May 12, 1967. Evening.

Physical recognition is not everything. Aurélien recognized me as easily as I had recognized him, which was surprising in view of the time lag. Then we didn't know where to begin. What do you say to an old lover after thirty years? As I walked up to his table, I said "Hello, Aurélien," just as if we had been recently separated. He said, "It's Anne Cumming, isn't it?" rather formally. We shook hands. I don't know why we didn't kiss. Perhaps because of the boy. The boy had not stood up when Aurélien rose to greet me, but he looked up at me quizzically. It was a mischievous look. Then Aurélien introduced him. "This is my son, Jean-Louis." The boy stood up and kissed my hand. There was something ironic about the old-fashioned gesture coming from a teen-ager in blue jeans. It was very French, but then they were both French. They didn't join us because they were expecting friends, and I refused Aurélien's invitation to sit with them at their table because I needed time to get over the shock. After standing for a few minutes in conversation, we agreed to have dinner together that night. I rejoined Rudi and sat down, feeling rather shaken. Rudi was fascinated—more by the son than the situation, however. I can see I shall have to make myself very beautiful tonight and seduce the son as well as the father to avoid a diplomatic incident. I can't have Rudi seducing my ex-lover's child!

The evening went off very well. Aurélien took us to La Mère Besson, just behind my hotel. It had just the right atmosphere of chic informality, and the food was delicious. It was rather too crowded for conversation, but we managed to fill in the years between.

Aurélien had married late, hence the boy's being so much younger than my own daughters, although Aurélien himself was a few years older than I. Jean-Louis was an only child because his mother had died when he was quite young. Aurélien had recently married again to a woman his own age who was past childbearing, and they now lived in Draguignan, about an hour inland from Cannes.

"I'm a provincial lawyer, my dear, and I like it. I worked in Paris for a time, where Jean-Louis was born; but when his mother died, it was difficult for me to look after a small boy in the big city. I went back to Draguignan, where my own parents were living. My father was ready to retire, so I took over the family business. Then I married my present wife, Marie. She isn't with us today because she's visiting her mother in Marseilles."

Aurélien was a mixture of country squire and sophisticated Côte d'Azur *roué*. I imagined he got around quite a bit and had a few mistresses on the side. He still had the old sparkle, although he looked very middle-aged. Perhaps my view of this was biased because most of my lovers since Rudi had been so much younger than I—in their twenties or thirties. Even Rudi was eight years younger than I was, which made him only forty-two then. Aurélien must have been about fifty-five, which was the right age for me, but I didn't feel of his generation at all. In a strange way I felt nearer to the boy.

I was very flirtatious with the child, consciously making him feel grown up. He reacted like a man too, but went on looking like an angel.

"You bloody cradle snatcher," Rudi said to me later as he walked me home, after the father and son had disappeared into the hills in their little car.

"I only did it to keep *your* hands off him," I replied.

"You could have flirted with *me* instead!"

"Rudi, I told you years ago I never wanted to sleep with you again. All that coming and going we did for so long wore me out emotionally."

"I liked it. I'd do it again."

"You're a sweet egotist."

"What does that mean?"

"It means you're selfish. Now go off cruising and find yourself a nice young man and leave me alone."

I kissed him warmly and went into the Grand

Hotel. It was altogether too grand for me, but the film company was paying. It was so grand that I didn't fancy any of the guests, since I'm not usually attracted to the very rich. Some of the staff looked quite promising, though. There was a young man behind the reception desk I had my eye on.

The young man stayed on his side of the reception desk. He was not interested in older women. Why should he be, with all the starlets around, plus the demi-mondaines who moved in for the festival season to console the tired businessmen? The Croisette was covered with pretty girls. Anyway, I was too tired and bleary-eyed from viewing wide screens from 10 A.M. to midnight to have much social or sex life. I had to content myself with the American and Swedish hard-porn films shown in the cinemas along the Rue d'Antibes.

Aurélien's wife phoned me one day and invited me up to Draguignan, but I explained that I didn't have time to come. I asked all of them down to Cannes again for a drink or a meal. I was curious to meet Marie. She sounded charming. We arranged a day, and I looked forward to it. The day came, and I found a note canceling our rendezvous when I got back to the hotel at lunch time.

Note found at the Grand Hotel. Cannes. May 17, 1967.
Mr. and Mrs. Laroche regret they cannot come to dinner tonight. Their son will come in and explain this afternoon at about 4:30 P.M., after school.

After school, indeed! It had not occurred to me that Jean-Louis was still a schoolboy. It had been a

Saturday when we met on the Carlton terrace. He must be in his last year at the Lycée.

I spent the afternoon working out a publicity stunt for the film I was there to launch. The Big Name Star of our picture had plenty of "tits and ass," to use the photographer's expression, but she was well into her thirties and had had two children, and her vital statistics were sagging. Rudi had come along to help me get the publicity stills I needed, sufficiently nude to please the press, but dressed up enough for me to be able to create the new image I was planning for her: "Sex symbol becomes a dramatic actress."

"What am I to do, Rudi? She looks like a tired baby doll, and she can't really act."

"Hmm. It's a problem. Black underwear looks kinky. Colored lace looks vulgar. We'll have to come up with something new."

Rudi went out and combed the Cannes boutiques for me. It was very sweet of him, but then he *is* a sweet egotist, and he loves his job and hates to be idle. When I lived with him, he made me change my clothes a dozen times a day so he could plan which earrings went with which skirt. I got so bored with it all that I have never cared much for clothes since, and the jewelry I inherited from my mother either lies in the bank or was given to my daughters when they married. Let *them* lose it, I said; then they can't blame *me*.

Rudi got back at the same time as The Big Star. They swept in together. He slightly upstaged her, a thing he is rather good at.

He had armfuls of saris, caftans and Indian jewelry.

"We're inventing the Indian Look," he said.

In 1967, the Indian Look had not yet been over-done. Perhaps Rudi really did invent it then. The Big Star was very impressed that I had Rudi along to help, and he made her look wonderfully glamorous and sexy and, at the same time, dramatic.

"A touch of Marlene Dietrich in *Morocco*," he said, standing back to view his handiwork. "Mixed with the mysterious magic of the Far East!"

The photographer moved in and arranged the lights, while Rudi draped the clothes and hung the recumbent Star with glittering gems. We were all set to shoot the stills.

"One minute!" shouted Rudi. He rushed forward and removed some dangling chains. "Always get dressed, put on your jewels, and then take off something. That's the way to avoid vulgarity."

Rudi was always right.

I sat outside the Grand Hotel after the photographic session ended, having left a message at the hotel desk to say I was on the terrace. I ordered tea and waited for Jean-Louis. He strolled up from the Croisette and across the lawn outside the Grand Hotel, so I was able to watch him coming. He was extraordinarily confident for a schoolboy. No shy slouch—more of a springy bounce. I caught myself looking at him the way Rudi looked at boys.

"How old are you, Jean-Louis?" I asked as a greeting.

He smiled, and his blue eyes twinkled. "Sixteen and three-quarters. How old are you?"

"Didn't your mother teach you not to ask ladies their age?" I parried.

"I didn't have a mother, really. Mine died when I was four, and my stepmother didn't come along until two or three years ago. My father brought me up."

"Then I must speak to Aurélien about it! I'm about five or six years younger than he is, if you want to know. I was fifty last December."

"Then you're a Sagittarian?"

"Yes. With Jupiter rising. What do you know about the Zodiac? Do they teach that in schools nowadays?"

"No, but I'm very interested in astrology. So I know that you're independent and adaptable and will travel far."

"And Jupiter's child is fortunate in middle age."

"You don't look middle-aged to me!"

"Well, I'm glad your father has taught you *that* much. Follow up a gaffe with a compliment!"

We both laughed. The ice was broken. The generation gap was closed. Jean-Louis sat there drinking tea with me like an old friend. He was adorable, as edible as the fresh ripe strawberries in the tarts they brought us. I wanted to pop him into my mouth at once, feel the slight crunch and the sweet juicy taste. It was just as well he had an appointment to go sailing with some young friends.

"By the way," I said as he got up to go, "you were supposed to explain to me why you couldn't all have dinner with me this evening. I was looking forward to meeting your stepmother."

"Of course. I quite forgot. They've both gone over to Marseilles. Marie's mother had to go into a hospital there for an operation. They may not be back for a few days. My father very much hopes you'll still be here when they return."

"You'll be here, though?"

"Yes, I stay with a family in Cannes during term time. I'm studying terribly hard for my *bachot* next month."

"Do drop in and see me again if you have time."

"I'd love to. I really would." He kissed my hand and was gone. I did not see him again, or his parents. I dined with Rudi that night.

"How was The Tasty Morsel?"

"Well named. I wanted to eat him up."

"Why didn't you?"

"Don't be silly, Rudi. I wouldn't know where to begin with a child like that!"

Rudi looked at me for a moment and then changed the subject.

"I shall want a credit line under those photos we took this afternoon. Photo by So and So. Designed by Rudi Von Hoffman."

"Rudi, you don't need more publicity. Your film's going to win you an Oscar."

"One can never have too much publicity in this business. You know that. That's what your job's about."

"I don't agree with you. You can burn yourself, as the Italians say."

"Not me. I've got too much good taste to over-expose myself!"

So I gave Rudi his by-line under the photos. And I went to the opening of his film on his arm, wearing a new dress he had made me buy for the occasion, and I put on what jewelry I had—and then

took off one thing. Perhaps one day I will shake off
Rudi's influence forever. At least I now have the
strength not to sleep with him anymore.

The rest of the festival passed as was to be expected: confusion and coordination in equal quantities. When you expected something to go wrong,
it went right, and vice versa. It rained quite a bit,
and we hid our summer dresses under umbrellas
hastily purchased at the Prisunic.

The film Rudi had designed won the award, but
it did not go on to win an Oscar. I forgot about the
Laroches and their son in my struggle to get The
Big Star to the right place at the right time and to
see that she hit the front covers of the best magazines, in spite of the fact that her film was the
worst entry at the festival. I was exhausted by the
time I got into my railway sleeping coach at Nice
to go back to Rome. They hadn't yet managed to
coordinate the French railways into the festival
and get the sleepers put on at Cannes. Rudi came
to see me off, bringing a dozen red roses. He was
driving back to Paris with friends to design a ballet
for the Paris opera. I promised to meet him there
in the fall when it opened.

"Good-bye, my treasure. Good-bye," he said as
the train pulled out of the station.

How many times had I heard Rudi say that?
Thank God it no longer hurt. I went into my compartment and sat down. As I crossed my hands in
my lap, I looked at my wedding rings. I wear
three. The first was given me by the children's father, my first husband, Robert, and just has the

date engraved inside. The second was from my second husband, Charles, and is made of pierced gold in Gothic script, saying "I love you more than yesterday, but not as much as tomorrow." It's in French, which is shorter, so it just fits around the ring. Rudi, whom I never married, gave me a gold ring on the day he left me. Inside were engraved the words "Always and Never." It's a very plain flat gold ring. "In very good taste, no?" Rudi said as he gave it to me. I wonder whether it is in really good taste to give a woman a wedding ring on the day you leave her?

Back in Rome it was very hot. Summer had started, and I had begun preparations for a new film, a big Italo-American co-production willing to pay for a publicist throughout the whole shooting, which was to start on September 1.

My daughter Vanessa and her toddler came in from the country to give her a chance to shop while I baby-sat. Matthew was an interesting child, very lively, astute and aggressive. "I think he'll do well in the Mafia," I told my Sicilian son-in-law. "I hope so," he replied.

Vanessa was still on the subject of my settling down. "Didn't you find a suitable suitor in Cannes?" she asked.

"Certainly not. I don't mind working in the cinema, but I'm not going to marry into it. Rudi was there, anyway. He's still quite possessive."

"Why don't you marry *him*?"

"Because he wants me for the wrong reasons."

The subject was dropped. I didn't tell her about

Aurélien, because the situation there had taken a turn she would hardly have approved of. A letter had fallen through my letter box shortly after my return to Rome and was now safely filed away in an old shoe box with other letters I wanted to keep.

Ma chère,

My English is not so good now as it was when we were both young. We grow rusty, although you do not seem to have aged. I saw you again with much affection and admiration. My wife and I regret very much that we could not meet you again, and it is her idea that I write to you now.

We have been worried about Jean-Louis. He does not have easy contacts with girls like his school friends. We were therefore surprised when the other day he said something about his meeting with you, which made us realize that he was physically attracted to you. I was quite jealous, but I understood it. In bed there is not age, only people. You have always been an exceptional person.

This brings me to the point of my letter. Jean-Louis is intending to go hitchhiking in Italy this summer. Would you ask him to stay and take on his sentimental education? He will just have had his seventeenth birthday. What a present! His father's ex-mistress . . .

I told Marie of how you flirted with him at our dinner party together, and she thinks you sound sportive enough to go through with my plan if you like our boy. But perhaps you have a jealous Italian lover who would not approve?

We are sending you many embraces. Jean-Louis will be setting off at the end of June, straight after his *bachot* exams.

Yours ever,
Aurélien

Aurélien's letter brought on a whole train of nostalgic reminiscences. My mother had sent me at eighteen to study French in Paris. I was lodged with a respectable French family near the Eiffel Tower. Their nephew, Aurélien, used to take me for walks at night in the gardens around the tower. One night, on a park bench where we had been doing "everything but," we finally went the whole hog. It was all rather uncomfortable, but the actual act of penetration didn't hurt—perhaps because I had been *nearly* deflowered the year before in Germany, at seventeen, but had lost my nerve at the last minute. In those days there was no Pill and not much general knowledge about contraception. However, my playing around with young men all over Europe certainly improved my languages. Since then, I had continued to enjoy sleeping dictionaries all over the world, although never yet an under-age first edition!

Letter from Rome to Draguignan. June 1, 1967.
Dear Aurélien and Marie,
   I'm amused and intrigued by your very French proposal, and I'm glad to hear that Marie is an equal party to this nefarious scheme. I don't want a jealous stepmother suing me for corruption of minors!

You seem very sure of Jean-Louis's cooperation. I got the impression that he is more interested in outdoor than indoor sports, but in spite of my advanced age, I feel the situation has possibilities. I'll give it a try. I have no jealous lovers at present, Italian or otherwise. After the last emotional disaster in my life, I decided to devote myself to passing fancies, and not have permanent live-in lovers.

Whatever you do, don't let Jean-Louis know about our scandalous scheming. If anything is to happen, I must engineer it so that he feels he has taken the initiative. I will write to him direct, inviting him to stay.

Your devoted friend and accomplice,
Anne

I was very busy for a few days, mainly with domestic problems, because while I had been away, my daily cleaning woman had fallen off a stepladder while spring cleaning. I had to do my own domestic chores until she recovered, as well as plan some pre-publicity for the new film, which included the difficult task of launching a Yugoslavian starlet with a new line in vital statistics. She had no breasts. We had to think up ways of getting the "tits and ass" photos, with little of the former and too much of the latter as our raw material. I missed Rudi, who would have draped her with clinging wet clothes or hung ropes of pearls in the right places. In the end we got some marvelous shots of her lying naked in a haystack with a kitten clutched to her nonexistent bosom. "Pussy on pussy," said the American photographer who had

been flown over from the States at great expense
by the publicity office. He was supposed to know
better than an Italian photographer what the American male wanted as his masturbation fantasy.

Eventually I got around to writing to Jean-
Louis. I can't say he was, as yet, my masturbation
fantasy, but I had caught myself thinking about
the possible pleasure of running my fingers
through those tumbled curls. When you have very
straight hair yourself, the springy feel of tight
curls is a real turn-on.

Dear Jean-Louis,

It was good to meet you in Cannes, although I'm
sorry your parents couldn't come with you on that
last occasion. However, it gave you and me a
chance to get to know each other better. I recognized many things in you. You have your father's
sense of humor as well as his twinkly blue eyes.
Recognition is one of the basic requisites of friendship, and I hope we *will* become friends this summer.

It seems that if you pass your *bachot* exams next
month, your parents would like you to have a holiday in Italy. I have a large apartment in Rome and
a little pied-à-terre by the sea. You would be a very
welcome visitor in both places. Now that my
daughters are married, I have plenty of room. The
generation gap did not loom too large over a café
table in Cannes, so perhaps we can close it still further on my Roman balcony.

Let me know if and when you'd like to come,

but don't let your parents force you into doing
something you don't want to do!

Love,
Anne

I hoped I had struck the right note of intimacy
and encouragement without scaring the boy off.
There was something in that twinkling, mischievous look of his that made me think he was ready
for adventure, but perhaps not yet ready for such a
mature woman. Was I ready for him? Yes, I think I
was. I had had two part-time lovers in Rome that
spring: my very snobbish diplomat and my very
butch truck driver. They had alternated at infre-
quent intervals and would be away for the summer. I could therefore do with something a bit
more constant. I waited quite impatiently for Jean-
Louis's reply, which was a long time in coming
and very terse and noncommittal when it arrived.

Dear Anne,

Forgive this awful postcard [a vulgar view of the
Croisette at Cannes in lurid colors, with the Carlton Hotel in the background], but it's the only one
I could find of where we first met. Sorry I didn't
answer before, but I was busy with my exams.
Would it be all right if I came to Rome next week?
I am going to hitchhike, so I don't quite know
when I will arrive. I think I've done quite well in
my exams. Father says I needn't wait for the results.

Yours,
Jean-Louis

Diary entry. Rome. June 25.

"Yours, Jean-Louis!" indeed! I wonder if he really will be mine? Now that I've accepted this strange deal, I'm not sure I really want to go through with it. I've had plenty of young lovers in my time—but Rudi is right; this is really cradle snatching. I didn't even have seventeen-year-old lovers when I was seventeen myself. I never feel my age, but this may finally make me feel it. I must keep our correspondence—it may be amusing to read one day.

Reply from Rome to Draguignan. June 26.
[On a carefully chosen postcard of two young people on a motorcycle embracing under garlands of hearts and flowers, speeding along a highway under a motto reading "A dangerous kiss."]

Dear Jean-Louis,
Come anytime. I'll expect you when I see you. The trattoria opposite has the key if I'm out. Top floor. Name on the door. Love, Anne

Note found on the hall table in Rome. July 13.
Dear Anne, I've arrived. You weren't here, so I let myself in with the key from the trattoria. Your house is just like you—it's very beautiful. I'm sunbathing on the top terrace. What a view! The Pincio Gardens and the Spanish Steps and all those red roofs. Come up and join me. J-L

I found the child sunbathing in the nude on my top terrace. What do you say to a guest who is lying stark naked on his stomach? I said, "What a pretty little bottom!" He laughed and asked, "Are you going to come and spank me?" So I did. He pulled me down on top of him to stop me. It was as easy as that. It was really *he* who seduced *me*.

He was not as inexperienced as his father imagined. It always surprises me how old the young are. *I* was as nervous as a young girl. It was *he* who put me at my ease. He told me later he had planned the whole sunbathing bit as an opening gambit and had been lying there for hours waiting for me!

A few days later I felt I must write to Jean-Louis's parents and tell them something. But how much? I knew Aurélien too well and his wife Marie not at all. It was a ticklish task. I phoned my second husband, who so conveniently lived around the corner with his new wife, and asked his opinion. Charles is a well-balanced, quiet man and has remained my pillar of support. "Write as little as possible, but come straight to the point," was his good advice. "And do bring the boy around to see us."

Letter to Monsieur and Madame Laroche. July 16, 1967.
Dear Marie and Aurélien,

Your son is safe and sound and in my bed. Everything is going according to plan. I think it's better for his sake that we never refer to the sexual side of this strange relationship again. He is just visiting his Fairy Godmother. The fact that he has also become her lover is neither here nor there. He has come to see Rome and improve his English. (Incidentally, he has an early Charles Boyer accent just like his father's!)

I shall take Jean-Louis down to the sea on August 1. I have a little apartment in Sperlonga, a fishing village about two hours from Rome on the way to Naples. I'm taking a month's holiday before starting a new film, but will come into Rome once a week to pick up mail. Or you can write to us there—Poste Restante, Sperlonga. The village is so small, it has no proper address system; you just say "in the street where the lady sells fresh eggs" or "over the bakery." Everything revolves round Giuseppe's bar in the cobbled piazza.

Best wishes to you both—and thank you! This is a valid experiment for me, too. As I never had a son, I'd missed out on that part of the human experience. In a way I'm having it now. I realize my life might have been very different if my daughters had been sons.

Yours ever,
Anne

After ten days, our life together had already fallen into a workable pattern. Like all the very young, he liked to sleep late. This gave me time to get most of the part-time preparatory work for the coming film done in the mornings, while Jean-Louis got up leisurely and went out to play tennis or to swim in the Olympic pool. When he came back, we had a late lunch on my terrace under the straw awning. I was glad we were going down to

the sea on holiday the following month, as a busy
sex life was *not* conducive to work. It had complicated my social life, too. I knew that some people
would consider our relationship to be a socially
bad match, however sexually good it was for us.
The combination of an older man with a younger
girl is more readily acceptable to society. There
were a number of occasions when I hesitated to
take the boy along with me, except as a "godson"
or "nephew," and I hated to stoop to such hypocrisy. However, I discovered that the problems with
a young boy were *only* social. Sexually, everything
was fine. Jean-Louis had no preconceived ideas of
sexual roles, and so he didn't try to dominate in
spite of his strong inborn qualities of curiosity and
initiative. He was self-confident and had a natural
talent for love-making. He was not shy and didn't
have any complexes. Why should he? He was a
beautiful boy, happy in his own healthy, sun-
tanned body. His smooth penis had been circum-
cised, so that in repose it had that rosebud look. On
erection it became rather fierce, very hard and flat
against his belly. He liked to have it played with,
but equally he liked to play with me. "It's like a bi-
ology lesson, exploring a woman," he said. "I love
to see you react as I touch you." I could not match
his youthful curiosity, and sometimes I felt almost
guilty to have done it all before—so many times, in
so many places, with so many men. I told him this,
and he replied that my experience was what put
him at his ease and made him function well. His
few attempts with schoolgirls his own age had
frightened him because it frightened them.

"I preferred to masturbate," he said when he was telling me about it, "although once or twice I went with my school friends to a prostitute they knew. She was a nice, motherly sort of woman who taught me what to do, but until I met you, Anne, I didn't particularly want to do it. I just went back to masturbating—it seemed easier than trying to pick up women."

"Didn't you feel guilty about masturbation?"

"No .. on the contrary. It seemed less complicated than getting involved with girls. Then you came along and began flirting with me that night in Cannes—and it all seemed so easy."

I smiled, but he went on without noticing.

"When your letter came, Anne, I made up my mind to seduce you. Reading between the lines, it seemed to me that it wouldn't be too difficult. . . . It wasn't, was it, chérie? You wanted me too?"

I laughed and kissed him. I didn't tell him that I had flirted with him initially to save him from Rudi, or that my letter had been written at the instigation of his parents. Perhaps, with the innocent sexual optimism of youth, he had struck on the real truth, which was that I had been ready for the pure sexual drive of a very young lover. It was a remarkable cure for the oncoming menopause, which I had just begun to feel.

We made love every night, usually both before and after dinner. And again if we woke up in the night, or in the early morning, after which I patted him as I got up to work, and he curled up like a warm puppy and went back to sleep. During

lunch the exhilaration of proximity usually sent us
back to bed again for the siesta hour that Italians
so wisely build into their daily lives. The shops are
closed till four and it's hot in the streets, but it's
cool behind the brown or green shutters that flank
every Italian window and are pulled shut by bare
arms on hot summer afternoons.

Later, Jean-Louis usually amused himself, read a
lot, played the record player, or came out shopping
with me. When we came in to get ready for dinner,
either to change and go out or to begin preparing
something at home, I would see him watching me
as I moved about the house. I stopped dead in my
tracks when I felt him giving me The Look. Then
I looked back, sinking into his sensuality, feeling it
turn me on. I hadn't had such a busy sex life for a
long time. I had thought I never would again, but
it generated its own pace with ease. The more you
have, the more you want. But it did take up too
much time and made me forget my family and
friends. I felt guilty about this aspect, but not
about anything else. So I began to get in touch
with a few friends again. I called my daughter in
the country and invited her and her little boy in
for the day. I knew I must get back to normality—
keep my balance.

Note left on the bedside table. July 26.
Darling Jean-Louis,

My daughter Vanessa is coming into Rome for
the day—so when you get up, please move all your
things into the spare room. If she guesses what is
going on, it can't be helped, but I would prefer her

not to know. I am not ashamed of our affair, and I
hate hypocrisy—but this is a question of good
taste. When I come back from my shopping, we'll
decide if it would be better for you to go out for
the day and not meet her at all. Then I can just say
that a friend's son is here for a few days while
hitchhiking around Italy. She will think that quite
normal. It's not easy to hide a sexual bond, and
Vanessa is a sophisticated young woman with no
illusions about her mother. However, I try to keep
my passing fancies to myself and just let her meet
my more serious long-term lovers.

I kiss you where you like it best!

Anne

Note folded and left on the hall table. Rome. July 26.
Dear Teacher!

What a lot of lessons you are giving me, in bed
and out. Now I have to learn the etiquette of how
to behave with my mistress's daughter. To avoid
the issue, I've gone off to the Etruscan museum.
Since you're always telling me to think more about
culture and less about sex, I'll stay out all day and
give you a call about teatime to see if the coast is
clear. I'm afraid to meet Vanessa anyway; she's too
old for me.

Your devoted student,
J-L

P.S. I can just hear you saying, "I'll slap his pretty
little bottom for that remark." But *you're* not too
old for me. You're young and gay and I'm mad
about you. This evening you can beat me as much
as you like. We haven't tried that yet!

I took this note and hid it with the other letters in my shoe box marked "Letters from Lovers." Then I spent a pleasant afternoon with my grandchild. We walked up to the Pincio to see the Punch and Judy show in the Borghese Gardens. Matthew had learned to walk quite well since Easter. He loved the show and particularly liked the scenes where the policeman beat Mr. Punch with his truncheon. It seemed as if all the boys in my life were suddenly into flagellation. No sooner had Vanessa claimed her one-year-old and disappeared into the dusk to catch her bus back to the country, than my seventeen-year-old reappeared, and we sat on the terrace watching the swallows swoop down from the sunset. He brought up the subject of beating, too.

"You remember when I first arrived, Anne, and lay naked on the roof waiting for you to come home?"

"Of course I do! That's when it all began."

"It had begun long before then for me. I'd been having masturbation fantasies about you ever since you flirted with me at that dinner with my father and Rudi. When your letter came, I was so excited I got a hard-on as I read it. I could hardly wait to get here. I just knew you'd let me fuck you, and that gave me the courage to lie naked and wait for you. I had an erection for hours up there on the roof, then I was suddenly so nervous when you actually walked in that I lost it. You know what turned me on again?"

"No. Tell me."

"When you smacked my bottom. Or pretended

to. Let's try it again. Beat me really hard this
time."

Flagellation was not a success; neither of us
liked it. A certain amount of rough and tumble,
yes, but actual beating, no. We tried it both ways
around, and we decided that neither of us liked
suffering or inflicting pain, so there was no point
to it. We tried bondage, too, and disliked that as
well. It was claustrophobic and frightening. I
think there was a certain innocence about both of
us, and although I had tried these things before, I
had quite forgotten my reactions to them.

I now began to concentrate on domestic matters
and to get our seaside holiday organized. I was to
be free of work for most of the month of August,
and I was looking forward to a sybaritic seaside
idyll with my young lover. I quite ignored my other lovers and just wanted to concentrate on Jean-
Louis. It was as though I thought this affair was to
be my Swan Song—an aging woman's final fling
with the youngest of them all.

Conversation on a train. Rome—Sperlonga. August 1.
    "Can you hire boats? Is there water skiing?"
    "Yes, I think so. It's a simple fishing village, but
I think they've got as far as that."
    "Haven't you done any? Don't you like it?"
    "Not anymore. I'm young enough to fall down,
but too old to get up!"
    He laughed but looked at me critically. Perhaps
he was beginning to see me as I really was, not as
the sexual fantasy he wanted me to be.

"Is there a discothèque? You do dance, don't you?"

"Yes, I love dancing, but I don't often get taken out dancing anymore."

"I'll take you out every night."

"We'll see. There'll be plenty of young people for you to go out with, don't worry."

"I want to go out with *you*."

He gave me a long, intimate stare. My heart flipped. I wished we weren't in public. . . .

"It's very inconvenient, having such a young lover. I can't even kiss you in front of an audience."

"Just do it, and I'll say, 'Oh, Granny, leave me alone,' and pretend I don't like it!"

We both got the giggles at this and rolled about with laughter in our seats. The other occupants of the carriage looked at us disapprovingly. I didn't care. I was being childish, and I was enjoying it. That's what our relationship was about. It didn't make me feel maternal at all. It made me feel young.

We arrived in the village at dusk, off the rickety bus from the station. Sperlonga is about two hours' ride from Rome through flat country until you reach Fossanova. Then the mountains come down to the sea, gray and rocky with yellow broom and rosemary on their lower slopes and with an occasional lone umbrella pine. You don't glimpse the sea until you get to Sperlonga, because the railway runs inland.

The dusty road from the bus stop leads to a bridge, and suddenly the blue sea is below you. A

long beach stretches away to more mountains, a
grotto, and a medieval tower. The whole village is
a fortress on a rock, standing high above the sea
like a white casbah. A maze of narrow alleyways
and arches runs between tall, whitewashed walls
that reflect the sun on one side and are plunged
into deep mossy shadow on the other. No car can
penetrate beyond the little piazza by the bridge.
The alleys are so narrow that you can stretch out
your arms and touch the houses on either side.
They tower above you, each one inhabited by several peasant families, one to a floor. They are the
original medieval form of apartment house, where
people huddled together for warmth, protection
and economy. My little attic apartment was at the
top of a house overlooking the sea. It was once the
granary, and the view was fabulous. You looked
down steep green slopes to the beach on one side
and up the mountain valleys on the other. Between
the two, there were fields of artichokes and the Roman ruins of an old port used by Tiberius; this was
his first stopping place on his way to Capri, by sea
or by chariot. It was a view combining both nature
and history, and one never tired of it.

*A conversation a few days later, hanging out of the
window in the moonlight.*

"You danced beautifully tonight. Far better than
all those girls."

"Years of practice. I was born to the Charleston
and worked my way through fox trots, one-steps,
waltzes, tangos, to the twist, the shake and rock."

"Your body's so soft and warm and—how do
you say it in English?—pliable?"

"You didn't have to wait till we were on the dance floor to find *that* out!"

He thought about this for a moment, then he said, "In bed I'm too busy thinking of what it's like inside you. I don't stand back and look at you."

He was standing behind me at that moment, pressed against me, running his hands up and down my body.

"Look at the fishing boats out there. They've all congregated in the silver path of the moon across the sea. I wonder what they're doing?" I said dreamily.

"May I go out with them one night? I'd like to see how it works, with those big lamps on the prows."

"Of course, darling. I'll arrange it for you to-morrow. The family below are fishermen. I'll ask Maria if her husband will take you."

His hands had lifted my long skirt and were pulling down my panties as I talked. I was still leaning over the windowsill. I parted my legs and leaned over further still as he pushed into me from the back.

"God, how hard it is!" I exclaimed.

Our sighs and groans floated out into the scented night. I even forgot my fear of heights. He was silent, as usual; his activity was always entirely physical, never verbal. I clutched the windowsill, lifting my buttocks to meet the thrust. He was clasping me to him by my thighs, occasionally running his finger down my clitoris. He was a good student; he'd learned just what I liked.

We reached orgasm together, perhaps the first time it had ever been so simultaneous. I screamed with delight, but he quickly cupped his hand over my mouth.

"For God's sake, you'll wake the neighbors!"

We both collapsed on the windowsill with laughter and total relaxation, his penis still inside me. It always took a long time to go down, something I particularly appreciated. The cooling-off period can be very important.

Eventually we fell into bed and slept till dawn. As the first light seeped through the shutters, I could see him curled up beside me. He had another erection in his sleep, the typical morning erection of a healthy young male. My first husband used to call it a "by-erection." It was very tempting. It turned me on terribly. I bent down and began to tickle the tip with my tongue. He didn't wake up, but rolled onto his back, unconsciously spreading out so I could get at it better. As I took it all into my mouth, he woke very slowly. He lifted me onto him for full penetration; he didn't really like to be sucked off; it was the only thing he was still a little shy about.

"Tell me what you want, teacher," he whispered, raising his arms and pinching my nipples. "Is that enough, or do you want me to touch you down there too?"

I could hardly speak with excitement, and my eyes were already closed.

"No, no, it's not necessary. I can rub myself on you as we move." The words came out as a series of gasps.

I opened my eyes again to watch, as I slowly circulated my pelvis. Now *his* eyes were closed, but his fingers still played with my hardened nipples.

He came very suddenly and unexpectedly, ejaculating as I was on the upward movement, so his penis was almost fully exposed, and the semen ran down it and onto his stomach.

"I'm sorry," he apologized sweetly. "You weren't quite ready, chérie."

"Don't worry," I gulped feverishly, leaning right back but keeping his penis still inside me.

I balanced on one arm and used my right hand to pick up some of his sperm on my middle finger. I rubbed it slowly over my clitoris, masturbating to climax. He watched intently, too fascinated to even take over.

His penis began to harden again, though it was too soon for him to have another orgasm. However, it made it wonderful for me. I loved the double sensation of masturbating and having him inside me at the same time.

Later I told him this, lying beside him, before we fell asleep again. When we woke again at ten, he remembered, and we made love with me lying backwards on top of him, his hard little penis moving inside me as his fingers ran all around the area between my outstretched legs. This time I came first, and he let me roll off him and go down on him. He even kept his eyes open and watched me suck him off, pulling the second pillow under his head to prop it up and see better.

"You're learning too fast," I told him when it was all over. "Soon I shan't have anything left to teach you."

The days fell into a sunlit pattern of sex and sea. He was beginning to do lots of things without me:

water skiing, fishing, long trips with friends in
their sailing boats. I introduced him everywhere as
my godson, but nobody was fooled by this, and we
became quite hardened to curious stares. He kissed
me in public quite shamelessly between his com-
ings and goings, and treated me like an anchor to
moor him to the mainland, to tie up to at night. I
spent my time on the beach, in the market, at a
café table in the piazza with friends, or getting
meals ready in the cool house with its three-feet-
thick stone walls. I was very happy. In spite of the
age difference, it was proving to be a very successful affair.

Jean-Louis discovered the camping ground and
the youth hostel, which was full of young people
of all nationalities. He made friends with two rather hearty English girls who were delighted to find
such a handsome boy who spoke perfect English.
He introduced them to me on the beach, and I
wondered what he had told them about me. His
godmother? His aunt? Or his mistress? Perhaps he
was bright enough to know it would make him
seem more sophisticated and desirable if he told
the girls the truth about us. I was amused, compassionate and jealous all at once. It was time for me
to look the facts in the face. I decided to be bravely
unpossessive and go to Rome alone to pick up the
mail.

Note left on the windowsill. Early morning. Sperlonga.
August 12.
Darling,
   I have gone to Rome, leaving you sleeping, be-
cause I hate even temporary good-byes. I shall be

back the day after tomorrow on the last train. I have a few things to do in the city, and I want to pick up my mail.

I know you'll find this note at once, because you always get up and look out of the window at the beach before doing anything else. I can see you standing there and stretching, shaking your long hippie curls and looking like a Botticelli angel. I'm sorry I'm not there to give you coffee and push you right back into bed. The 'fridge is full, but I'm sure you'll eat out with Les Girls. See you late tomorrow night. Enjoy yourself—but not too much!

Kisses,
Anne

Back in Rome it seemed quiet, hot and stuffy, oppressive. It made me feel my age again. Rome was full of domestic responsibility, bills, letters from people I didn't want to hear from. Most people were out of town. My daughter Vanessa, with her husband and child, had gone to an island off the coast of Sicily. I didn't want to see anybody, although I knew I should. It would be good for me to get back to a normal life. I couldn't go on forever pretending to be a swinging teen-ager. The point was that I really felt like that inside at the moment. I wanted to break every mirror in the house to keep from seeing my middle-aged self. I was also worrying about Jean-Louis and those girls. I longed to get back to Sperlonga the following evening and find out what was going on.

Note found on my pillow. Sperlonga again. Midnight. August 15.

Chérie, You said you'd be late, so I've gone out dancing. I'm with those girls from the youth hostel—you know, the English ones you said were "jolly hockey sticks." It was such a funny expression, it made me laugh. You always make me laugh. I love you.

J-L

He came back very late. I had steeled myself to ask nothing and to be told nothing. I was longing to say "Had a good time?" with irony and intent. I wanted to know and I didn't want to know. I had examined the bed, which was neatly made, as soon as I arrived. Who knows who had slept in it last night? Or would his good taste have prevented him from bringing a girl to my bed? Perhaps he had had them both on the beach—or an orgy of girls in the youth hostel. I preferred the idea of numbers to that of just one.

I decided not to speak at all, just to open my arms. I did just that. He fell into them without a word. Soon I opened my legs. He fell into them, too, without a word. I was blissfully happy again. Twenty years old again.

Conversation on the beach. August 16.

"Hello, girls. How are you? I'm glad you've been looking after Jean-Louis."

"How was it in Rome, Mrs. Cumming?"

"Hot, very hot. But do call me Anne."

"Thank you. We just came to ask Jean-Louis if he'd like to go into Gaeta to the cinema tonight. There's a German boy with a car who'll drive us in."

"How nice! Do go, darling. I rather wanted to see Bianca and Salvatore this evening. I know they bore you."

"Are you sure?"

"Of course, darling."

I kissed him, just in case the "darlings" had not sunk into their innocent hockey-stick minds.

Diary entry—a few days later.

I should be glad he is going out with those girls. If this is an incestuous mother-son relationship, I should want to see him enjoy himself. I don't. Unless I am a part of his enjoyment, I get jealous. Is this going to be a positive relationship for him and a negative one for me? Am I becoming a possessive old woman when I feel like a passionate young girl? Am I deluding myself? The physical side is getting a bit out of hand, too. Throughout the day I catch myself giving the child lascivious looks. I like to watch him from the back when he is unaware that I am looking. His shoulders are still narrow, and the shoulder blades stick out with a youthful skinniness, which is touching. His hips swell out to a rounded bottom and heavy legs. He would be bottom-heavy if it were not for the lightness of his springy walk. When he turns his head, the hippie ringlets swing across his eyes as he gives me that blue-blue, twinkling look. His teeth are a little too big and his nose a bit too small, but the result is somehow very sexy. He's a Brigitte Bardot of a boy. I want him in my bed all the time. I coax him back from the beach at lunch time so we can spend the long, hot afternoons making love. He jumps out of bed again with that Bardot bounce, and I watch from the window as he runs down to the sea and swims fast and far out to wash off the sweat and surplus sperm, and perhaps the feel of having been possessed. His is the age of freedom, and I must be strong enough to let him have it. If it weren't for those damned girls, watching and waiting on the side lines! Maybe it's time I sent him home to France. We have to go back to Rome at the end of next week anyway. I must prepare for work again.

Conversation in the Trattoria da Peppino. Evening. Sperlonga. August 25.

"Darling, do you realize we only have two more days here? Perhaps we should make some excursions into the hinterland."

"But it's so wonderful here, Anne. I'm having such a marvelous time."

"I know. But when you look back on a holiday, it's not always the marvelous times that matter. You often remember the place more than the people in the end. You haven't seen much of the surrounding country here."

"But I don't ever want to move from this beach. Be my teacher, Anne, but don't be an old schoolmarm!"

The words hurt, but the fact that he called me "Anne" instead of "chérie" hurt me even more. He had learned all he needed from me, and now he wanted to move on elsewhere. He didn't realize it yet, but I did.

"Are you going dancing tonight?" I asked casually, as if changing the subject.

"I might. Do you want to come?"

"No, thank you, darling. I've got some things to do about the house. You go, though. We'll be together tomorrow for our last night here."

"Well, I might go over to the discothèque and see who's there."

"Okay. But you won't be too late again tonight, will you?"

I got him back to Rome, but not without difficulty. He wanted to stay on in the youth hostel. His excuse was that he didn't want to go back to the hot city. I was sorely tempted to let my work go to hell and take him on somewhere else. I would have liked to extend my holiday to be with the boy, but I had a new film coming up, and the one from the Cannes Film Festival went on general release in September, and I had to begin the advance publicity. This would involve running around for most of the day seeing the editors of the monthly magazines, who were already closing their September issues. Jean-Louis had to amuse himself. He spent too much time sitting on the Spanish Steps or in the Piazza Navona in doubtful company.

The police were allowing the hippie kids to sell their handmade jewelry on the Steps, and they rolled out their bundles of beaten nails and leather thongs on the worn Travertine marble where the

azaleas had stood at Easter. I suspected they rolled
joints, too. The Italian police are very tough on
any kind of drug scene, so I was quite relieved
when I received a letter from Aurélien.

Letter from Draguignan to Rome. September 6.
Dearest Anne,

Marie and I are delighted to get such happy letters from Jean-Louis. He is obviously never wanting to come home! *Apropos* of which, do you think
he would be embarrassed if we drove to Rome for
a week to fetch him? We could stay at the Hotel
Inghilterra, which is near you, no? And then take
Jean-Louis back with us in the car, showing him
Florence and Lucca and a few other places of
interest on the way home. We do not want to be
interrupting your idyll, though. To us there is
nothing more natural than that our boy is "spending a holiday with his Fairy Godmother," as you
so cleverly put it. I know that you are sophisticated
enough, ma chère, to handle the situation of our
parental visit in the middle of a honeymoon—but
is he? The last thing we want to do is to be spoiling
your fun. I rely on you to write and tell us honest-
ly how you both feel.

I embrace you,
Aurélien

Diary entry. Rome. September 10.
How do I feel? Partly amused, partly annoyed
and partly relieved. It *is* a little irritating to have
the idyll interrupted, and to come down to earth

again. However, is it still so idyllic? The boy is
running around a great deal by himself while I am
working, and who knows what he gets up to? I am
partly jealous and party worried. He is becoming a
responsibility. Perhaps it will be a good thing if his
parents come to claim him. It would be a neat and
clean ending to our affair. I will ask him how *he*
feels about it this evening.

Snatches of conversation over dinner on the terrace.

"I had a letter from your father today. Your parents are thinking of driving down to get you."

"Oh, *merde!* That's the last thing I want!"

"It will be much more comfortable than hitchhiking back. What upsets you about it?"

"I don't know. They just don't seem to belong
here, that's all. Why can't they stay at home?"

"My dear boy, even we old people deserve a holiday sometimes!"

"You see? You're already taking their side! It's a
fucking bore!"

I went around and sat on his knee and ruffled
his hair, which brought things back into perspective again. The generation gap between us had
loomed rather large for a minute, but when he
kissed me, we forgot it again. Later, in bed, we got
back to the subject of his parents' visit.

"Where are they going to stay? Not here, I hope,
in the next room! That would be too much!"

"No. Your parents are very tactful. They will
stay at the Hotel Inghilterra down the road."

"What do you mean—'very tactful'? Don't tell
me they know I go to bed with you?"

I hid my smile in his curly hair and kissed him

behind the ear. It would have hurt his male vanity to know it was all originally a put-up job. It was difficult to know what to say next. I put my tongue in his ear. It had a slightly salty taste and a fringe of fine golden hair around the lobe.

"Your father knows me very well. I think he would be quite disappointed if he thought I hadn't seduced you."

"Good God! You must be joking! He's much too square to think of a thing like that."

"No, I'm not joking, darling. We always see our own parents as doddering old creatures with antediluvian ideas and no sex life. I'm sure you can't even imagine them in bed together."

"No, I certainly can't! What a ghastly idea!"

"You see? You're the one that's square! Your parents are pretty swinging."

"How do you know?"

I weighed my answer very carefully, then took the plunge.

"Your father was my lover years ago. He's not an old stick. He's a very passionate man."

For a moment I thought the child was going to faint. Then he looked as if he were going to hit me. Then, to my relief, he burst out laughing.

"Christ, how funny! It's like an old movie I once saw—*Les Parents Terribles*."

"It was a *new* movie when your father and I were young. I think we saw it together. We identified ourselves with the young couple then. Now we're the parents. Life itself doesn't change, but time forces us to exchange roles. I was only *your* age when your father seduced me."

"Good God! What was the old man like in bed?"

"I never discuss one man with another," I said firmly, but added, "He's much more sophisticated than you think. He taught me everything I've taught you!"

"Oh, my God, my God! You mean to say all those . . . you've done all those things with my father?"

He was looking a bit pale again, terribly young and defenseless. Perhaps I had gone too far. I put my head against his shoulder and snuggled up as if I were the child.

"Darling, you're a grown-up man. You must meet your father as an equal now. You can laugh about it and compare notes."

"Heaven forbid!"

I ran my hand down over his breasts. "Look, you're getting hair on your chest!"

"Oh, fuck off! You're a monster!"

But he didn't push me away. He hugged me to him. It was as if he were taking me back from his father. He made love to me furiously, angrily, holding me down and not thinking about my pleasure at all. He didn't even look at me; he turned me over and rammed me from the back and came with a great shout for the first time. He had never made any noise before. Then he rolled over and lay separately from me, also for the first time. He usually lay in my arms for a long time.

"Fucking bitch," he said. "You're mine now."

Letter from Rome to Draguignan.
Dear Aurélien,

Everything will be all right. We are both looking forward to your visit. You will find your son quite capable of handling the situation. You must be careful not to make him feel a little boy again. Let me know your dates so I can reserve your hotel room.

Love,
Anne

Things turned out rather differently than we had planned. Marie's mother was taken very ill again. She sent Aurélien down to Rome alone. I wonder why? Jean-Louis could easily have gone back by train. Anyway, Aurélien turned up, looking very dapper, and father and son were very funny together. Jean-Louis was the least embarrassed of us all in the end and carried it off beautifully. I was proud of him. He had just the right air of restraint, without actually trying to hide anything. His manner was quietly proprietary, as if to put his father in his place. Aurélien and I smiled at each other behind his back sometimes. My heart went out to both of them.

Note found on the hall table Friday evening after work.
Dearest Mistress Mine,

I hope you're not going to be cross with me, but I felt like a last weekend of swimming, so I've taken the keys to Sperlonga and gone off for a couple of nights to the seaside. After all, you have father to look after you! He invites you to dinner tonight, incidentally, and will call for you at eight. See you Sunday night. Father says we must leave on Monday.

Love,
J-L

I was furious at first. And jealous. I knew it was
those wretched hockey-stick girls he'd gone down
to see. I was sure Aurélien had put him up to it.
The two of them had become as thick as thieves
now. Aurélien had sent the boy off so he could get
me back himself. I was being hoisted by my own
pétard, to be passed back and forth between father
and son. Only the French could be capable of such
complicity!

Diary entry. Saturday morning.

I suppose there is something to be said for one's
own generation, after all. Aurélien is still asleep in
my bed.

It was quite an interesting evening last night. I
had no tendency to compare the two men. They
are quite separate entities to me. Of course I never
knew Aurélien when he was J-L's age; he was over
twenty-four when I met him, an older man to me
then, and an older man to me still. Now he is also
an old friend, and there is a nostalgic quality to our
love-making. It is cozy and intimate and less intense than with his son. I like them both, without
making comparisons or even linking them in my
mind. They are two different individuals who
haven't even much in common except me.

Conversation in bed on Saturday afternoon.

Aurélien woke up late, then took me out shopping and to lunch. We went back to bed again to
have a siesta with sex. The hair on Aurélien's chest
was quite white, though the hair on his head was
barely gray. His body was well preserved for a
man of fifty-five or -six.

"What does it feel like to go to bed with an old man after a teen-ager?" he asked.

"Aurélien, we agreed not to discuss your son. Anyway, you're not an old man, and he's not a teen-ager. You're two individuals, and there's no connection in my mind. I just said so in my diary."

"You keep a diary?"

"Intermittently."

"I thought only young girls kept diaries?"

"Sometimes I still *am* a young girl. Do you see me as old, Aurélien? Or do you see me as I was when we first met?"

"A mixture of both. And you?"

"I can hardly remember you at all. It's like a new affair with a different man. It's not that age has anything to do with it—it's just that I have no memory. I never have had."

"Someone once said 'The only really happy man is he who has no memory.' You're a happy woman, Anne."

"Have you been happy, Aurélien?"

"Not always—but there are many things I have to be grateful for. I'm grateful for Jean-Louis. He's a fine boy, and you've helped me to see it. He's very 'together' for his age. He never talked to me before—now we're very close. We even talk about you, man to man. He's not as reserved as you are about your love-making—he tells me the sexual details!"

"You bastards! I expect you're exchanging stag jokes about me!"

"Now stop it. You should be glad we both appreciate you in bed."

"It's immoral."

"So what? Who's got any use for morality? Only the insecure."

"This whole situation is getting beyond me."

"You provoked it."

"What do you mean? *You* wrote to me proposing the whole bloody thing!"

"You flirted shamelessly with my son at the Cannes Film Festival. I saw you deliberately turn him on. I was jealous and pleased at the same time."

"What pleased you about it?"

"I was pleased that my son was following in his father's footsteps. That he could appreciate a real woman. We all want to see our children grow up in our own image. Or is it our own image in our children?"

"It's a mistake to live vicariously through your children, Aurélien. Don't tell me you sent Jean-Louis here just to re-live our old love affair second-hand?"

"Not exactly. I'd hardly be here in your bed if that were true."

"Why *are* you here now? You and Jean-Louis are playing games with me. It's not what I expected."

"Did *you* want to play with *us*? Did you think I was sending you a pretty toy?" His voice had a dangerous edge to it.

"Oh, shut up and make love to me again," I said, trying to get back on safer ground.

"Anne, I'm fifty-six. Are you trying to kill me?"

"Come on, Aurélien. Your son can get it up twice running."

"You little bitch!"

Aurélien hit me. I had known the aggression of

comparison would arouse him, and it did. Under similar circumstances, the son had been stimulated into a childish rage. The father displayed controlled fury, domination and possession. He shook me like a rat, then crushed me against his body as he penetrated me, as if he wanted to annihilate me by swallowing me up. I felt the adult power behind the drive. There was certainly nothing childish about Aurélien.

After the rigors of the afternoon, we decided to sleep in our own beds. Aurélien was also a little afraid that Marie might call him and not find him at the hotel. I was relieved, because Jean-Louis might phone me, too, from Sperlonga, and I didn't want to speak with him in front of his father.

We had dined out of doors in Piazza Santa Maria in Trastevere. Ambulatory musicians came around singing old chestnuts like "O Sole Mio," old crones sold flowers, setting their wares right on the table, children played ball in the piazza, and the illuminated mosaics on the façade of the church glittered behind the sparkle of the fountains.

Aurélien had bought me a handmade gold chain with a jade heart on it. I was touched by the gift. His son had never thought of bringing me a single rose in all the time he'd been staying with me. There was something to older lovers, after all.

The wretched boy did not telephone. He was probably out dancing with those wretched girls. There was a nightclub on the beach near the camping site, from which it was all too easy to walk along the dunes and get lost in the clumps of bamboo. I was not exactly jealous, only sad that it wasn't me among the bamboos, and that I wasn't seventeen too. I had always known that I'd lose the boy, but that knowledge couldn't protect me from emotion. I missed him intensely.

On Sunday morning I made breakfast and took it outside on the terrace; the morning glories were coming out, electric-blue trumpets heralding the sun. The glass table was cracked, and my wrought-iron chairs needed painting. A previous lover had once said, "Anne achieves what we all strive for—stylish dilapidation. She's a slut with class!"

The telephone rang. My heart leaped. I was furious with myself for caring so much. I was even more cross when it wasn't Jean-Louis but the American star of the picture I was about to work on. He didn't like the piece by Moravia in the Sunday paper. I explained that I hadn't written it myself, but he said it was my fault for letting a cheap journalist interview him. Stars are all the same—they're mad if you get them publicity and even madder if you don't.

I quoted Oscar Wilde to him: "It doesn't matter what they say, just as long as they talk!" He'd never heard of either Oscar Wilde or Moravia. I explained that Moravia was not only one of Italy's greatest living writers, but also wrote the film reviews in *L'Espresso*, the Rome intellectual weekly. The American then calmed down and invited me for lunch. Stars are often very lonely. People all think they are having a glamorous time, and therefore don't dare to invite them. Often they just sit in their hotels, afraid to go out and be recognized, afraid to be seen alone without some dazzling companion. That's why most of them have secretaries to trail around after them. It's not so much to cope with the fan mail as it is a bulwark against the loneliness at the top.

"I'll come to lunch, but I have to bring a house guest. He's a charming man—you'll like him—a French lawyer."

"Does he speak English?"

"Yes. I taught him."

"Okay, then. The Grand Hotel at one?"

"Fine; we'll be there."

It would amuse Aurélien to meet an American movie star. We could have a wonderful lunch, because I knew the star was getting $100 a day for expenses. He also had a car and a chauffeur at his disposal, and we could go out to the Appia Antica district to eat.

Conversation on the way to the Grand Hotel. Rome. Sunday. September.

"I had a phone call from my son this morning."

"He called *you*! The little beast! I hoped he'd call me."

"He wanted to know whether I'd like to be alone with you another day or two. He thought of staying on at the sea."

"He could have asked me that too. But I suspect he was not thinking of us—he wants to stay on with those English teen-agers at the camping site."

"Anne, I believe you're jealous! Don't tell me you've fallen in love with my son!"

"Would that be so strange?"

"But he's only seventeen."

"I was eighteen when you and I fell in love with each other. Have you forgotten?"

"But you're fifty now."

"I don't feel it when I'm with Jean-Louis."

"No, I suppose not. It seems a little ridiculous but ... well, it's rather charming. Very nice for you both, in fact."

"It's been *very* nice, thank you. Of course I didn't expect it to last, but I would have liked it to go on a bit longer. It was very rejuvenating."

"Do I make you feel your age?"

"No, you make me feel young, too—but in a different way. I feel protected by you. I even feel like a spoiled child again. It's nice to sit in an expensive restaurant for a change, and to know the table has been reserved in advance, and that the bill will be taken care of, and that if I order the most expensive things on the menu, you'll enjoy my enjoyment of them. With the boy, *I* feel protective; *I* do the spoiling."

"So I'm still a father-figure to you?"

"In a way. The six years between us means nothing now—we're equals—but when I was eighteen and you were twenty-four, it seemed like a lot."

"I'm sorry. I never felt fatherly toward *you*. You were my first Grand Passion."

"Of course, darling. For me, too." I stopped in the middle of the busy street. "I not only love your son, Aurélien, I still love *you*."

I kissed him in the middle of a pedestrian crossing. A taxi screeched to a halt and the driver leaned out and shouted angrily, "*Basta!* You two! You're old enough to know better!" We laughed and went on. I realized I had hurt Aurélien's feelings and tried to make amends.

"Don't you understand, darling, the boy has nothing to do with us. If I ate a delicious ripe peach yesterday, it's not going to spoil the strawberries and cream I have for lunch today, nor the chocolate cake tomorrow. It only sharpens my appetite. Your son is a tasty morsel; you are a succulent mouthful."

Aurélien looked slightly more confident again. Really, all men were such boys!

"You're both tasty dishes," I went on, trying to lighten the atmosphere and be more frivolous. "Maybe I could have you both for the same meal one day." I squeezed his arm.

"Are you suggesting a *partouse* with me and my son, you terrible woman?"

"Why not? I'm sure it's done all the time."

"Not in my family, thank God!"

"Well, think it over."

We had reached the Trevi Fountain. We were making a slight detour, so Aurélien could throw in his coin. He had refused Jean-Louis's suggestion to stay on longer. The boy was coming back that evening as planned, and father and son would leave in the morning together.

We walked down the steps, hand in hand, to the great florid fountain.

"It's too baroque for me, and there's too much water. I really think the French do fountains better."

We were photographed by some irritating *papa-*

razzi, and agreed it had been a mistake to go there.
It was very hot at noon, too, and you could smell
the chlorine in the water.

"The magic is not here at midday!" Aurélien
said.

The star was propped up in the gloomy bar of
the Grand Hotel, drinking a concoction of Camp-
bell's consommé and vodka. He was pretending to
himself that it was nourishment rather than alco-
hol, and he was talking to a redhead, obviously an
expensive whore. Little did she know that this fading he-man was a well-known alcoholic. He would
not be much of a client; she might get an auto-
graphed photo out of him at most.

We drove right down the Appia Antica and
back, trying to decide on a restaurant, before
choosing the Escargot at the beginning of it. It was
a beautiful drive, the cypresses black in the hot
sun. Old Roman villas crumbled along the road-
side in front of new Roman villas, where the nouveau riche were basking around their swimming
pools set in formal Italian gardens. Beyond were
open fields with grazing sheep and fallen aque-
ducts.

Under the arbor at the back of the Escargot, we
were protected from sightseers and gasoline
fumes, wrapped in expensive damask napkins, and
presented with huge menus. The two men were
ultra-polite to each other, both bowing to an imagined superiority each thought the other possessed;
but the star was a phony, struggling to stay young
at the top, whereas Aurélien was a *real* man, sure
of his position and not ashamed of his age. All

those women sighing in the aisles for the star would have had a much better time in bed with Aurélien, I thought.

We dropped the star at the Grand Hotel to sleep off his liquor, and, as there is nothing I like better than making love on a long hot summer afternoon, we went home to my apartment and got into bed again. I tried not to think of Jean-Louis's imminent return, but I couldn't relax in Aurélien's arms and didn't fall asleep as usual.

"I suppose I must let the boy sleep here to-night," Aurélien said, as if reading my thoughts. He was wiping the sweat off my breasts with the sheet. His tone was grudgingly generous.

I made a big effort to ignore the temptation to accept.

"I don't think that's a good idea, Aurélien, from anybody's point of view. Why doesn't he stay with you at the hotel? You've got a double room. Then you'll be all ready to set off together early in the morning."

"Don't you want a last night of love with youth?"

"No," I lied. "I hate long Russian good-byes and studied farewells. It's much better *not* to know when you've gone to bed with someone for the last time. He'll be here soon, and I'll just help him pack."

"Then I'd better get up!" He got out of bed and began to dress. "Bring him and his luggage over about 8:30, and we can go around the corner to Ranieri's. Does that seem a suitable place for a formal family farewell dinner?"

I smiled, although I didn't feel amused. I got out

of bed too and kissed Aurélien tenderly, and the tenderness was genuine. It was just that I no longer felt that "high" with Aurélien that only drugs or new love can give—a lightheaded, dizzy vibrancy that you know to be an unhealthy hang-up, but which is irresistible.

"Why don't you stay here and receive the prodigal son with me?" I asked, afraid I would not refuse the boy unless the father was still there.

"No, you two have things to say to each other that I don't want to hear," Aurélien replied, now fully dressed and making for the door.

"Nonsense, Aurélien. All that's a thing of the past already," I said—and as I said it, I knew it to be true. But after letting Aurélien out, I purposely kept on my transparent summer dressing gown.

"Anne, darling Anne, how I've missed you!"

Jean-Louis burst into the house, bronzed and bouncy, his golden curls tumbled, his blue eyes shining. He'd had a wonderful time, but he was sweet enough to pretend otherwise for my sake. It was touchingly obvious. The knife turned in my heart, but the smile never left my lips.

"Hello, darling, I've missed you too."

"Didn't father console you?" He looked at me quizzically.

"You know I never tell one man about another!" I kept my tone bantering.

"Is he having dinner here tonight?"

"We're going to a formal restaurant for a formal farewell. You're sleeping at the hotel with your father for an early start."

He pouted. "What, no last lessons with my favorite teacher?"

"The last lesson is that it's better to skip the last lesson. Then you're never left with a taste of bitterness in your mouth."

"What a marvelous woman you are!"

He kissed me, but I could tell he was secretly relieved. He had been worn out on the hockey field behind the sand dunes and didn't need me anymore.

"You know, I don't think I'll come out to dinner tonight," I said as I helped him with his packing. "Your father will understand."

"Shall I tell him you're skipping the last lesson?"

"Yes, he'll know what that means. Now come on and we'll finish your packing. He's expecting you at 8:30."

We bustled around the apartment collecting things. Every now and then we kissed. He pinched my breasts, I felt his balls.

"They seem a bit empty!" I commented.

He blushed. "Who are you to make accusations? What have *you* been doing? And with my own father, too!"

We laughed and went on packing. It was only a game after all.

At last he was ready to go. The fatal moment had come. I mustn't cry. I mustn't cry. I picked up his camera and hung it on his shoulder. It was probably full of snapshots of the hockey champions. There was one snap in it that I had taken of him on a rock, and one he had taken of me on the beach, sitting on my Union Jack towel. He sent them to me later with an inscription.

I walked him to the elevator with all his bits and pieces.

"Will you be able to manage it all as far as the hotel? Do you want me to come with you?"

"No, I'd rather say good-bye to you at your own front door."

"Good-bye, then. Come back and have your pretty little bottom slapped from time to time."

"You bet I will. Every year."

He pressed the button, and the elevator moved away.

"Tell your father I'll miss him," I shouted.

"You'll fucking well miss us both!" His voice floated up to me.

It was true. I'd miss them both.

I began to cry as I went inside. "You silly old bitch," I said to myself. "Pull yourself together. Sentiment is for the young."

I went out onto the terrace. The morning glories had shut their blue trumpets for the night. The music and dancing were over. Aurélien had been a nostalgic reprise of the main melody. Jean-Louis had been the song itself. The evening air seemed very still.

2 ∽ London Bridge
Is Burning Down

In December 1967, I decided to take a month's holiday in England. I was exhausted after the film with the drunken American actor. Keeping him out of the papers had been even more difficult than getting him into them!

Every now and then, one should go back to the land of one's origins to see what is going on, so I was going to London for Christmas with my daughter Fiona, and would also be seeing Rudi.

Rudi was designing an Italian opera for Covent Garden, and I had asked him to reserve a little furnished flat for me in his Chelsea apartment hotel. Like that, we could be together—but not too much so. I had not seen him since autumn, when he had paid me a brief visit on his way to see his father, the old Baron Von Hoffman, a distinguished elderly widower with a Franz Josef moustache, who lived in Vienna in the winter and in a crumbling old castle near Salzburg in the summer. Rudi had gone to move him from one to the other, intending to return to Rome, but had then been summoned to Covent Garden. I had been left with Rudi's heavy luggage and an invitation to join him in London for the Gala Performance.

I stepped off the train at Victoria Station, to be confronted by a billboard with a blown-up photo of a maniacal face bearing the legend "Wanted for Murder. If you've seen this man, go to your local police station."

"There's nobody like the British for a juicy murder," Rudi said as he met me at the barrier. "You're just in time for the witch hunt."

I had come by night train, because I had too much luggage for the plane. Most of it was Rudi's. I was bringing it to him in London, so he could eventually go straight on back to New York. It all sounded very Jet Set, except that I was traveling second class by train, Rudi having gone directly to London by first-class plane. I was his slave of love as usual.

"It might be a good idea if we left the heavy suitcases at the left luggage place," I suggested. "Then you can pick them up here again when you take the boat train to Southampton."

Rudi was going on to New York after Christmas, on the *Queen Elizabeth*. We therefore directed the porter to the left luggage depot.

"There ain't no left luggage office no more," he told us, grinning happily. "Bloody Irish terrorists and their bombs. Can't take care of no unaccompanied suitcases nowadays. 'Ad to close down the 'ole bloody office."

"Oh, dear! The Irish have upset the British way of life, Rudi, and I was so looking forward to enjoying it again."

"What do you mean—again? You've never really lived here."

Rudi was right. I'd spent very little of my life in England.

My parents had never lived in England, but they were very English. We had lived everywhere, from the wilds of South Africa to the South of France. My childhood had been spent moving from colonial backwoods to continental boulevards, while my parents searched for a congenial way of life between the two wars. The main trouble was that they were not congenial to each other, so the search ended in divorce, and my brother and I ended up in London in the 1920s with our mother.

Life in London in the twenties and thirties was a cozy indoor life of comfortable chairs and intellectual conversation around gas fires, toasting muffins with a long brass fork. Dinner parties were held by candlelight in spacious dining rooms with open fireplaces and high Georgian windows. On summer days the windows would hastily be thrown open to let in the weak sunlight. In winter they were kept hermetically sealed against the encroaching gray. I had grown up enjoying an outdoor life of beaches and terraces, closing shutters against the hot sun. I did not take kindly to scuttling across wet pavements under an umbrella in my navy serge gym tunic, nor to the English boarding school where the water froze in glasses left on bedside tables in bleak dormitories. I was relieved when my mother took an Italian lover after the divorce and went back to live on the Côte d'Azur, taking us with her.

Now, years later, I was still looking for the England of my childhood. No wonder I didn't know where to find it, with such a confused background.

"My treasure," Rudi said to me the morning after my arrival, "I need some reference books on the eighteenth century for my costumes."

Rudi had always prefaced his daily demands on my time and energy by calling me his "treasure," the slight Austrian accent emphasizing the first syllable.

"Books on costume in particular or the eighteenth century in general?" I asked hesitantly, feeling my holiday evaporate.

I knew my role in Rudi's life—slave of love. He knew how to turn the screws (in every sense of the word) with such charm that he got excellent work out of all his willing slaves. Rudi *was* charming, the most charming, self-centered egotist I knew, with a rare quality for getting the last ounce of everyone's flesh without anyone feeling the slightest pain. I had sold myself voluntarily into his human bondage fifteen years ago, and had not yet managed to extricate myself from it. Rudi might have strayed from my bed, but he had remained fixed in my heart.

"I need scenes of everyday life by famous painters of the period," he went on. "Painters have the artistic eye already; they single out character and atmosphere. So get some books from the public library, darling, and go and buy any that you know I'd want to keep." He smiled his sweet, affectionate and winning smile. "After all, who else would know just what to get?" he added cunningly.

Who else, indeed? My holiday had gone. I was to be a part-time, unpaid assistant to one of the world's great designers and my own ex-lover.

The next day I was in Zwemmer's bookshop on Charing Cross Road, having spent the previous day in reference libraries. Human bondage might possibly be better than boredom, but I did feel as if I deserved a little light relief on my holiday. The light relief turned up in heavyweight form in Zwemmer's.

"One moment, sir. Where are you going, please?"

The shop assistant spoke from the top of a ladder, which effectively barred the way to the back regions. A young man had just entered the shop and was crawling under the ladder with a certain amount of difficulty on account of his enormous size.

"I'm going into the back room to see if you have Chadwick's *Decypherment of Linear B*," came the reply in a voice so smooth and mild and gently upper class that I wondered who had spoken. Surely not the enormous young man?

He was now standing on the far side of the ladder. His manner had been mild, but his appearance was so extraordinarily barbaric that I quite understood why the assistant had tried to impede his passage. He looked as if he would knock down bookshelves rather than buy their contents.

His hair was wild and reddish, and he had an aboriginal look about him, not from the jungle perhaps, but from some distant mountain stronghold where young men were warriors, all slightly over life-size, and sporting fierce moustaches and square red Assyrian-type beards. He bulged out of a black rollneck sweater, stretched to its utmost by the huge muscles of a weight lifter. That he should be ferreting out obscure books on archaeology in the back room of Zwemmer's was incongruous.

"*I'm* looking for unusual books as well!" I exclaimed, galvanized into instant action. "May I join you?"

"Madam," came those soft, dulcet tones from that massive frame, "let me be your guide." He held out his hand, indicating that I should crawl under the stepladder too.

I got down on all fours and joined him on the other side. "How do you do?" he said. "My name is Gregory."

Bad Gregory, as he came to be called (to distinguish him from Good Gregory), was a very unusual young man. He took me home for tea after helping me choose books. His home, not mine. It was a studio on a roof in Parson's Green, full of beautiful Persian carpets and not much else. There were also some books and a hi-fi, but the focal point was a huge double bed made out of assorted cushions. It was a bit lumpy, and I found myself falling from one cushion to another, but it was all in a very good cause. Bad Gregory always knew what he was doing, in bed or out, with a singular clarity and precision and attention to detail.

"Why do you know so much?" I asked him after he had expounded on a dozen subjects between the bookshop and Parson's Green.

"It's quality, not quantity, that counts."

"But he's got an oversized brain as well. He knows everything about everything. Touch on any subject and he rambles on in depth and detail for hours."

"What does he do?"

"He preserves ancient monuments. He's an archaeologist in an office."

"The more you tell me about him, the more unlikely he sounds. Are you sure you didn't make him up?"

"No, really. I'll show him to you. He's coming in for a late tea after work, on a bicycle."

Gregory appeared in a yellow raincoat and a sou'wester. It was one of those English days where the rain is so fine you wonder whether it is really raining or not; whether you should leave your umbrella at home or take it with you. His outfit was therefore excessive for the occasion, but so was everything he did.

Rudi and I were staying in the Chelsea Cloisters, an apartment hotel which was more like a ship than a cloister. Built in the shape of a rectangle around a central courtyard, the long windowless corridors opened on either side into tiny, one-room apartments like ship's cabins. Some faced inward and were quieter, some faced outward and had more light. It was significant that Rudi had chosen the darker quiet and I had chosen the noisy light. It was even more significant that we were on separate floors—so near and yet so far. This was part of our new life-style together—separate lovers, separate lives.

My new 170-pound lover *and* his bicycle entirely filled my tiny cabin.

"How on earth did you get your bicycle up here?" I asked him.

"In the lift, of course."

"Couldn't you leave it outside?"

"And get it pinched?"

"But this is England. Nobody steals anything."

"You're joking!"

"No. I'm just living in my long-lost girlhood. Now take off your raincoat and sit down and have a cup of tea."

Gregory leaned the bicycle against the wall and undressed. Completely.

"You're wet?" I asked.

"No, just an exhibitionist."

He sat on the single divan, which sagged to the floor with his weight.

"Fuck first or tea first?" he asked calmly.

"Well, I was going to ask a friend down for tea."

"Does he like to watch?"

"I've never asked him."

In the end I phoned Rudi and told him to come down in half an hour. It was too soon; we were still hard at it. Gregory's approach to sex, like everything else, was excessive, detailed and scientific. He systematically worked through all the positions in the almanac. I told Rudi to walk around the block. By the time he came back, the gymnastics were over, and I was in my dressing gown. Gregory was still naked, however, drinking his cup of tea, his penis now limp but obvious. Fortunately the central heating was good, and

Rudi was sophisticated enough to take it all in his stride. He and Gregory chatted amicably enough for half an hour, then Gregory dressed and left us.

"It's unusual for such a big man to have a big cock," Rudi commented when Gregory had gone. "Usually it's the other way around."

"You mean little men have big cocks?"

"Yes, haven't you noticed?"

"Maybe I've had less experience than you have!"

"Or you're just less observant," he said, refusing to be put down by my bitchiness.

It was a difficult situation for two people, once passionate lovers, to get onto a totally different footing. Rudi and I were still working at it. With a heterosexual man, there would have been a lingering sadness; with Rudi in his present homosexual phase, there was a kind of spirited rivalry. In a way it made things easier.

Diary entry. London. December 5, 1967.

I can't decide which has changed more, England or myself. Here I am, facing my fifty-first birthday, living in a cloister. But not, however, like a nun. I have given up love, but I have not given up sex. Do I like this new situation? It has its advantages. I am no longer torn with anguish and doubts. Sex has become, like eating and drinking, a necessary and often pleasant pastime. The disadvantages? I need several people instead of one. Love and desire, friendship and affection, trust and security are no longer all rolled up in one person. I love my children and grandchildren; in other ways I still love my husbands and Rudi. I feel friendship for my friends, desire for my lovers, affection for them all. Perhaps, in a way, this is healthier. You can't be let down so hard and so often. My security is in myself. I no longer expect it from others.

I spent my fifty-first birthday in bed with Gregory. He had taken the day off from work.

"I've brought you a present, Granny," he said as he arrived. He had found a way of padlocking his bicycle to the banister in the downstairs hall. The management had not yet objected. They probably thought he was the window cleaner.

"I don't know if I approve of my lovers calling me 'Granny.' My name's Anne."

"Too late now, Granny; I've got used to it."

He gave me an enormous hug. He was like a warmhearted, well-trained Russian dancing bear. He had noticed that I wore Arpège and had brought me matching soap and bath powder. There was a poem with it:

For Granny on Her Birthday
Paradox.
In a world where everything grows smaller
How long does a stillborn hope
take to disappear?
                              Love,
                                  Gregory

I don't know to this day what it means, but I was very touched. I put it away to add to my collection of correspondence from young lovers.

"And now comes the real present. Get into bed, Granny."

The real present was a long trip around all the erogenous zones. Somewhere along the line I was bound to come, maybe even twice, although I'm not a multiple-orgasm girl. Gregory himself took hours to reach orgasm. It was a little tiring, but you can't always achieve perfection every time with every man; you must be grateful for small mercies and big cocks—or vice versa.

Rudi came to see us during the day. He handed me a small, flat box—not from Cartier but from Ken Lane. Inside was a pair of chandelier earrings. They hung nearly to my shoulders.

"Wear nothing else, or just black satin," he said. "I want you to scintillate at my gala performance."

It was fun being fifty-one—like crossing the Rubicon.

The next morning I went looking for Rudi in the vast scene-painting studio at Covent Garden and found him with a new assistant. He was introduced to me as Caspian, a name I found as fascinating as the young man himself.

"I think Nureyev must have leaped straight through a piece of scenery and they took the silhouette and made Caspian out of the mold," I said to Rudi. "Where did you find him, and are you in love with him?"

"Of course I'm not in love with him. I'm in love with my friend Tom in New York, and I'm too busy to be unfaithful to him even in my *mind*—although I admit Caspian's a temptation!"

"So you haven't had him?"

"Not in the sense you mean—alas! He's straight. He has a very pretty girl friend who comes to call for him every evening."

The girl friend was named Kate, and that night I met her at the stage door. She and Gregory had both been waiting there and got into conversation.

"Let's all go and have supper together," I suggested, when Caspian had joined us.

Rudi wouldn't come. He was still sticking pieces of silver paper onto the scenery to make highlights. Rudi is one of the hardest workers I know. His work has always been my biggest rival.

"I'll cook if we can find someplace open to buy the food," Gregory offered.

I thought it very generous of him, but I realized later that Gregory's cooking was as thorough as everything else he did and was based on a desire to dominate the situation. He had to be in charge. Kate and I tried to help, but we were eventually banished from the kitchen. We joined Caspian in the big studio room and played records from Gregory's classical collection until a marvelous cordon bleu meal arrived.

"You're a continual delight to me, Gregory," I complimented him. "Where did you learn to cook?"

"My Russian grandmother," was the surprising reply. "She'd been brought up in St. Petersburg, left very much in the care of the servants, and there was a French chef in the kitchen where she spent much of her time. When her family fled the revolution and lost everything—including the

French chef—it turned out she was the only one who knew how to cook. Then she married and had my mother, who became the intellectual she still is—again my grandmother became the cook and this time looked after *me* in the kitchen."

All this was related with a flamboyant flourish of egg whisks and wooden spoons. Like everything he did, Gregory played to his audience. While we were lying about later on the cushions, he began making love to me. Caspian and Kate were over by the hi-fi choosing records, but he paid no attention to them. I could feel it was a turn-on for him to make love in public. I didn't like it and said so. It didn't stop him. I even struggled, but he held me down in a viselike grip—he had studied karate—so I gave in gracefully, but I couldn't come. The rhythm of the music was at counterpoint with the rhythm of the love-making—and I prefer to make love in private.

For the first dress rehearsal, Kate and I were allowed to sit in the upper circle, or grand tier as it's called at Covent Garden. Rudi and Caspian were busy rushing from the front of the house to backstage to supervise the singers' costumes as they came on. Rudi had managed, as usual, to create a magical atmosphere, light but sumptuous. Misty pastels were interspersed with deep colors. Gold and silver glinted through their subtle depths like flashes of lightning on a summer's night.

"I wish I were going to be here for the gala," Kate whispered to me.

"Why aren't you?"

"I've got a job in a touring company. It's my first real part."

"I didn't know you were an actress."

"Yes. That's how I met Caspian. We were at drama school together. I hate to leave him now, but I've got to go up north for our Christmas show. We open in Liverpool on Christmas Eve, and there's a week of rehearsals first."

So Kate left for Liverpool and Caspian moved in with Gregory in order to sublet their apartment. Kate was not going to be back for at least six months, and, as Gregory needed a flatmate, it seemed like a good idea for the boys to double up and share expenses. I was a bit worried at anybody moving into Gregory's territory—he was very possessive—but it wasn't my business, as I was soon leaving London anyway.

As the gala performance approached, Rudi was very nervous.

"The Queen Mother is coming," he told me. "I'm to be presented to her afterwards in the Crush Bar at a little champagne party. You're to come too, Anne. I'll see that you're introduced."

"I've already met her, Rudi. She's a vague relative of Robert's, although I first saw her years ago at Buck House when I was presented to her in-laws."

"What do you mean 'her in-laws'?"

"George the Fifth and Queen Mary. I was presented at Court in their Jubilee Year in white satin with the requisite three feathers on my head and a long train—you've seen the photo."

"Then you've got to be particularly beautiful still. What are you wearing?"

"Don't worry—I won't let you down, but it will be a surprise. I'm an independent woman now, Rudi. You don't choose my clothes anymore!"

At the gala opening, Rudi was in a dark brown velvet suit, I was in black satin with Rudi's birthday earrings, and the Queen Mother was all tinsel and tiaras. She looked as if she had just stepped down from the top of the Christmas tree in the foyer. Princess Margaret and Lord Snowdon were with her. Flunkys in white wigs and knee britches held back velvet curtains for them all. Waiters in tails brought champagne on silver trays. The Royals smiled, and glittered, and proved once again that fairy tales still exist for a public that still believes. In that respect England hadn't changed.

When it was all over, Rudi and I couldn't find a taxi. We went home in the underground in full evening dress. That hadn't changed either. I remembered that too from my childhood; people in evening dress in an underground train.

"There's that man again," I said, pointing to the blown-up poster that was still being displayed in all stations.

"He's got eyes like Gregory," Rudi said. "Don't get murdered. You know what the English are. Specialists in kinky sex murders. He'll put your corpse in a cupboard and bring it out on Saturdays for necrophiliac practices."

"What do you mean?"

"He'll fuck your dead body."

"Oh, Rudi, he's such a cuddlesome young man, like a great big Russian bear. He'd never do a thing like that!"

But the remark left a nasty taste in my mouth.

There *was* something strangely menacing under Gregory's mild but dominating manner.

The whole family was converging for Christmas at Fiona's. Vanessa was flying from Italy with her husband and baby. Robert, the father of both my daughters, was coming up from Wales from his stately home. Charles and his wife would be in London and would come down to Fiona's for the day. My ex-husbands were very good friends. That's how it all began.

"Now, mother, you can bring one lover," Fiona stipulated. "Who will it be?"

"Rudi, I suppose. I have nobody else suitable at the moment."

"Is he still your lover?"

"In a manner of speaking. We don't go to bed together anymore, but does that matter?"

"Only if it matters to you."

She's such a sensible girl, my elder daughter.

Christmas is a milestone in family life, marking chronological and social changes in the construction of any family group, although the traditions always remain the same. My lovers had dispersed, my ex-husbands had arrived. Rudi had decided at the last moment that he must go back to Vienna to see the old Baron, his father, and Gregory had left London to go and visit his parents.

Robert arrived from Wales with bronchitis and settled in at Fiona's with his hot water bottle and a poultice on his chest. Vanessa, with husband and baby, flew in on a charter flight. Charles and his wife were to drive down. There were not enough bedrooms in Fiona's house for the entire assortment of Christmas guests.

"Only *you* could have conglomerated such a mixed bag," Robert said to me as I made up his bed on the sofa.

"I don't know why you have to make yourself so uncomfortable, Robert. You could have shared the spare room with me."

"Certainly not. Very improper. Haven't slept with you for twenty years. It would make my bronchitis worse."

There was no arguing with Robert. We sat by the fire like Darby and Joan while our daughters organized an English Christmas for us, identical with the Christmases we had once organized for them.

"Don't forget to put a tangerine in the toe of the stocking," generations of English grandmothers said on Christmas Eve. I said it once again too.

"Can we wake up now?" generations of children asked on dark northern Christmas mornings, bouncing about with excitement hours earlier than usual and trying to see in the darkness the outline of a knobby stocking on the end of the bed.

I was sleeping with my English grandchildren, since Robert had turned me down. This enabled us to give Vanessa the spare room for her little Matthew, who had afternoon rests and went to bed late like the little Italian he was.

"Granny, can we wake up now?" two little English voices cried in unison at 5 A.M. on Christmas morning.

"No, certainly not," I replied, fighting a losing

battle. "Keep quiet till six. Then you can open your stockings and get into my bed for a story."

I tried to doze off again through their protests. They were head to tail in one of the twin beds, while I was in the other. They began fighting and teasing each other, and I was sorely tempted to hand over the stockings to keep them quiet.

"If you don't shut up, your mother and father will come in, and they'll be even more cross with you than granny."

There was a momentary pause in the activities in the other bed, then a loud wail from the little girl. She was the younger, but a born troublemaker. Her brother was an angel and, like all male angels, was being henpecked by the domineering female. I could see their matrimonial futures in the making, shaped by the children's games they were already playing. Their present sibling rivalry would turn into the war between the sexes as soon as they began playing adult games. How could I help them? The die seemed already cast at the ages of three and four—perhaps it was even cast in my daughter's womb. Should I have spoken to *her* when she was in *my* womb? Could one tamper with heredity and the genes before one even conceived? Take a fetal tranquilizer? Choose a different mate? Go in for human husbandry to improve the race? This was Christmas morning. How did the Virgin Mary conceive such a Christlike child? She should have left her recipe, together with the Scriptures.

"Granny, he kicked me."

"She kicked me first."

"No, I never!"

"One of you come over here and lie quietly in granny's bed till six o'clock."

"I'm coming . . ."

"No, I'm coming . . ."

Struggles, scuffles, an old-fashioned slap from granny. Then they both got in, one on either side of me. We settled down quietly for a few minutes. I pretended to fall asleep; then it started all over again. I foresaw generations of children waking sleepy parents; my mind stretched back into the past and forward into the future. Finally I gave in and officially woke up.

"Get me the set of Beatrix Potter books, Malcolm. . . . No, you stay here, you little minx."

So we read about Mrs. Tiggywinkle and Tommy Titmouse and Peter Rabbit till the light filtered through the curtains and the central heating came on. Then I let them get out of bed to get their stockings. The little girl plunged into hers and swiftly unwrapped all the tiny parcels, throwing them around the bed. The boy sat for a long time feeling the lumpy shapes and wondering what they were going to be. Then he cautiously peeped inside.

Later little Matthew toddled in, and we all helped him unwrap his stocking. We had breakfast in our dressing gowns. Then we dressed and spent the rest of the day eating. The port wine was passed clockwise, as we stood to drink the Queen's health. She spoke to us from the new television set, still in her "My husband and I" period. I can't remember the rest of the programs, as I fell asleep among the crumpled wrapping paper on the sofa till it was time to leave.

I traveled back to London with Charles and his wife in their rented car. I wanted a few days alone in my cloister.

As I sat in the car, I thought hard about the mutability of love. Charles had once been the most dramatic of my great loves, but now he was only a quiet friend. It hardly seemed possible that I had run away with him across five European countries all of twenty years ago, and then run away *from* him eight years later. His wife was like a sister to me. I felt no sense of rivalry or loss. I had just moved on, forward and far away.

"Come to dinner, Anne. Caspian and I are going to make a New Year's banquet," Gregory's soft voice came over the phone. He had just got back from the holidays with his family. I hadn't seen him yet.

I found a dozen young people for dinner in Gregory's studio when I got there. Gregory himself was so busy cooking that he didn't notice one of his friends cuddling up to me on the divan. It was very cold, and there was no central heating. While we sat around eating, we were given plaid rugs from the Scotch House to keep us warm.

"I believe this is called 'bundling,' " I said as a young man called Peter or Paul snuggled up to me.

There were both a Peter and a Paul present, but I never learned which was which. One of them wrapped around me like a spoon between the courses. He was rather drunk and had a hard-on. He lifted my skirt under cover of the rug, and, with a little wriggling of underwear and bodies, he slipped it in. Once in, he never moved again. I looked around and found that he had fallen asleep.

Everyone clapped as Gregory brought in some crêpes suzette. This woke Peter or Paul. He slipped out as quietly as he had slipped in and went on eating as if nothing had happened—and indeed nothing had.

It was a strange vacuum period in my life, a holiday period during which nothing much mattered, least of all sex. The boys came and went. Gregory and Caspian and their friends seemed to like having me around, and they all flirted mildly with me when Gregory wasn't looking.

"Why do I appeal to such very young men?" I asked Rudi, who had turned up again in England to take his boat from Southampton to New York.

"You act available," Rudi answered. "Young girls play hard to get."

"I suppose you're right, Rudi, but I don't consciously chase young men—I just automatically react to them, and I suppose it shows. Men like to be desired, so they react back."

"A chain reaction, you might say?"

"Yes . . . and that's how a habit starts."

I asked Gregory and Caspian the same question. The subject was beginning to bother me. "Isn't it grotesque to go to bed with somebody my age?"

"Not while we're still so young," Gregory answered. "But if a middle-aged man were to go to bed with his grandmother, it might be a bit kinky."

Caspian said, "After twenty-five, we'll all get set

in our ways; now we're still experimenting with what to do and who to be, both in bed and out."

Encouraged by this remark, I thought I might experiment with the beautiful Caspian. Kate had already been away two weeks, and he was getting sexually restless. Better nice old Granny than some girl who'll take him away from Kate, I thought!

I often stayed the night with Gregory, so one morning while he was still asleep, I went into Caspian's room. He had asked me to wake him.

"Your alarm call," I said, slipping into Caspian's bed.

But his alarm did *not* go off. Nothing I could do would even give him an erection. He lay there passively, slightly embarrassed, while I worked over his beautiful body with my tongue and fingers. Nothing moved. I was not as infallible as I thought. I got quickly back into Gregory's bed before he woke up, feeling my age. I decided from then on I would wait to be chosen, not do the choosing. I didn't like failure.

Rudi had returned from Vienna in low spirits. He had not had a happy Christmas. His father was failing in health, and this had made Rudi depressed about illness, old age, family ties and domestic responsibilities.

"My father is clinging to a way of life that doesn't exist anymore," he said, sitting on the bed in my cloister. "If I try to change anything, it's as if I'm asking him to die."

"Then there's nothing you can do, Rudi, except

leave him alone. You obviously can't live with him—your life's in America, or wherever your work takes you."

"Yes, you and I are beautiful nomads, Anne. We have to travel light."

"Well, you're not doing *that* very efficiently! Look at your luggage."

Rudi's luggage had been moved down to my cloister just before Christmas. It was piled around us. The idea was for him to stay two nights with me and then take the boat train to Southampton. There was only one single bed, and we had not discussed whether we were sharing it or whether I was expected to go to Gregory's. Actually I didn't want to sleep with anybody at that moment, but I was forced to choose the lesser of two evils. I decided I was less likely to get hung up emotionally with Gregory than with Rudi. When Rudi was depressed, I longed to take him into my arms. We then risked a *retour de flamme*.

I was a little embarrassed at being alone with Caspian and Gregory again, and I wondered if they had discussed my wandering into Caspian's bedroom. Evidently not, because when I turned up late that night after dining with Rudi, they both seemed relaxed and undisturbed by my presence. Gregory was roaming around naked as usual, in spite of the lack of central heating, and Caspian was in pale blue pajamas like a track suit. They made a handsome pair.

"How lucky I am to be going to bed with the two most beautiful boys in London!" I exclaimed.

"Who said you were going to get us both?"

Gregory queried, but his tone was quite receptive. Caspian just smiled.

I threw myself down on the big pillow-bed in the studio, where Gregory now slept since Caspian had moved in.

"I thought we were becoming rather a good *ménage à trois*," I said, looking up at them and relaxing back into the cushions with my arms and legs outstretched—seductively, I hoped.

Gregory towered over me, naked, his penis hardening encouragingly.

"Come and help me pull off her boots, Caspian," he said.

One took either leg. My boots came off quite easily, then my panties. I was wearing black stockings rolled around garters.

"Stockings turn me on. I don't like tights," Caspian said. I was happy to see the telltale bulge in his pajamas.

"Shall we leave the stockings on, then?" Gregory consulted him.

"Yes. Let's leave them on."

"I want the rest of me to be naked," I said. "And I want to have a pee first."

I got up and went into the bathroom, shedding the rest of my clothes on the way—throwing them around the room.

"Don't lose your erections, boys," I said before I closed the bathroom door.

It had been my lifelong habit to have a pee before sex, quickly washing the area afterwards and slipping in my diaphragm. The latter routine was no longer necessary, although I still menstruated.

My gynecologist had told me that it was very unlikely a woman could conceive after fifty, so I'd dropped that part of the ritual. However, I always washed myself carefully between the legs, usually rubbing on a little cream afterwards as the soap and water made me too dry. I couldn't find anything greasy in the boys' bathroom—but at least I was clean. With two of them, we were sure to get into oral sex.

"I'm all yours," I said, standing for a moment in the bathroom doorway, carefully posed, naked except for my stockings.

Both boys were lying on the bed, Caspian still in his pajamas.

"Come on, off with your clothes," I insisted, kneeling down and tugging at Caspian's trousers.

He giggled a little, but let me undress him. I was relieved to see that he still had his erection. Gregory was actually lying back and fingering his.

"My God! This is an old lady's dream—the perfect masturbation fantasy," I exclaimed. "And it's all for real!"

I looked at them for a moment—Gregory, redhaired and heavyset, his muscles bulging; Caspian, perfectly formed, although much smaller, his pale blond Slavic beauty in direct contrast to Gregory's huge fierceness. They were certainly a turn-on. I leaned forward and grasped a penis in each hand. I enjoyed taking the initiative.

After a while Gregory said thickly, "Which end of her do you want, Caspian?"

He raised himself up and pushed me back, as usual wishing to dominate and stage-manage the

situation. Then he knelt between my legs, pulling
me onto him. This left Caspian no option but to
straddle my chest and put his penis into my
mouth. I raised my head to take it.

Later we all lay back exhausted and fell asleep.

The next morning I awoke first, with one on either side of me. Both had erections in their sleep. I
couldn't resist taking them into my hands again,
and massaged them both slowly into awareness.
They rolled over onto their backs and let me do it,
neither asleep nor awake. Presently they began to
masturbate themselves, leaving me free to do the
same. We lay there in a row, bringing ourselves to
climax. It was so exciting seeing and hearing the
boys jerk themselves off that I came first, thrash-
ing about the bed between them. Caspian came
next, and I was sufficiently recovered to take it
into my mouth at the last minute and swallow it. I
did the same for Gregory later. He took a long
time as usual, but I sucked out every last drop.
Afterwards, they both fell into a deep sleep, and I
was the only one to hear the alarm.

"Boys! It's time to get up!"

Neither of them moved, so I decided to get up
and wake them with coffee in bed. I had nothing to
wear, so I took Caspian's pajamas from the floor,
put them on, and went into the kitchen. There was
no milk in the refrigerator.

I had heard the milkman making his rounds as
we lay masturbating, and I knew there would be a
bottle of milk on the doorstep. I found Caspian's
bedroom slippers and flapped all the way down-

stairs in them. As I stepped out to get the milk, the front door slammed behind me.

"Oh, shit!" I said out loud, because I knew the bell didn't work. Gregory had disconnected it because children were always ringing it. The bedroom windows were all at the back of the house, so there was nothing I could do but walk around the block into the next street and shout.

Some passersby looked strangely at me as I slopped along the cold morning streets in my oversized men's pajamas, the slippers flapping on the damp pavement. But this was England, and no one made any comment or offered to help. It was my own private business unless I stated otherwise.

"Gregory! Caspian! Gregory! . . . Gregory!"

To my surprise a head came out of a nearby window and shouted back, "Yes?" An unknown young man was staring at me.

"Hello," he said. "Do I know you?"

"I don't think so," I replied, confused. "Who are you?"

"Gregory."

"Oh . . . well, you're not the right one."

"Are you locked out? Or do you usually run around the streets in somebody else's pajamas?"

"Yes . . . I mean, no. I mean I *am* locked out."

"I'll let you in so you can use my phone. I presume the other Gregory does have a telephone?"

"Yes. What a brilliant idea! Thank you. Where are you exactly? I'll come right around."

"Nearly next door to Gregory No. 1, I should imagine. 25 Chisholm Road, the bell marked Arundel."

Gregory Arundel was waiting for me on his doorstep when I got around to the other street. He was a tall young man, willowy and giggly and divinely beautiful. He must have been a male model, I realized at once. Nobody else could be that elegant at 7:30 in the morning. He was fully dressed too, in a smart dark suit.

"I just got in," he said by way of greeting. "That's why I heard you."

"How do you do.... This is very nice of you. I'm Anne Cumming."

We shook hands formally. He led me upstairs to a tiny flat. "There's the telephone," he said. "Can I get you some breakfast?"

"No ... you must come to breakfast with us ... if I can wake them both up."

I was dialing as I spoke. Caspian answered sleepily. I explained the situation. "I'll come down and let you in," he said, "but I can't see my pajamas anywhere."

"I've got them on."

"Oh! What am I supposed to do? Wear your clothes?"

I giggled. "Put on a bath towel!"

"It's January," he replied a bit grumpily. "What a way to start the day!"

I insisted on the new Gregory coming with me, and we all had breakfast together in various stages of undress—except for Gregory, the Good Samaritan, who was naturally still in his dark evening suit.

"I'll call you Good Gregory," I said to him. "You saved my life. I would have died of exposure or been arrested by the police for soliciting." He giggled. It was an endearing habit. He giggled at everything I said.

"I suppose I'm considered Bad Gregory because I locked you out," said the Russian Bear, now dressed and putting on his bicycle clips, ready to go to work. "Silly bitch! Can't even open a door without it shutting behind her."

"That's the story of my life," I commented sadly. "Doors shutting behind me."

I saw all three of them off. "Drop in whenever you like," both Gregorys said to each other simultaneously on the doorstep. Bad Gregory then bicycled off, Good Gregory went home to sleep, Caspian went to the underground, and I went back into the house to tidy up and wash the dishes. Then I went home to Rudi.

I saw Rudi off on the boat train. He didn't seem very happy to be leaving Europe, and I wondered whether the affair with his friend Tom was going well in New York. We seldom discussed it, because Rudi still felt guilty at having left me and gone back to homosexuality.

"They were the happiest years of my life," he often said, referring to our five years together.

"Nonsense, Rudi," I always used to reply. "We were totally unsuited to each other. I'm glad you left me. I'm having a much better time now." It wasn't always true, but I always said it. Recrimination and vengeance are useless and always negative.

"I wish I were coming with you. I haven't been to New York for a long time," I said at Victoria Station.

"Why don't you come?"

"Too expensive. And I can't think of any real reason."

"Because I invite you. I'd like you to meet my friend Tom."

"Good God, Rudi, what next? I'm in one *ménage à trois* now. I don't need another."

"I'll put you up in a hotel near us. If you can find a cheap charter flight, Anne, I'll pay for the ticket. You've been a great help to me here, and I'd like to do something for you."

It was just like Rudi—egotistical to the point of selfishness one day, sweetly generous the next. I kissed him good-bye and promised to think over this sudden invitation. I still had a month's holiday left and no particular plans. It might be a good idea to move on. I wanted to see my friend Kurt in New York.

Good Gregory called me. He came around to see me in my cloister.

"You always look so glamorous," I exclaimed. "How do you do it?"

He giggled. "I've just been crimped, and I've also been shrunk."

"What do you mean?"

"I've been to my hairdresser and to my analyst."

"You? To an analyst? But you always seem so giggly and happy."

"I was in a psychiatric clinic last year."

"What for?" I asked casually, as if it were a common occurrence.

"Depression. I couldn't get over an unhappy love affair."

"You're gay, I suppose?"

"Yes, but it isn't always as gay as they say. We have all the usual emotional problems, as well as our own particular ones."

"I'd never thought of it that way."

I liked Good Gregory and began to see quite a bit of him. Bad Gregory and Caspian liked him too, although he couldn't have been more different from them. He had started to make himself very useful to them. He did their shopping, paid the milkman, and took in parcels. He was the perfect next-door neighbor, in fact, and what Bad Gregory liked best about him was that he could be dominated—manipulated—and always came up smiling and giggling. He also fitted in perfectly with my busy last week in London, being most helpful to me too.

I had decided to take Rudi up on his offer and go to New York. It was true that he owed me a great deal, but that was not why I was accepting his invitation. I was curious to meet Rudi's boyfriend Tom. Winter was a slack time in the Italian cinema anyway. I had nothing to do till March.

"Aren't you jealous of another man having taken your place?" Good Gregory asked me when I told him about Tom and my trip to New York.

"Not anymore. Just mildly nostalgic for half-remembered bliss."

"The idea of homosexuality doesn't disgust you?"

"Why should it? I like a nice hard cock myself, and I don't mind where I put it. I'd be a terrible hypocrite if I pretended to be shocked at finding out that others like the same thing."

"I wish there were more people like you, Anne. Then we wouldn't finish up in psychiatric clinics with guilt complexes."

"I'll tell you a big secret, Gregory. Most heterosexual men don't like cunts either. It's the ultimate goal, but they don't really like them. They prefer a woman's breasts, her hair, her legs, her beautiful eyes, her pretty face. They like to grasp her around the waist or cup her neat little bottom in the palms of their hands and pull her to them. They don't really want a close-up view of her cunt. Very few men even look at it. But when a woman wants a man, she immediately grabs for the penis—she's not afraid of it."

Good Gregory giggled. "That's just how I feel, too!"

"Of course. That's why women usually get on so well with queers. We like the same things."

Bad Gregory did not take so kindly to my ideas or my imminent departure. He was not in love with me, but he liked having a mature woman at his beck and call. He enjoyed his power over me, in bed and out.

"I won't like it here without you," Caspian also said. "Gregory wants to run my life for me. I know it's his flat and I'm only a paying guest, but on the nights when you're not here, he becomes impossible."

"I can't stick around just to be a catalyst, Caspian. My life is really elsewhere."

"So is mine. I'm going to look around for a new job, doing my own thing. I can't go on painting other people's scenery, living in other people's homes, fucking other people's women. It will probably mean going to a small theater outside London, but I'll be better paid, more creative—and I can get married to Kate."

We embraced. "Good luck to you and Kate. Tell her I only shared a little bit of you—just to keep it in the family!"

I didn't see any of the boys for the next two or three days. I was busy getting myself ready for departure, seeing other friends and family, going to the dentist, and being a good grandmother. Fiona brought the children up to London for the day. She went shopping for wallpaper while I took the children to the Natural History Museum. Caroline wept because she wasn't allowed to stroke the stuffed animals, and Malcolm whined because he wanted to go and see "the stuffed trains" in the Science Museum instead. I was quite relieved to put them all back on the train.

As I opened the door to my cloister, the phone was ringing. I stumbled over a chair in the dark as I ran to pick it up. It was Good Gregory.

"Anne, you'd better come at once. The other Gregory has tried to kill Caspian."

For once Good Gregory wasn't giggling when he met me at the door of Bad Gregory's house.

"I don't know exactly what happened," he gasped, "but when Caspian got home from work, they had a row. You know how strong Gregory is, and with all that karate training, Caspian didn't stand a chance."

"You mean he's dead?" I felt deathly cold myself.

"No, no. Just in a hospital recovering from shock. Gregory pinned him down and then strangled him. Caspian thinks he actually died, because the first thing he remembers was being brought back to life again by mouth-to-mouth resuscitation. Gregory evidently realized what he'd done, and so he brought him around again. Caspian then broke away and ran next door to me and collapsed in total shock. I called an ambulance and had him taken to a hospital. Then I called you."

We climbed the stairs to Bad Gregory's place. "Are you frightened, Good Gregory?" I asked.

"No; only by the idea that Bad Gregory might try to commit suicide now. It goes together. Suicide is another hostile act."

I was very frightened, frightened of what we might find upstairs.

"I'll go in first, Anne. He has nothing against *me*."

I was amazed by sweet, smiling, giggly Gregory's command of the situation, and said so.

"You forget that I've been in a psychiatric ward myself," he said. "That teaches you a lot."

We knocked. Nothing happened, but I could hear music. Bach's Cantata in E Minor, one of Bad Gregory's favorites.

"Surely you wouldn't put on a record and then commit suicide?" I said to Good Gregory.

We knocked again. Bad Gregory opened the door to us this time. He was in a kind of catatonic trance and looked more than ever like a big unhappy Russian bear.

I took him into my arms and kissed him. It seemed a strange reaction to a near murder, but that's what I did. I kissed the murderer. Friends in trouble are still friends. Lovers always need love.

"What's the matter, Gregory?" I asked, leading him over to the pillow-bed.

He sank down beside me and laid his great big head in my lap. Good Gregory sat opposite us and lit a cigarette.

"Caspian wouldn't listen to Bach," was all he would say.

I looked across at Good Gregory. "I think we'll be all right," I said softly. "Will you go to the hospital and see how Caspian is and come back and tell us?"

"You're sure you don't mind being alone, Anne?"

"No, don't worry. But come back soon."

"What's really the matter?" I asked Bad Gregory as I heard the door close quietly behind the other Gregory.

He looked up at me. Rudi had been right; his eyes were too close together. I remembered that even my brother had once said to me, "Anne, never get involved with someone whose eyes are too close together."

"What do *you* think's wrong with me?" Gregory asked.

"I think you take too long to reach orgasm," I heard myself say. "I'm sure it's symptomatic of something, but I don't know what. Will you see a psychiatrist, Gregory?"

I often have an instinctive understanding of things I know nothing about. I looked down at the huge young man in my lap. Behind that bristling Genghis Khan moustache and dominant manner, there was that soft, well-mannered voice. The two did not go together.

"I think you're Dr. Jekyll and Mr. Hyde, Gregory. You build things up and then you knock them down. You've a destructive streak in you."

"Are you afraid of me?"

"Yes," I answered. "Quite frankly I am."

"I want to make love to you, Anne. . . . I haven't seen you for days."

I hesitated, then I took a deep breath. "What do I do if you try to strangle me, Gregory?"

"You poke two fingers into my eyes as hard as you can and kick me in the balls at the same time," he said calmly.

I smiled, feeling more relaxed; the conversation seemed quite normal.

Gregory was staring up at me, unsmiling, and he said very seriously and tenderly, "Thank you for reminding me of what I've just done. You're never afraid of the truth, are you, Anne?"

"Often, but I try not to show it."

When Good Gregory came back, we were lying naked in each other's arms. Bad Gregory was curled up in a fetal position with his head against my breast.

I decided it was better to leave London in spite of everything. Good Gregory had persuaded Bad Gregory to go into the clinic he had only just left. Although Caspian had no intention of pressing charges for assault, awkward questions had been asked in the hospital before they let him go. I helped him pack his belongings and move out of Gregory's studio. Fortunately, he had already heard of a job out of town.

"I think that was part of the trouble, Anne," he told me. "I had just broken the news to Gregory that I had another job and wouldn't be staying on. He felt he was losing his hold over both of us."

"What was that story about Bach's Cantata?"

"Well, after I'd told Gregory I'd be leaving soon, he put on the hi-fi full blast. Then he asked me if I'd heard from you. I told him no, maybe you'd left without saying good-bye; and then I went over and turned down the volume on the record player. The noise was deafening me. Gregory shouted, 'Don't touch my record player!' and hit me. I hit him back, and I don't remember anything else except his hands around my neck. When I came around he was on top of me, breathing into my mouth. We hadn't even had an argument."

I saw the doctor in the psychiatric clinic. Gregory was a voluntary patient and was being allowed to go to his parents' home for a few days' rest, provided he came back as an outpatient. I had telephoned his mother that he had been ill with flu. How could you call someone's mother and say, "Your son has just tried to murder his best friend"?

Peter or Paul, or whatever his name was, took it very calmly. He promised to round up all of Bad Gregory's friends and to keep an eye on him after my departure. Good Gregory said he would move in with him for a while, if necessary.

"It's like Alcoholics Anonymous," Good Gregory explained. "Once you've been through that psychiatric-clinic bit yourself, you're ready to help others."

"Should I feel guilty at all?" I asked the psychiatrist.

"I'm not here to judge," he replied coldly. "Only to cure. Something has sparked off latent paranoia in an unbalanced young man. Hostile violence is often turned against the people you love best. I should have thought a woman your age might well ask herself why she was mixed up in a situation like this. It might be your turn next time. I would stay out of the way for a bit."

It was not a happy note on which to leave for New York, but I figured that it would probably be better if Bad Gregory forgot both Caspian and me for a while. He was under analysis and would eventually find a new relationship to satisfy every side of his complex nature. In the meantime, his friends would look after him. The New Young felt very responsible for each other, I noted. I admired them for it.

As if to clear the air, another bomb went off, this time in a letter box in Baker Street station. Everyone began to forget his personal troubles in the face of the Irish trouble.

At London airport, overworked security officers were looking for bombs and hijackers instead of smuggled bottles of Chanel No. 5. The billboard with the face of the wanted murderer was still around. Britain of the Swinging Sixties was coming to an explosive end.

3 ‹ "New York, New York. It's a Wonderful Town"

At the end of January 1968, I flew off to New York by Air India, thinking it would look and taste more exotic than British Airways or Pan Am. I can't say I traveled in Oriental splendor, except for the presence of a charming hostess inclined to trip over her long sari. But a jet is a jet, and plastic curry in plastic containers on a plastic tray is barely distinguishable from plastic *boeuf bourguignon*. Oh! for the days of leisurely ocean liners! I first went to New York by boat before the war with Robert, a blushing bride with a dozen suitcases and a huge cabin trunk. Only Lindbergh and Amy Johnson flew the Atlantic then.

Robert and I had traveled second class on the old *Aquitania*, all mahogany cabins and damask tablecloths, lounging on the deck in cushioned chaise longues while handsome waiters circulated with silver trays of cocktails, beef broth or English tea. It was luxurious and leisurely.

Now, you are sucked into a windowless maze of airport corridors carrying your own bags, and you don't even get a good night's sleep because they fly the Atlantic so fast. Travel has lost its glamour.

Diary entry. New York. January 20, 1968.

Rudi and his boyfriend came to meet me at Kennedy Airport and left me here in my hotel to sleep off the jet time-lag. Rudi has generously paid for a suite in the Fifth Avenue Hotel near Washington Square for a month because it's only a few blocks from their apartment. Rudi's friend Tom seemed delighted to see me. I suppose it's difficult for him to imagine that Rudi and I were once lovers. I'm just a middle-aged visitor from another world. Tom has never been to Europe. He's a healthy, normal white American male who just happens to be homosexual. He's much younger than Rudi and obviously worships him. It's the disciple-at-the-feet-of-the-master situation, and Rudi is obviously enjoying it. It's just right for his present state of evolution, and it's a direct parallel to my own relationships with young men—only I seem to need more of them!

New York has changed less than most European cities. The dawns are still mauve, and the sidewalks are still covered with snow and garbage in equal quantities, representing the beauty and squalor that make up this exhilarating city. A walk around the block is a walk around the world. You go from skyscraper to tenement, from Hamburger Heaven to chic restaurant, from austere bank to plush health spa, from the New School of Social Studies to the sleazy porn movie houses, and from laundromat to liquor store. Heaven and hell is right here in one block, with people of all colors, races, shapes and sizes, wearing incredible clothing with nothing matching and nothing making sense; the ugly and the beautiful are mixed together here into one grotesque melting pot which is called New York.

I was invited to lunch at Rudi's. When we had lived together, he never boiled an egg or made a cup of tea; but now, seven years later, he was going to cook for me.

"Come in; come in! How nice to have you here." It was not Rudi who greeted me, but his boyfriend Tom. In a way he was playing the host, while Rudi cooked in the kitchen.

The roles in a homosexual partnership are less clear and more involved than most heterosexuals realize. I had seen a great many of such "marriages" in my life, but it was the first time I had seen Rudi living openly with a man. It did not make him seem effeminate, I noticed; rather, the contrary. Tom was much younger, so Rudi was the father-figure: decisive, responsible and dependable. With me, he still used to slip back into the little-boy-lost syndrome.

"I can see I got the wrong years of your life, Rudi," I said when the lunch was over. "I should have waited around for the cooking period."

"But didn't he cook when you were together?" Tom asked.

"I was brought up to believe you should be spoiled by women," Rudi interposed smugly. "I left Vienna when my mother died, in search of a job and someone to go on spoiling me. I found both the job and the woman in Rome."

Tom looked at us inquiringly. "So that's where you two met—in Rome."

"Yes, in a restaurant," we replied together.

"We took pity on each other," I elaborated. "I'd just left my second husband and needed someone to love, and Rudi needed to be loved. It was as simple as that."

Tom took me for a walk around the Village after lunch, which was very different from the Village I remembered from my last visit. The setting hadn't changed, but the cast was different. The hippies had taken over. We sat for a while in Washington Square, which had once been so elegantly Bohemian in a Henry James way, but was now simply squalid. The Beat Generation might have their own form of elegance, but it was not based on cleanliness and order.

"Come back and have a cup of tea at my hotel," I invited Tom. "It's too cold here."

Back in the Fifth Avenue Hotel, comfort and luxury kept out the cold, and the casual Tom, with his neat haircut and clean blue jeans, could fit into any ambience. We felt strangely at ease together. I asked him up to my room, and we lay on the bed and gossiped for hours. I could see why, living with him, Rudi had become more of a man. "All that crap about passive and active roles—who needs it?" Tom said. "I'm a man; I like other men because they're men. What I do in bed is just gymnastics; it doesn't change my personality." We even went into physical details and compared notes. "Rudi is mainly a narcissist," I ended up. "As long as you flatter him, it all works!"

Finally Tom looked at his watch. "Christ! We've spent hours together. I'd better go. We don't want Rudi getting jealous, do we?"

We kissed each other on the lips. How much it meant, I don't know. It was becoming a fashion among the young. I hugged Tom to me.

"I'm glad you're with Rudi," I said.

"I'm glad you're with *us*," he replied.

I went uptown to see my old friend Kurt. Kurt is my pet psychiatrist, and I only use psychiatrists as pets. I don't seem to be able to get into analysis, although once long ago, my second husband sent me to a Freudian lady because *he* was having problems. After two sessions, I turned around to the Freudian lady and said, "Now *you* do the talking. I'm not going to spend all this money listening to myself." I never went back. Perhaps I didn't need to. I had Kurt.

I first met Kurt when I was a student in Germany before the war. My mother had sent me there after my English boarding school and before Paris. Kurt was a homely, round-faced Jewish medical student in Weimar. We used to take long walks together, talking about Goethe, and then I would cry on his shoulder and tell him all my problems, most of which were young men. One day I stopped crying and began going out with another student who was a storm trooper in his spare time. I had no idea what a storm trooper was, as Hitler had only just come into power. I only knew that I liked the dashing black uniform and the highly polished riding boots, and the only problem was whether to lose my virginity or not. Soon I was crying on Kurt's shoulder because the handsome storm trooper treated me badly because I wouldn't go to bed with him. Then came the day when storm troopers began treating Jewish students badly, and I fled to London, taking Kurt with me. His family followed, and they settled in London. Kurt continued medical school and became a psychiatrist. He has been one of my best friends ever since.

Throughout two marriages and two divorces and endless love affairs, I had consulted Kurt, not as an analyst, but like the oracle. I would pop in on a friendly visit, give him a kiss, say "What do I do now?" and rush out again. Half the time I didn't even listen to the answer; it was enough to know that he was there. One day he wasn't there anymore. He had emigrated to America. However, he often came back to Europe on holiday, and I always looked him up when I was in New York.

"Darling, darling Kurt!" The past flooded back as I embraced this portly, middle-aged man.

Kurt had married, but the marriage hadn't been a success. He was now a bachelor again, so he took me to a Hungarian restaurant on the West Side. First we caught up on family news, and I told him all about my daughters and grandchildren. Then he said, "And what about your love life?"

I told him all about Bad Gregory, and he consoled me and explained similar case histories. I also told him about Rome and my stable of young part-time lovers: my simple, satisfying, uncomplicated truck driver; my law student; my diplomat; and busy Bruno of the five-minute fuck.

"Most women have one man for all seasons. You seem to have several men for each different occasion," Kurt commented. "Don't you sometimes find it confusing?"

"No. The confusion sets in when I settle down with one man," I replied.

"Well, I hope you're resting on your laurels here in New York. I think you should take a holiday from sex."

"I think I'm falling in love with Rudi's young man."

Kurt looked at me disapprovingly. He already disapproved of Rudi.

I had hoped Rudi and Kurt would become friends when Rudi emigrated to the States, but it didn't work out that way. Kurt had said, "I don't think Rudi has ever been in love with you. He's just a spoiled young man." Rudi had said, "Kurt has always been in love with you, and you've ruined his life." Neither statement was quite true, but the two men had not become friends. They distrusted each other.

"Why are you falling in love with Rudi's young man?" Kurt asked. "To get even with Rudi?"

"No, I just like him. I think I like him better than Rudi."

"Well, that's a nice change, but I still don't think it's a good idea."

"Then who shall I go to bed with next?"

"No one."

"You always say that, Kurt. And I never listen to you."

"One day you will. How old are you, Anne?"

"I've just had my fifty-first birthday."

"Do you ever stop to think?"

"Not yet. I'm keeping that for my old age."

We both laughed and held hands across the table.

I was not holding hands with a fat, middle-aged man, but with a plump, round-faced boy. I always see people as they were when I first met them.

I didn't go to bed with Tom, but I saw a lot of him. I dropped in and out of their apartment, and if Rudi was busy, he would send us out together.

Tom was an abstract painter, and his time was his own. It often became my time, and we had a wonderful time together. It was one of the best holidays I ever had. Through Tom I met new young friends, discovered the "underground" cinema, spent my evenings in off-Broadway theaters, and learned that there was a new New York under the old New York. I even found a new young lover, but that had nothing to do with Tom.

Kurt had been right when he said that it was unhealthy to see so much of Rudi and Tom. It was becoming another *ménage à trois*. I often turned up when they were still in bed together, and even sat on the edge of their bed. But I needed a new bed to sit on. I began to frequent other old friends and, through them, met other new friends.

Among my new friends was a very witty, campy queer who just *loved* my accent, *adored* my dresses, found me *too too* divine. It was all very *déjà vu* after the new-look New York that Tom had introduced me to, where homosexuals were masculine young men in surplus army clothing. But now I slipped back into a queer world I had always known.

One evening I sank into the lush, close carpeting of my new friend's upper-class, Upper East Side apartment on my way to what I expected would be a chic homosexual dinner party. The apartment

was all marble, brocade and ormolu, with a collection of miniature obelisks like a forest of phallic
symbols. The party seemed to be going on in the
kitchen. There was a confusion of cooking sounds
and raised voices, and in the kitchen I found a
woman and three elderly cooking queens.

"Too many cooks spoil the broth!" said my host,
as, sweeping into the kitchen and trying all the
sauces, he added his contribution to the confusion
of ingredients.

I was introduced to everybody. To my surprise,
the only other woman bore a name like Astor or
Vanderbilt or Stuyvesant, an old social-register
name. She was an ex-wife of some social scion,
pretty, chic, fortyish. She held out a wooden
spoon; I shook it.

"And this is the gymnast," someone said, back in
the sitting room again.

On a white brocade sofa was a Pink Pearl. Glowing among that artificial group was a beautiful
blond nature boy, with a pearly pink radiance
born of youth, health and perfect cleanliness. He
sat patiently and decorously on a corner of the
sofa, destined for an old queen too busy cooking
to pay him much attention. He was the Birthday
Present, the Midnight Cowboy, a juvenile male
whore, seemingly as yet untouched by human
hand. He looked as if it was his first night out anywhere.

Everyone was drunk on dry martinis. The Pink
Pearl and I were the only ones who didn't drink.
Suddenly we found ourselves alone on the sofa.
Everyone else was either in the kitchen, or in the
dining room laying the table and arranging flow-

ers, or in the bathroom being sick. The Pink Pearl
kissed me on the lips.

"Look, I think there's been some mistake. You
were invited here for someone else."

"There's plenty of time for that," he replied
quite naturally, as if referring to some future job.
"Let's go into the television room for a little
while."

He was evidently familiar with the apartment,
and led me into a small study lined with books. I
felt guilty rather than self-conscious. I didn't want
to steal someone else's trade. I made a quick dash
into the kitchen and explained the situation to our
host.

"That's quite all right, dear. Dinner's not *nearly*
ready yet," was the only reply I got.

"Well, if anything goes, I'll have a go, then," I
said.

"Yes, darling, be our guest."

I returned to the other room, where the television screen was flickering in the dark and the Pink
Pearl was sitting on the floor. I turned off the
sound, and we lay on the thick carpet, fully
dressed, in front of the screen. What took place
was warm and spontaneous and even innocent:
children's games climaxed with adult orgasm. The
voices in the other rooms were like sounds from a
distant playground. We were still lying peacefully
in each other's arms when the door opened and
dinner was announced. The Pink Pearl's attitude
toward sex was completely open and natural and
guilt-free. He picked me up from the floor, zipped
up his fly, and offered me his arm to go into the

dining room like a well-brought-up child with a maiden aunt. He didn't even smell like a man yet.

"How old are you, Pearl?"

"Fifteen."

I gasped. "It's the first time I've corrupted a minor."

"What's corruption?" he asked. "Who's a minor?"

He wasn't kidding. He simply didn't know the words. The gymnasium where he worked out was his only source of education. He had quit school at thirteen, lived with a widowed mother in Atlantic City, and spent each day on the beach collecting shells. He was innocent only because he had never heard of decadence, although he had been a juvenile hustler for the last year. He had been picked up on the Boardwalk at fourteen by a cruising queer, who had brought him into New York and then abandoned him to fate. It did not occur to the boy that what he did was wrong. He came up to New York whenever he wanted pocket money. He unzipped his fly, stuck it in someone's mouth, and got paid.

"That's all there is to it," he said.

"You don't actually screw anybody or roll over yourself?"

He looked slightly shocked. "No. I'm strictly trade."

He told me all this during dinner in a soft, serious, childlike voice while the others were screeching and falling about with sophisticated drunken laughter. I was appalled and fascinated at the same time, not by the facts, but by his attitude.

The meal was excellent, and the Pink Pearl and I had worked up hearty appetites on the floor of the television room. I had one glass of wine, and he had a glass of milk.

"I'm in training for a gymnastic display," he explained.

Everyone took this the wrong way and roared with laughter, much to the Pink Pearl's surprise.

Afterwards, we offered to do the washing up; we were the only ones who could have held a slippery plate by then.

"What do you want to do when you grow up?" I asked him as we dried the silver.

"I'm saving up to go to California," he replied. "I want to be a surfer."

"But that's not an activity that pays very well. How will you live?"

"I'll hustle some in the evenings, so I can be on the beach all day."

"What else will you do?"

"Eat, sleep, find myself a girl."

"But after that . . . ?"

"You mean when I'm old? When I'm about twenty-five?"

"I mean in about six months' time, when you're bored."

"Why should I get bored?"

"Doing nothing all day."

"That won't be nothing. I only get bored doing things I don't like."

"I can see we'll have to have this conversation again in twenty years. When you're *very* old, in fact—like thirty-five!"

He had no idea what I was driving at. He was a

young animal who lived by instinct alone. His unawareness of moral values made him perfectly content with the life he was leading.

Off the kitchen was an unused maid's room. The Pink Pearl took me in there when he had finished the dishes.

"They let me sleep here sometimes," he explained, with no resentment in his tone. He was used by others and then put away in this cupboard, but he didn't seem to mind at all.

He began undressing, and I sat and watched as if he were one of my grandchildren going to bed. His body was superb, a pale, translucent study in male perfection, but his mind was completely undeveloped. I had never seen a centerfold pinup, boy or girl, so beautiful, so succulent and so appealing.

I ran my finger down the center of his body, and his penis came up to meet it. There was a symmetry and rhythm in him that made it almost nonsexual, like a cuckoo clock springing into hourly action.

"You get undressed too," he said.

Again I had the feeling that I was involved in children's games. I was a little shocked, not at him, but at myself. For an aging woman, I was behaving in a strangely irresponsible manner. But was I seducing a child or was the child seducing me?

The innate beauty of his body was irresistible. Making love with the Pink Pearl was like an art-appreciation course. Each position and move was an esthetic delight. I never once shut my eyes.

Suddenly the door flew open. The screaming queens had sobered up over coffee, and three of them fell on us like vultures, stripping off their

clothes and jumping into bed with us. I was afraid
the Pink Pearl would be torn apart in their efforts
to make love to him, but he took it all with relaxed
acceptance, letting their eager tongues and mouths
work over his entire body. It seemed like some
strange tribal rite. A couple of them just stood on
the sidelines and masturbated while they watched
the other three at work. I left them to it and
slipped out, taking my clothes into another bedroom to dress. Mrs. Social Register had passed out
on the bed in there, fast asleep on a fake leopard
bedspread. I left her undisturbed and went into
the sitting room. I felt a vague social obligation to
await my host and say good-bye.

Presently all the men emerged in various stages
of undress. The Pink Pearl was fully dressed but a
little rumpled, like a small boy who has been in a
fight. I didn't feel disgusted, only vaguely maternal. I took a comb out of my handbag and tidied
his hair.

"Shall we go home now?" I asked.

"Sure. I'd like that," he replied.

We said our formal good-byes. My host gave the
Pink Pearl a $50 bill, which seemed a lot to pay for
what little they'd got, or did it cover my entertainment too?

"You must be tired," I said in the elevator.

"No, you get used to it."

He looked more like a Norman Rockwell cover
for *Saturday Evening Post* than a centerfold pinup.
He was incongruously the all-American boy, and
that shocked me most.

"Do you get freckles in the summer?" I asked,
touching his nose.

He looked puzzled. "Yes. Why do you ask?"

"I just wanted *something* to fit the image."

He had no idea what I was talking about, but it didn't matter. He was pretty and cuddly, and later snuggled up in bed in my arms like a plush toy. He reminded me of a pink teddy bear I had owned as a child, whose ear had fallen off and whose stuffing kept coming out. Would anybody look after the Pink Pearl when he grew old and his pretty ears fell off and the stuffing came out?

He stayed with me off and on for the rest of my visit. As I had a two-room suite with kitchenette in the hotel, they couldn't object to overnight visitors—however unusual. They were already used to Tom's coming and going in the day; now I just added the Pink Pearl at night. Rudi referred to my suite as "Boys' Town." He didn't approve of the Pink Pearl. He wasn't jealous this time, just shocked by the Pearl's age, his class, his lack of intellectual promise, and his way of making a living. Rudi began calling me Mother-of-Pearl and referred to the boy as the Seed Pearl.

"You might at least have got yourself a man-sized pearl," he said.

"Sour grapes," I replied.

I found the Pearl a pleasant enough companion. He was used to running errands and cleaning up the house; and if he was only adequate in bed, rather than inspiring, he made up for it by being decorative. I loved looking at him, and that was all I needed for the moment.

"I've got a job tonight," he said occasionally, in the same tone of voice as when he said, "I think I'll go home and see my mother today."

He would then go off to "work." It paid well and didn't take long, and he would come back and sleep it off in my arms. I didn't mind at all. I was not emotionally involved, and he was young and healthy enough to have plenty left over for me. For a time it was all very amusing; then I began to think.

Thoughts can be very depressing when issues are big and solutions are hard. Thoughts send some people to the bottle, but fortunately I don't drink. I keep myself busy with the little things of everyday life instead.

I was on holiday, so I tried not to think. I took my shoes to be repaired because I couldn't repair the state of the world; I ironed a dress as if this would smooth out the sufferings of humanity; I painted my nails as if I were whitewashing my sins. Then I phoned Kurt and invited myself to dinner. Kurt could think for me—he'd been doing it for years.

"What's worrying you?" he asked me right away. "You've got your 'whom-shall-I-sleep-with-next' expression on your face."

"This time it's whom will *he* sleep with next," I replied. "I'm going back to Europe soon, and I feel bad about leaving my Pink Pearl to a fate worse than death."

"Are you morally involved?"

"What do you mean?"

"Does his 'trade' bother you?"

"Should it? Is giving pleasure a sin? Are puritan values always right and pagan values wrong?"

"I don't know; I'm asking you. I deal with the

guilty and the troubled, but you and your pearl are not of that breed."

As I saw it, giving physical pleasure to others was quite justified. Film stars and athletes sold their handsome bodies too, giving visual pleasure for financial gain. That's all the Pearls of this world were doing—giving pleasure. They were well-trained sportsmen giving a night of love instead of an evening of knocking someone down in the boxing ring or kicking a ball around a stadium.

I ended up by saying, "Isn't the human need for affection and a sexual outlet more important than spectator sports?"

Kurt smiled. "Perhaps, but not everyone would agree with you," he replied.

"One man's meat being another man's poison?"

"Yes. . . . Or you could ask, Who are the guilty, the Pearls or the Swine? Should you put prostitutes in jail, or their clients?"

"Neither. Perhaps prostitution should be part of the National Health Service."

"Masters and Johnson might agree with you, but I don't think the government would."

Tom was busy working for Gay Liberation. *He* wanted a society where prostitution was not necessary.

"If there were more sexual freedom, there would be less vice," he said.

Tom and I were having one of our evenings together. Rudi often went out, leaving Tom behind, just as he often took me and not Tom. Rudi was not sexually liberated; he was still undecided as to who should know what he did with whom. Tom, on the contrary, was very open about his sexuality.

"I'm so open, I might even start sleeping with women again soon!" he said to me.

"Why did you give it up?"

"Too much of a hassle. No man really wants all that courtship bit. They want to get their rocks off as quickly as possible. If friendship and affection come later, that's fine; you stick with the person. If not, you move on. Other men understand that."

"And love? And children?"

"There's a time for those. It's not my time yet. I'm too busy with my work at present."

"Do you love Rudi?"

"Of course. I love being with him, in bed and out. Isn't that love?"

"A simplified version."

"Why complicate matters?"

"That's my philosophy too."

We were lying on my bed because it was the only comfortable place to be in my hotel room. Tom kissed me. Should I encourage him to go further?

"How bisexual are you, Tom?" I asked. "Do you like men much better than women?"

"Cocks are more stimulating. Cunts are more satisfying. I'm into stimulation at the present. I may go back to cunts later when I want relaxation."

"I hope I'll be around," I said.

Time was running out. I would soon be going back to Rome and work. I decided to give a farewell cocktail party and mix all the dramatis personae of this strange holiday period. I had made a lot of friends.

"But you can't invite them all together," Kurt gasped.

"Of course I can. That's the whole point of a cocktail, the unusual mixture."

So they all came: Rudi and Tom, Kurt and the Pink Pearl, the Swine, the Wasps, the Jews, the Beautiful People and the Ugly Ducklings. Friends from uptown, downtown and out of town.

"You see, Kurt, that's what New York is all about. Variety. It's the most exotic town I know."

"I hadn't thought of it like that."

"You think too much. Just *do* for a change."

It was Kurt who came with me to the airport. I wanted a quiet send-off. No Rudi, no Tom, no Pink Pearl; no tears at parting, neither real nor false. I had said too many sad good-byes in my life. It was a relief to slip away into the night sky and fly back to my real life. The holiday was over.

4 ⌒ The Revolutionary in Gray Cashmere

I came out into the spring sunshine in front of
the Paris air terminal on May 16, 1968. I had arrived to do the publicity for a film on the life of
Rimbaud, the French poet. I looked up toward the
Invalides across a square full of horse chestnuts in
full bloom, some pink, some white. The perfection
of the spring day was marred by only one thing—
there were no taxis. The result was utter confusion. People and their luggage crowded the
sidewalk. There was talk of a strike, of insurrec-
tion among the workers, of a new French revolution. On such a day in Paris, it all seemed quite
ridiculous. You could think only of sitting at a
sidewalk café, or strolling along the Seine looking
at the secondhand bookstalls and searching for old
picture postcards. Or you could buy a bunch of lilies of the valley to take home to your mistress or
your wife, whoever cooked better. Revolutions
were for ominous gray days in November when
there was nothing better to do, nothing to look forward to.

However, one thing was clear. Even if the taxi
drivers called off their strike, it would take hours

to clear away the accumulation of travelers and their suitcases from under the chestnut trees. So I picked up my suitcase and began walking toward the Quai d'Orsay, where I could get a bus down to the Ile St. Louis.

I had taken an apartment there, because the film was a big co-production and would take about four months, in and around Paris, so I was settling in for a long stay. I liked working for the French; there was no nonsense about them. You knew where you were, and their aggressiveness was stimulating. After the ambiguous charm of the Italians, so anxious to please, so determined to create the *bella figura*, and so full of unkept promises, the take-it-or-leave-it attitude of the French was refreshing. I was looking forward to the job. I was also looking forward to seeing my brother who lived in Paris, although he was temporarily out of town at the time of my arrival.

My suitcase was heavy. I was bringing clothes for all eventualities. I was even trailing a fur coat, a traveling rug and a camp stool for use on the set.

I reached the Quai d'Orsay and realized that the one-way traffic ran up one side of the Seine and down the other. I would have to cross over the river to get my bus. In the middle of the Pont Alexandre III, I collapsed and sat down exhausted on my camp stool, wondering whether to take my luggage to the air terminal or to struggle on.

A young man was leaning over the bridge, gazing through binoculars at the Chamber of Deputies, in front of which a great many police were milling about. He had that left-wing look of the young intellectual. Although his corduroys were rumpled and his shoes were dirty, I noticed they were good English Clark's desert boots, and his shapeless sweater was a washed-out cashmere. The boy himself was small and ugly, and wore oddly shaped glasses. I don't know why he caught my eye. The only beautiful thing about him was his curly black hair, worn in a big fuzzy bush, a style which was later to become so fashionable among the young. This was the first time I'd seen it. I have a thing about thick dark curls. I always want to run my fingers through them, feel their crisp vibrancy.

"What's going on?" I asked.

"We were organizing a protest march along the Quai d'Orsay. I think it must have been diverted. Too many *flics*."

As he spoke, a whole new contingent of police appeared and began barricading the other end of the bridge. We were sandwiched between two police cordons at either end of the Pont Alexandre III.

"Come on," he said, "or they'll think we're trying to blow up the bridge. Put on your fur coat and look rich and respectable. I'll carry your suitcase."

He put away his binoculars. We set off toward the Rive Droite. The police made way for us politely, and we turned down the quai toward the Louvre. It was very peaceful walking along under the plane trees. After about a hundred yards, the young man leaned my heavy suitcase against a mottled tree trunk and looked across the Seine again.

"You're very useful," he said. "If I'd been alone, they would have arrested me. I can see that I must borrow your Vuitton suitcase for the bombs tomorrow and have you walk beside me in your mink coat. What a pity you wouldn't do it."

"Why not? I'm a nonviolent anarchist, but if the bombs are to blow up places and not people, I might consider it—as long as the cause is a good one."

"The cause is good. We want a new educational system and better buildings. They've pushed my entire faculty out to Nanterre into prefabricated pigpens. The misuse of public money is appalling."

"Then I'll consider it. Is it the pigpens you're going to blow up?"

"I can't tell you. How could I trust an anarchist who wears a mink coat and owns a Vuitton suitcase?" He smiled behind his funny glasses.

"The mink coat is secondhand, and the suitcase was given me by a satisfied film star I once worked for. She still has eleven others. How did you know it was a Vuitton suitcase?"

"My mother has one."

"How can you trust a revolutionary whose mother has a status symbol suitcase?"

"*Touché.*" He laughed and looked more relaxed.

We had begun walking again, and carried the suitcase between us. We stopped several times at bus stops, but there were no buses running. I gave him a cup of coffee at a café hemmed in by birdcages. We had reached the quai, where they sell plants and small animals on the sidewalk. The morning passed very agreeably in his company.

He was witty and talkative and had tremendous charm. Our rhythm of thought was the same, a tremendous asset to conversation. I enjoyed being with him.

There seemed to be no more disturbances, but there were still no taxis and very little traffic. It was abnormally quiet.

"Are you sure there's a revolution going on?" I asked when we were about level with the Palais de Justice.

"Yes. You can have a revolution in one part of the city without the other part knowing what's going on. Tomorrow it will be different. If the workers come out with us, there'll be a general strike."

"Then it's unlikely my film will start on Monday."

"Oh, are you an actress?"

"No, I'm a journalist and do film publicity. I get news and photographs out to the media during the shooting."

"I'm going to be a journalist too when I get through the university. As a matter of fact, I've already published several political pieces."

"Congratulations! You hardly look old enough to read and write!"

"I'm nineteen, but when you've always been skinny and ugly, you learn to try harder in order to get there quicker."

"Do you think looks make all that difference?"

"They facilitate things. You saw for yourself how we walked straight through a police cordon because you're beautiful and distinguished looking. I'm sure your whole life has been like that."

I enjoyed the direct compliment. He was a very direct young man.

"You're probably right, although I'd never thought about it. In fact, I never think much at all; I just carry on."

"If I were tall, handsome and athletic, they might not stop me either. Whenever there's trouble, they automatically pick up the ugly, scruffy ones. In drug raids too. My mother says only ugly men go in for politics. My mother is very apolitical. She disapproves of my activities, but backs me up in everything I do."

"And your father?"

"I hardly ever see him. They're divorced. My mother brought me up. She's a wonderful person. I adore her."

"So you're not the usual teen-ager, rebelling against your parents?"

"Not at all. My mother's a dream. I never want to leave her!"

"That sounds like incest."

"Have you anything against incest?"

"I've never thought about it."

"I shall have to teach you to think."

"I don't know that I want to. I get by very well on instinct."

We'd reached the Pont Marie. I was nearly there. I offered to take the suitcase.

"Shouldn't you go on your way now—wherever that is? Presumably to the Far Left."

He laughed. "The Left can wait. It usually does."

We walked on together over the bridge and on

to the tiny island in the middle of the Seine where the inhabitants jokingly say, "Shall we go over to the Continent?" when they have to take the Métro. We collected my key from the concierge and struggled up the stairs. It was a four-floor walk up to the apartment I had taken. On arrival, we took the suitcase straight into the bedroom and exhaustedly flopped down on the bed together. It had been a hard climb after a long walk. I was still in my mink coat, sweating profusely.

"Would you like a glass of cold water?" I asked, getting up and taking off my coat at last. "There's nothing else in the house yet."

"What I'd really like is a cold shower. Might I have one? I shall probably be fighting at the barricades all day, and then we're going to stage a sit-in strike at the Faculty of Medicine tonight. Who knows when I'll get home. It's rather far from here anyway." He got up and looked out of the window.

"Where do you live?"

He looked embarrassed. "In the 16th arrondissement."

"A very chic district for a revolutionary."

"Well, Karl Marx lived in bourgeois comfort, dressed like a bank manager, and planned his revolution sitting quietly in the Reading Room of the British Museum. You don't have to dress like a revolutionary to be one."

"Yes, I noticed your cashmere. Take it off. I'll light the gas water heater. We both need a shower."

When I came back from the bathroom, he had slipped off his gray jersey. He was painfully thin, almost like a child out of Belsen. He must be Jewish, I thought; that type of whiz kid usually is. I asked him his name as I slipped off my own dress and opened my suitcase to take out a bathrobe.

"Joseph Dreyfus," he replied, stepping out of his trousers.

It was one of the best known Jewish names in France.

"I'm Anne Cumming," I said, standing there in my slip.

He was wearing white cotton underpants, like a little boy. They bulged ominously. He had an erection and was embarrassed by it. I was touched. I went over and put my arms around him. I lifted the elastic band away from his thin belly with one hand and took his hard penis in the other.

"Don't be shy. I want you too." I smiled encouragingly, and he kissed me. It was a strong, aggressive kiss, as if he needed to conquer me; but then the tough militant student suddenly crumpled in my arms and became a shy, hesitant lover at first. He lost his erection when we got into bed, and when we got it back, he came too soon. He was all nervous intellect. I would have to teach him to calm down and use his body instead of his brain.

"It doesn't really matter. Relax. It's enough for me that you felt like making love to me," I said comfortingly.

It wasn't quite true. I was aching to reach orgasm, but I didn't want to embarrass him further by saying or doing anything about it then. It wasn't the moment for masturbation. At nineteen, I knew he would soon be ready to make love again, and it would be worth waiting quietly on the brink. I was right.

The second time was full of intense passion for both of us. It was always to be like that, from then on. Whatever else went wrong—and so much did—sex was always perfect between us. That and a sense of humor. We were an exceptionally ill-matched couple otherwise, but we could cut through to the essential common denominator in seconds. Our basic rhythms in life were the same.

Telephone call. May 7, 1968.

"Hello. We're barricaded in the School of Medicine. I'm afraid that if I try to come and see you, I'll be arrested as I leave the building. The *flics* are everywhere. It's hell."

"Politics are inconvenient."

"No, *love* is inconvenient."

There was complete silence for several days. For all I knew, he was dead or in jail. I made myself get on with the work of setting up my office, and I tried to put the strange encounter out of my mind. It had been a one-night stand on a spring afternoon. Why feel so intensely about it? The last thing I needed was emotional involvement with an unsuitable child. But love is like influenza: it often strikes when least required.

I felt a quiet desperation that led me to search for Joseph's name in the telephone directory. It was difficult, because I didn't know his mother's first name or the exact address. All the Dreyfuses in the 16th arrondissement were men, mainly doctors. Perhaps his mother had left the phone in his father's name.

What could I say to his mother anyway? "I'm a middle-aged woman who's slept once with your son, and I can't get him out of my mind. Where is he? I'm worried about him." What could she reply but "I'm worried about him too, madame," and hang up on me.

I waited another two or three days without doing anything. Then one night I dialed the first possible-looking number in the book.

"Hello. Excuse me, is this the home of Joseph Dreyfus?"

A charming woman's voice said it was, but he wasn't in at present. Could she take a message?

"No, I'm sorry—I have to speak to him personally. Could I call back later? Do you know when he'll be in?"

No, she didn't know when he'd be in. She sounded a little worried. She asked my name, but I didn't want to give it, although she was only being polite, not curious.

"My name would mean nothing to him," I said quickly. "I've a message from someone else. I'll try again in a day or two."

He was probably rolled up in a sleeping bag on the university floor with some liberated political girl. My name *would* mean nothing to him. He would have forgotten me in the excitement of the student revolution.

But I was wrong. When I got home from work the next day, he was sitting on my doorstep. Or rather, he was on the landing, leaning his woolly head against the seventeenth-century balustrade that had been listed as a historical monument. He had been there for hours, having lost my telephone number.

"I was afraid you'd be with someone else," he said as soon as he saw me.

I ran up the rest of the stairs and knelt down beside him. I was so relieved to see him that I threw my handbag down to free my hands to touch his hair. Then I threw myself down beside him, and we lay on the top step in each other's arms, kissing feverishly. The handbag rolled down the stairs, spilling out its contents along the way. We couldn't bear to let each other go for long enough to allow me to rescue my belongings. His nervousness had turned into violent passion. I finally broke away to get the keys or he would have made love to me on the stairs. Not that I would have minded. In due course we made love everywhere in that apartment: on the floor, leaning over the dining room table, propped up against the refrigerator. There was one particular Persian rug in front of the fireplace that I remember well.

"The patterns become extraordinary just as I'm reaching orgasm," he once said. "You're my marijuana. You turn me on more than any drug I've ever had. With you, I can escape into a better world, a world without violence and filled with love."

It was remarks like that which made me take our affair seriously. He seemed to need me to complete a complex, brilliant destiny.

Diary entry. Paris, May 15.

It's ridiculous to have fallen in love at my age with an ugly little boy. Apart from the age difference, which is grotesque, he isn't even my type. For some reason my defenses are down, and I'm allowing myself to turn illusions into reality. Perhaps I've been having too many lightweight romances recently and need some deep emotion for a change, even if I don't want to get involved. Then why choose someone so unsuitable? But does one choose, or is one chosen?

One Sunday Joseph and I were walking along the Quai d'Anjou in a spring rain on our way home. We stopped for a moment under the dripping trees and watched the river, swollen with spring rain, whirling past like molten gray metal.

"How long do you give our relationship?" Joseph suddenly asked.

"About a month," I replied casually. I was sure of myself then. I thought I could live without him.

"Don't say a thing like that so flippantly."

I looked at him with amazement. He had gone dead white and was leaning against the river wall as if he were going to faint. His black curls were sprinkled with tiny raindrops, and his funny square-framed glasses were misted over. When he took them off to wipe them, I saw fear in his eyes. For once, he looked like a child. He usually looked like a strangely immature old man.

"How can it last? It's grotesque! I'm fifty-one."

He didn't answer. I moved over to him under my umbrella and took his arm, and he walked home in silence, as if in a state of shock. At my door he said, "Don't ever frighten me again. When the time comes to leave me, just go. Don't ever threaten me."

He made love to me that night in a frenzy of possession. He held me down and his nails dug into my wrists at the moment of climax so there were five purple marks on each arm the next day. They took a week to fade. Could the intensity of his love be based on fear? What fear?

Note found under my door. Monday, May 29.
MY PERSONAL MANIFESTO. A FIVE-YEAR PLAN FOR ANNE.

I can't come to see you for a few days. Probably I shan't be able to telephone either, but I want to feel *with* you. Above all, I want you to know that, although I am so involved with politics, I am also involved with *you*. Up to now, sex has meant very little to me. It was a physical curiosity to be experimented with because it was there. Now I want a full sexual experience. I want to live with you for a long time; otherwise, I'll become an arid and limited political instrument instead of a human being.

1. I think five years is a good period, because I should get my degree in five years' time.

2. I shall eventually marry, because I want children.

3. My wife will be a gray, mousy girl who works for the Communist party and adores me.

4. I shall never love her as I love you. She'll be part of Phase 2.

5. Will you be my Phase 1?

The above is *not* just rationalization of the fact that I have suddenly awakened to the pleasures of fucking—although that comes into it too. Politics seem pale in comparison to sex—but let's never tell the Communist party!

Joseph

My immediate reaction was one of relief and intense happiness. Like any woman, I was relieved to know that my love was returned. It was only later that I began to envisage the difficulties this plan would involve. I was *not* a young woman. I did not live in Paris. I could not suddenly change my whole life.

I was glad to have a few days to myself to think things over and to get on with my neglected work. My mind had not been on the job, although fortunately shooting had been delayed by the political upheaval, and nothing much was being expected of me at the moment.

The Cannes Film Festival had started, and I decided to go down and see what was going on. New films by Fellini, Louis Malle and Roger Vadim were in the program. My brother Max decided to come with me. He had just returned from Morocco, where he had been painting near-abstract desert scenes of spectral delicacy. Although Max and I suffered from the usual sibling rivalry and seldom saw each other, our love-hate relationship was often closer and more intense than my relationships with other men. The fact that he had not been in Paris when I arrived may even have contributed to the fact that I had fallen in love with Joseph. Max might have filled the void, and Joseph would have remained a *divertissement*.

Max and I left on the Blue Train. "Do you remember those journeys with our mother when she was always in such a hurry to get back to Juan les Pins and Count Nicki?" I asked.

"We used to travel first class then," Max replied. "The whole of life was first class, too. Mediocrity didn't set in till the Second World War."

"Not for us at least. I remember the big boxes of marrons glacés that Count Nicki used to bring us. Now I take my grandchildren little tubes of Smarties."

Cannes had a certain glamour, but it was forced and artificial. We were quite glad when the Festival was interrupted by student manifestations there too, and the whole thing had to be called off. We beat a hasty retreat to Paris. I just had time to telephone Aurélien. Jean-Louis was away, at the University in Grenoble. I still didn't get to meet Aurélien's wife.

When I got back to Paris, the first thing I did was call Joseph. I had left without seeing him and expected him to be as eager to see me again as I was to see him. He told me that he was studying for an exam and had decided not to see me for two weeks—until the exam was over. Two weeks! I accepted this ultimatum as I had accepted his manifesto: with a grain of salt. I was sure he would relent after a few days.

We now started our film in earnest, shooting scenes by a canal on the far side of Paris. It was little used for commercial traffic anymore, but it was very useful to us. It doubled as the Thames for scenes of Rimbaud's visit to London and as the port from which he departed for Africa. We were out every day at dawn on a little tug, chugging up and down the still, black waters between disused factories with that bleak late-nineteenth-century-industrial-revolution atmosphere that would make anyone want to emigrate forever. It was my duty to spread the word to the press that this was a film about the original "dropout," a young man who wanted an alternative society, and whose turn-of-the-century poetry was as modern as anything being written today. This was the only angle that would make the film a commercial attraction. It was unlikely that the general cinema public had heard of Rimbaud.

"Anne, would you look after Verlaine? He seems to be upset about something," a voice greeted me as I went on board one day.

It was the director, an American who had difficulty in communicating with some of his actors because of the language barrier.

"Where is he, Phil?" I asked.

"Down in the hold somewhere drinking coffee. He's unhappy about the color of his hair."

I went down a rickety ladder and found the well-known French actor, who was playing Verlaine, with a thermos in one hand and a paper cup in the other. The makeup man was holding up a mirror for him, and he was tilting his head from side to side, waving the coffee in exasperation.

"But it's not the same color as it was yesterday. It's much redder, and it doesn't suit me. Where's the hairdresser?"

The makeup man too was American in this

Franco-American production, for most of the
money was coming from the States.

I translated, the interpreter being busy elsewhere.

"The hairdresser is on shore, back in the makeup caravan. What's happened, monsieur?"

"They touched up my hair this morning, and it's
come out quite differently. I should have worn a
wig—I always knew I should have worn a wig."

He was beginning to get a little hysterical. He
was a stage actor, made doubly nervous by the
presence of the camera and the unaccustomed
dawn rising. I sympathized with him.

"How can I play a big emotional scene with the
wrong color of hair?"

I went back up and had a quick consultation
with the director.

"Get the wardrobe department to put him in a
hat for today. Is the costume designer on board?"
he asked.

"I think so. There's a hamper of costumes for
dressing up the extras. I'll go down and see what
can be done."

"Thanks, Anne. What would I do without you,
honey?"

"Make a wonderful movie that's going to break
all records."

"I hope you're right, baby. I hope you're right.
I'm not sure. I'm out of my depth here in Europe."

"Then don't jump overboard. It's cold down
there."

He laughed, and I left him looking through his
lense-glass at the rising sun.

I went home and collapsed every evening, hoping Joseph would appear to relieve my own personal tensions. His absence and silence tormented me. I began to think he was doing it on purpose— to see just how far he could go with me.

One evening, to while away the time and to lighten my emotional state, I wrote an answer to his manifesto. I planned to read it to him as soon as he turned up again.

Paris. June 10.

Darling little lover with big ideas,

Thank you for your touching offer—or was it a command? I am not used to political manifestos.

I can only think of negative answers.

1. Five years is a long time.

2. Paris is where you live. Rome is where I live.

3. Fifty-one is more than thirty years older than nineteen.

4. Your parents would be horrified. (I would be, in their place.)

5. On my fortieth birthday, I decided never again to live with a man on a permanent basis. I had done my duty to domesticity, with two husbands, two children and many houses. From now on, sex was going to be just fun, unrelated to responsibility. I'm sticking to my credo.

"F" is for Freedom as well as for Fucking!

Anne

My letter lay on the bedside table for three days—a terrible three days. My real feelings for this young-old political child bore no relation to

the above principles of non-entanglement. It was a
purely intellectual declaration. The truth was that
I wanted to be free, but I also wanted to be with
Joseph every minute.

I went over to see my brother in Montmartre
one evening and to cry on his shoulder.

My brother had always lived alone and liked it.
He had known from the start what it had taken me
two husbands and a dozen lovers to find out: sleeping around should be fun; otherwise, avoid it.

"I'm going to give up sex," I said to Max. "This
time I mean it."

Max smiled. He was making mint tea. Since the
war, he had spent most of his time in North Africa, so he was full of little Arab ceremonies. We sat
on a low divan in front of a brass tray from Fez.

"Sex is the most difficult habit of them all to
kick," Max said. "Remember?"

I remembered. William Burroughs had first said
it when we were all living in the Beat Hotel in
Paris in the late fifties.

"So what do I do?" I cried.

"Learn to live with your habit," Max said, rolling a joint of the best kif from the Rif Mountains.

I went home refreshed. Could I learn to live
with Joseph? Through him, I was once again involved in the cosmic optimism of youth. At his
age, I too had been a Communist and a revolutionary. Was it possible to turn the clock back?

The mirror told me it was not impossible. A
lively and interesting face stared back at me. I was
fading, but not yet old; and Joseph was such a
strange-looking child, a veteran child prodigy so

weighed down by his own wisdom that he looked as if he might grow old before I did. We were ill-assorted, but in a compatible way.

The telephone rang, but it was not Joseph. I was quite annoyed with the kind friend who was inviting me to dinner. I didn't want to go out for fear of missing Joseph, so I refused—and then hated myself for refusing. That night I masturbated to calm myself down. I was fast asleep when the telephone rang again. This time it was the call I had been waiting for.

"Are you alone?" came Joseph's voice.

He didn't sound as if he minded; he was just curious, playing cat and mouse. I tried to keep cool.

"Of course I'm alone. Where are you? Are you coming over?"

"Probably. But if you don't see me within an hour, it means I can't come and will call you in the morning." Then he hung up.

I leaped out of bed, tidied the house, did my face and hair, sprayed on a little Arpège. "My mother uses it too," he had once said. I rearranged my negative declaration—the letter answering his manifesto—on the night table. I planned to read it to him as soon as he arrived.

I didn't read it to him. I forgot about everything in the excitement of his arrival. Like a bitch in heat, I had extrasensory perception, for I heard his bright, springy footsteps in the street, then in the courtyard, then on the stairs. My mind blocked out all other sounds as my ears strained for signs of his approach. My blood pressure rose, my pulse raced, my nipples tingled, and my vagina dilated in anticipation. I opened the door and fell into his arms.

"You've been away so long!"

"What's a few days in a five-year plan?" he protested. "It's the thousandth part of a quarter of one percent."

"My heart is not a computer like your brain!"

I began kissing him all over. To hell with restraint and decorum and being my age.

"Hey, let me get my breath!"

He was pleased just the same. I was playing up to his power complex, making him forget those basic fears that lurked deep in his nature and which I had not clearly understood.

"Hold off a minute. I want to call my mother."

He sat on the bed and picked up the telephone. I knelt behind him and nuzzled the black curls at the back of his neck.

"Do you mind if I give my mother your phone number?" he asked before dialing. "I want to tell her where I'm sleeping."

"Is she that understanding?"

"Of course. She knows all about you."

"Is she jealous?"

"She says not, although she admits that a woman her own age is more of a threat than a young girl."

"You have an incestuous relationship with her! I know it. I feel it. *I'm* the one who's jealous!"

"Shut up and lie down." He dialed. "Allo? Maman? I'm all right. I'm spending the night with Anne. Would you like to take down the number? If anything comes up, you can call me here."

There was a pause while he listened, and I wondered what she was saying. What would I say under similar circumstances? Probably "Have a good time!"

He hung up the phone.

"What did your mother say?"

"Have a good time."

I burst out laughing and told him why.

"You're not at all alike, really. Her lover is fifteen years older than she is."

"Lucky her! I'm tired of teen-agers."

He hit me. Quite hard. I was surprised to find I rather liked it. I goaded him on.

"Fucking Nazi! Jews never hit women."

"They forgot to circumcise me."

He hit me again. Harder. I bit him.

"*Merde!* I have enough trouble during the day staying away from violence." He pushed me back against the pillows, and for a moment I thought he might strangle me. I was just about to poke my fingers into his eyes (the trick Bad Gregory had taught me) when there was a knock on the door.

"It's the police! They must have followed me!"

He crumpled with cowardice. The student-revolutionary became a frightened little boy. I got up and went into the hall. I was just as frightened as he was, but refused to show it.

"Who's there?"

"Telegram for you."

I opened the door and was handed a blue envelope.

"Thank you." I signed the receipt for it and went back to the bedroom, ripping it open and tearing the text in my hurry. I read it with relief. "Arriving Paris June 16. Book hotel near you if other half your bed not free. Love. Rudi."

I passed it over to Joseph, who read and spoke English very well.

"Who's Rudi?"

"He's an Austrian stage designer who specializes in opera. He's probably coming over to work here—we're always in touch. We lived together for five years after I left my second husband."

"How long ago was that?"

"About ten years ago."

"So he keeps coming back to you—expecting to share your bed?"

"They *all* keep coming back."

"You're an earth mother for incestuous boys."

"With very little earth and not much maternal instinct. Anyway, Rudi's not a boy; he's nearly my age."

"Then why didn't you marry him?"

"He didn't want responsibility, or a home or children. He only really loved his work—my greatest rival."

"So you would have married him?"

"Probably. I missed my husband Charles terribly. I still liked marriage then."

"So it wasn't you who left your second husband?"

"No. I never leave anybody. I just add; I don't subtract. However, one day Charles came back, but I'd lost my eternal optimism by then. I could no longer make a go of it."

We were lying in each other's arms, touching each other gently. Our violence had died with the knock on the door. Through the dark, cool air drifted the song of a bird.

"Listen," I said. "It must be a nightingale."

"In the middle of Paris?"

"Why not? It probably lives in the Jardin des Plantes, or even in the Zoo. They're only just across the river from here."

"Maybe you're right. My mother says she can hear them in the Bois de Boulogne. We live near there, you know."

"It must be easy to be a revolutionary from the comfort of your mother's house in that snob *quartier*," I said as I curled up with my back to him.

He wrapped himself around me and pulled me roughly to him as an answer. I could feel a big hard-on against the base of my spine. It amazed me that such a little boy had such a big penis. He now slipped it in quickly from the back. I gyrated slowly, then faster and faster as the nightingale sang louder and louder. Its music exploded in my loins and up into my whole body. Then it slowly ran down and ceased, like an old phonograph record. We fell asleep still joined together. I completely forgot to read him my negative answer to his manifesto.

We were awakened by the telephone. I had forgotten to put the alarm on.

"Allo? Bonjour, madame," a woman's voice greeted me. "May I speak to my son Joseph?"

"Of course, madame. I'll just call him."

I put down the receiver and shook him, whispering, "Wake up; it's your mother."

Then I called out as if he might be in another room, "Joseph! Telephone!"

He rubbed his eyes and sat up. He was very

shortsighted without his glasses, so I put the telephone into his hands.

He greeted his mother in a sleepy voice, "Allo, maman."

They talked for quite a while. Then he passed the receiver back to me. "Maman wants to invite you to lunch. Speak to her."

I had a moment of panic. The sophistication of the situation was a bit intimidating. I felt that his mother was in the room with us as I took the telephone from him.

"Hello, madame. Yes. . . . Yes. . . . That's very kind of you, but I'm supposed to be at work. Yes. . . . Thank you. Perhaps I could come on Sunday instead . . . ? Please don't bother about lunch, though. I can just drop in for an apéritif. . . . Well . . . if you insist. At one o'clock, then? . . . Thank you. . . . Yes, on Sunday."

I put the telephone back carefully and looked at Joseph, who was feeling around for his glasses.

"Do you think your mother really wants to see me?"

"Of course. She's longing to meet you. She likes to take part in everything I do."

"But doesn't she have a busy life of her own?"

"Not really. She's at home a lot. Her lover's married, so they don't go out much."

"Does he come to see her while you're there?"

"Yes, of course. He often stays with us."

"How do you feel about it? Are you jealous?"

"No. It's like having a stepfather." He smiled complacently. "And I know she loves me best."

"Conceited little bastard!"

"Shut up and get my coffee."

He liked ordering me about. I enjoyed it too. The whole setup was so inverted that it amused me.

When I'd brought his coffee, I said, "I'd better call my office. I'll tell them I'm out seeing some magazine editor and that I'll be on the set this afternoon."

"Where's your office?"

"In the studios at Billancourt. It's really part of the production office."

"Where are you shooting today?"

"On the docks by the canal. Rimbaud and Verlaine have to stagger out of an opium den after an all-night session, cross the road in the fog, and plunge into a blind alley."

"But it's a beautiful sunny day!"

"Special effects. We burn sulphurous smoke candles. Wet the streets from a fire hydrant if necessary."

"May I come and watch?"

"Why not? There's always a crowd when we shoot out of doors."

So we forgot the revolution for a while. We got up slowly, had lunch, and took the Métro to the canal. We were in love; time didn't matter; age didn't matter; politics didn't matter.

When we got to the canal bank, the crew were doing their best to hold up traffic while Rimbaud and Verlaine crossed the road. The hooting cars were not interested in anything but getting to their destination, but we couldn't have a modern car passing two turn-of-the-century gentlemen.

"Hello, Anne. Where have you been?" Kisses all around. I was welcomed back into the fold. The intense duet between myself and Joseph became a confused orchestration of cacophonic modern sounds and activities. I was buffeted around, torn from Joseph's side, taken off to talk to the director, the actors, the police. We were working without a permit and holding up traffic. I tried to flirt unsuccessfully with an outraged *flic* who had arrived from the local police station on a bicycle, his navy blue cape flapping around him like a bat's wings.

"But, monsieur, it will only take a minute!" I begged.

At that moment the special effects man lit the sulphurous smoke flares and a choking yellow fog drifted over the road. The policeman was incensed and asphyxiated at the same time. I kept him talking, watching the scene out of the corner of my eye, trying to keep him interested till it was all over.

"You see, that's the young American actor Norman Kent playing Rimbaud, and that's your great French tragedian Boissevain, from the Comédie Française."

He was not really listening to me; he began blowing his whistle. Fortunately, I managed to keep him by me until Rimbaud and Verlaine had crossed the road and were headed down the alley. Then he broke loose. Everyone was very polite and apologetic, and, as the scene was in the can, we moved on peacefully. The policeman thought we were obeying his orders and was satisfied that he had done his duty.

I looked around for Joseph. He was gone. Why had he gone without a word? Desperately, I began to search for him. I was furious with myself for feeling such an acute sense of loss over a nineteen-year-old boy. I was sure he had disappeared on purpose, without saying good-bye, just to annoy me.

Diary entry. Paris. June.

Two days have passed and Joseph has not called. I'm supposed to go to lunch at his mother's tomorrow—or am I? I shall have to call her, check that the address is the one in the phone book, and that she really wants to meet me. It's rather strange that a boy who has declared he wants to live with me for five years, and who nearly faints when I suggest leaving him, would not have taken the trouble to give me his address himself. We've been together over a month, and it has always been he who gets in touch with me, arranges our meetings, sets the pattern for our relationship. I've rather enjoyed being a "slave of love" again, but now it's got to stop.

It was Saturday night. Rudi had arrived, and I had taken him to a hotel. Over apéritifs I explained to him the Joseph situation and promised him that while I was out of Paris on location, he could stay in my flat. Until then, I had to be there on my own, awaiting Joseph's random visits. I told Rudi all about my obsessive feelings for the child—how I was hooked on the habit of love again.

"My poor girl. You've got it badly."

"No worse than when I was with you. Now that I think about it, Joseph's not unlike you. You too were always disappearing without valid reason. In our case, it was your boyfriends. Here, it's politics."

"Did I really make you suffer? Looking back, I always feel it was the happiest and most tranquil period of my life. Wasn't it for you?"

"In a way. I loved you so much that I forgave you everything. The men you went to bed with worried me less than if they had been women. I felt you would always need me, that I was the only woman who could understand the ambiguity of your sex life, and that as long as you still enjoyed going to bed with me, you would always stay with me."

"I would have. It was the offer from America that tempted me, not another person. I went to live with Tom because he was American and could help me start a new life over there. You couldn't come because of your children, remember?"

"Yes. I couldn't leave them while they were still in school, could I? Now they've grown up and married—but it's too late for us."

"I'm always glad to come back to you."

"It's not the coming back I mind; it's the going away. You were once a great love, Rudi. Then you became like a series of casual affairs, at inconvenient moments."

"What was so inconvenient?" Rudi looked surprised.

"You know perfectly well. You used to come and stay and then expect me to drop whoever else I had around. I'd put you in the spare room and treat you like a guest, and the next thing I knew, you were back in my bed because it suited *you* at that moment."

"You make me sound like a terrible egotist."

"You are. A sweet egotist."

He came over and kissed me. I purposely kept it a sisterly kiss.

"Come on. I'll take you out to dinner. Let's go to those nice girls at Les Chimères."

"I'd better call Madame Dreyfus first and see what's going on."

I was undecided. I wanted to have a quiet dinner with Rudi, but I longed to see Joseph. Perhaps if Joseph was at home and answered the phone, I could get him to join us. Madame Dreyfus answered.

"This is Anne Cumming, Joseph's friend. You were sweet enough to ask me to Sunday lunch. I haven't seen Joseph for a couple of days, and I wondered whether the invitation was still convenient for you?"

She said it was. Joseph had been so busy, she'd hardly seen him herself. She apologized for him. But the fact remained that *she* had seen him.

"If he comes in this evening, would you tell him I'm dining at Les Chimères? He knows where it is. I'll be home by about midnight."

She promised to do that. I had the impression that she sensed my anxiety, understood my longing to see her son, and sympathized.

"Thank you so much, madame. I'll be there at one tomorrow, then. Is the address the one in the phone book? Avenue Henri Martin?" She said yes.

I hung up slowly. Rudi was watching me.

"You don't seem very happy. What's wrong?" he asked.

"Nothing I can put my finger on. Joseph declares eternal love and devotion, and then keeps disappearing. It's unsettling."

"He's young. He's busy. There's a revolution on. Perhaps he's just not the type who keeps in touch."

"Love always keeps in touch—that's what it's all about."

I slipped on a jacket, combed my hair, and we set out for Les Chimères.

The restaurant was crowded. We found a table in the far corner. It worried me because I couldn't see the door. I spent the meal looking up, but Joseph never came. I tried to content myself with the warm pleasure of seeing Rudi again, even toyed with the idea of asking him to come home with me, more with the idea of infuriating Joseph if he turned up and found us in bed, rather than as a way of consoling myself. I didn't, though. I went to bed alone, and Joseph didn't even call.

Lunch with Joseph's mother went better than I had expected. I had arrived in a panic, after walking up and down the tree-lined streets of Passy, where the tall chestnuts stand like sentinels to guard the respectability of the upper-middle-class inhabitants. I had started off too early in my nervousness and had to mark time by walking around the district, observing the staid French families returning with their children from a Sunday walk in the Bois. The children wore long white socks, had expensive bicycles and expensive pedigreed English dogs of breeds no longer fashionable in England—cocker spaniels or wirehaired fox terriers. Everything still had a 1930s look; time had stopped still in the 16th arrondissement.

Joseph and his mother lived on a modern block, one of the few in the area. I was relieved when Joseph opened the door and took me straight into the kitchen, where his mother was putting the finishing touches to the lunch. She held out her hands in instant friendship.

"What a pleasure!" She squeezed my hands between both of hers. "Joseph is right. You *are* very beautiful!"

"And *you* are much younger than I expected! Couldn't you have been a bit nearer my age?"

We both laughed, and the ice was broken. Joseph was not nervous, I realized. He was actually enjoying the simultaneous presence of two women who adored him. He was an only child twice over, so to speak.

"I'm the only Frenchwoman you know who's no good at cooking," Françoise Dreyfus said. "Do you think this *gigot* is done?"

There was a delicious smell of garlic and herbs. I poked the lamb with a fork and pretended a knowledge that I didn't have.

"It looks delicious; just right."

The whole ritual was symbolic. We were two women, accomplices in life and love, getting together over a Sunday lunch. The rest of the conversation was easy. We chattered on about subjects both serious and frivolous. I really didn't want to leave.

"Why don't you come for a walk in the Bois

with us?" Joseph asked when I got up to go. "Then we'll go to the cinema."

"I don't think I'll go today," Françoise said quickly. "I think I'll have a nap."

I realized I was interrupting a family tradition. The only son spends Sunday with *maman*.

"It's very sweet of you, but I want to prepare some work for tomorrow. If Joseph would like to drop in later . . ."

We left it like that. Françoise and I embraced. Her parting shot was perfect.

"I'm trying to get Joseph to wear contact lenses. Will you help me? See that he puts them in when he gets up in the mornings."

I spent the rest of the day in a calmer frame of mind. I had passed the test. I was the official mistress of a nineteen-year-old boy—with parental approval!

Joseph had walked me to the Métro.

"I told you it would be all right," he said. "Maman accepts everything I do."

"But I don't. Why didn't you say good-bye to me on the film set the other day? Why didn't you call me? Why do you say you want to live with me for five years and then disappear for days? You can't still be at the barricades; they've taken them all down."

"Women! I was busy. I'm studying for my exams. I gave you my written declaration; I come whenever I can; what more do you want? Now go home and stop being obsessive. I'll come for dinner."

I made no reply. I took his point. We stood at the top of the Métro steps, where a thousand lovers must have kissed good-bye in front of the art nouveau bronze railings. Ours was a very passionate kiss. It had to be. It was bridging time and space and a thirty-year generation gap.

When Joseph arrived for dinner, Rudi was with me. He'd dropped in for an apéritif. I wanted them to meet, but Joseph was strangely reluctant and hesitated at the door.

"Shall I leave and come back later?" he whispered when I told him Rudi was inside.

"Don't be silly. I met your mother. You can meet my ex-lover."

"But a lover is different."

"You'll meet quite a few if we are to be together for five years! I have lovers, not mothers, and I told you—I add; I don't subtract."

There was nothing he could say to that.

"Rudi, this is Joseph, my revolutionary from the 16th arrondissement," I said as we went into the sitting room.

"How charming! All the best families should have one."

Joseph held his own very well. I thought he would be annoyed at our teasing, but he teased us back. He responded to Rudi's wit and charm with a surprisingly mature brilliance of his own, and I could see that Rudi was fascinated by him. While I was cooking in the kitchen, Joseph insisted that Rudi have dinner with us. I had wanted to be alone with Joseph, but at the same time I was amused at

Joseph's taking over the man-about-the-house position. It was as if he were putting Rudi firmly in the past, saying "I am in residence now. I am the host."

"Are you sure it's all right, Anne?" Rudi asked. "Is there enough to eat? Can I go out and get something?"

"No, everything's under control. How lucky I am to be having dinner with the two men I love best in the world!"

I embraced them both with equal affection and went to set the table. They went on talking like old friends, conscious of their common bond.

"You sit on my right, Rudi, as you're the eldest," I said.

Rudi smiled. "I can remember when I was the younger man in your life. You seemed so much older than me then, although it was only by five years."

"Of course I seemed older. I'd had two husbands and two children. We were worlds apart. Now things have evened up. We're both just middle-aged."

The conversation rambled on pleasantly enough. We seemed like one big happy family. It occurred to me that if Rudi and I had conceived a child the night we first met, he would be about Joseph's age. I put the idea out of my mind—I didn't like it.

"I think I should leave you two together now," Rudi said when we had finished eating. He kissed me good night and shook Joseph's hand. "I hope we shall see a lot of each other," he said to Joseph.

"Call me tomorrow evening, Rudi," I said as I showed him to the door.

Joseph was lying in front of the fireplace with his head on a cushion when I came back into the room.

"May we light the fire?" he asked.

"But it's summer!"

"It doesn't matter. I've always wanted to make love in front of an open fire."

I undressed while Joseph laid the fire. When it was burning well, he turned out the lights and put his glasses carefully on the coffee table, then changed his mind and put them back on.

"I want to see you by firelight," he said, and lay looking at me while I knelt naked beside him.

He was lying on his back, stretched straight out, staring up at me. So was his penis. It stood straight up in the firelight, swaying gently, sometimes giving a little bounce. I wet my finger and ran it around the tip to moisten it as I swung my left leg over him, facing away.

I bent my head so I could see his balls and began playing with them. I rubbed them softly against my own labia on the inward thrust, which tickled us both simultaneously into a state of intense excitement.

"You're mine! You're mine!" he cried, arching his back and pushing right up into me as he ejaculated.

His body shuddered under me, and he kept on crying, "You're mine! You're mine!"

Finally we both relaxed. I lay back over him, and he took his hands from my waist and cupped

my breasts, holding them tightly as if afraid to let
go. Then, little by little, his hands relaxed too, and
fell to his sides. I lifted myself off him and turned
to look at him.

"Was it like that with Rudi too?" he asked.

"I never tell one man about another's sexual performance. Anyway, it's different every time."

"Has he got as big a cock as I have?"

"Find out for yourself!" I teased.

"*I'm* not a bloody queer!" he shouted, and
slapped me across the face.

I hit him back, and we rolled about on the floor.

"Mind my glasses! Mind my glasses!" he
screamed.

I took them off him, put them on the coffee table, and threw myself on top of him again. We
fought like fiends, naked in the firelight.

"It's like that scene in *Women in Love*," he
gasped.

"Don't you believe it. It's more like a grotesque
detail in a Hieronymus Bosch painting: a ghastly
old grandmother being fucked by a little black
demon."

"Do you feel like that?" he asked. We had
stopped rolling about.

"No. I feel we're both young and beautiful and
in love."

We had calmed down and were looking at each
other almost sentimentally. He kissed me.

"I love you, Anne."

"I love you too, Joseph. But it's a disaster. When
I go away to the country, I think we should break
it off."

"Why?"

"I'm emotionally tired. I don't want to be in love anymore. It takes too much out of me."

He didn't answer, just began making love to me again, tenderly, gently, in the dying glow of the flames.

That's how it was for the next month. Alternate flames and dying embers. Joseph came and went, fascinating and exasperating in turn. He often disappeared, forgot to call, even forgot to come to dinner when it was on the table. Sometimes I sat alone in front of a table set for two, near tears. Or I called Rudi. Thank God for Rudi, who was designing some sets for the Comédie Française and would be in Paris for a couple of months. He too was alone, as his boyfriend Tom was back in New York, so we saw a lot of each other. He enjoyed Joseph when the boy was there. And Joseph purposely revealed all his hidden charms, his extraordinary wit and knowledge in front of the older man. Rudi was enchanted. A bit too enchanted, I thought.

The film proceeded on its normal course. We were now shooting interiors in the studios at Billancourt—bedroom scenes—Verlaine with his wife when he insisted on having Rimbaud to stay; nude shots of the two men in their London lodging house and the Brussels hotel. It was an intellectual film, but with some porn thrown in for good measure.

The young American actor playing Rimbaud was surprisingly uptight about playing the nude homosexual love scenes. I found this rather suspicious. Nobody in Europe in the Swinging Sixties was bothering too much about macho images, and those who hotly denied homosexual tendencies were suspected of being closet queens.

"The lady doth protest too much," said a French actor playing a bit part, who rather openly flaunted his own homosexuality and arrived on the set every day with a new boy, each more beautiful than the last. "An actor should be prepared to act. After all, I often have to play love scenes with a *woman*!"

We all laughed, but the American director defended his star and agreed for a stand-in to play the love scenes, particularly the scene in which the young Rimbaud comes to Paris for the first time at seventeen and is raped by soldiers in the barracks where he takes refuge.

"Just as well he *doesn't* want to expose that flat *derrière*," said Verlaine. "We must find a stand-in with the most beautiful body in Paris so I can play *my* love scenes with him for real. I'll find him myself."

"He must be very young and the right height," the director insisted. "Then I can use him in long shots for the boyhood scenes in Charleville, too."

"Don't worry," said Verlaine. "He'll be perfect."

And he was. Not a transcendental beauty, nor even terribly sexy, but with a perfect body except for one small detail: he had a swallow tattooed on the right side of his groin.

"It will never show," said Verlaine. "We'll keep him permanently on his stomach, and with a bottom like that, he should *always* be shot from the back."

I felt sorry for the boy, who was a very young dancer from the Paris Opera School. He was both narcissistic and shy. He would stand around in ballet positions, very conscious of his beautiful body, but psychologically insecure. As always happens with stand-ins and extras, he was treated like dirt, pushed around like an object, and often completely forgotten.

I found him hanging around disconsolately one day and took him into my office with me. Joseph had made one of his disappearances and hadn't telephoned for days. I was lonely and dispossessed and felt I also needed a stand-in for Joseph. The two boys were roughly the same age and size, although the similarity ended there.

"Come in, Antoine. I'll show you some of the stills of your beautiful bottom."

I gave him the magnifying glass I kept for looking at contact prints. He studied the scenes in the barracks where his trousers are pulled down and three hefty soldiers take turns to bugger him. The scene would have to be considerably cut in the end, but it was still pretty crude in the present version.

"The sad thing about the cinema," Antoine said, "is that everything is reduced to short, sharp scenes with an artificial continuity put in later. However surprising real life is, it flows."

I looked at the boy with new eyes. He was not just a pretty piece of trade, after all; he was an intelligent, sensitive boy. I grew to like him. He often dropped into my office after that.

"You've got a stand-in," I said to Joseph when he finally reappeared. He had been beaten up by the police and his glasses broken. He was finally wearing the contact lenses his mother had bought him, but he looked even plainer without his funny glasses.

"Is he as ugly as I am?" Joseph asked about Antoine.

"No, he's rather pretty. He has a beautiful body with a tattooed swallow flying into his pubic hair."

"Oh, so you've got that far, have you?"

"Jealous?"

"No. I want you to have a good time."

I was furious. I wanted Joseph to be madly jealous. He was frightened of losing me, but didn't care who I went to bed with. It wasn't good enough. I wanted him to be obsessively possessive about me as I was about him. I decided that I *would* go to bed with little Antoine the next time Joseph disappeared, and I hoped he'd come back and catch us in the middle of it.

I didn't have long to wait. Joseph spent two days with me, and then a very earnest young girl called for him, her arms full of pamphlets and posters. They went off together to a factory to convince the workers to go on strike.

"I won't be back for a day or two," he said. "We're going out of town."

"Call me tomorrow," I pleaded.

I heard nothing for days, but when I called, Françoise told me he was back in Paris.

I invited Antoine for dinner. We went home in the Métro from Billancourt. It was a long ride, and he told me all about himself on the way. He was a French Canadian who had come over to study ballet against his parents' wishes. They had cut him off without a cent, and he did all kinds of odd jobs, including extra work in the cinema, to pay for his schooling. He missed his family terribly, particularly his mother.

"Let me be a mother to you," I said ironically with an ambiguous smile. I was sure he was going to be fair game, and I wanted to make Joseph jealous.

We bought cheese at the cheese shop with a hundred cheeses, and a black currant sorbet at the ice cream shop opposite, and then tiny tournedos at the butcher's.

"Let me do the cooking," Antoine said. "It's been so long since I was in a real home."

We did it together, with plenty of innuendo and shared playfulness. After we had eaten, we sat on the sofa.

"Could I see your swallow?" I asked.

He stood up and dropped his trousers as obediently as he did on the set and stood half naked beside me. The little bird covered an appendectomy scar. I ran my finger down the scar to the swallow's beak. There was no reaction. His penis hung there limp and pretty, but quite lifeless. I reached his pubic hair and combed it with my nails. Nothing moved. I took his penis into my hand and fondled it. He just stood there looking at me rather sadly.

"I don't think I can get it up for someone who reminds me of my mother," he said softly.

I bent over and tickled it with my tongue. Nothing happened, no matter how hard I tried.

"Perhaps you don't like women?" I queried.

"No, it's not that. It's ... well, it's just that I think of you as being so much older than me. I've never thought of going to bed with someone ..."

"With someone old?"

"I suppose that's it. Are you upset? Have I offended you, Anne?"

"No, not at all. I'm in love with somebody else, as a matter of fact. Someone your age. It's just that I miss him when he's not here."

"Doesn't he live in Paris?" Antoine asked, sitting down beside me again.

"Yes, he does. That's the point. He keeps saying he wants to live with me forever, and then doesn't even come to stay. I get lonely."

Antoine put his arms around me.

"Shall I stay the night just to keep you company, then?"

"There's only my big bed. The sofa's not very comfortable."

"That's all right. I'd like to sleep beside you."

And he really meant sleep. He lay in my arms, both of us naked, and the swallow never stirred. I pressed my own pubic hair into its wings, but they didn't even flutter. He soon fell into a deep sleep.

I lay awake for a long time hoping Joseph would come and find me in this compromising position, but even that didn't occur.

The next morning I phoned his mother, and she said Joseph had not been home all night.

"He isn't here, Anne. I thought he must be with you." She sounded perplexed.

"He's obviously being unfaithful to both of us," I said. I was trying to sound gay, but ended up sounding bitter.

"Oh, I'm sure not," Françoise tried to reassure me. "He adores you. There's nobody else."

Joseph was lying in the bath, and I was sitting naked on the lavatory seat watching him. He was giving me a very poor excuse for not having come to see me the previous night, immediately on his return from the trip to the factories.

"I went to see my father. My stepmother likes a little drink after dinner, and I felt I had to drink with her. I was too tired and drunk to go home, and they persuaded me to stay the night."

"Then why didn't you call your mother?"

"I never do. She's not as obsessive as you are."

"I don't believe a word of it. You're bored with me; you're unfaithful, and you only care for your family. *When* you care!"

"For Christ's sake, stop it, Anne," he said raising his voice. "You're getting to be unbearably possessive."

"You're right—it's got to stop," I shouted back. "I hate you, Joseph. I hate you for turning me into this. You're manipulating me to show your power over me, and I hate myself for allowing it. Keep your power games for politics!"

I began to cry. I was sitting naked on a lavatory seat crying. The ridiculousness of the situation hit us both simultaneously.

"You silly bitch," he said, and threw a sponge at me. I threw it back. It hit him square in the face. He got out of the bath dripping wet and came over to me.

"I bet you've never been fucked on the WC before," he said.

"I don't think it will be very comfortable," I replied, still near tears.

It was very uncomfortable, and we finished up in bed. He was still wet, but I didn't care. When it was all over, I said, "Don't think you can always settle everything with your big prick. I'm leaving you for good when I go on location to Charleville next week."

We had Françoise to dinner. I wanted to return her hospitality before I went away. Rudi came too, to make a fourth, and it was gay and charming, and we all had a good time. After dinner I took Françoise to one side.

"Come and chat in the bedroom a moment," I said.

We sat on the bed.

"I hope you're not really leaving Joseph," she said at once.

"He's told you, then? I wanted to talk to you about it. What do you think?"

"Perhaps I'm being selfish, because from my point of view it's been perfect. He's never been so well or so happy. But I must try and see it from your point of view. Does he make *you* happy?"

"Yes and no. It's not his age that worries me, it's his lack of real emotion. He plays games. I'm sorry to say this about your son, but I think he's basically unloving and unsacrificing. I don't think he's a real Communist at all. He takes what he wants by enchanting us all, like a little spider spinning a beautiful web. Then he leaves us entangled in his web, struggling in one corner, so he can visit us when it suits him."

"You're probably right. Divorced parents often overcompensate. I expect I've spoiled him."

"Maybe. Anyway, I don't think he's ready for a relationship that makes demands on him. Perhaps he never will be."

"You must do what's best for yourself," Françoise said generously. "But I think you still have a lot to give to each other, so perhaps you can remain just good friends?"

"Not a hope!" I exclaimed. "Not for a long time. The atmosphere is too electric when we meet. We find each other very stimulating. God knows why!"

Françoise smiled. "You and I will remain friends anyway. Promise me you'll come and see me whenever you're in Paris?"

"Of course. Now we'd better join the gentlemen."

We went back to the other room.

"Your mother's a darling," I said when Françoise and Rudi had gone. "I'm not jealous of her anymore."

"Why don't we all live together, then? That would solve everything," Joseph exclaimed.

"Was that part of your Five-Year Plan?"

"No. I was coming to live with you."

I protested, although I was pleased.

"I couldn't be the reason for your leaving home. That will have to wait till you get married."

"You don't really want me, do you?" He began to put on that frightened little boy look.

I handed him my answer to his manifesto, which had been lying around unread all this time.

He read it and handed it back. He made no comment, but later he made love to me in that frenetic way he had when he thought he was losing me. He dug his nails into my flesh so hard that I found blood on the sheets the next morning. Once again he shouted "You're mine! You're mine!" at the moment of orgasm.

Later, when we were lying back, I said, "One day you'll shout 'I'm yours! I'm yours!,' Joseph. But I don't think it will be with me."

He looked at me strangely. Again he had nothing to say.

We were getting ready to leave for Charleville in the French provinces to shoot the scenes of Rimbaud's childhood. Antoine was to come with us to play most of the scenes in long shot, as they needed boyish movements of which our American actor was no longer capable. It required great effort on the part of the makeup man to make him look like a fresh twenty-year-old for the rest of his role. He was only in his late twenties, but lack of exercise and too many martinis were taking their toll. No tricks of the trade could have made him look like a high school boy again. Antoine was delighted. It was his summer holiday period, and he now had a good reason not to go back to Canada at once.

"I'd much rather spend my holidays with you,

Anne, instead of my real mother," he said when he heard the news.

"Antoine, I'm not very maternal, and I have a tendency to jump into bed with my son-figures. We've tried that, and it didn't work. Take my advice and stick to your real mother."

He hugged me, but still with a filial devotion. "Darling, Anne, please don't turn me down because I can't get it up!"

"For heaven's sake, child, I'm not turning you down. You turned *me* down! I'm merely keeping our relationship where it's supposed to be. Unhappiness is so often caused by expecting the wrong thing from the right people."

He gave me another kiss and leaped out of the room, like Nijinsky in *Spectre de la Rose*.

"Your understudy is coming with us to Charleville," I told Joseph later that night. He didn't react. He was lying naked on the sofa, his head in my lap. We had made love as soon as I came in from the office. As he now had my keys, I often found him waiting for me.

It was hot, and we had not bothered to get dressed again. We often wandered about the apartment naked, now that the warm weather had arrived. I ran my fingers through his black curls which, owing to the position of his head in my naked lap, were mingling with my own pubic hair.

Joseph turned his head so that his nose was in my crotch. "I like the smell of sex," he said in a muffled voice.

"That's very French of you," I commented, still idly stroking his curls. I glanced down his body to see if he was getting another erection. He was, but he was also scratching at his pubic hair.

"Joseph, why are you scratching like that? Don't tell me some scruffy revolutionary girl has given you crabs?"

"What do you mean, crabs?"

I thought perhaps I had used the wrong word in French. I had used "lice," but perhaps they had another word for pubic lice.

"You know—those horrible little insects that burrow into the roots of pubic hair and crawl around the world from one crotch to another as people make love."

"How disgusting you make it sound. We have a much prettier name for them in French. *Les papillons d'amour*—the butterflies of love."

"I've always thought of love letters as the butterflies of love, flying around the world from one lover to another. This is something quite different."

"Well, I've never received a love letter, and I've never had crabs."

"There's always a first time. Let me look. Turn around."

Joseph obligingly lifted his head off my thighs and substituted his pelvis, lying across my lap like Christ down from the cross.

"We look like a *Pietà*," he commented. "You're bending over me like Mary Magdalene."

"Don't be sacrilegious!"

I was dividing the hairs very carefully and examining his pubic mound. I couldn't see very well and needed my glasses.

I got up and went into the bedroom to get them, and then I remembered I had something better. I had the magnifying glass with which I examined the contact prints.

"Now let me have a look," I said, kneeling down beside him as he lay supine and untroubled on the green velvet sofa. I peered through the magnifying glass.

"Oh, my God! You filthy child! You've got a whole family of them!"

"Well, you must have given them to me."

I ignored his remark. "Let me look at your armpits too. They get there as well."

I moved the glass up to his armpits. There were two under his left arm and three under the right. I told him so.

"They must be a married couple under the left and a *ménage à trois* under the right. How chic!" He laughed.

"It's not chic, it's revolting. And I've nothing to put on them. I'll have to pick them off with my eyebrow tweezers. Don't move."

I got my eyebrow tweezers and a piece of Kleenex. I picked them off one by one and dropped them onto the paper. Then I made him look at them.

"So that's what your revolution is about. Fucking dirty girls in filthy fleabags."

"It's not true. You must have given them to me."

"And where would I have got them, may I ask?"

"Antoine."

"So you *are* jealous!"

"No. Just logical. Now kindly examine yourself."

I looked at my own bush with the magnifying glass. I found two crabs nestling together.

"Oh, my God! I think they're mating!"

"You see? It's all Antoine's fault. It's a particularly promiscuous strain."

I wasn't going to give him the satisfaction of telling him that I had not made love to Antoine. We had lain together, though. I suppose it was just possible.

"You've got more than I have," I protested. "You must have got them first."

"No. It's just that they prefer teen-agers. My understudy's probably been breeding them for years, ever since he gave up keeping white mice."

"I'm sure Antoine never kept white mice. He's a pure, beautiful boy, and he hasn't got crabs, either. You'll meet him if you come to Charleville, and you can see for yourself."

"I'm certainly not going to examine my rival's pubic hair. I leave that to you. Now throw away that piece of Kleenex, or they'll start walking around the world again."

I threw the Kleenex into the lavatory. Then I went back and lay beside Joseph on the sofa.

"We'll have to get some of that special powder in the morning and sprinkle it on ourselves. We'd better put it on our heads too," I said as he took me in his arms.

I felt contaminated and sensual at the same time. Sensuality won. It seemed that nothing could come between us, not even the butterflies of love.

Something did come between us. Several hundred miles of France. The whole crew was shipped off to Charleville by bus, by car and by train. I tried to get Joseph to come with us. I had forgotten my firm intention of separating from him. In a macabre way, the crabs had drawn us together again. He had come to me nightly for treatment, so, during my last days in Paris, we had really been together.

One night as I sprinkled on the white powder and rubbed it in, we discussed where the crabs could have come from.

"Did you ask Antoine?"

"Yes, I did. He'd never even heard of them. When I explained, he said his swallow would have kept them away."

"So he's got a sense of humor too?"

"Of course. I keep telling you that you'll like him. Come with me to Charleville, and you'll meet him. Why don't you want to come? The university's closed and you're on holiday now."

"I'm going somewhere with my mother."

"Where?"

"We haven't decided yet."

I called Françoise. I was desperate at the idea of leaving Joseph, and wanted to know their plans. They seemed vague. Françoise was waiting to hear if her own lover could get away. She was perfectly happy to let Joseph come with me to Charleville. I could even have got him a small part as one of the schoolboys in the scenes where Antoine would be doubling as Rimbaud.

"You'll enjoy being with Antoine," I insisted. "You'll officially have to share a room with him."

"Me, with a baby faggot from the ballet? You're mad!"

"He's not a faggot. I'm sure he's not even decided *what* he is."

"Well, you should know."

"Then come and protect me from him."

But there was no way I could persuade Joseph to come. Even Rudi tried. He was moving out of his hotel and into my apartment while I was away, and had brought his things over.

"Go with Anne. You'll have a wonderful time. It's great fun on location," Rudi insisted on my behalf.

"No, I can't leave Paris. The revolution needs me."

"Fuck the revolution," I said bitterly. "The fourteenth of July is over."

In point of fact, I left for Charleville on July 17. Joseph didn't even bother to see me off at the station. When I got to Charleville, I wrote him a long letter.

July 18, 1968.
Dearest Little Love,

When you first suggested your Five-Year Plan, my immediate reaction was to refuse. The vast difference in our ages would make it an impossible relationship. Then I thought of it as an interesting challenge, a daring experiment. I like adventure and revolution. Perhaps I *could* settle down with a very young man. No older man has tempted me into any kind of long-term contract over the last ten years.

Adolescence and middle age have something in common—a fear of the future. I could help you with your fears, but could you help me with mine?

I should need to feel really loved for as long as the relationship lasted. I think you are too egotistic to be capable of real love. You demand it, but you do not give it. It is partly your age, but mainly your nature. Your basic charm is your volatility. You come and go, take me and leave me, with frenzied haste. It takes time and effort to give.

I shouldn't be expected to put my whole life into reverse unless it's for a reasonable period. Five years is reasonable—but you aren't capable of total commitment for five minutes! It requires too much personal sacrifice, which I don't see either in your personality or in your politics. Your Communism does not go very deep; it's mainly in your precocious, overdeveloped mind. Humanity and awareness of others are not your strong point.

As destiny has put 300 miles between us at the moment, perhaps it would be better to make a clean break now than suffer prolonged anguish later.

I love you—that is the trouble.

Anne

I posted my letter with relief—but relief soon died, and longing took its place. I began doubting my motives for having written. Was it really from mature good sense, or was I hoping that Joseph would refuse this ultimatum and arrive on my doorstep, declaring himself capable of giving me everything I wanted? Was *I* playing games now?

The weather turned hot and stuffy, and summer took over. I wanted to lie in the arms of a full-blooded lover, not a will-o-the-wisp child. The trouble was that in bed, this child was a man; his fragile frame managed to possess me and satisfy me by sheer strength of will—another famous Jewish survival quality he'd inherited.

If I hadn't been waiting anxiously for the answer to my letter, I would have enjoyed my stay in Charleville. We were shooting in and around an old stone farmhouse, and we spent the warm, sunny days in the green fields sprinkled with poppies, or in the courtyard and barns of the farmhouse where Rimbaud wrote his first poems as he hid in the hayloft from his severe and disapproving widowed mother.

The whole troupe was lodged in the same small provincial hotel, which made it easier for me to get closer to the actors and to discover those little foibles that make good copy for publicity articles. We also had a television crew down from Paris, and I was kept busy organizing this junket, seeing that their cameras did not get in the way of ours, and persuading the actors to give off-the-set interviews. I had to interpret Rimbaud's interview as we went along, as our American actor spoke no French. His film mother, a well-known French actress, was so living the part that it was quite clear why Rimbaud ran away to Paris at eighteen to get away from her and all that she and French provincial life represented.

One of my favorite scenes was played in the rain outside the Charleville cathedral. The entire Rimbaud family, with the sisters and mother, were under umbrellas on their way to Sunday mass. The local fire brigade was paid to make the rain. We had no stand-ins except for Antoine, and all the actors got very wet and bad-tempered. The next day we were back in the sunny fields again, and I got hay fever.

"Are there any letters for me?" I asked as I got back to the hotel every evening. There were often letters from my daughters, but nothing from Joseph.

I went up the wide wooden staircase to my old-fashioned bedroom with its mahogany cupboard and its two brass bedsteads. I had set up a little office in the corner on a big round table they had kindly brought in from the hall. Every evening I sorted through photographs, interview tapes, and my notes. I called Rudi occasionally. He had moved into my flat and was busy and happy. I called Jopseh once to see if he had received my letter, but Françoise answered and said he wasn't there. We had a friendly chat, but I didn't like to call again, in case she might think I was pestering the boy. I left my number, but Joseph never returned my call. I made up my mind to forget him, as he seemed wise enough to be forgetting me. He had read my letter well and was taking me at my word.

A charming French actor came down from Paris to play Rimbaud's headmaster. He was a man about my age, and was put in the bedroom across the hall. We met on the stairs on his first night, and went in to dinner together. I explained my work to him.

"Could I see some of the photographs later?" he asked.

I knew he was asking for more—and why not?

"Of course. We'll go to my room after dinner."

We both smiled, we both knew the score, there was no hurry. We had a leisurely dinner with coffee and liqueurs in the bar afterwards, and then we went slowly upstairs together.

In my anxiety to forget Joseph in his arms, I got a little frenzied. He obviously liked a quieter approach and patted my thigh as if to calm down a spirited horse.

"We've got all the time in the world," he said. "We're not so young. We must make it last."

I held back, but I missed the urgency I had known with Joseph.

"That was an excellent cure for a bad case of teen-age fever," I said when it was over. "I've been living on a steady diet of juvenile lovers. I hope you've broken me of it."

I enjoyed these mature charms for the three days the actor was with us. He was a smooth, urbane man who took his pleasures calmly. It did me good to move in a more relaxed tempo. When he left, I was genuinely sorry to see him go, but we did not exchange Paris phone numbers. Probably he was married; in any case, we didn't ask each other any questions or plan any future meetings.

His room was empty for a few days. Then a covey of journalists came down to visit us for the night. One of them was left without a bedroom, for we had completely filled the hotel.

"I have an extra bed in my room," I said tentatively.

"Madame is very sporting," said the leftover, whom I naturally thought the best of the bunch.

"When the ball is thrown into your court, at least you pick it up," I said. "You needn't go on playing if you don't want to."

We had a very pleasant "game and set" that night. It all helped to pass the time. It was a fortnight since I had left Paris.

I had stopped expecting a letter from Joseph. I had accepted the fact that probably he was wiser than I was. He knew that if you intended to break off a relationship, it was better not to write. I was therefore surprised when the plump blond girl at the reception desk stopped me one day as I came in and held out a cheap white envelope.

I waited till I got to my room before opening it. I sat down on the brass bedstead, but not the one I usually slept in—where I had lain in the arms of other men. I sat on the unused bed to read Joseph's letter.

Dearest Anne,

You are not the first person to find me arid and unemotional. It is probably true, but in my own way I love you to the full extent of my possibilities. I can't do more. I want you. I need you. Please come back to me.

Joseph

My first reaction was to run downstairs and look up the trains to Paris. Then I calmed down. The letter did not tell me anything I didn't know, nor did it offer anything that I needed. As usual, it was what *he* wanted. As an answer, it was two weeks overdue, and it was very short, considering the time and trouble I had put into my own letter. I must wait quietly and maybe give him one more chance when I got back to Paris in two weeks' time. I wouldn't even answer till I got back.

But I couldn't wait two weeks, and I couldn't resist answering. I phoned him and found him in.

"You could have called me before" was his first remark. "You've been gone nearly two weeks."

"It's nearly *three* weeks, and you could have called *me*," I replied.

There was a slight pause, then he said, "Why don't you come up to Paris for the weekend? You promised you'd come back for a weekend."

"Joseph, I wrote you a long letter explaining that I was breaking off our affair and trying to forget you."

"But you didn't mean it?"

"It was up to you to find out. You could have written or phoned or come down to see if I meant it."

"Please come up to Paris this weekend."

"No, Joseph. It's you who must make the effort. You know where I am. I have a double room. You could come on Friday night."

"But it's so complicated!"

"It's complicated for me too."

I hung up at that point, pleased with myself for having been so firm. I then spent the next two days in a panic, thinking he wouldn't come. I hadn't been very encouraging, but I stopped myself from calling again. He didn't call either.

I had to take some local journalists to the set on Friday. As I went out, I told them at the reception desk that my godson might come down for the weekend. He could be shown to my room if he arrived.

When I got back, he was lying on my bed reading Proust.

"It's a bloody long train journey," he said. "Thank God for *La Recherche du Temps Perdu*."

I threw myself on top of him, forgetting entirely that I was supposed to be playing hard to get.

"Be careful of Proust!" he protested, waving the book in the air.

"Fuck Proust! It'll do him good. Constipated old French queer!"

"He wasn't old . . ."

Joseph never finished the sentence. Nothing more was said. The book dropped to the floor.

It was a Madame Bovary weekend; we hardly went out. On Sunday afternoon, I finally dragged him to the Rimbaud farmhouse, where we spent most of the time in a nearby hayfield. The bees had never buzzed louder, and the poppies took on a more intense red.

"Love is better than marijuana," I observed. "It makes everything more everything."

"You're not leaving me, then?" He smiled happily.

"Of course I am. But not till the film is over. Why don't you call your mother tonight and stay on here a bit?"

Joseph stayed for a week. Away from Paris, everything went much better between us. He was witty and amusing and everybody loved him. Camp followers are a common phenomenon with a film crew on location. Nobody seemed to think of us as an odd couple, and his presence was justified by his being given a small part. He was Rimbaud's school friend, and even had a few lines and got paid for two days' shooting. He became bosom friends with Antoine; the two boys became inseparable.

"You see, I knew you'd like Antoine," I said. "Just as I knew you'd like Rudi. Why are you so hesitant about meeting people?"

"Only queers. I don't want to meet any queers."

"How can you be so intolerant?"

"I'm not intolerant. I'm just selective."

I let the matter drop. When I went out to the set the next day, Joseph and Antoine were sitting side by side, deep in conversation. They were both dressed as old-fashioned schoolboys, perfectly cast, two school-leavers—one dark and one fair. They had to run down a hill together as if coming out of school for the last time, throwing their books away into the long grass as they ran. They repeated it several times till the director was satisfied. It was a charming, youthful scene.

The rest of the week passed all too quickly. When neither of us was working, we explored the little town, visited the museum, and behaved like any young lovers on holiday. Sometimes we ate with the rest of the crew, but more often we went off by ourselves to a little bistro frequented by passing truck drivers.

"I've got a truck driver for a lover back in Rome," I told Joseph.

"Will you go back to him when you leave Paris?"

"Would you mind?"

"I'd rather you had that kind of man if we have to be separated for a time. I'm not jealous of what you do in bed. I'm jealous of your heart and your mind."

It was an intellectual reaction, quite alien to my own way of loving.

"You needn't be jealous. I'm not planning any long-term relationships," I assured him.

"Not even a Five-Year Plan?"

"I'm thinking about it, Joseph. I like Paris, and I've been meaning to take time off to write a novel."

"What about?"

"Love. It will be called *Beyond This Limit*."

"What does that mean?"

"I took the title from a sign in the Paris Métro: 'Beyond this limit tickets are no longer valid.' It could well be set in France. When this film is over, I could give up my movie work for a time and write my book in Paris."

"Do that, Anne. Give it all up and hurry back to me."

He held out his hands across the checked table-cloth, and I put mine into them.

"By the way, when do you come home from Charleville?"

"About another two weeks. And please remember the Île St. Louis is not my home—it's a rented apartment. I only have it for another month."

"Take it for five years."

I didn't answer.

Joseph left early the following Monday morning. He swore he'd call me every night. He did call twice and sent me a funny postcard. I sent a post-card nearly every day on the premise that it would be ridiculous at my age to write proper love let-ters. The time passed more quickly, and there was hope in the air.

Rudi also phoned from Paris to say that he didn't think he could wait for my return; he would have to leave a day or two earlier for Salzburg. He promised to come down and see me in Rome when I got back there in the autumn. He sounded happy too.

We had nearly finished shooting in Charleville, and there seemed no reason for me to stay on to the end. I could be more useful in Paris preparing for the crew's return. I decided to surprise Rudi and turn up on his last morning to say good-bye.

I took a milk train to Paris so I could get there in time to wake Rudi with a cup of coffee. It was a last-minute decision, so I didn't let Joseph know I was coming, either. I wanted to resume our rela-tionship on another level and with another rhythm. Sex would inevitably still be the basis, but frenzy and haste must go if it were to last. I would see Rudi off before getting in touch with Joseph again.

I arrived back in Paris at eight o'clock in the morning, and as the taxi turned over the Pont Ma-rie, I was surprised to see fishermen on the quais already, optimistically casting their lines into the murky water.

I struggled upstairs with my bag and baggage and let myself in with my keys. I opened the bed-room door softly and peeped inside to see if Rudi were awake. He was not awake, and he was not alone.

"Oh, excuse me!" I said involuntarily, although they were both fast asleep, curled around each other.

In the darkened room, I couldn't even see if Rudi was sleeping with a man or a woman. I was not particularly embarrassed. In the ten years since our separation, I had met many of his lovers. In New York I had even sat on the edge of their bed. I would just make an extra cup of coffee to take in.

I was about to slip out of the room when the stranger heard me and sat up. It was not a stranger. It was Joseph. The whole thing was unbelievable, unnecessary, and in bad taste. I mustn't make things worse by showing my horror.

"Good morning," I said, keeping my voice down so as not to wake Rudi. "I came back to get you both breakfast."

In the back of my mind, I suppose I wanted Joseph to get out of bed, come with me into the other room, and produce some miraculous explanation.

Rudi woke up. "Oh, hello!" he said, relatively unconcerned. Then he sat up, and the bedclothes fell away. Both men were completely naked, and I could see there was to be no miraculous explanation. Rudi's pajamas were hanging untouched behind the door, and Joseph's white cotton underpants were on the floor.

"I came back to get you both breakfast," I replied inanely. I was too upset to think of anything else to say. I went into the kitchen.

Rudi presently appeared in a dressing gown. I could hear Joseph in the bathroom.

"Why did you do it?" I asked, without rancor but in great pain.

"It was his idea. You told me you'd given him up, so I saw no harm in it. Teen-agers are great seducers. It's we older people who usually think twice."

"Why did *he* do it, I wonder?"

"You'd better ask him. Perhaps he needed a father as well as a mother." Rudi went into the bathroom too.

I went on making breakfast, trying not to show my distress. I set the table in the living room, and Joseph came in fully dressed. He looked a little sheepish, but not unduly disturbed.

"I think I must run along now," he said. It was the first time I'd ever heard him say anything banal.

I walked to the door with him.

"Why did you do it?" I asked again, as if the reason were more important than the fact.

"Communism, I suppose," he replied quickly with a forced levity. "Share and share alike."

I could see he was frightened.

"I see. Communism 16th arrondissement style. Very sophisticated." I tried not to sound bitter. I never believe in revenge.

"Good-bye, Joseph."

He went out the door without kissing me or even shaking my hand. He turned at the top of the stairs, where I had once dropped my handbag and had lain down beside him.

"I'll call you," he said.

I shut the door and went back into the sitting room. Rudi came in from the bathroom.

"Breakfast for two," I said. "The child has run out on us."

I was determined not to cry.

"Are you very upset?" Rudi asked. "Forgive me. I didn't realize it was so serious. We've shared lovers before." We sat down opposite each other, and I poured out the coffee.

"I would have preferred *not* to share this one."

"I'm sorry. He's a fascinating boy. He called me and asked to come to dinner. I couldn't resist."

"I didn't even know he had homosexual tendencies."

"I didn't corrupt him," Rudi answered me. "He'd been to bed with men before."

"That's what hurts me most—the fact that he didn't have the courage to tell me. Particularly when he knew all about you and your relationship with me. He pretended to hate homosexuality, and he was even very jealous of your hold over me."

"Then he probably did it to weaken my hold."

"Could be. But it's not the reason that matters now, it's the hypocrisy I can't bear."

"He's a very interesting young man, but I can see he'll drive you around the bend if you stay with him."

"I won't stay with him, although not on account of this. After all, I was unfaithful to him myself while I was away. I can't stand living with half-truths, Rudi. I have to know where I am."

Rudi looked at his watch.

"I must pack. My plane leaves at midday."

"And I'm supposed to be in my office."

I cleared away the breakfast things and washed the dishes. Rudi finished his packing. We might have been any bourgeois couple at the beginning of their humdrum day.

"I'd better go now, Rudi," I finally said when I was ready. "We'll see each other in Rome."

He came over and took me in his arms.

"Do you forgive me?"

I kissed him.

"There's nothing to forgive. Perhaps I should thank you. You've probably saved me from wasting a lot of time. Five years, maybe."

We kissed again. He accompanied me to the door.

"*Ciao!*" he said.

"*Merde!*" I replied as I ran down the stairs.

I was glad no one was in the office when I got there. I sat at the typewriter with tears streaming down my face.

Dearest Joseph,

If the truth has to come, then it's better that it comes quickly. I blame no one but myself for my present suffering and delusion. At my age, I can't waste time on illusions. It's not because of what has happened that I'm turning down your Five-Year Plan, but I couldn't go into a serious relationship with someone who doesn't put all their cards on the table. You had three months in which to do so, but you hid your true self behind your big prick and your revolution. I enjoyed them both, and I could again, but right now I don't think I'd enjoy the real you.

Tell your mother I'll call her on my next visit to Paris. If I don't meet her again at the moment, it's because I'm protecting myself from *you*. She'll understand.

Call me if you want to. I'm not refusing to see you.

Anne

He never called. The film finished, and I went back to Rome. On arrival, I slipped Joseph's manifesto, with his letter and postcard, into the shoebox file. Antoine wrote to me from Canada, and I put his letter in there too.

I wondered for a moment if the two boys had ever made love in Charleville while I was busy. Perhaps Joseph had passed the crabs to Antoine after all. But it seemed unlikely. By then, the butterflies of love were dead.

5 ∽ A Roomful of Rainbows

Evaristo fell out of the sky—literally. He was carrying a rainbow in his hands, a roomful of rainbows, with which he lit up my life for over a year. He is still one of my best friends.

In the spring of 1969, I was flying back to Rome after an Easter visit to see Fiona and the children. I was traveling by Sudan Air to save money. Like all the Arab airlines, they have a fuel stop in Rome and take on passengers for that leg of the journey at cut-rate prices.

We were in midair halfway across France when Italy decided to have an air strike. All Italian airports were closed, and our first stop, Rome, was canceled. There were only two alternatives: to go straight on to Khartoum, or to get off in Germany. France didn't want us, so we found ourselves in Frankfurt. I would have loved to go on to Khartoum, but everyone else was a little hysterical. One woman would have jumped off while the plane was still in flight had she been able.

"Let's go on to Khartoum," said a voice behind me.

I looked around to identify this kindred spirit and was surprised to see a very inconspicuous young man whom I hadn't even noticed before.

"I'd like to go to Khartoum too," I said to the Captain, who had kindly appeared in person to talk to us. "I've always wanted to see the Aswan Dam and Abu Simbel."

The Captain smiled. "We appreciate your spirit of adventure, madam, but the airline can't offer free trips around the world. You'd have to pay your passage back."

The young man and I looked at each other re-gretfully. He was holding a strange parcel in his . though it were breakable; otherwise, he ap-pea. ery ordinary, and I wouldn't have given him a second glance.

"Couldn't we find somewhere more amusing to go to than Frankfurt?" he asked. His English was good, but he had a strong Italian accent. "What about Paris?"

"At this moment, we're closer to Frankfurt, where we have special connections," said the pilot. "You will be taken to a hotel where we shall pay for your meals and for an overnight stay, if neces-sary. We shall also arrange for connections to Rome as soon as the strike ends."

The pilot went back to the cockpit. The plane veered to the left and soon began to lose altitude. I had never been in Frankfurt and began looking forward to it.

"All transit passengers to Rome will leave the plane here. Don't forget your hand baggage."

"But our other luggage? What will happen to

our other luggage?" a hysterical middle-aged Italian woman shouted. "My daughter is waiting for me at Rome airport. Will she know what has happened to us? Oh, Mamma mia! I've just had an operation on my heart. My aorta isn't working properly. Oh, Mamma mia!"

She was shouting in Italian, so not everyone knew what she was saying, least of all the calm hostess.

"The lady is worrying about her registered luggage," the young man with the parcel translated. "She's afraid it's going on to Khartoum."

We were assured that the luggage for Rome would be unloaded in Frankfurt. A young German with a neat blond military moustache took charge when we landed. He was polite and efficient, like all airline personnel anywhere in the world. He herded his ill-assorted sheep into the huge modern terminal and penned us into one corner, where we sat for half an hour till we were moved to the vast departure area, which gave us false hope of early departure. We sat or strolled about for three or four hours, as false rumors and the blond moustache came and went.

"Time to spare, travel by air!" said the young man who had wanted to come to Khartoum with me. He had parked his curious parcel on top of an expensive-looking overnight bag. Gucci? He was not as ordinary as he seemed.

We began to form groups. There was an amusing American girl who was shuttling between London and Rome trying to decide between two fiancés. There were two smooth Italian queers carrying a terribly heavy canvas sack between them. They were antique dealers weighed down with English silver. There was a Milanese businessman agitated over missing vital appointments. There was a Philippine girl with wide, frightened brown eyes, who was shy and breathless and terrified of missing some secret rendezvous. We formed the "sophisticated" group. The others were little families, traveling salesmen, a couple of schoolteachers on holiday, a priest, and some nondescript girls going to work in the Food and Agricultural Organization.

Time began to weigh very heavily after the first hour. We were offered free soft drinks by the airline, which was like being inadvertently invited to an ill-assorted cocktail party where you knew no one. We did our best to fraternize. The American girl showed us her two engagement rings. The antique dealers showed us their silver. And I found some photos of film stars whose biographies I had been preparing for pre-publicity. It all helped us to pass the time and to get to know one another. The Milanese businessman kept disappearing to make international phone calls, and the Philippine virgin sat and read the Bible.

"Do you think she's going to Rome to become a nun?" I asked the young man, who sat clutching his curious parcel again.

Before he could reply, our shepherd with the military moustache announced that there was no hope of the strike being lifted that night, and that we would now be taken to a hotel. We all got up and followed him meekly through halls echoing with tantalizing multilingual announcements of other departures to less problematic destinations.

"May I walk beside you?" asked the young man with the parcel. "If we are being led to the gas chambers, I would like to die in the arms of a beautiful woman."

His remark surprised me. I looked at him with new eyes and new ideas. He was small but tough. His Gucci bag was slung over broad shoulders, his clothes fitted well over a thick chest, well-rounded bottom and strong thighs. He was not handsome, but when you looked more closely, there was something sexy about him. Not sex at first sight, but sex at the end of the season, I said to myself, paraphrasing Oscar Wilde. One could do worse for a one-night stand between two airplanes.

"Before you die in my arms, you must tell me what is in your mysterious parcel. My lovers are not allowed to have secrets."

"I shall unwrap it for you tonight, but only in private. It's a roomful of rainbows," was all he would say.

We were about to get into the same taxi when the heart-case passenger had a new fit of hysterics.

"But my luggage? Where is my luggage? I am not going to the hotel without my luggage," she screamed in Italian.

Our German shepherd turned to us, seeking elucidation. I was already in the taxi, but my young man was still outside and had just passed me the parcel.

"Would you hold this for a minute? Keep it this way up," he said and hurried off to interpret. The two antique dealers got in beside me, their heavy bag of silver on their knees, squashing my precious package.

"Oh, do be careful," I said instinctively.

"Why? What is it?" they asked as the taxi drove off, though the driver had not been told where to go.

"I don't know what it is. It belongs to that young man."

"What young man? We didn't see any young man!"

They looked at each other for confirmation of this strange fact. They would obviously have summed up any possible young man with their cruising, homosexual eyes.

"He's rather inconspicuous at first."

"That's dangerous. It's probably a bomb. They always choose the inconspicuous ones to place the bombs."

"He said it was a roomful of rainbows."

"Isn't that just what you'd see if a bomb went off?"

"Well, I can't just throw it out of the window! It may be something very valuable."

We were passing through a thick forest. The whole situation was getting unreal. It had the feeling of a modern Grimm's fairy tale—at any moment we would come to the ogre's castle.

Sure enough, there it was—a second-rate Hilton-type hotel. Steel and plate glass outside, Hänsel and Gretel's cottage within, all carved wood and pewter beer tankards. A girl with golden braids and a peasant dress showed us to our rooms. I put the mysterious parcel on my dressing table, washed, and went down for the free dinner.

"Come and sit with me!"

It was the girl with two fiancés. She would probably steal the young man from me if he reappeared, but I was tired and not really interested anyway. The contents of the parcel had become more interesting than he was, and that was already in my possession.

To our surprise, the Milanese tycoon came in with the future nun. She had changed into a pale blue dress and had removed her rosary. They sat at a table in the corner by themselves and seemed very interested in each other.

"Strange bedfellows," commented the young woman.

"Perhaps he's doing a deal with the Vatican in black-market nuns!" I said.

The antique dealers came in and joined us, but there was no sign either of my young man or the hysterical lady.

We had a very expensive meal and a comfortable, air-conditioned night to go with it. I toyed with the idea of opening the mysterious parcel, but only got as far as listening to see if it ticked. It didn't, but I put it into the bathroom before falling asleep, as a precaution, and left my bedroom door unlocked, as an invitation. If the young man came to claim either of us, he could get in.

I was awakened by a telephone call at 7 A.M., requesting all passengers to be ready by 8 A.M. in case Rome airport opened and we could leave on a 9 A.M. flight.

We assembled breakfastless in the hall. There

was my young man with his Gucci bag on his shoulder.

"Where's my parcel?" he asked in consternation.

"Oh, my God, I've forgotten it. It was in my bathroom," I replied. "I'll go and get it."

"I'd like to come with you. May I?"

"Why not? I expected you last night."

"I didn't know your name. How could I ask which room you were in?"

"I see." I introduced myself. "I'm Anne Cumming of room 427."

"I'm Evaristo Nicolao."

He kissed me in the elevator, making up for lost time.

"I hope you like sex before breakfast," he said.

We got to the room and found a fat German fräulein making up the bed for the next client. The parcel was still in the bathroom, but the girl glared at us when we walked into the bedroom. She crossed her arms and stood her ground, even when Evaristo produced the sign saying "Do not disturb."

"I think we'll have to give up the idea," I said.

Downstairs in the hall everyone had gone, but we hadn't missed the plane. They were all having breakfast in the Beer Cellar.

All planes for Rome were still grounded, and we were told to stand by until midday, so after a hearty breakfast, we gathered in the hall again. We were forbidden to leave the hotel, but we no longer had a bedroom to go to. I noticed a sign on the reception desk that said "Swimming Pool and Sauna on the top floor."

"Let's go for a swim," I suggested.

The young man came, carrying his parcel, and the doubly engaged girl with her two rings, and the antique dealers with their silver. Our valuables were left in the dressing rooms, and we rented bathing suits. The young man was given a very small bikini, which revealed the fact that at least one part of him was not at all inconspicuous. The antique dealers noticed it first, and their comment drew my attention to it.

"Someone's got a jumbo jet!" they said to each other.

After that, it was a race to see whether they were going to get him into the men's Sauna, or I was going to smuggle him into the women's. Neither of us won, for we were summoned to the hall again for a special announcement.

"You have three choices," said our guide with the military moustache, clicking his heels and reading from a Telex sheet. "You can go back to London, remain here at your own expense, or go on to Paris, where a Syrian plane will be leaving for Rome, whether the strike is lifted or not. As theirs is only a small plane, they may be given emergency landing rights, as their fuel will not hold out until Damascus."

Pandemonium broke out. No one could decide what they wanted.

My young man and I tried to be helpful by arranging people into three groups: we had "Back to London," led by the Milanese tycoon and the future nun—who no longer seemed in a hurry to get to Rome; "Stay here," led by the antique dealers, who did not want to drag their silver back through any more customs; and "On to Paris," consisting only of Evaristo and me. The doubly engaged girl had decided she would seize the opportunity to have another look at her English fiancé, and was going back to London. The "Stay heres" would be offered a Lufthansa flight to Rome when they began again. Evaristo and I were to fly Air France to Paris and hope for the best.

"Where's my parcel?" he asked me once more. This time it was he who had forgotten it in the dressing room of the swimming pool. We went back to get it together. On the way up in the elevator, he kissed me once again.

"I hope you like sex before lunch," he said.

"Especially in a swimming cabin," I replied.

But a gauleiter in swimming trunks barred the way to the dressing rooms. He got the parcel for us.

"What's inside?" he asked.

"Arc in Himmel," I invented, with a sweeping gesture. I couldn't remember the German for rainbow.

He looked at me in amazement and handed over the parcel so quickly that Evaristo nearly dropped it. We found ourselves back in the elevator.

"We'll try again in Paris," I said. "Are you in a hurry to get to Rome?"

"Certainly not! I'm going back to Italy to do my military service."

"Then you can only be twenty years old!"

"Nineteen, but I haven't wasted a minute."

His self-assurance was infectious. I didn't want to embark on any more young lovers, but this one was too stimulating to miss. Part of the fascination was his apparent innocuousness and mediocrity.

Back in the hall, we were told to go to the airport and check in with Air France. Our guide with his military moustache escorted us to a free taxi and gave us a salute halfway between a wave and a Heil Hitler.

"Young soldiers never die," said Evaristo.

"Don't laugh at him. You'll be in uniform yourself on Monday."

"Being a soldier is not an Italian talent. We make excellent waiters, barbers and ladies' hairdressers, and passable lovers. I shall be as bad a soldier as all the others, but I am determined to enjoy myself. I intend to get into the parachute corps and jump straight into bed with the Colonel's wife."

He kissed me all the way to the airport. Our plane was delayed, and we were given a free lunch. We then went looking for a secluded spot, but as soon as we had found one, our plane was announced. We were soon sitting side by side in a sleek Caravelle. Evaristo had his famous parcel on his knee. I touched it experimentally.

"If I put it under the seat, will you go on touching me?"

I smiled. "Wait for Paris. When you unpack *your* parcel, I'll unpack mine."

We got to the new circular Charles de Gaulle airport, all glass and open-plan. Moving conveyor belts took you from one place to another. We pressed together for a moment somewhere between Arrivals and Departures on the travelator, just long enough for me to confirm how well hung he was, although you could hardly say it was still hanging. It was pressing its urgent way from my thigh to my navel. Before I could do anything about it, we were decanted into a transit lounge. Syrian Airways was determined to take us on to Rome and Damascus. No night of love in Paris.

"Don't worry. We shall have a thousand and one nights in Damascus if Rome doesn't let us land," I promised.

As if to underline my statement, an Arab gentleman in the departure lounge took out a small prayer rug from his flight bag, calmly unrolled it, knelt down facing Mecca, and said his evening prayers.

"Well, at least we know it's sundown," Evaristo said.

"When are you supposed to report to your barracks?"

"Tomorrow morning at eight."

"So it's tonight or never?"

"I presume I shall sometimes get leave."

"If the Colonel's wife lets you."

"I always get everything I want. Sometimes two of everything. I mean to have you *and* the Colonel's wife."

"What about a few younger girls as well?"

"I've no time for young girls. Life's too short. You have to jump right in where everybody knows what they're doing."

"I can see that of all the young men in my life, you're the most likely to succeed."

"But I'm not in your life yet."

"You will be."

But I really didn't believe it. Young men don't

fall out of the sky into your arms. The whole thing was surely just an aging woman's sexual fantasy.

Our rickety old army surplus plane took off and came down safely. We made an emergency landing in Rome, where we had to dive into the belly of the plane, drag out our own luggage, and carry it for miles across the Tarmac. Evaristo took our cases, and I took the package of rainbows. The airport was deserted—no customs, no police, no anything. Fortunately taxis were not on strike.

"I'll drop you off and then go on and say hello to my family," Evaristo said. "I'll pick up my kit ready to leave for the recruiting station, and then I'll come over and stay the night at your apartment."

I still didn't believe any of this was going to happen. When I got out in front of my apartment building, he kindly helped me unload, but I noticed he took the parcel with him.

"You don't have an entry phone," he observed before getting back into the taxi. "How will I get in later?"

"Any key opens my front door."

He caught the double meaning and smiled.

"I'll be back in half an hour. I've got a big key waiting."

"And the lock's well oiled," I answered.

We kissed, and I thought it was really good-bye. All the rest had surely been just a flirtatious verbal game. His taxi disappeared into the night.

I had only been gone two weeks, but my apartment looked unlived in—too tidy. I threw my

things down on the couch and at once it looked
better. I opened the accumulated letters and
turned on the hot water. It was after midnight
when I got out of my bath and into my bed. I still
didn't really think Evaristo would show up—the
whole thing was too unlikely. He was probably being tucked up into his bed right now by a doting
mother, and, at best, he might give me a passing
thought as he masturbated one night in the barracks.

I was fast asleep when my bell rang. Through
the spy hole in my front door, his mini-toughness
was reduced to midget proportions; but even at that
size, there was something compelling about him. I
opened the door. He was holding the famous parcel and a military kit bag.

"I underestimated you."

"People often do."

He put the parcel carefully on the hall table,
dropped the kit bag on the floor, and followed me
into the bedroom. When he took off his clothes, I
was stunned by what I saw. There was nothing
nondescript about *that*—the biggest penis I had
ever seen was rampant and ready. Its performance
lived up to its looks.

I got up at six and brought him breakfast in bed.

"You won't get this again for a year. Enjoy it."

He put the tray on the floor and pulled me down
on top of him.

"First things first."

There it was again—incredible in size, inex-
haustible in performance. We ate breakfast, the

tray between us, still joined like Siamese twins
lower down. Then he looked at the time.

"Duty calls."

He leaped out of bed—sturdy, energetic, determined. He took a shower, dressed and brought the
parcel from the hall.

"Open it."

I did as I was told. It was a glass prism made of
pastel colors. He stood on a chair and hung it from
the center light over the bed, then opened the shutters. The morning sun glinted off its many facets
and filled the room with glancing, shifting rainbows. It was as if all the fantasies in the world had
come true.

He bent down and kissed me, picked up his kit
bag, and was gone.

Postcard from Avezzano Barracks.

They've sent me a hundred miles away. Perhaps
compulsory military service was designed to prevent the corruption of minors by middle-aged
nymphomaniacs.

                                                    Evaristo

The little bastard! Just who seduced whom?

Postcard from Rome to Avezzano Barracks.

Hurry up and get leave so I can slap your face!
                                                    Anne

Postcard from Avezzano Barracks.

You can slap my face on Saturday, May 16. I

have other intentions, but we'll see who can get which in first!

E.

I began to wonder whether they censored soldiers' mail in peacetime.

Letter from Avezzano Barracks. May 19.

Adored one, I'm sorry I got so drunk on Sunday afternoon. Sunbathing on your top terrace with a bottle of whisky and you naked beside me was too much for me. I'll have to learn to hold my liquor better before I get to be a general.

E.

Postcard from Rome to Avezzano Barracks. May 25.

Please don't become a general. Get a dishonorable discharge immediately and hurry home. Perhaps you could claim to be a queer.

A.

Letter from Avezzano Barracks.

I followed your suggestion. Told the doctor at weekly medical inspection that I was a homosexual, and military life was too much of a temptation for me. He took a long look at me and picked up a copy of *Playboy* from his desk. He opened it at the centerfold pinup and handed it to me without a word. I got an erection immediately, which in my case is difficult to hide. "Fuck off," the doctor said. "Stop wasting my time."

Any other suggestions?

E.

Postcard from Rome to Avezzano Barracks.

Only one suggestion left. Tell the Colonel your grandmother's dying. She is. Dying to be with you.

Letter from Avezzano Barracks.

Grandmother's life and my sanity may be saved. I have become a male nurse instead of a parachutist. It is less romantic, but more convenient to have my feet on the ground. If I am ever found missing at night in the barracks, they will think I am on night duty at the military hospital. There's a midnight train to Rome and one back at 5:00 A.M. You will see me at least once a week. The hospital backs onto the railway station.

E.

The whole summer passed agreeably in this fashion. A little figure in a white coat would be revealed on my landing as I looked through the spy hole. I didn't always know when he was coming, and once there was somebody else in my bed. Evaristo took it in his stride. He walked into the bedroom, shook hands, and got into bed on my other side.

"You don't mind, do you?" he said to my friend. "All's fair in love and war."

The other gentleman was rather amused.

"Go ahead."

"No, after you."

"Please . . . you got here first."

I took matters into my own hands, or rather, one matter into my mouth and the other into my vagi-

na. Then we changed around. Eventually Evaristo
got up and put on his white coat again. He shook
the other gentleman's hand once again, thanked us
for our hospitality, and disappeared into the dawn.

"Did that really happen, or was I dreaming?"
the remaining gentleman asked.

"Of course you were dreaming, darling. Could
any little boy have such a large prick?"

"Never," he said, and went to sleep.

Letter from Avezzano Barracks. September 1969.

Disaster! I'm being transferred to Northern Italy on maneuvers. I shall be eight hours away from
you instead of two. No more illegal journeys on
midnight trains to be back in time to faint on pa-
rade the next day. What can absence teach me?

E.

Postcard from Rome.

Abstinence. It makes the heart grow fonder.

A.

My heart had grown very fond and I missed
him, but like the rainbows, I knew he would always reappear. Other men would come and go, but
when most needed, he and his arc of bright colors
would illuminate my life again. A long leave, a
short weekend, a carnival evening, a hot summer
night, a winter's day, and a lot of letters, all of
them lighthearted, with never a complaint or a

word of recrimination or a false promise. Nothing ever marred our unusual relationship.

One of Evaristo's charming communications was a *collage*. The letter with it read:

Dearest Anne, I have lots of time on my hands here and nothing to read but cheap magazines. I've put two and two together and made you a little book entitled "Why I Love Her." Here it is with my deep affection and endless longing.

Evaristo

Enclosed was a little booklet made out of cutouts from glossy magazines. The first page simply said: I LOVE HER BECAUSE ... Then followed a series of witty pictorial comments relevant to us alone. Each page was a different *collage*, and the whole made a touching love letter.

I looked at it for a long time, then I put it with the rest of the letters I was keeping in my shoe-box file. The box was getting rather full. I would have to get some more boxes and sort the letters out a bit. I found two more shoe boxes and sat down to work out a filing system. How can you classify the remnants of love?

Finally I labeled the boxes: LETTERS FROM HUSBANDS, LETTERS FROM LOVERS, and LETTERS FROM MY BOYS. The third box was to contain letters only from those under twenty-one. I put Evaristo's booklet beside Joseph's manifesto. I reread Jean-Louis's first postcard and Gregory's poem. There was something very touching about their youthful fervor. Evaristo's little booklet was truly a labor of love.

Diary entry. Rome. Early October 1969.

The time, trouble and imagination that has gone into Evaristo's declaration has left me wordless. How can I reply to such unpretentious, casual, throw-away humor that is nevertheless a touching testimonial to my basic virtues? It's a real expression of love. Words alone will not suffice as an answer; too many letters have been written. I must *do* something.

I did something. I traveled twelve hours by three different trains to a village in the Dolomites where the army was practicing mountain warfare. A visit was the only answer to such an adorable tribute.

I asked on the telephone from the station buffet for the Colonel's office. The Colonel's personal aide-de-camp answered. "Who did you say you are, signora?" He sounded on the defensive, but probably my foreign accent had put him slightly off guard. I evidently didn't sound like an Italian mother checking on the welfare of her little boy.

"I'm an English journalist doing a series of articles on the welfare of the armed forces. I've come to visit your regiment."

There was a silence, then he said, "I'd better put you through to the Colonel. One minute, signora."

The Colonel sounded as peaceful as a peacetime Colonel should. He had a roof over his head and regular meals provided by the government, and, unless he was singularly inefficient, advancement was assured. Relatively happy and slightly bored, he was delighted to have his monotonous routine interrupted by an unexpected visitor, and sent his car to the station for me.

"I'm from the *Sunday Times*," I lied.

"Enchanted, signora. I suppose you were sent from Rome?"

"Yes, of course. The Ministry of Defense has been most kind. We are doing a series of articles from the woman's angle on what happens to the boys of various countries when they join the army." I smiled at him. "It's always the mothers who worry, of course."

"They worry me too, I can tell you! I get hundreds of letters a month asking me if their little dears have changed their underpants and eaten their dinners."

"Now I don't wish to take up *your* valuable time. If it's possible, I would like one young soldier from each department to show me around his own section. A cook from the kitchen, a young man from the laundry, a medical assistant in the infirmary, and so forth. You get the idea." I uncrossed my legs and leaned forward seductively. "And then if I could come back and steal another moment of your time . . . ?"

We smiled at each other understandingly. Well, why not? If Evaristo could have the Colonel's wife, then I could have the Colonel.

His personal assistant guided me across the barracks square. I was passed from one young lieutenant to another. I was guided and guarded and whistled at and flirted with all morning. By the end of it, I was quite willing to join the army myself. I purposely left the infirmary till lunch time.

It was too much to hope that Evaristo would be detailed to guide me around the hospital, but who-

ever it was would be sure to know him. The young
doctor who was chosen to take me around knew
him very well.

"So you know Evaristo Nicolao from Rome?
He's a character. He keeps us all in stitches. He's
like a court jester. You'd like to see him, of
course?"

"If it isn't undermining military discipline. It
must be about lunch time . . . perhaps he has a little time off?"

"I'll see to it that he has. Would you mind waiting in my office?"

While I was waiting alone in the office, the
phone rang. I answered. It was the Colonel, checking on how I was getting along. Would I have
lunch with him in half an hour?

"I'd be delighted. I just want to inspect the dormitories first. Is that all right?"

"Yes, certainly. Have you got someone to take
you? Are you being properly looked after?"

"Beautifully. I've even met the son of an old
friend in Rome. I had no idea the child was here!"

"Oh, good. I'll see that the sentries let you into
one of the dormitory blocks, then come on over to
my office."

Evaristo appeared without his white coat. He
had been promoted to hospital administration, and
wore an ordinary uniform. He may have looked
just like an ordinary soldier, but I knew better.

"I was just passing by, and dropped in to say
thank you," I said casually. "Will you take me to
see your dormitory?"

"But we're not allowed in till the end of the

day—and certainly not with a woman. How the fucking hell did you get in here at all?" He was suitably amazed, and a little nervous.

"I'm on a state visit to inspect the troops."

"You're mad. I'll be court-martialed! I'll be put into solitary confinement for life! I'll be shot down at dawn!"

While he was saying all this, he was kissing me. When he let me up for air, I said, "It's all right. I'm a visiting journalist. If anyone's shot, it will be the poor Colonel, who never stopped to check my credentials. He's even told the sentries to let us into the dormitory block."

So it was then that I discovered that a hard army bed and a rough blanket and a sweaty uniform are more aphrodisiac to me than silk sheets. While the siren sounded for lunch, and army boots tramped across the square outside, and male voices were raised, and military orders were shouted, I held Evaristo's tough little body in my arms in the hush of an empty dormitory.

"This is all of my masturbation fantasies come true," he gasped. "You've no idea how often I've dreamed of you in this bed. I wish I dared to undress you now as I've done a hundred times in my mind."

"We'd better not risk it. Anyway, it turns me on to see your secret weapon sticking out of your uniform like that."

It raised its swollen head with pride and nuzzled its way between my legs. It seemed even bigger than usual.

"Instant home leave!" Evaristo exclaimed with a sigh.

"Mmmmm . . . mmm . . . Right on target!"

We had no time to waste, and we didn't waste it. I wasn't even late for lunch with the Colonel. I left Evaristo straightening the bed.

"I'll see that you get a long leave and rail pass," I said from the doorway. "You deserve it. Your little book was the most beautiful letter I've ever received."

The Colonel dismissed his driver, after taking me way out of town to an inn on the edge of a pine forest. It was autumn, and we took a long walk in the woods before lunch. We took another walk in the woods *after* lunch. My panties were full of pine needles by the time his driver came back for us.

"By the way," I said as the Colonel marched me along the platform to my homeward train. "My friend is very ill—the one with the son who works in your infirmary. A little compassionate leave wouldn't do any harm."

"I'll see what I can do," he promised. He saluted and stood to attention as the train moved out.

I could hardly stay awake enough to change trains twice along the way.

The Colonel had sent for Evaristo a few days after my visit.

"Nicolao, we had a very interesting visitor the other day. Said she knew your mother."

Evaristo's heart sank. His mother had been dead for years, and this information was presumably on file, but he would let the Colonel do all the talking before venturing any kind of statement.

"Yes, sir."

"The lady said she was writing articles about the armed forces."

"Yes, sir."

"Headquarters in Rome seems to have lost track of her; don't seem to have heard of her, even."

"No, sir?"

"They're very badly organized in Rome. Lose everything. Can't count on them at all. What this country needs is Mussolini back again."

"Yes, sir."

"I see you're a sensible young man."

Evaristo swallowed hard. He could not have been more left wing.

"Yes, sir."

"Now, I'd like to find that woman again. Want to read what she's written about us. Very attractive woman, too."

"Yes, sir."

"Do you know her address?"

"I'll ask my family, sir."

"By the way, I hear your mother's ill."

This was getting too specific. Evaristo knew nothing of what had happened between the Colonel and me. He hadn't seen or heard from me since I had left him in the dormitories, so he had no idea of my subsequent adventures, or where the Colonel had got this misinformation.

"She *was* ill, sir, very ill," he said tentatively.

"Perhaps you'd like some compassionate leave? And while you're in Rome, you can find that charming English lady and bring back a copy of her article."

"Yes, sir. Of course, sir."

So Evaristo got a week's leave at the end of the

month. When he got back, he told the Colonel that the English lady had gone back to England, and that his mother had died. The Colonel expressed his double regrets. No doubt he is still waiting to receive a copy of my article.

Maneuvers were over, and Evaristo was transferred once again, this time to Trieste, on the Yugoslavian border.

His next long leave was a week in the middle of December. He arrived on my birthday. So did Rudi.

I would not have invited Rudi, who was on his way to design an opera in Milan, if I had known Evaristo was coming. However, it was my fifty-third birthday, it was near Christmas, and I had not see Rudi for a long time.

"You dare lay a finger on Evaristo, and I'll never have you to stay again," I told him. "Separate lives, separate rooms, separate lovers, remember?"

"But Anne, I've never taken anyone you really wanted," he protested with saccharine sweetness. A Viennese Sacher Torte wouldn't have melted in his mouth. "I only borrowed Joseph because you were giving him away."

Rudi's Austrian accent only appeared when he was being consciously charming.

"I was *not* giving him away. I was trying to get him out of my system, which was an entirely different thing—a sort of cooling-off process."

"Look, in one night I got him out of your system for you. You even *thanked* me."

"I still do in a way." I went over and kissed him. "But hands off Evaristo!"

Rudi kept his hands off all right, but not his eyes. He became a sort of voyeur. He observed our every move. I felt as if I were under sexual surveillance, as if a moralistic branch of the CIA were checking up on me. But I was determined not to let it cramp my style. It didn't.

Evaristo arrived one afternoon. He burst in wearing a crumpled uniform with an incongruous fur glove on one hand. This was my birthday present. The palm was made of crocheted gold thread and the back was of smooth black mink. It was a massage glove.

"The only thing you can give a woman who has everything is a new experience!" he announced. "Go into the bedroom, Anne, and take off your clothes. We'll try it out at once."

"This is Rudi . . ." I tried to interpose.

"How do you do? You can borrow the glove later. Now, please excuse us for a minute."

He swept me into the bedroom, leaving Rudi speechless. I was amused and rather pleased to have Rudi ignored. If I had planned it, I could not have had a sweeter revenge. For the first time since Rudi had left me, he was completely shut out of my life. He was an innocent bystander forced to witness a whirlpool romance, without being sucked into it at all. Evaristo was polite and considerate to Rudi, treating him like the older man he was, but continually putting him into the past tense. It was as if he were saying, "You had her once, and you gave her up. Now it's my turn. You have no further rights." I could never have said it so forcibly myself.

Rudi was jealous. He paced up and down at

night. He went out on the cold terrace under the wintry stars and walked up and down in front of our bedroom window. We paid no attention. We even played to our public. We drifted around the house half-dressed. We were both on holiday. It was our first sustained honeymoon. Rudi's presence was not going to stop us from enjoying it.

Evaristo disappeared as swiftly as he had come, leaving the fur glove and Rudi behind. The army was not giving him Christmas leave. Rudi, on the other hand, wanted to stay for a family Christmas with us. Why not? His opera was not opening until January, his father was going to a sister in Vienna, and I was getting used to having him in the spare room on an impersonal basis. At least Evaristo had achieved that. Neither of my ex-husbands were with us for Christmas, but Fiona and family flew out to stay with her sister. It was Vanessa's turn to make Christmas, and she did it beautifully in her old stone farmhouse with its huge open fireplaces. It was a mixture of Italian and English ceremonies. After Christmas, they all came into Rome to buy toys at the stalls in Piazza Navona. I took my grandchildren from church to chruch to see the different Nativity displays, each parish vying with the next to have a more elaborate crèche—some of them were even clockwork. Christmas cards from all over the world were crowded on my mantelpiece and wrapping paper littered the floor.

Soon the pine needles began to fall to the floor under my tree, and, after Twelfth Night, I swept everything and everybody out of the house. Rudi left for Milan, Fiona and her family went back to England, and Vanessa retreated to the country.

Family life was swept away for a few months, and
my working life returned. I was offered a new film
in Yugoslavia.

Postcard to Private Nicolao in Trieste Barracks. January 16, 1970.

I will soon be just across the border from you.
Perhaps we can declare war and meet in no man's
land.

                                                    Anne

No man's land was farther than I thought, and it
was peopled exclusively with men. I had chosen
the film to be near Evaristo, but found myself behind the iron curtain making a war picture on the
wrong border. We were nearly in Romania. I was
farther away from Evaristo than I had been in
Rome.

Our filming had taken us to a one-horse provincial town in central Yugoslavia where even the
horse had already been consumed in the restaurant
of our third-rate hotel. There were not enough single rooms to go around, so most of the crew were
sharing and grumbling. I was lucky. I had a room
with three beds in it, but at least I had it to myself,
because it also had to serve as my office. The
weather was icy, and the wind blew uninterrupt-
edly straight from Siberia across the vast plains.

"Russia is nearer than you think," said the cameraman, rubbing his frozen fingers. "Thank God
for my automatic Ariflex. Imagine if I was D. W.
Griffith winding the camera with my bare hands."

"I'll knit you some mittens," I promised.

"Thanks. And while you're at it, make a cock-

shaped one, or that'll fall off too. It's even too cold
for fucking."

But it wasn't. It never is. Two months away
from home and wives, and the lusty Italian crew
was not going to starve, either sexually or otherwise. The hotel restaurant was persuaded to serve
spaghetti at every meal, and the hotel manager
sent to Belgrade for reinforcements to his female
staff. A resident prostitute or two were part of the
hotel personnel, and, as the hotels in Yugoslavia
are State-owned, the girls were civil servants with
all the usual Social Security benefits. I got quite a
few *unusual* fringe benefits from the Communist
State myself. Being a war film, the entire Yugoslavian army had been placed at our disposal, and I
personally disposed of quite a few of the younger
officers. The State provided, I decided, and some
important reconnaissance work took place in my
bedroom.

Postcard to Trieste Barracks. January 20, 1970.
I am doing my military service too. It's very
good for my Serbo-Croatian.

Anne

Postcard back to Novi Sad.
Don't wear your Serbo-Croatian out. Remember, I'm being demobilized this summer.

Evaristo

Postcard to Trieste Barracks.
What rests, rusts. You wouldn't want that,
would you?

Anne

I didn't rust, but I froze. It was a long, hard winter and a long, difficult film. Nearly every night I allowed officers of various ranks to hang their uniforms at the foot of my bed in an effort to keep warm. The hotel was out of bounds to other ranks—Communism was not for privates.

I managed to get into Belgrade occasionally for the weekend. Once I was sandwiched into the elevator of the Metropole Hotel with a good-looking Slav, who later followed me to Novi Sad.

"Camp followers," the cameraman commented. "They come in all sizes and sexes nowadays."

"He's my blow for women's lib," I replied. "Now that we girls go off to the wars too, we're entitled to full military benefits."

I was afraid my camp follower was going to follow me all the way back to Rome. A great many Yugoslavs are just waiting for susceptible lady tourists to take them back to democracy. This one was also inclined to ask for a loan even before orgasm had worn off. I longed for Evaristo, who was in it only for fun.

Postcard to Trieste Barracks. March 8.

My war is over. We're retreating to Rome next week for the studio work. Can you get leave and join me there? I'm tired of Slavic melancholy, and need your sense of humor.

                                                   Anne

Postcard received in Rome.

My sense of humor needs you too. I can hardly

keep it down. But leave is hard to come by, now that my demobilization is in sight.

Evaristo

However, we managed a one-night stand in Bologna. He traveled halfway down Italy and I traveled halfway up, having chosen Bologna for this happy reunion simply because it was Italy's most famous railroad junction for express trains from all directions. It is also famous for its cuisine. We met at the railway station, and walked to the nearest hotel.

"There isn't time for both eating and fucking," Evaristo said, "unless we combine them."

We got into bed, started our love-making, and ordered a vast meal. When it arrived, we sat up naked, eating *tortellini alla crema* in bed.

"I don't know which I'd rather eat," I said with my mouth full of tortellini drowned in cream and parmesan cheese, "you or these delicious little lifebelts."

Later I tried Evaristo's local specialty. I had forgotten how big it was. It hardly fitted into my mouth.

"Mmmmm . . . heavy cream!" I said when it was all over. "I could write a thesis on the quality and taste of male sperm. Yours is very thick and tastes bitter."

"That doesn't seem to put you off, does it?"

"Nothing puts me off my food. There's food for love and food for nourishment, and I need both. A really sensual woman is neither squeamish nor fastidious."

"When I'm in love, I'm not hungry," Evaristo

stated, reaching out for some more of the dessert—
that delectable concoction known to the Italians as
"English soup" and to the English as trifle.

"Then you're not in love with me. Your appetite's enormous."

"After a year in the army, I'm hungry for everything—food, sex, friendship, love, money. You
combine them all; no one else does. I want *you*.
Isn't that love?"

"It sounds like greed!"

"I'm happy with you. Isn't *that* love?"

"If happiness were love and love were happiness! Love is also suffering and sacrifice and disil-
lusion."

"I don't want to find that out yet. I'm only interested in the positive things in life."

The conversation stopped there, because he had
finished his trifle and was trifling with my left
nipple instead, which drove all thoughts out of my
mind. Next morning we separated at the station—
he to get back to barracks by Sunday curfew, I to
get back to home and work. I had six hours on the
train to think about happiness and love again.
Happiness, I thought, can be tiring. Was it time I
settled for simple, undemanding contentment?

Letter to Rudi.

Carissimo, I'm beginning to feel my age. When
you left me, I decided that men would be *divertissements*, not involvements and undertakings. Now,
even the *divertissements* are tiring me out. Evaristo
has been the most diverting of them all, but he

needs more than I can give. I'm emotionally exhausted. I've given it all. What shall I do now?

Anne

Telegram from Rudi.
  Learn to take. Rudi

I planned what was to be the first of a series of wonderful weekends together that spring and summer. Whenever Evaristo got weekend leave, we met in a different place. I planned my work in such a way that I could leave on a Friday night and fall into his arms on a Saturday morning. He would have to travel overnight from Trieste on his military pass, so wherever we ended up, the first thing we did was to have breakfast in bed. We would then put the tray on the floor and look deep into each other's eyes.

"Let's try a different position every time we meet," Evaristo said, "at least for the first fuck. Then we can go on to our favorites."

I had just given him, as a present, a pornographic zodiac chart I had found, with twelve couples in twelve different positions of love instead of the usual zodiac symbols.

"I don't know how you have the energy to even *think* of such an ambitious program," I said. "You've only just got here after a ghastly journey."

We were lying in a fabulous antique French bergère bed, all gilt, carved wood and intricate caning, under a real Vigée-Lebrun portrait in delicate pastels. In the bathroom where Evaristo had just taken a shower was a Picasso.

"A minor one. Only suitable for a bathroom," our host had told us.

We were staying with my cousin in his eighteenth-century palace in Tuscany. My cousin is the last of the world's great gentlemen. He has also been described as "the nicest man in the world." The description fits him admirably. His money was inherited, and it has been put to the use for which it was intended—to provide gracious living. The house has ninety-nine rooms if you include the Piranesi-like cellars and storerooms, a park with a Swiss chalet like Marie Antoinette's "hameau," a Roman amphitheater for private theatricals, some Etruscan tombs, a Turkish folly, and a heated swimming pool.

Evaristo had traveled overnight to the nearest station, then hitchhiked at dawn to the great wrought-iron gates, where a night guardian had let him in. The guardian had opened a little side door of the enormous house and had given Evaristo a map I had drawn the night before, so that he could find his way to my bedroom.

"What shall it be this time?" Evaristo said, turning our erotic chart upside down to understand one of the complicated positions.

"Something French, I suppose, to please the lady over the bed," I suggested.

We ended up in the sixty-nine position, not my favorite, but it seemed right for the occasion. Evaristo was always right for every occasion. Before I put his enormous member into my mouth, I said, "Little men make big lovers." To which he replied in French, "An old hen makes good soup."

The sun was high in the Tuscan sky when we

got up. As we walked out into the garden toward
the swimming pool, a gardener appeared from an
English rose garden and preceded us into the
Turkish folly, from which he extracted cushions
for the chaises longues and peacock feather fans
which he laid out on bamboo tables beside the
pool. Decorated lacquer umbrellas from Thailand
were raised to provide shade.

"It's too much," said Evaristo. "It's like a fairy
tale. I need a stiff drink to pull me together."

"Go into the Turkish folly, then—you'll find a
bar there."

I heard him gasp as he entered it. The folly is
round, and in the center is a table containing a var-
ied liquor supply and all varieties of suntan creams
and lotions. Around the sides are cushioned bench-
es with sarongs and exotic hats laid out for the
guests' enjoyment and adornment.

Evaristo chose for himself a bright red sarong
over a tiny black French bikini, from a range of
bathing suits for guests who had come unprepared.

"Those trunks barely cover your sense of humor," I commented.

At that moment my cousin appeared and over-
heard me. "How lucky you are, my dear, to have a
young man with such a large sense of humor!"

We kissed good morning, and a parlormaid
emerged from the house, beyond the lotus pool,
with a plate of quails' eggs to nibble with the
drinks.

"There's only one thing missing, darling," I
teased my adorable cousin. "I need a Nubian slave
to fan me with the peacock feather fan."

As if on cue, a beautiful Indian boy dressed in

white came down the garden path. My cousin's latest import from the Far East bowed and kissed my hand and began fanning me with a delicate movement of his fragile wrist. I noted that he wore a small, square Cartier watch, with a sapphire set in the winder. Evaristo floated in the turquoise pool, his sturdy little body in direct contrast to all this refinement and luxury.

"What would you like for lunch?" my cousin asked.

I can't remember what we had for lunch—probably something with a cream and truffle sauce. Or possibly just a marvelous joint of English roast beef from a Tuscan cow, with fresh culled peas. My cousin also has the kind of simplicity born of great good taste, and, in spite of his setting, he is a modest man.

If I can't remember the meals, at least I remember the positions. We tried all twelve of them during that short weekend.

"Aren't you going to leave *one* of them for next time?" I begged at one point. We were in the woods near the Roman amphitheater on a long, hot Sunday afternoon.

"I may not get home from the wars again, and I want to try the position for November," Evaristo insisted, making me kneel down on the fallen ilex leaves and pull down my white lace panties. "Your bottom's all pink from the sun," he added, and kissed me on both cheeks.

We had a last moonlight walk before the chauffeur took Evaristo to the night train. I was staying till Monday morning. We strolled to the very end of the garden, where an ornamental pool grew

three different kinds of water lilies. I particularly
remember the way the yellow ones glowed in the
moonlight as we said good-bye. We lay on the edge
of the pool, on a wide travertine marble border. As
we turned to make love for the last time, I remember a blue water lily from Lake Bunyoro in Ugan-
da exploding in my face at the moment of orgasm.
It was a fitting end to position number twelve.

Dearest Coz (I wrote later),
   It's going to be very difficult to match your life-
style anywhere else. I've promised Evaristo an exotic weekend for every leave. What can I do next
when you're the ultimate? I should have kept you
to the last! Thank you for having given us such a
marvelous beginning. Yours gratefully,

                                                        Anne

It was indeed a standard difficult to keep up.
However, Evaristo's youthful exuberance kept up,
so wherever we were, we had a marvelous time.
But I had begun to worry about how things would
be when he was discharged and back in Rome. I
didn't think our relationship was lit by the steady
flame of love. It was more like a series of evening
fireworks. How would I feel about him when he
was back to stay? Had I the staying power myself
anymore? Could I bear a day-to-day relationship
with him?

   The first thing Evaristo did when he was demobilized and got back to Rome was to come
around and remove Rudi's photo from my dressing
table. It had been there, among the silver brushes

and bottles, since the day Rudi had bought me this delicate little *table de toilette* in the Via dei Coronari. His half smile in its silver frame had greeted me every day for nearly twenty years, and I missed it. Evaristo was the first lover who had objected to it. Even my ex-husbands, when they came to stay, had accepted it as part of the interior decoration of my life.

"I'm not sure I like this symbolic gesture," I said to Evaristo as I put the photo into a drawer. "Isn't it rather presumptuous of you to think of eliminating the other men in my life?"

"I *am* presumptuous. I'm living up to my reputation. Little men make big lovers. There's no room for anyone else while I'm around."

He was around a great deal. It made me nervous. In a series of brief encounters, he had been the perfect protagonist; on a long-term engagement, he was exhausting and possessive, and he made me feel my age.

"I shall have to give up very young lovers," I said to my friend Franca, one of the few really liberated Italian women I knew. "Would you like Evaristo?"

"You'll miss him. You'll never get another like him—he's unique."

"I know, but I haven't got the physical stamina to keep up with him, or the psychological strength either. I don't want another Joseph."

"You're going to be lonely."

"I'll risk it."

"And Evaristo will never leave you."

"He doesn't have to. He just has to become less intense."

"I'll be interested to see how you manage it."

It wasn't easy. Every time I tried to slip away, Evaristo's charm and bounce won me back. His mind was stimulating, his body was satisfying. Some outside force would be needed to dislodge him from my life.

"*Aou, Anne! Amore! Come stai?* Where the fuck you been?"

There was no mistaking the rough Roman accent. It was my favorite truck driver. He drove in and out of my life from time to time, and fate had sent him back at an appropriate moment. I hadn't seen him for a long time.

"I've been away, and I've been in love, and I've grown old."

"*Ma!* What the fuck do I care? I'm coming over anyway. Are you alone?"

"Yes, I'm alone."

Evaristo was going out with some university friends. He had enrolled in the faculty of architecture, but was treating it as lightly as he had treated the army. I was encouraging him to frequent his college companions in the hope that he would catch some of their fervor to study. It also gave me some evenings to myself. This was one of them.

"*Aou!* I'm coming over right away! I'll leave my truck in the market. It won't matter at this time of night."

It probably *would* matter. Cars left there all night were towed away the next morning. Once Pietro had left his empty truck there, and no one had quite known how to deal with it. We'd gone down in the morning and found the stalls all grouped around it and someone selling oranges out of the back.

"Right. Come on over. You'll do me good," I said, anxious to break Evaristo's spell a little.

I had lain in Pietro's strong arms, and smelled his strong masculine odor, and let him do all those things he did with the prostitutes along the highways. He was like the force of nature, and everything he did seemed right and wholesome, although in another man, it might have seemed vicious. This time he got up at dawn, before they began to set up the market. I heard him rev up his five-ton truck and drive away. No problems. I was at peace.

Evaristo buzzed in at lunch time. It was Saturday, and I wasn't going to work—they had finally brought in the "No Saturday working except on location" rule, so long overdue in the Italian cinema.

"I had a visitor last night," I told Evaristo.

He stiffened, but said nothing, as if he hadn't heard. I hoped he'd make it easier for me to tell him.

"Aren't you going to ask me who it was?"

"We've never asked each other questions. We've always known the answers and kept them to ourselves."

"Perhaps I'm beginning to ask *myself* questions."

"Like what?"

"Like . . . Aren't our ages too incompatible? Do I have the strength to go on giving so much of myself to one man? So many other people want little bits of me—my family, my friends—have I enough left for an affair like ours? I didn't want another permanent lover."

Evaristo had been striding about the room. Now he stood still, but tensely.

"Is there somebody who could make you happier than I do?"

"No, I don't think so. It's not a question of personality, but of timing. Do you know the old saying: 'If you want to be happy for a day, get married; if you want to be happy for a week, fall in love; if you want to be happy for a lifetime, cultivate a garden'? Maybe the time has come when I should give up men and grow roses instead."

He relaxed a little. I realized that his tension had been due to suppressed jealousy. We had never been together long enough for it to show itself before, and during our short spells together, I had always been completely dedicated to him. He had never asked what I did in between.

"Can't I become one of the roses in your garden?"

He came over to me and took me in his arms. I could feel all the usual responses, physical and psychological. Perhaps I was not quite ready to take up gardening. I made a last effort to protect myself.

"There may be other roses . . ."

"Which is your favorite?"

"It's a rose called 'Peace,' with pale pink edges."

"I'll do my best to have pale pink edges."

We went into the bedroom. It was a sunny afternoon, and the crystal prism was filling the room with rainbows.

Vanessa and my son-in-law liked to come in from the country, leave Matthew with me, then drive on and spend a weekend of freedom elsewhere. Matthew, now aged four, enjoyed his visits because he could boss his grandmother around. He showed every sign of becoming a potential "godfather." Sicilian blood will out. So will Sicilian jealousy.

"Granny, whose is this yellow toothbrush? Mine is blue and yours is green; there never used to be a yellow one."

"Granny has a friend called Evaristo who often spends the night when you're not here."

"Does he sleep in your bed?" he asked, a mixture of jealousy and possessiveness in his voice.

I paused for a moment. I don't like telling lies.

"Where else would he sleep? I wouldn't like to put him in yours, even when you're not here."

Matthew didn't answer. He went back to play, and I thought I had successfully got over a difficult hurdle. But when Vanessa took him home to the country and Evaristo came to stay the night, he couldn't find his yellow toothbrush.

"Where can it be?" he asked.

"I can't imagine," I said. "I haven't touched it."

My daughter called the next day. "Matthew had a yellow toothbrush hidden in his paintbox. He said it was an old one you wanted to throw away, but it doesn't look very old to me."

"It isn't, but he can use it for paints or throw it away if he wants to."

We went on to talk of other things, but the yellow toothbrush suddenly took on new importance for me. Perhaps the time had come when my grandson could rightfully object to my having strange toothbrushes in my bathroom.

The weather had suddenly become hot and stifling. My friend Franca came to supper with us on the terrace one evening, wearing a marvelous 1930s dress she had found in her mother's cupboard. She had tremendous style and didn't look much older than Evaristo, although she must have been over forty. She was going through a bad time because her lover had left her and she had to change apartments all at the same time; but she was one of those women who took things in her stride. I could see that Evaristo admired her.

"Would you like to go to bed with her?" I asked Evaristo when she had gone.

"I wouldn't mind. I'd like to have both of you in 1930s underwear—crêpe de chine step-ins or camiknickers or whatever they called them."

"I wasn't suggesting the two of us together. And I'm too old for that 1930s bit. I'd just look as if I'd been wearing them since then."

"It's both of you or nothing. You're not going to get rid of me so easily."

Franca's new apartment, which she moved into the following week, was near Evaristo's home. I called her to wish her well.

"Will you be in this evening? I want to send you a housewarming present."

"How exciting! What is it?"

"An old-fashioned bed warmer."

I meant Evaristo. He mustn't suspect anything, but must find himself in a position where the seduction of my best friend would seem inevitable and irresistible. I prepared the way.

"Darling, you must help me lighten Franca's

life," I said to Evaristo that evening. "On your way home, I want you to take her a housewarming present."

"But I wasn't going home," he protested. "I was staying the night with you."

"Well, you can always come back again. But you owe your family a visit, and the present is so fragile, it must be delivered by someone responsible."

I had bought an opaline glass vase in the shape of a hand, filled it with yellow roses, and wrapped the whole thing in cellophane. In a sealed envelope, I had put a short note:

Put the roses in the sitting room and take Evaristo into the bedroom. His sense of humor is the biggest in town. I'll be glad to share it with you. I need peace at least every other night.

Anne

I told Evaristo that I was worried because Franca was so hard to please that she would be unable to forget her old lover by jumping into bed with somebody else, and I told Franca she was to play hard to get. The whole situation must present a challenge any self-respecting young man would find hard to resist.

"Are you sure you won't regret it?" Franca had asked. "I don't want anything to spoil our friendship."

"On the contrary, you'll be doing me a good turn. We'll never let him know that I know, and it will take the emotional pressure off me and give me a rest physically. He's got plenty of energy for both of us, and enough spirit of adventure to enjoy the situation, provided he thinks he's invented it himself. Never let him find out we've ganged up on him."

Evaristo buzzed off in the bus, and I spent the evening happily gardening. I tried not to think of him in Franca's arms, but I felt more jealous than I had anticipated. He meant a great deal to me, but that was the reason I was getting nervous—he was undermining my principle of the *divertissement*. I must be prepared to go through a short season in hell to prevent long-term suffering. I didn't want to become a pathetic old woman clinging to a lusty lover. I must have the strength to give him his freedom before he wanted it himself.

I applied myself vigorously to my weeding. I told myself that the old saying was right: love was for a season, but gardening was forever. But I wasn't persuading myself. To hell with gardening!

I went inside and washed my hands and got undressed. I felt sure that Evaristo would jump out of Franca's bed and hurry back to mine. He wouldn't be able to resist the temptation to have both of us in one night. I looked forward to Evaristo's ten-inch sense of humor and a nightful of pleasure. I must have been mad to think I was old enough to do without it.

I put on a virginal white nightgown and looked at myself in the mirror. I saw that I did not look like a pure young bride, but like a nineteenth-century grandmother. My face was quite firm and fresh, but my eyes looked tired and over-experienced. My body sagged a little.

I lay awake all night, but Evaristo did not come. Nor did he telephone, although Franca telephoned next morning to thank me for my housewarming gifts.

"The vase is divine, and the bed warmer functions beautifully," she said.

"Give him my love."

"I will if I see him, but I expect you'll see him first."

"Isn't he with you still?"

"No, isn't he with you?"

Neither of us saw him for two days; then he went to see Franca again. She phoned me the following morning.

"He had read the note before he brought me the vase, and he's offended with you," she told me.

"But I sealed the envelope." I was upset too.

"Well, he must have opened it. All's fair in love and war, I think, and, after all, he's in love with you. He didn't like being given away."

"If he's in love with me, he'll give me a second chance."

But Evaristo did not give me a second chance. His pride was as big as his sense of humor, and he stayed away. Eventually I sent him a note:

My bed is getting cold.
                    Anne

That night at midnight my bell rang. I leaped out of bed. I was wearing the virginal nightdress again, and I ran to open the door to Evaristo. Instead, a strange young man was standing there—one of the most beautiful young men I have ever seen. In his hand he held an opaline vase in the shape of a cornucopia; inside the vase was a single Peace rose.

The young man stepped inside. He neither smiled nor spoke, but held out a letter to me.

"Thank you," I said, at a loss for anything more appropriate to say. "Won't you come in?"

The young man sat on the sofa holding the vase while I read the letter. Like all great beauties, he was willing to sit quietly and be admired.

Dearest Anne [wrote Evaristo],

A rose is a rose is a rose is a rose, but I prefer not to be one of a bunch. Nor do I like to be given away. However, I wish you peace.

The young man has been paid for his night's work at the usual Equity rate, plus extra for night shooting, and indemnity for nudity. I hope you enjoy him.

Evaristo

I put down the letter and looked at the young man. As if on cue, he smiled, coolly, professionally, but pleasantly enough. He held out the vase to me. I put it down on the table and, to my own astonishment, began to cry.

The young man didn't know what to do. It was not the scene he had expected to play, any more than it was the one I had hoped to enjoy.

"Shall I come back another time?" he asked.

"No, that will not be necessary," I sobbed.

He went to the door, hesitated, and said, "Goodbye, then."

He was embarrassed by my weeping, and so was

I. There was nothing he could do for me, so I showed him to the front door.

The elevator took him down, and he went out into the night. At that moment, I didn't regret his hasty departure. Beautiful as he was, he could not have replaced a rainbow.

6 ∽ Life May Cease

I woke up in London one mid-September morning in 1971 with extraordinary pains. At the end of a week, I realized I must see a doctor.

I phoned my brother Max. He was on a visit to London to arrange a show of his paintings, living in a comfortable flat borrowed from a friend on holiday. I had been staying in an uncomfortable flat that I had rented and found full of fleas. I had just had the County Council in to fumigate it.

I was spending my holidays in London to see Fiona and the children, and had timed it so I could also help Max with his exhibition. It looked as if he were going to have to help *me* instead. I was practically doubled up and could hardly walk. I felt almost ashamed, sure that my pains must be psychosomatic.

"Max," I cried over the telephone, "I've got some ghastly kind of hysterical paralysis—I'm in great pain, and I can hardly move!"

"Don't be an idiot," my brother said. "You're the least neurotic person I know. It can't be a psychosomatic illness. You've got rheumatic fever, or galloping arthritis, or infantile paralysis."

"Infantile paralysis at my age? I'm fifty-four, Max. You don't get infantile paralysis at fifty-four!"

But I realized with a shock that he might be right. My hands and feet *were* now paralyzed.

The next day my brother took me to see our family doctor. The taxi driver had to help him carry me into the waiting room.

"Good heavens, Mrs. Cumming! Why did you wait so long before coming to see me?"

"It just crept up on me. I didn't realize it was so serious. I thought I was imagining it all to hide some subconscious pain."

"Really! Psychiatry first taught patients to imagine they were ill. Now it's teaching them to imagine they are *not* ill! My dear girl, you're partially paralyzed. I'm not a specialist, but I shall send you to one immediately."

Before I knew what was happening, there were telephone calls, another taxi, then an ambulance, and I was carried into the outpatient department at Queen's Hospital on a stretcher.

A famous specialist, Mr. Llewellyn-Jones, examined me. He stuck pins into my hands and feet: I couldn't feel the pricks. He hit my ankles and wrists with a little hammer: there were no reflexes. He hit my knees and my elbows: they barely twitched.

"Your feet and hands feel as heavy as lead? You have pins and needles all the time?"

"Yes."

"Hmm . . . classic symptoms."

"Symptoms of what?"

"Peripheral neuritis."

"I've never heard of it. Is it serious?"

"Not if it stops in your extremities, which it seems to be doing."

"Will I get better? I prefer to know the truth."

"I can't answer you until we've made some tests. We shall have to establish the cause before we can start any treatment. I advise immediate hospitalization."

I was helped from the stretcher into a wheelchair, and my brother wheeled me into the admittance office.

I lay in the corner of a ward in a rough cotton hospital-issue nightdress. My brother had gone home to get my personal things. A group of young medical students were gathered around my bed, all looking very grave. They were allowed to feel my limbs and ask me questions. One of them was singled out by the professor to stick pins into me again and hit my reflexes. I still felt nothing.

"Nesbitt, this is your case. I would like you to make a particular study of it," said Mr. Llewellyn-Jones.

"Yes, sir. Thank you, sir," the young man replied.

Then they all moved on to the next bed. I watched the earnest-looking young men in white coats move down the long ward full of women. I liked the one who had been allotted to me best. He had a boyish twinkle in his gray eyes. But then, he *was* a boy. He looked back at me from the end of the ward, and we smiled at each other.

I now understood the meaning of the word "patient." It meant a sick person who had to wait patiently. I didn't know what I was waiting for, except pain that nagged and nudged its way forward, taking me over completely till I was possessed by it and could think of nothing else.

I had no visitors except my brother, who was himself a visitor to London. My daughter Fiona lived miles away and couldn't keep trailing up, dragging the children behind her. I had indeed persuaded her not to do so. I hadn't told any of my friends where I was yet, and certainly none of my former lovers. I didn't want to upset them. I'd rather they were offended than distressed. I've always hated to bother other people with my troubles.

My only real human contact in the hospital was with the young man named Nesbitt, who was studying my case. He stayed behind after every ward round to check on my condition, which remained the same.

Something was happening between Nesbitt and me that made our relationship different from the professional contact I had with the other doctors and nurses. It was not wishful thinking on my part; we'd had a strange conversation one day that was certainly an overture to something. As my bed was in the corner of the ward and the next bed was temporarily vacant, I enjoyed a certain privacy, and we would talk quietly together.

"I'm sorry to bother you, but I need your blood," he said, coming back after the usual ward round with my specialist, Mr. Llewellyn-Jones.

"Have as much as you like. Everybody else has been helping themselves."

He handled the syringe so delicately that I hardly felt the prick. I found him very attractive up close, and noticed how long his lashes were around the cool gray eyes. My blood was beginning to fill the syringe.

"It's a nice color," he commented.

"A good vintage. Old bottles contain good wine."

He smiled. "It doesn't seem possible that you're fifty-four."

"How do you know about my age? You don't study the admittance cards, do you?"

"Sometimes. I'm following your case as part of my training. I have to get the full picture, as there seems to be no medical reason for your illness. It's definitely not a hysterical paralysis, either. Your motor nerves have been killed off for some reason—so I needed to know who you were and where you came from."

He had got up to transfer the blood to a test tube. He stood there with the syringe in his sensitive fingers, looking down at me. His hair was longish and fell over his forehead. He looked like a young musician rather than a future surgeon, except for that cool, calculating look. He squirted the blood into a test tube.

"I've never met anyone like you before. You're from another world. I can't imagine who you are or how you live," he said, looking at me again.

I was surprised, and smiled at him. His interest made me suddenly feel less like a guinea pig and more like a human being.

"One day I'll tell you who I am," I said.

He looked down at the kidney-shaped dish in his hand with its test tube of blood and said shyly, "I'd like to know you better."

"Why?" I asked.

"You're very beautiful," he said, and walked away.

Diary entry. September 21.

Many women have sexual fantasies about their doctors, but it would perhaps be more natural if my biological urges were directed toward the famous specialist—a man my own age. Why do I want Nesbitt, the young man with the gray eyes? And why *that* particular young man? Since Evaristo left me a year ago, I have led rather a quiet sex life, mainly with my steady beaus, some of whom are nearing forty—although none of them have been my own age since Rudi left me. After a long absence abroad "en poste," my diplomat had a spell in Rome again at the Ministry of Foreign Affairs. My truck driver has driven in and out of my life at intervals, and there is always little Bruno to fill the gaps. Even he is nearly thirty. But now that I'm confined to a hospital bed, I suddenly long for my younger lovers. Waves of nostalgia for Jean-Louis, Joseph and Evaristo sweep over me. I even miss Bad Gregory, and perhaps I will let him know I'm here. Behind his paranoia is a loving and caring heart—perhaps even because of it. He would come and see me at once and not be afraid, even if I am dying.

I have never had sexual fantasies before, because I have had too much of the real thing; but it occurs to me now that perhaps my very young lovers were a concrete form of sexual fantasy. Now that I'm immobilized and removed from any real sexual contact, I'm beginning to fantasize for the first time in my life, in spite of my pain and suffering. The young medical student, Nesbitt, who fills my thoughts, looks as if he had just left high school. I seem to have acquired a taste for teen-agers, and the physical aspect of this is beginning to worry me. It's becoming a habit—the Boy Habit. I *like* the feel and the smell of smooth young skin. I enjoy running my hands through thick, healthy hair. Love-making with a very young man is like the enjoyment of spring—a sensual, physical pleasure. I hope Nesbitt comes back to see me soon.

"Good morning. I've come to do your lumbar puncture. It'll be a little unpleasant, but it doesn't really hurt. Would you lie on your left side?"

A young doctor I'd never seen before was standing at my bedside. I rolled over as directed and closed my eyes.

I was stabbed in the back by a long needle that went right into the spinal column, allowing him to withdraw spinal fluid. It was anything but pleasant, and I tried to put myself into a kind of yoga trance so as not to feel it. I imagined myself lying on a bed of nails, walking through fire—anything to cancel out the thought of that long needle in my spine sucking out my life forces. I tried hard to rise above it all with transcendental meditation, to become unconscious, but the young doctor's voice cut in.

"Mrs. Cumming? Are you all right?"

He sounded anxious. Perhaps he thought I'd fainted.

I realized that he was as nervous as I was and had probably not done this very often. Possibly he even thought he'd killed me.

"I'm still alive," I said. "You can't get rid of me so easily."

He smiled with relief and triumphantly held up a little bottle of colorless liquid for my inspection—the vital spinal fluid. It looked like water.

This was the first of a series of ghastly tests— some worse than the illness itself. Over the next few days, I had my blood taken every few hours for diabetes. Then I had a myelogram—I was turned upside down with air pumped into the delicate membrane over the brain and spinal cord to check for a rupture or compression of the vertebrae. The next test was electromyography—I had horrible little electrified darts stuck into my legs to induce muscular action and check the extent of my paralysis. My lungs were x-rayed, my life history revisited. Was I an alcoholic? Had I ever suffered from malnutrition? Every day I grew more and more depressed. At night, when the lights in the ward were turned off and the night nurse turned on her little table lamp, they came around with sleeping tablets. I began saving mine in case I was to be paralyzed for life. I would rather crawl away somewhere and take them all at once than be obligated to others for the rest of my life.

My specialist, Mr. Llewellyn-Jones, had news for me one morning, but not of the kind I was expecting. He told me there was nothing wrong with me. All my tests were negative.

"Nothing wrong except that I'm partially paralyzed and totally bored," I exclaimed impatiently. "What happens now?"

"Just be patient, Mrs. Cumming," he answered. "We're still studying your case. We're taking good care of you."

He moved on, smiling to himself. Nesbitt, my gray-eyed student, was instructed to stay behind and check my heart and blood pressure. We were left alone in my corner. We began to talk like old friends. I felt he was as glad to see me as I was to see him. We were curious about each other. I wanted to know more about him. His accent suggested that he was probably a clever, working-class boy who had got where he was through scholarships. His background interested me.

"What's your first name?" I asked him. "I can't call you Dr. Nesbitt. You're too young."

"Grant. Grant Peregrine Nesbitt."

It sounded fictional. I would have been more convinced by a name like George Albert. He obviously wanted to become someone and innocently supposed that changing his name would bring him nearer to his ideal. His romantic longing touched me.

"I'll call you Grant of the Gray Eyes. It sounds

like a medieval knight," I said, playing up to his fantasy.

He touched my hand, pretending to examine my fingers, more venturesome than I had expected, so I went on, "I rather fancy you, Grant, if you want to know."

He looked up, startled.

"Nobody's ever said that to me before. You're a very outspoken woman. I didn't know people in your class could be like that. Is it because you've lived abroad?"

"I don't think so. It's just that at my age I know what I want." He put down my hand and placed his stethoscope on my breast.

"I know what I want too," he said, "but I wouldn't dare tell you."

"Go on, tell me."

He was bending over me listening to my heart with his stethoscope, and I thought for a moment that he was going to kiss me. It obviously passed through his mind, but we were in full view of a ward of inquisitive women, so he stood up reluctantly.

"I would like to learn all about women from you," he said boldly. "I think you must know a lot. I need experience."

"You're not a virgin, are you?"

"No. I've had several experiences. Last year I had a steady girl friend, a schoolteacher much older than me."

"How much older?"

"Twenty-eight."

I burst out laughing. "And how old are *you*?"

"Nearly twenty-one. Are you laughing at me? Is it so ridiculous to be young?"

"No. It's ridiculous to be old. I must be older than your mother. How old is she?"

"I don't know. She ran away with a policeman when I was six, and we've never seen her again."

"Who's we?"

"My father and I. He brought me up alone. I still live with him."

"What does he do?"

A slight pause. "He restores antique furniture."

The pause was significant. There was some mystery about the father. Probably he was just a simple carpenter, and the boy was ashamed of his origins. He stood by my bed like the little chimney sweep from *The Water Babies*, who comes out of the dark chimney into a big room and stands at the foot of the bed of a poor little rich girl with golden curls, lying sick under a spotless white sheet. I began to feel maternal—incestuously maternal, of course—and I held out my hand to him again. He took it in his.

A nurse hurried up to us. "Let's get ready for your little trip downstairs, dear," she said briskly, handing me my dressing gown. An orderly was approaching with a wheelchair. I was being taken down for another test.

"See you later," Grant said, standing up quickly, but hesitating and wanting to say more.

"Good-bye," I said, helping him to go.

When he was out of earshot, the nurse said, "That young man seems to have taken a fancy to you, dear."

"Nonsense, nurse," I protested. "He's just taking his job seriously." In my heart I knew better.

The orderly helped me into the wheelchair. I was being taken downstairs to the x-ray department for a cerebral angiography—a colored liquid would be injected into my veins and its passage through my brain studied to see if there was any blockage. Since my motor nerves were not functioning, perhaps my brain was not sending out the correct messages. It was not a pleasant prospect. The results could mean a brain tumor.

That afternoon I was surprised to see Grant come into the ward. He didn't usually appear in the afternoons, and there was something strange about him. He seemed on top of the world, as if he were drunk.

"I want to see your legs," he said, coming straight up to me.

His shy, romantic manner had gone. He seemed purposeful and sure of himself. The little-boy-lost quality had gone, too. He had evidently made some decision as well as taken a strong drink. He sat down beside me.

"How much do your legs hurt?"

He ran his hand down the leg nearest him. It was more of a caress than a scientific investigation.

"Quite a lot."

"What kind of pain?"

"A sharp ache; not a dull, nagging pain like rheumatism, or a stabbing pain like a twisted ankle or a sprained knee. I've never had this kind of pain before, so it's difficult to describe."

"Do the pain killers you're taking help?"

"For a couple of hours, but they soon wear off. The nights are worst because the pain keeps waking me up."

"Don't they give you sleeping tablets?"

"I don't take them. I'm against taking too many pills. I'm a sort of nonviolent Christian Scientist."

He laughed and began playing with my toes. I couldn't feel anything as my feet were numb, but I could see what he was doing.

"Tell me when you begin to feel it."

He was pinching my ankle and working his way up to the knee. Halfway up my thigh, I said "Ouch!" His hand was under my nightdress. He stopped pinching and stroked my upper thigh. It was a very pleasurable sensation.

"I can certainly feel that! I never thought I would again."

I smiled at him encouragingly, glad there was no one in the next bed to hear us.

He gave me his new look of cool determination. The pupils of his eyes were very dilated, very black against the pale gray. He spoke in a low voice, bending over me.

"The patient will probably recover. She obviously still has the capacity for sex, and I shall make love to her before she leaves this hospital."

I was speechless with surprise. He in turn looked quite frightened at what he had said and done, but quite resolute. I felt again that his manner was in some way artificial.

"Have you been drinking?" I asked as my power of speech came back.

"No," he said, lowering his voice still further. "But I did have a joint at lunch time."

"Do you smoke a lot?"

"Quite a bit."

"I wish you wouldn't. I'd rather help you get over that than your sexual inexperience."

"We'll work on both."

"But where? How?"

"There are lots of very private places in this hospital. You'd be surprised."

"I'm already surprised. In fact, I'm astounded."

At that moment, we saw the head nurse advancing. Grant got up quickly and went to meet her, said a few words, and left the ward with her. After a few minutes she came back, bringing a wheelchair and my physiotherapist, a sturdy, sensible girl who had obviously been head of her class in gymnastics and who stood by my bed in her short tunic as if she were still a senior schoolgirl. She talked to me as if I were one of the juniors.

"Now, Mrs. Cumming, you're going to the gymnasium with me. I'll show you some useful remedial exercises to keep those muscles from atrophying."

"I see. Then I'd better try and *walk* to the gymnasium. Have you any crutches?"

"We'll get you some later. Now, put your arm through mine and lean on me."

I swung my legs over the bed and stood up gingerly. Then I took her muscular arm and tottered forward.

When we reached the gymnasium, I realized how little of the hospital I had seen. There was a whole area devoted to brain surgery. Crawling about on the floor or on mattresses were patients who looked like spacemen. Their heads had been shaved, some were still swathed in bandages, and most of them were in striped pajamas. They were all incapacitated, off balance, and could scarcely move, in spite of the enormous efforts they were making.

"We're all cripples!" I blurted out, realizing it for the first time.

"Only temporarily," replied my muscular guardian angel. "Now come over to the parallel bars."

I looked around at the patients on the floor. The ghastly part about it all was that this was not a psychiatric hospital. Everybody was conscious of his own condition, struggling against terrible odds, with little hope but with tremendous courage. I took a deep breath and took as firm a step forward as I could.

As I skirted the squirming bodies on the floor, I realized that none of them could stand or walk. They had been helped out of their wheelchairs and laid down on mattresses, where the only movements they could make were wormlike ones. There was I, a superior being, who could *walk*.

I was so carried away by my sense of comparative strength that I let go of the therapist's arm, wobbled, lost my balance, and fell to the floor.

I found myself lying on a mattress beside a strange gentleman—in my nightdress, he in his pajamas. He smiled at me. He had very dark eyes that crinkled at the corners. I could tell at once that we were going to like each other. The situation struck me as funny, and I couldn't help laughing.

"It's been a long time since I've heard anyone laugh," he said rather wistfully. "Thank you. It's done me a world of good."

I propped myself up on my elbow and looked down at him. He was lying on his back, and I quickly realized that he couldn't move anything but his arms, and even those not very much.

"Forgive me for joining you so abruptly," I said. "I do usually wait to be asked before jumping into bed with a man."

It was his turn to laugh. It must be good for him, I thought—and saw myself as an instant Florence Nightingale. I must make this man laugh again. The fact that he was a strong-looking, dark, handsome man in his early forties was going to make it easier. I was very happy lying beside him. There was only one fly in the ointment.

"Are you going to get up and come to the parallel bars, Mrs. Cumming?" the fly was saying. I looked up at her, then turned back to my new friend.

"Look, I'll be back later. Now don't go away, promise?"

"I can hardly do that, can I?" He made a hopeless gesture with his hands.

"Men are always running away from me. Thank God I've found one who can't. You're going to be the great love of my life."

He looked at me with amazement, because he could see I meant it. I struggled to my knees, but found I couldn't go any farther. My physiotherapist stepped forward and lifted me to my feet.

"I don't usually fall for a man and then end up in a *woman's* arms," I explained, looking down at him. He laughed again.

"Come back soon," he said.

The next day Grant came again to see me alone. He pulled the curtain around my bed, enclosing us in a cozy green cubicle.

"I'm supposed to have a nurse in here with me while I examine the patient. Shall I call one?"

"Is that a question or a proposition?"

"Both. We are advised to protect ourselves from possible charges of rape. You've no idea how many hysterical, sex-starved women there are in the world just waiting to be seduced by their doctors. Then they complain later to assuage their guilt."

"And do you expect me to complain?"

He smiled and shook his head.

"I would say that you're a low-risk patient, so if you agree, I'll spare the overworked nurses and give myself the pleasure of being alone with you."

"Agreed."

"Then would you take off your nightdress?"

He kept the sheet over me as much as possible during a complete and serious medical examination: the stethoscope, the pins, the hammer, my pulse, my blood pressure. He noted the results on my chart. There was only one difference this time: his cool, gray eyes looked into mine the whole time. The result was electric, not unlike a pleasant version of the electrode test. My nerves tingled, my vagina became moist, and my nipples hardened. I forgot my pain; I forgot the dark stranger made of stone I had fallen in love with yesterday in the gymnasium; I forgot the twenty other women beyond the curtains; I forgot the risk we were running. I just wanted this young man to go on touching me.

"Except for the lower arms and legs, I would say that your nerve endings are exceptionally sensitive and alive," he said, his eyes twinkling mischievously. "May I examine them further?" His hand was already straying over my breast.

I didn't need to reply. During the previous examination, he had already felt my pulse quicken and seen my nipples harden. Now his fingers ran over them in confirmation. He knew my answer.

He sat down beside me, pulling the sheet over me but leaving his left hand under it between my legs. I have never known such a delicate, inquiring touch. While his left hand stayed below, his right hand explored every inch of me. He started with a soft caress to my hair, ran his hand around my face, one finger down my nose to circle my lips and press between them, then the whole hand caressed my throat, cupped my breasts, lightly pinched the nipples, before a finger strayed on down my stomach and around and into my navel. Finally it traced a line down into the pubic hair, where it met the left hand. All this time, his left index finger had been plunged boldly into my vagina, with his thumb resting on my clitoris. He had been rotating them carefully, testing for the exact pressure and speed that gave me the most pleasure. He watched my face intently all the time, checking that the movements of the right hand heightened the pleasures of the left to such an extent of excruciating ecstasy that it was all I could do not to cry out. It was the most thorough and expert titillation I have ever known. He took it all in, watching me coolly, but breathing heavily. As I began the first spasm of an orgasm, he quickly withdrew his right hand from my pubic hair and put it over my mouth to remind me where I was. It was just as well, because I was lost to the world. I would have cried his name. As it was, I only whispered it.

I came down slowly from my private plateau. I stretched out my right hand and touched his thighs and then his crotch. He had a hard erection under his concealing white coat, which was partially hidden when he stood up.

"I want to do something about that," I said, still fondling it as he stood by the bed, leaning over me.

"Not now. We've taken enough risks for today." He bent down and kissed me. It was our first kiss. "We'll find a way to do more, don't worry. Now put your nightdress on."

I slipped it on, obedient as a child, fascinated by his mature command of the situation. Our roles were suddenly reversed because of his newly acquired sexual power over me. He opened the curtains and raised his voice.

"Thank you, Mrs. Cumming," he said. "Your case is very interesting, although we still do not understand certain aspects of it. You'll need further examination."

"Anytime, Dr. Nesbitt, anytime." I tried not to smile.

"I'm not a doctor yet," he corrected me.

"You're doing quite well, all the same!"

The rest of the day passed as if in a dream. A ten-minute episode had changed my whole attitude toward life. What had happened was astounding enough, but it had also taught me an extraordinary fact: although I had little or no sensation in my hands, they had "felt" Grant's erection. However limited my life was to be from now on, I would still be able to "feel" everything. The real erogenous zone is in the mind.

The following day I was on a starvation diet. They put a notice on the end of my bed saying "Nothing by mouth." It was Diabetes Day. My blood was taken every hour on the hour. By afternoon I was starving, having missed breakfast and lunch and seen the food carts disappear forever into the bowels of the hospital; so when the physiotherapist came for me, I explained my problem.

"Look, I haven't had anything to eat all day because of a diabetes test. I'll faint if I do my exercises on an empty stomach. Is there a cafeteria in the hospital?"

"Yes, I think you can get sandwiches and tea in the outpatient department. I'll get someone to take you down in your wheelchair."

"If I had two canes, I think I could manage it myself."

The lady in the opposite bed offered her crutches.

"Are you sure you don't mind?"

"It's not as if I'm going anywhere!" she said sadly.

So I set off by myself, with a promise to go up to the gym in half an hour.

I swung briskly down the ward on the crutches. I was surprised at how fast I could go. I took the elevator down and swung along the corridors to the outpatient department.

I felt a bit strange in my dressing gown here on the ground floor, where everyone else was in street clothes. At the end of the outpatient waiting room, with its tank of tropical fish and leatherette armchairs, I found a small counter where a stout lady from the Women's Voluntary Services was serving tea, sandwiches and plum cake.

"Could I have a little of everything? I'm starving!"

She looked at me strangely, not quite sure what I was doing there.

"How are you going to manage it all with your crutches, dear? Here, let me put the tray on a little table for you."

She kindly came out from behind her counter and settled me into an armchair by a coffee table, where I sat eating and watching the tropical fish. Except for the crutches beside me, I might have been in any English tearoom. Presently she came and took my tray.

"I have to clear away now. We shut down at five. The morning's our busy time, really."

"You mean this whole part of the hospital is empty at night?"

"Yes, of course, dear. Only day staff work here."

I thought this over as I swung back to the elevators at the front of the hospital. What was to stop me from going there with Grant in the evenings? During visiting hours, ambulant patients often took little walks down the corridors with their visitors. I could slip into an elevator and disappear into the darkened regions of the outpatient department every evening between 6:30 and 8:00 and meet Grant there!

When I got to the gymnasium, I looked at once for my paralyzed friend. I had been physically unfaithful to him, and I felt guilty. He was there on his mattress, trying to learn to roll over by himself. I flopped down beside him and gave him a kiss. It was like coming home to the husband you really loved after a casual infidelity with a sexy young stranger.

"Shall I give you a push, or isn't that allowed?" I asked.

"What I like about you," he said smiling, "is that you're not afraid of the truth. Everyone else pretends nothing has happened to me."

"What *did* happen?"

"I ran a high temperature for a couple of days, had aching pains all over, thought it was flu, and woke up one morning unable to move. I'm a doctor myself, but I didn't know what was the matter with me."

"What did you do?"

"I couldn't do anything. I've lived alone since my divorce. There wasn't even anyone who could hear me if I shouted."

He said all this in a matter-of-fact tone of voice, but I could clearly visualize the horror of the situation. He was a brave, wonderful man, and I loved him.

"So what happened then?"

"Fortunately I belong to a car pool. A friend picks me up every morning, and we go to work together. Usually I meet him on the street corner so he doesn't have to park. When I didn't come down, he called from a phone booth. I heard the phone ringing, but I couldn't get out of bed to answer it. That was the worst moment."

"Oh, my God! And then what happened?"

"He was going to drive on, thinking I'd slept at some woman's house and forgotten to call him. By a lucky chance, he saw a parking space and decided to come up, in case I was in the shower and hadn't heard the phone. When he rang the bell, I shouted. He had to get the police to break down the door."

My physiotherapist had just seen me. She came over quickly.

"Now, you two, what's going on?"

"I'm busy dispensing my own form of therapy to my friend," I said, giving him another kiss.

"She's doing me more good than anybody." He smiled as I used my crutches to help me get up.

"See you later," I called as I swung over to the parallel bars.

Before my dark-haired doctor friend was taken back to his ward, he had the orderly wheel him over to ask if I would visit him next day.

"I'm in the Nuffield Wing. Can you walk that far? Are you allowed to go out of your own ward?"

"If I stick to visiting hours, I don't think anyone can stop me. We're not in prison, are we?"

"In a way we are—imprisoned in our own bodies. But you, my dear, are going to get out soon."

I could tell by his tone that he knew his own case to be hopeless, but he spoke with the serenity of total acceptance, and his courage amazed me. I leaned forward, supporting myself on the arms of his chair, and gave him another kiss in tribute. There were tears in my eyes. I found it difficult to be as brave for him as he was about himself.

By the next evening, I had got myself two canes and given back the crutches. I set off resolutely for the male wards.

The hospital had quite a different atmosphere on the weekends. There were fewer doctors and no medical students. I hadn't seen Grant since our sex scene. Perhaps he was frightened at what he had done. Perhaps he had finally woken up to the difference in our ages. I had no idea what he did on weekends, or where he and his devoted father lived.

The male wards were even more dreary than the female wards. They were unkempt. We women, natural homemakers, carefully set out our toilet articles and personal belongings. We had more flowers, and we tidied up our own beds and put photos on our night tables.

My friend was in the first bed on the right as I entered—which was just as well, because I didn't know how to ask for him. We had not introduced ourselves; it hadn't been necessary. We had fallen into this friendship, bypassing the social preliminaries, and would probably have fallen deeply in love if there had been any possible future for the relationship. I was already slightly in love, but I recognized that he was a doctor—a man who had never lived by fantasy and never would. He would expect and accept from me only what he himself could return.

"Hello," I said brightly as I held out my hand. "Shall we start again now that we are meeting on new ground? My name is Anne Cumming. How do you do?"

He took on a social tone. "I'm Ian Bromley. I'm glad to meet you!"

He was propped up on pillows and could turn his head to look at me, but had difficulty in holding out his hand to take mine.

"Let's practice shaking hands," I said quickly, realizing my initial mistake. "I can put out my hand, but I can't squeeze anything."

I took his hand several times, exaggerating my own trouble, and we made it into a children's game, one hand on top of the other as if we were playing pat-a-cake. We laughed at our own inefficiency, happy to share even that. Then I sat down beside him.

"Now that we've finished being formal, could we go back to just kissing?" he asked. "You've no idea how much good it did me to have you fall from the skies and kiss me as though you didn't notice my condition."

I leaned forward and kissed him on the lips, measuring the length of the kiss to express affection rather than passion. I was not sure how far to go to give him pleasure without the embarrassment of making him realize his impotence.

"It's a new sensation, being kissed by a beautiful woman now. I feel it emotionally, although there's no longer the usual physical reaction."

"Does that worry you?"

"I don't mind so much the realization that I'll never again feel physical pleasure, but I *do* mind the idea that I can't give another person pleasure."

"You must have been a good lover, then. Most men feel more for themselves than for the woman."

"For me, the ultimate turn-on has always been to see desire in a woman's eyes. Now I couldn't even touch your hand if I saw it."

I knew then that he understood the kind of woman I was—too volatile and sensual to be interested for long in any static situation—and that he was only too aware that his own situation was the most static of them all. He would be grateful for my breezy presence occasionally and my throw-away kisses, but he would know how to limit his emotions to fit his other limitations. He did not want to see desire in my eyes. I wished I could be like him. I told him so.

"I admire your acceptance and restraint, Ian. I still want too much for my age, let alone my condition. It's often undignified."

"No. I'm sure it's right for *you*. Go on wanting it, and you'll get it to the very end. I can see you at ninety in some young man's arms."

"God, I hope not! *I* may not know when to stop, but surely the young men will?"

"I doubt it. I think you'll be seducing virgin boys on your deathbed."

We both laughed at the idea. I longed to tell him about Grant, but that would really be a blow below the belt. I would have to keep both men in separate compartments, giving and taking as much as I could while we were still in the hospital. Then I hoped to leave and forget it all back in Rome, even

if I got there on crutches. I would work so hard
that I'd even forget the pain.

I told Ian my hopes and asked him about his. He
wanted to talk about it, and again his words hurt
me more than they hurt him. He told me about the
rehabilitation center where they would teach him
to do as much as possible, and from there he would
go to a home for incurables, where life and work
was organized on a level commensurate with the
capacities of people like himself. He hoped to do
research on his particular medical specialty—allergies and asthma—and to write textbooks about
them.

My spine ran cold at the words "home for incurables," but he talked about it as though it were the
name of a hotel. I realized that my own thoughts of
suicide had shown cowardice rather than courage.
Ian was a truly heroic figure. In spite of his touching gratitude, he was doing me more good than I
was doing him.

Visiting hours were soon over. We had talked of
our pasts, and had discussed our marriages and
other successes and failures. Then the bell rang,
and visitors had to leave.

"I'll have no more emotional struggles in life,"
he was saying. "It's quite a relief. From now on,
my problems will be purely physical."

I hadn't expected my absence to be noticed, but
the head nurse was justifiably cross that I had gone
without telling her where I was going. I explained
the situation, and she forgot her annoyance.

"It's just that you had a visitor, and we couldn't
find you."

"What visitor? I wasn't expecting anybody."

"It was that young man—your medical student. He left you those flowers. He said he'd come to take you for a walk. Doctor's orders. Just fancy! You've made a conquest!"

She was all for romance. How could I explain to her that it was only sex I wanted from Grant? Romance created too many emotional responsibilities.

Sunday visiting hours began in the afternoon, but I stayed in my ward. I felt bad about not going to see Ian Bromley, but I was afraid that if I moved, I would miss Grant again. Ian knew I had a brother and would presume that he was visiting me and that I couldn't get away.

I waited and waited, but Grant didn't come. I was disappointed. After a time I gave up hope and got ready to go down to see Ian.

I was waiting by the elevator to go down to the men's wards when Grant stepped out. In another minute I would have missed him. He had a package in his hands and was wearing a classic Harris tweed jacket.

"Dad sent you this cake. He baked it himself."

We stood there looking at each other on the landing. I put both canes into one hand so I could take the cake.

"So your father cooks?"

"Yes, he cooks very well. We always have a big Sunday lunch together, then I help him with the dishes, and we take the dog for a walk in Hackney Marshes near our flat. It's not a very elegant flat, but we've made it quite nice. It's full of valuable antiques."

I smiled, not really believing this fantasy. Like his name, it was probably invented.

I was still holding the cake. He took it back from me.

"Shall I put it by your bed?"

"No. Let's take it downstairs with us. We can go to the outpatient department. There's nobody there in the evenings, but they've got chairs and tables and a coke machine. We'll have a tea party!"

And that's how it all began. We sat in front of the tropical fish tank, with paper cups of coke and the cake on the table between us. We had to break it with our fingers because we didn't have a knife. Grant popped pieces into my mouth, and I bit his fingers tenderly and looked deep into his gray eyes. He stood up and shed his jacket, then he lifted me and took me into his arms. No one came near us, although distant footsteps made us a little nervous and we sometimes stopped to listen. His hands lifted my nightdress and robe, and I unzipped his fly. At last I saw it—long and slim and terribly hard, just as I had imagined it.

"Take me over to that high table. My balance is bad."

There was a long table with magazines against the wall. We walked there, his arm around me, his penis sticking out of his trousers pointing the way. I leaned over the table, my chest pressed down on *The Lady* and my face turned sideways on *The Illustrated London News*. My rear end stuck out naked as I pulled up my clothes again.

"Put it in. Oh, my God! Put it in!"

He did it gently, carefully, hugging my thighs

and pulling them back into him as he thrust forward. He moved slowly at first, and, in spite of his own pressing urge to ejaculate at once, I could feel him holding back. Then the long, pencil-slim penis swelled up and exploded suddenly. I was almost left behind, but the feel of the warm semen gushing out and filling my vagina brought on my own orgasm as his subsided. It seemed as if we were coming for hours. His penis went on throbbing, and my spasms kept repeating themselves. It was a long time before I lifted my head from *The Illustrated London News*.

I turned around as he withdrew. He held me in his arms, knowing I would fall if he didn't, and I laid my head on his shoulder, my face against his neck. We stood there for some time without speaking, and I felt the sperm running down my thighs. Before we sat down, he found some paper napkins on the cafeteria counter and cleaned us both neatly and efficiently, as if he were doing a surgical dressing.

We sat down side by side, squashed into the same armchair, and talked and talked as if the sexual act had released words from some hidden source, which was indeed the case. It was the open sesame to his secret hopes and fears. He told me all about his life, which, as I had suspected, was that of a working-class boy trying to imitate those he considered his betters. He read extensively, alone with his father in the evenings, and he was a strange mixture of this fictitious, fictional world and the real working-class world around him. His clothes were what he thought a gentleman should wear, although boys his age from expensive private schools were in dirty old jeans and windjackets. All this gave him an old-fashioned air, the romantic troubadour of the Lady of Shalott. I now understood what he saw in me—an aristocratic mistress coupled with a lost mother. There were other things I did not understand.

"You puzzle me, Grant. Sometimes you seem such a sensitive boy, then a tough, assertive young man takes over. It's positively schizophrenic. You're like two different people."

He looked embarrassed, began to say something, and then stopped. Then he started again.

"If you'd been brought up in my neighborhood, gone to my schools . . ."

"No, it's not quite that. It's uncanny—not quite normal."

He looked embarrassed again and dropped his cool, gray gaze, speaking very fast without looking at me.

"I'm on Speed. I started taking it for my exams, and it helps a lot. It gives me the courage to do all sorts of things I ordinarily find difficult. I could never have approached you without it."

"I see."

"Does it worry you?"

"Yes. I'm frightened of drugs."

"Perhaps I shouldn't have told you."

"No, I'm glad you did. I want to understand you. I think that's what you're looking for in me— understanding and appreciation."

"And what do you want from me?"

I smiled and made a vulgar gesture.

He laughed.

We kissed, and our love-making began all over

again. I never moved from the chair; I just spread
my legs. He slipped to the floor on his knees. My
whole pubic area was widely exposed. He leaned
over and examined it.

"I've never looked at one before," he said, "except in medical books. I've only touched them in
the dark."

"Is it disgusting?"

"No. It's like a flower. A passion flower."

He took his hard penis out once again. I pushed
back the foreskin.

"And yours is like a bud. There's even a drop of
honey on the tip."

No one had seen us go down in the elevator together, so it was easy for me to slip back into the
ward and for Grant to go straight out the front
door as if we had never met. So we did it again and
again and again. Every night, in fact, I would go
into see Ian on my way down, and then meet
Grant in the outpatient department. I was impatient on the nights my brother came to see me, so I
would take him down to see Ian with me, explaining that it would be tactful if he left us together
after a few minutes, so my brother never stayed
long. Ian tired easily, so he was not surprised or offended when I would leave very soon after my
brother. We held hands, exchanged loving words,
understood each other deeply—and that was
enough. He was no longer capable of the physical
consummation of love, no longer needed it, and I
simply got it elsewhere. I literally fell into Grant's
arms every night.

One evening we were nearly caught in the act. A black, off-duty nurse came in with some fish food.

"I forgot to feed them this morning," she explained, going over to the tank.

"What a hospital! A tropical nurse for the tropical fish!" I said, swiftly adjusting my nightdress.

We all three laughed, and she left us together, looking rather puzzled but saying nothing.

"What do you think she thought?" Grant asked.

"Nothing. She'd only see me as an elderly patient sitting with a favorite nephew."

"But why would we be down here?"

"Family business too private to discuss in the public ward. Why? Are you worried?"

"A bit. I could be expelled from medical school for seducing a patient."

"In this case, I think *I* would be expelled for corruption of a minor!"

"Perhaps you're right. I shouldn't worry so much." He laid his head on my shoulder. "That's how I started using Speed, through anxiety. It's been tough keeping up in medical school; the Old-Boy class system keeps coming up. They're always asking what your father does and whether you play rugby. It's their way of finding out if you went to a private school."

"Good God! In this day and age they still worry about things like that? What has it got to do with being a good doctor?"

"Don't ask me—ask them."

"Ask who?"

"The powers that be. You wouldn't understand. You were born with a silver spoon in your mouth."

"Fuck that. All it does is choke you!"

We laughed. We laughed a lot during our illicit evenings. We made love and we laughed. I was walking much better. The exercise with Grant was doing me more good than the physiotherapy in the gymnasium!

I had written to Rudi, telling him of my illness. I got two letters back from New York—one from Rudi, one from Tom.

My treasure [Rudi wrote; he did not write English as well as he spoke],

I also am having my difficult moments, although my pain and suffering is not physical. Tom has left me and will shortly be getting married. He will write to you himself, because I have told him where you are. I used the excuse of your illness to phone him. I am trying to keep in touch, as you do with all your lovers, but I don't think I have your strength or generosity, so it isn't working very well. I feel lonely. I would like to come to you at once, but I have to go to San Francisco to design *Cinderella*. I remember you once said to me, "Prince Charming only exists in the imagination— you have to invent your own Prince Charming when you need him or sit by the fireside alone forever." I shall try and invent a new Prince Charming, and I know you too will dance again at the ball. You are a force of nature, Anne, and your love of life will make you get well, even if the doctors don't know how.

I need you, and will come and see you soon.

                                              Your Rudi

It was typical of Rudi that he was more worried by his problem than mine, but he needed me, and I liked to be needed. That had always been the basis for our relationship, and I found it strangely consoling that nothing could change that. He was convinced of my strength even in my moment of weakness. I couldn't let him down.

I opened Tom's letter with curiosity. It was very short:

Hi! You can't die! You must come over and meet Sharleen. She's a great girl, she reminds me of you. She has two small children, and I'm into children at the moment; all my paintings are about the beginning of life. Two men don't make one whole— they remain two separate halves—so the composition was wrong. I had to get things into perspective or lose my artistic balance. I'm sending you a new drawing to help you get well and show you what I mean.

Love,
Tom

There was a little black-and-white sketch enclosed of curious abstract forms moving upwards and outwards. You could see that they were growing organisms—like Tom himself. There was nothing static about him or his work. He'd have to move on.

"Good morning, Mrs. Cumming." It was Mr. Llewellyn-Jones on his ward round. "Good news for you today. Your myelogram and pneumoencephalograms are negative. We found no trace of brain damage or other obstruction. No sign of any tumor."

"Thank you. That's nice to know. What *is* the matter with me, then?"

"We know what's the matter with you, but we may never know the cause."

As usual, Grant was standing behind him. I had never tried to catch his eye since we had become lovers, but this time I looked to him for help. He spoke for me.

"It is true, isn't it, Professor, that in such cases the patient generally recovers without treatment?" Grant asked, knowing what I wanted to hear.

"Nature is a great healer, and we doctors can only help it along. In this case there seems nothing extraneous to remove and no germs to destroy, so we can only wait and see what happens. Fortunately, our patient seems to be getting better, not worse."

"But it's all so slow!" I moaned. "How long will I be like this?"

"About a year, I should think. But you'll see a marked improvement after six months," he added consolingly.

"My God, a year!" I exclaimed. It seemed like a lifetime.

I joined Ian on his mattress in the gymnasium.

"I'll be like this for a year."

"I'll be like this forever."

"I won't even be near you to come and visit you. I'll be in Italy. But I'll write to you every week."

"And I'll look forward to your letters, but don't

write if it upsets you. You may want to forget this whole time. I certainly do. All I want now is peace."

"What do you mean by that? That you don't want to live?"

"No. I'd thought of that, of course, but I'll try living. However, I'll live with people and with situations that have no connection with the man I once was. I'll be a physical vegetable, but a creative vegetable, I hope, living with my books. If I lived with a woman, I would always wish I were still a man."

"But I love you as you are. Can't I go on loving you?"

"I don't think so. You belong to a different type of love. You're my fond farewell to all that. In a way, you've made the transition easier for me. Sad, but sweet. It could have been just sad."

The next evening I was downstairs early in the outpatient department. I didn't go to see Ian first, because I wanted to think over what he had said. I watched the tropical fish while waiting for Grant. Were they happy in their heated tank? Could they remember the freedom of tropical seas?

I could hear Grant's footsteps coming down the corridor and felt the sudden lift that only sex, love and drugs can give. He stood for a moment in the entrance in a wet raincoat. I wanted to run into his arms, but my feet were frozen to the floor with sickness and my canes were propped against the table.

Grant moved fast, however. I was pressed to the

wet raincoat and carried into one of the consulting rooms and laid on a hard examining table.

"I wish I were young and healthy for you," I said.

"You're to stop worrying about your illness. I'm going to lock the door and keep you here till you forget who you are and where you are."

"That's the trouble; I can't forget. I'm an exotic fish who's used to swimming freely in warm seas. I can't be hemmed in. Even Ian sees that. He understands me much better than you do."

"Probably. He's much older. And he comes from your world."

"You're jealous!"

"Yes, I am. Even though, poor bastard, he can hardly take you away from me. But I'm jealous of all those things you've both done that I've only read about in books."

He walked quickly to the door and locked us securely into our own little world. He was in one of his cool, determined moods.

"You've been taking drugs again. You're too sure of yourself."

He didn't answer, but began to undress me even before he had taken off his raincoat. He immediately began kissing me all over. He drew my nipples into his mouth, ran his tongue into my navel, and then on down into what he called my "passion flower." I automatically spread it out before him. His tongue licked around the labia and then centered on my clitoris. I immediately felt the sharp tingling of the oncoming orgasm.

"No! No! Wait, darling, wait. I want to come

with you. Oh, no! Please wait ... please ... please...."

But he didn't wait, and I couldn't wait, and I writhed and gasped and clutched at his hands which were holding my thighs apart.

When it was over, he came up and leaned over me to kiss me on the mouth. I shivered a little in his arms, and the wet raincoat pressed my naked body. I tasted my own taste and didn't like it.

"Undress. It's your turn now," I said.

"No. I want to wait till you're ready to come again."

"That'll be quite some time."

"Don't worry. I like to work up to it slowly. I often walk about for hours with an erection, just thinking about sex. I've got a huge hard-on now, and I'm going to keep it that way until you're ready for me."

"All right. But I want to see it. Let me undress you slowly," I said, sitting up. "You can't stand there all night in a raincoat."

I instinctively touched his crotch first, felt the swelling in my hand, and opened his fly. Out jumped his jack-in-the-box.

I sat back and admired the effect. He laughed and flapped the sides of his coat, and his penis bounced up and down as if it were beckoning me.

"You're making a fetishist out of me! Raincoats and exhibitionism, for Christ's sake!"

He slipped his raincoat off, then the rest of his clothes, and stood naked for a long time beside me, caressing me with that cool, exploratory manner that was so typically Grant's. His penis got harder and harder until the telltale drop of lubrication oozed out at the top, and I began to feel my own answering wetness. He automatically knew, and climbed on top of me. The bed was very hard and very narrow, so my legs dangled down over the sides to make room for him to enter me. It was a good position, bringing my clitoris into easy contact with him. It was impossible to tell who came first or finished last; it was one of those rare occasions of joint orgasm to the point of physical fusion. We clung together for ages, pulsating in each other's arms until the mechanism finally ran down and was still. We lay in silence for a long while.

"I've got to get you out of here." He raised his head to look at me. "We've got to go somewhere where we can always be together like this."

"Grant, dear, when I get out of here, I'm going back to Rome."

"I'll come with you, then. I'll follow you there. You can't just run out on me."

"Run is hardly the word. I shall limp back into life, hobble back to Rome, and try and forget you."

His head dropped to my shoulder. He didn't say anything. He was crying.

I had followed up my impulse to get in touch with Bad Gregory. He was now working on a project in Bath, but he came up to London especially to see me. His enormous frame loomed in the doorway one visiting hour, startling the nurses, because he was carrying a tree.

"I thought flowers insipid," he said, "so I've brought you the Tree of Life."

He put it down by my bed, where it bloomed for the rest of my stay. Nobody had ever been given a tree before, and the head nurse had to be summoned to give her permission for it to stay in the ward.

"You can't take away the Tree of Life from a dying woman," Gregory said firmly.

"I don't think Mrs. Cumming is dying," the head nurse replied tartly. "Suppose everyone started importing trees—we'd soon have a forest in here."

"Better a forest than a graveyard," Gregory retorted, his eyes narrowing and appearing even closer together.

The nurse beat a hasty retreat. She probably recognized incipient paranoia when she saw it. My tree stayed.

When she was gone, Gregory made me dress and then picked me up bodily and carried me downstairs and out into the gardens in front of the hospital.

"I don't want to see you on crutches or in a wheelchair," he said. The nurses were too surprised to protest.

We sat outside talking as dusk fell. Gregory seemed quite sane and adjusted to his life and loves now. He had a girl friend who worked with him. He gave me news of Caspian and Kate, Good Gregory, Peter and Paul, all of whom he still saw. I explained to him that I didn't want any of the others to come and see me in my present state.

"You're different, Gregory, and you always will be. I like you because you and your behavior match—they're both larger than life. You're barbaric, and you're never boring. In a way, we suit each other. We're both grotesques."

He smiled and hugged me gently—that Russian bear hug of his. He was a giant, not an ogre.

When it grew too cold outside, he carried me back upstairs, undressed me, and popped me back into bed as if I were a doll. Then he kissed me and left. I told him not to come again; the journey was too long. I knew we would meet again, and we have—many times.

"That was an unusual visitor," said the lady in the next bed, who was prone to understatement. "Is he a relative?"

"In a manner of speaking. We do relate."

I did not feel I could explain further.

The weekend came around like a punctuation mark. I decided to have a bath and get dressed so I could hobble boldly out the front door with a cane to sit in the gardens with my daughter when she came. We could take Ian with us in his wheelchair. It would be my gesture toward carrying our friendship into the outer world, my refusal to accept his decision that our relationship might end. Ian and I would continue to see each other when we left the hospital. Grant and I would not. One has to make a distinction between lust and love.

My decision was reversed, through no fault of mine. Ian had left me! The one man whom I thought could not run out on me had done precisely that.

I went down immediately after lunch to find his

bed empty. That did not surprise me, because there were a number of places where he could go in his wheelchair. I sat down to wait. The man in the next bed looked at me strangely, but said nothing. Then I noticed that the night table had no books, no clock, and no jug of water.

"Where is Dr. Bromley? Has he changed wards?" I asked his neighbor.

"No. He left the hospital. Didn't you know he was leaving? His sister came for him this morning."

"You mean he knew all along he was going today?"

"Yes, I think so. He's gone to his sister's for the weekend; then on Monday he goes to a center for paraplegics."

I limped over to the nurse's office and asked for his sister's phone number.

His file had already gone down to the administration office, which was closed till Monday morning.

It was Saturday afternoon, and my daughter came up from Monmouth with the children. It was a big sacrifice for her, because the children were noisy and troublesome on the long train journey and too obstreperous to stay long in the hospital. They were fascinated by the gruesome details of hospital life, from bedpans to blood transfusions, and ran about the ward examining everything. Fiona did her best to keep them quiet, but after half an hour, we agreed they had better be taken home. I was dressed, so I went downstairs with them to the front door, put them into a taxi, then limped across the road to sit alone in the public garden. It was my first outing. I had intended to do it with Ian, and I felt cold and miserable and alone. Grant was not coming because of the family visit. Ian could have fitted into such a day, but Grant could not. I staggered back to my hospital bed.

Next day, Sunday, I had a pleasant surprise. I was sitting quietly with my brother Max in the dayroom when a little man came in with a crumpled paper bag. He looked around, and when he saw me, his face lit up, and he came straight over to me.

" 'Ullo! You must be Lady Anne Cumming," he said.

"Yes and no," I replied. "I'm just plain Anne Cumming."

"That's me son all over. 'E can't leave anything the way it is. 'E 'as to romanticize it all."

"Good heavens! You must be Grant's father!"

"Right first time. 'Ere, I brought you a cake. Made it meself." He placed the crumpled bag in my lap. I peeped inside. It was an old-fashioned plum cake.

"How lovely!" I smiled up at him. "Thank you, Dad."

A broad grin spread over his face. "I'm glad you called me Dad. It's more natural like. Grant's learned to talk posh, and 'e calls me 'Father' now. It ain't what we're used to around our way."

"I've always thought of you as 'Dad,' so it just popped out. I'm glad you don't mind."

I introduced my brother and asked Dad to sit
with us. My brother looked mystified, and Dad
was pleased as Punch when they shook hands.

"Glad to meet you. I've 'eard a lot about Anne,
but I didn't know she 'ad a brother in London.
Grant says she lives all over the world."

"So she does," Max replied. "It takes an illness
like this to hold her down long enough for me to
be able to catch up with her." He looked at me inquiringly. "I don't think I know Grant, do I,
Anne?"

"No, I've only just met him myself. He's the
medical student who's been assigned to my case."

Dad beamed proudly. "Ever so bright. Got 'ere
through scholarships. Never stops working, my
son. 'E's determined to get to the top, and I bet 'e
will. 'Ere, 'e sent you this."

Dad pulled an envelope out of his pocket. My
name was written on it with a great flourish. The
writing, like Grant himself, didn't seem quite real.

"I'll read it later. I take it he isn't coming this
evening?"

"No, 'e's gone away for the weekend. Down one
of 'is caves. Speli . . . something or other 'e calls it."

"Speleology," my brother put in. "He sounds
quite a remarkable young man, your son. Does he
often go down into caves, Mr. . . . er . . . Mr. . . . ?"

"Call me George. George Percy's the name.
Same as me father and same as me son, only 'e likes
to be called Grant Peregrine! Why, I can 'ardly
pronounce it meself, but if it makes 'im 'appy, it's
okay by me."

It was my turn to smile. George Percy, indeed! I
felt a rush of tenderness, but I knew I'd tease

Grant unmercifully for denying his Cockney heritage, his name, and this darling little man who wanted to be plain "Dad."

"Well, I must be running along now. I've got to do the ironing. I'm Mum *and* Dad, you see. Me wife buggered off with a policeman when me boy could 'ardly walk, but I've managed. 'E's never gone without nuffin'."

He shook our hands warmly. "Ta-ta for now," he said, beaming, and bustled out before I could thank him again for the cake.

"Well!" Max exclaimed. "You certainly haven't lost your touch for picking up strange men. What's the son like?"

"The answer to a bedridden old lady's prayer. He comes to see me every day and looks after all my needs!"

My brother looked at me curiously, then shook his head.

"I don't know how you do it, but you always fall on your feet, even when they're paralyzed!"

Later I got back into bed and read Grant's letter.

Dearest Love,

I felt you didn't want to see me this weekend, and I knew I wouldn't fit in with your family anyway. You will see what I mean when you meet my father, who insists on bringing you this note. He's an ordinary little man, but I know you'll be nice to him. He wanted so much to meet the beautiful lady I keep talking about.

Your devoted admirer and passionate lover,
Grant Peregrine Nesbitt

On Monday, the ward round stopped at my bed. Grant was back, with a faraway look in his eyes. I wanted to jump out of bed and welcome him back to my arms. Instead, I just had to say a polite "Good morning" to them all. To my surprise, Mr. Llewellyn-Jones informed me that I was to be a showpiece in the lecture theater. One of the Queen's physicians, the now-retired Lord Brighton, had come especially to give a talk on neurological peculiarities to a distinguished group of postgraduate students. I was asked to go downstairs immediately and wait outside the lecture theater. I didn't even have time to speak to Grant.

Three of the other exhibits were stretcher cases. Another was a brain operation, with shaved head, the black stitches showing at the temple and running back to his skull under a thin stocking cap of stretched white jersey. Only one other man in a wheelchair had leg trouble like me. I was the only one to walk in by myself, annoyed because we'd all been kept waiting outside for nearly an hour. I attacked poor Lord Brighton before he could open his mouth.

"Patients are sick people, and should be treated as such. I've been waiting in a drafty corridor without even a chair to sit on for three quarters of an hour, and I'm probably going to faint."

Lord Brighton tottered forward, picking up his own chair on the way. He was a very old man and walked no better than I did.

"Here, my dear. Sit down at once. And thank you for coming to see us." He gave me the chair.

He radiated such sweetness that I immediately apologized for my attitude.

"Forgive me. This is the only thing that is badly organized in this hospital, and I think it's because no one has the strength to protest. I'm a one-man protest march. Fair treatment for guinea pigs!"

Lord Brighton smiled and patted me on the head. He waved a quavering but authoritarian hand.

"Nurse! Send for the head nurse."

"Yes, my Lord."

A pretty nurse scurried out of the room while "my Lord" read out my notes.

"Now, has anybody any suggestions about this case?"

I looked around for Grant, but realized that this was a much older audience, and he was not among them.

To my surprise, an American voice asked, "Has anybody determined whether the patient has been poisoned?"

The audience, it appeared, was composed of young doctors from all over the world. This one had his name and "Mayo Clinic" on his lapel.

Lord Brighton turned to me with his sweet smile.

"Well, my dear, we must consider everything. Have you any reason to suppose you have been poisoned, by mistake or on purpose?"

Dr. Mayo Clinic hurriedly cut in. "I meant, does she follow some occupation that could bring her into contact with lead, arsenic, or other noxious material?"

Lord Brighton persisted, "The patient doesn't look to me like an industrial worker, but she looks beautiful enough to have been poisoned by a jealous lover. What do you say, my dear?"

"I'm very flattered, my Lord, but my husbands and lovers have always seemed quite glad to get rid of me peaceably," I replied. Then a thought struck me. "The nearest I've ever come to poison was when they sprayed my house recently for fleas!"

Dr. Mayo Clinic at once asked seriously, "What kind of spray did they use?"

"DDT, I imagine—I never thought to ask."

"Is DDT still used in England?" The young American doctor looked surprised.

At this point a very starched head nurse strode briskly into the room.

"You sent for me, Lord Brighton?"

"Yes, nurse. I want to know two things. Is DDT used in England? And why are patients kept waiting for hours when they are kind enough to come down and let us publicly examine their unfortunate conditions?"

"I don't know, my Lord. I'll look into both matters."

She left as briskly as she had entered, but the starch had wilted.

"Now," said Lord Brighton. "About poison. It is true that various poisons affect the nervous system. Since DDT kills insects by paralyzing them, I suppose in large enough doses it could kill people."

"We've had many cases of DDT poisoning among agricultural workers in the States," the young doctor said. "That's why it's now banned. Do you suffer from allergies, ma'am?"

"Yes, often. Hay fever, hives, urticaria, the lot."

"Then you'd be especially prone to the effects of DDT. Did you sleep in the house after it had been disinfected?"

"Yes, I did. Nobody told me not to."

Lord Brighton took over again. "We shall have to consult the Borough Council, the city exterminators, and the factory involved in making the poisonous spray. I had expected to give a purely medical lecture on this case, but it has turned out to touch on environmental problems. We shall send the patient's blood to the Ministry of Agriculture for DDT testing. If this was indeed the accidental cause of her illness, her body will slowly right itself and adjust to any slight incapacity which may eventually remain."

"You mean I may never be completely normal again?" I asked anxiously.

"None of us is normal, nor are we all the same," he replied consolingly. "Age and illness affect us all differently as well. A few of your motor nerves are permanently impaired, Mrs. Cumming, but you'll be able to walk again soon." He came up and helped me up from the chair where I'd been sitting, and handed me my canes. "Go back to the ward now, my dear. Your new nerves are already growing slowly, and at the same time, you are learning to do without some of them. The human body is the only machine with powers of self-adjustment and recuperation. We doctors can only help this natural process. You will cure yourself, Mrs. Cumming. I do not need to examine you further."

I was touched almost to tears as I thanked him warmly. His lecture had done *me* more good than his students. I actually left the room with the help of only one cane instead of two.

In the corridor, the three stretcher cases were still waiting their turn—unattended. As I limped away with both canes in one hand, their eyes followed me, full of silent questioning. I understood their inquiry and their apprehension only too well, and went back to comfort them.

"He's a marvelous lecturer today—a wise old man who knows what illness is all about. You'll feel much better after you've seen him. Look at me; I went in there propped up on two canes; now I can walk with one."

I staggered away again, waving to them with my free hand. All three waved back and smiled.

I was making for the administration office to get Ian's new address. I did not entirely believe in his desire to be altogether alone, and intended to write to him at once.

I was given the address of a rehabilitation center, which sounded better than a home for incurables, at least. I went on up to the ward to write my letter before tea, but before I could do so, Grant came in to see me.

"I've got lots to tell you," he said.

"I've got lots to tell *you*, too!"

We sat by the gas fire in the day room, and he took my hand. We both started speaking at once, as if we hadn't seen each other for weeks. He told me about his adventures in the caves, and how much he'd missed me, and "Dad," whom he referred to as "my father."

"He has a very lonely life. I don't know what

he'll do when I move away and come and live with you," Grant said.

"Grant, you're mad!" I replied. "I've told you we can never be together once I leave the hospital."

He was about to protest violently when a Portuguese maid came in to lay the tables. I pushed him out of the room.

"See you later," I said meaningfully.

I had not had a chance to tell him about the DDT.

Our meeting that evening was strange. For the first time, Grant and I did not make love. We still had lots to tell each other. I told him about Ian's silent disappearance and also about the DDT. Grant's reaction was mixed. He was naturally pleased to know that the cause of my condition—poison—was something that was over and done with weeks ago, and I would slowly get better. But this prospect revived the threat of my departure. Once again, his "mother" was leaving him, and his fear became pathetically obvious. He suddenly crushed me to him, and then let me go abruptly and went over to the coke machine. He stood with his back to me as it dispensed the liquid into a paper cup, but I saw him quickly slip something into his mouth and wash it down.

"What are you doing?"

He looked at me guiltily. "I was taking an 'upper.' I felt too down to make love to you. We've got so little time."

He strode toward me. I stood up furiously and grabbed my cane. My rage was a mixture of hurt female vanity because he needed a stimulant to

turn him on and maternal irritation because he
was doing something I had forbidden him to do.
My roles were getting as mixed as his were. Almost for the first time in my many relationships
with very young men, I felt my age, and that made
it easier to push him away.

"Grant . . . let's leave it till tomorrow. Don't
spoil it all now, at the very end."

"But it's not the end. It's the beginning. We're
going to be together, really together."

He was hugging me, kissing me, clinging to me,
a boy and a man in one.

"But I want you . . . I want you . . ." he kept repeating as he tried to pick me up and carry me
over to the magazine table. "I want you as I first
had you—with your head down, and your nightdress pulled up, and your body all mine."

"Grant, please . . . please . . . I don't want to
make love to you when you're pepped up on pills.
It turns *you* on, but it turns me off. I don't want
you . . . I don't want you like this. I don't want to
make love to a drug addict!" I practically shouted.

He dropped me at that, looked at me desperately, then turned on his heel and walked straight out
of the building. I crawled back to the elevators,
feeling old and tired and ill. It had been our first
row, possibly our last. I wondered if he would
come back.

Next day, I noticed at once that Grant was not
among the students. Mr. Llewellyn-Jones always
turned around automatically to him for my file
during the ward round. Grant was not there, so
another student stepped forward with it.

"Nesbitt's not here today, sir. I've got Mrs. Cumming's file, and the Ministry of Agriculture's report has just come."

"Nesbitt is often 'not here.' What's wrong with the boy?"

"Perhaps he's ill, sir."

"A doctor can't afford to be ill. Now ... where were we?"

He was studying the Ministry of Agriculture's report on my blood sample, then began reading it aloud: "The quantity of DDT found in this sample is high, but not much higher than is to be expected in the blood of all persons living in countries using modern sprays, fertilizers, powders, gases and even fly strips emanating insect repellent ..."

Grant had suddenly appeared in time to hear this last sentence. He too had a paper in his hand.

"Excuse me, sir," he said to Llewellyn-Jones. "I have just been to the Chelsea Council, who told me that their exterminator, who uses this product every day, has come to no harm, and that this is the first case to come to their attention. I also contacted the manufacturers, who maintain that nothing has ever happened to any of their hundreds of factory workers engaged in the production of DDT."

"Thank you, Nesbitt. I wondered where you were." To my relief, his tone was one of pardon, and he continued talking: "Very often, people suffer toxic effects without realizing what is wrong, but I think we can conclude, in this case, that Mrs. Cumming has suffered DDT poisoning. However, we shall never be sure it wasn't an unknown virus."

"In other words," I interpolated, "there's not enough proof for me to be able to sue anybody?"

Mr. Llewellyn-Jones smiled at me. "Mrs. Cumming has a way of coming straight to the point!" He patted my bare legs. "I shall be sorry to lose you, my dear. You have been an interesting patient, but I don't think there's anything more we can do for you."

I had just been dismissed. I was a redundant guinea pig.

He then turned to Grant. "Nesbitt, the head nurse can arrange for Mrs. Cumming's discharge tomorrow." Turning back to me, he said, "You will get well very slowly, Mrs. Cumming. Try to be patient."

He smiled at me and shook my hand.

The little group moved away. Grant and I were left alone, stunned by the rapid conclusion of events. Plans, words, projects, suggestions, resolutions, conclusions—all would have to come later.

"See you tonight" was all I could say to Grant.

The rest of the day was taken up with what seemed like the most hectic and complicated planning in order to move out of one small bed in the corner of a hospital room! Over a month of super-protection with restricted mobility had changed my whole orientation. I, who had always moved about the world rapidly and easily, now found it hard to contemplate getting from one side of London to the other.

I telephoned my brother and then my daughter, thinking I would stay first with one and then with the other. Obviously I could neither stay in the DDT-infested house nor go straight back to Rome until a reasonable convalescent period had elapsed. The hospital case worker came up to see me, offering to admit me to a State convalescent home for a month, and it flashed through my mind that I might be able to join Ian in his rehabilitation center. I sat down at once to write to him.

I was still not sure whether Ian had really wanted such a sudden ending to our relationship or whether he had done it for my sake. My letter was to tell him that I still wanted him in *my* life, but I would quite undertand if he didn't want me in *his*. I asked him to write to me at my brother's. I went downstairs and posted the letter in the front hall. Then I went out onto the doorstep and sniffed the fresh air.

The afternoon dragged until visiting hours. I was impatient for my final secret descent into the outpatient department.

Grant was standing by the tropical fish when I arrived. His pupils were dilated, his manner strange. He looked drugged. Anger surged up in me, but I didn't want to let rage color our last encounter.

"You're not going to leave me!" he blurted out before I could speak.

"I'm leaving the hospital, not you."

"But where are you going?"

"To my brother's. What else can I do? I can't go back to that flat full of DDT."

"Come to Dad and me."

It was the first time he had called his father "Dad" in my presence; that surprised me more than his offer, which touched me deeply.

"How could I? What would Dad think?"

"He would be honored—and happy. He's always afraid I'm going to leave him to live with a girl. He'd love the idea of the girl moving in with *us*."

"But I'm not a girl!"

"You're *my* girl. Come to Dad and me," he said, and looked into my eyes inquiringly.

"Not yet. Maybe I'll visit you later, but first I want to be at my brother's. He'll be out all day and away on weekends, so you can come and see me there sometimes."

"That's not enough. I don't want to lose you to your family, or to that other world. Our flat's quite good enough for you—it's full of beautiful antiques."

I didn't believe him, but I said nothing. I was worrying about the boy's attachment to me, not about his fantasy surroundings. For his sake, I would not see him once I left the hospital.

I was determined to be firm and decisive. Instead, it was Grant who was decisive. He pulled me over to the table, still with its old copy of *The Illustrated London News*, and bent me gently over it with my nightdress raised. He stood behind me, trembling and sighing and murmuring into my ear, as he penetrated me from the back to the utmost limit. Afterwards, he collapsed on top of me and cried his heart out. I cried too. We were still lying over the table in tears when the bell rang. The last visiting hour was over.

Diary entry in the middle of the night. Back in the wide world. Saturday, November 2.

I have weakened and allowed Grant to come for the weekend. My brother is away, and we are in his big double bed. It's the first time we have actually slept together. What a lot you can learn about someone, sleeping beside them! There are men who lie like silent stones, separate and alone. There are those who embrace you all night long, who want to possess you even in sleep. Those who want to be cuddled, those who want to escape, those who don't know what they want. Grant is a troubled soul, a very disturbed boy. He thrashes about, calls out, is never still for a moment. Between his restlessness and my own recurring pain, I am getting very little sleep. In desperation, I got up and decided to sleep alone in my own single bed in the spare room, where I'm writing these few words. I should never have allowed Grant to come and stay.

I was awakened by Grant bursting into the spare room, his hair awry, his eyes full of tears. He threw himself on me, sobbing.

"You left me! You ran out on me! You don't love me!"

I was amazed by the violence of his reaction.

"Why did you leave me? Why?" His tears turned to anger.

"Grant, I'm still ill. I have terrible pains in my legs all night, and I have to get up and walk about. I just didn't want to disturb you."

"I'm sorry. I forgot. When we make love, you never complain—never say I hurt you. You only seem to feel pain when I'm not there."

"That's true in a way. Put it down as a medical observation. 'When sexually aroused, the patient feels no pain.' "

"Then I'll just have to keep fucking you all the time. I'm not going to let you get away from me."

I realized he had had an erection all the time we'd been talking. How could you cry and have an erection? I had no time to ask him. He was inside me, and it was all over too fast for me to enjoy it.

"You didn't come?" He always knew; there was no point in lying.

"It's not the same without *The Illustrated London News*," I said lightly, and we fell asleep again, squashed into the single bed.

"Hello, you're up!" It sounded like an accusation. He was still suffering from a sense of rejection.

Standing in the kitchen doorway, naked, hair tousled, how defenseless he looked.

"Darling, you'll catch your death! I'll get you my brother's dressing gown."

"Kiss me first. I can't go to work without a kiss."

After breakfast, Grant left for the hospital. I asked him not to come and see me for a few days. I had resolved to leave for Rome, in a wheelchair if necessary, before the next weekend. It would be better if we didn't see each other again. I was in no condition to cope with Grant's emotional complications, and there was no point in prolonging a dangerous situation. I would have my checkup, leave Grant a note at the hospital, and fly off before he could get it. A quick, clean break would be best for both of us.

In the afternoon I went out, armed with the rubber-topped walking cane given me by the hospital. It gave me moral and physical support, but I felt slow and awkward as I waited at the bus stop. I finally decided to take a taxi to Regent Street, where I bought a one-way ticket to Rome.

When I got home, my brother opened the front door with the afternoon mail in his hand.

"Anything for me?" I asked.

"No. Were you expecting something?"

"Just a letter from Ian Bromley, my paralyzed doctor friend."

"Oh, yes. How is he?"

"I wish I knew."

"You were rather fond of him, weren't you?"

"In a way—but I fall in and out of love too easily."

"Lucky you!"

The next morning I decided to go to the hospital by bus. The conductor kindly helped me down. I limped slowly along the road, across the square with the dying roses, down the corridor to the back of the hospital.

"May I have your outpatient card, please?"

I fumbled in my handbag and pulled out my brand-new badge of office. I was now an official inhabitant of what had once been my own secret twilight zone.

"Take a seat, will you? Mr. Llewellyn-Jones will see you in a minute."

I sat in the big plastic armchair where Grant and I had made love so many times. It would never happen again. I would give the head porter my farewell note when I left, knowing Grant would not get it till the next day. It would be too late for him to do anything but burst into tears, which I was afraid might happen. But he would get over it, and would one day realize this was the best way to do it—cleanly and quickly.

"Will you come with me, Mrs. Cumming?"

The tropical nurse took me into the consulting room to see the doctor. She didn't seem to remember our previous encounter—when she had come to feed the fish—nor did she know that I could have found that particular consulting room blindfolded.

"Come in, Mrs. Cumming. You're walking quite well!"

"As you predicted, I'm learning to do without what I don't have, and I'm thankful to be able to get around."

"I'll just have a last check on your reflexes. Just take off your stockings—that will be enough."

I smiled slightly, remembering the other garments I'd so often discarded and dropped on this floor.

"Tell me when you begin to feel this."

He worked the hatpin up my foot, then banged the hammer on my ankles and my knees. Nothing happened; there was no reaction. Status quo. I was neither better nor worse.

"Come and see me again in about six months. You'll be walking quite well by then. And don't hesitate to call us if you are worried, or if anything unusual happens."

I put on my stockings, shook his hand, and thanked him warmly.

As I left, I gave a backward glance at the little room—so brightly lit, so sterile, so unlike the warm, dark cubbyhole smelling of sweat and sex and Harris tweed, where we had never dared to turn on the light. I walked slowly to the hospital entrance.

"Would you give this to Mr. Nesbitt tomorrow morning? He's one of the medical students." I handed my note to the porter.

"Do you want me to send it over to the medical school now?"

"No, no—just put it up on the bulletin board so he'll find it when he comes in tomorrow."

"Right. Shall I get you a taxi, ma'am?"

"No, thanks. I think I'll walk for a bit."

I crossed the square with the roses for the last time. Not one of them was still alive.

Dearest Grant,

When you read this through those long lashes, with your cool, gray look, I'll be in midair on the way to Rome. All that will be left in London will be a file saying "Not to be handled by the patient."

I have a guilty feeling, I've used you to satisfy my ego and my body. Young lovers are the ultimate ego trip, like having children. I shall probably miss you more than you miss me. You'll just be furious with me for disappearing. Get drunk, smoke pot, take a Speed, and forget me. But please get off the junk after that.

Write to me if you feel like it, but I'll understand if you don't. I shall still love you, miss you, think of you. Forget me, forgive me, and be happy.

Anne

I arrived back in Rome to find a pile of mail, a film of dust, and my telephone ringing. My life had begun again. My feet were still partially paralyzed, my hands were weak and fumbling. I walked with difficulty.

Rudi had sent me a beautiful silver-topped cane and some good advice from New York:

Get out and about, Anne. You've always been an example of vital energy and stoic good cheer. Don't let us down now.

R.

In November, and again in February, the rains hit Rome. They sweep right across Italy like monsoons, flooding the highways, destroying bridges and dams, causing havoc and dismay; and then they are forgotten. The sun comes out again.

I watched the November rains through my windows for the first few days, inert and listless. Friends came and went. My little maid called every morning. Charles and his wife were duly concerned, and my daughter Vanessa came in to see me whenever she could. She was pregnant again, and I tried to be happy for her.

Grant wrote to me every day—long, touching love letters. One of the saddest things about them was that they were not really addressed to me—the real me—they were addressed to some mythical, romantic heroine, not even to a mother-figure. I found it hard to reply. But I did, although any activity was a strain at the time.

My brother forwarded my mail from London, among which was an envelope that said, "Return to sender, addressee unknown here." It was my letter to Ian. Where was he? Perhaps he had gone to a different convalescent home, or maybe his life had ceased. I had no idea where to write to him. He would never know I had wanted to join him, that I still loved him.

Grant probably went back to drugs. At least I think so. It's easier for me to think of it like that. I feel less guilty if I remember that the problem was already there, so the blame does not all fall on me. Like the November rain, it falls everywhere.

I was watching the rain flood my terrace and wondering if I ought to go out and unblock the drainpipe, clogged with geranium leaves, when the postman appeared with a registered letter. The writing was unknown to me—a slightly illiterate hand. On the reverse side was the sender's name: George Percy Nesbitt—Grant's father.

There were three things inside. A school medal for long-distance running, a letter from Dad, and a newspaper clipping. I read the clipping first:

A young medical student, Grant Nesbitt, was found dead on Monday evening in the outpatient department of a London teaching hospital. He died of an overdose of heroin. He was not known to be a habitual user of heavy drugs, and it was not clear whether his death was the result of an accident or suicide. His body was found in an armchair near a tank of tropical fish. There was no note. The coroner's verdict was "Death by misadventure."

It was some time before I could bring myself to read Dad's letter.

Dear Lady Anne,
That's how my boy used to talk of you. I know you loved him and would want to know what has occurred, so I'm sending you the news, together with a keepsake. He once said to me, "Dad, if anything ever happens to me, send this to Anne. Tell her to keep running through life in spite of her legs." I didn't egsactly know what he meant at the time. He won it at Grammer School. He was a clever boy, but never really happy. I'm ever so grateful to you for having been interested in my boy. It meant a lot to him. I'm a bit lonely now, but life goes on, don't it?
Yours,
George Percy Nesbitt

Yes, Dad, life goes on. I have hung the medal for long-distance running on a silver chain. One day I may have the courage to wear it.

7 ✺ Barcelona Blues

It took me much longer to get over Grant's death than it did to get over my illness. But I did get over it—one does. I never expected, however, to have a very young lover again. But I did that too. I couldn't seem to kick the habit.

I spent the winter of 1971-1972 in Rome, hobbling through life like a ninety-year-old. I was fifty-five. Vanessa, with Matthew, came in to see me on my birthday, and Charles and his wife brought a cake. It was a very quiet and rather sad occasion, so different from my usual parties. I had suddenly grown old. Everything was an effort. My friends all rallied around, but to bring me their sympathy, not gaiety and laughter. My lovers came to see me, but they were suddenly just good friends. I wouldn't have wanted it any other way. I couldn't envisage sex with men who had known me previously. Grant had taken me as he found me—a cripple. He had loved me as I was because he knew no other Anne.

There were two bright stars on the horizon:

Vanessa was expecting another baby, and Evaristo came back into my life.

"I want to bring you a Christmas present," his voice came over the phone. "What do you need?" He had heard about my illness from Franca.

"But I'm not celebrating Christmas this year, except to go quietly to Vanessa's in the country. I can't go shopping, or to the theater, or out to parties. I'm suddenly an old lady, Evaristo. All I need is an old-age pension!"

"Then that's just what I'll bring you. I once gave you a rainbow—now I'll bring you the pot of gold."

Evaristo arrived with a Roman amphora—one of those huge terra-cotta jars. It was filled to the brim with chocolate money wrapped in gold foil. He emptied it all over me as I lay on the sofa. There must have been at least a hundred pieces. I was covered with them; the floor was covered with them. Pieces rolled under the furniture, to be discovered months later. I laughed and laughed until I cried. Then I laughed again.

"I'm going to start a trust fund for your old age. All your lovers will subscribe $10.00 a month. Anyone can afford that. You'll be a millionairess in no time. Now, how many lovers have you got? A thousand? Two thousand?"

We began enumerating my ex-lovers, starting fifty years ago with the schoolboy with whom I had played hide-and-seek, and who used to kiss me passionately behind the long velvet curtains of his mother's stately home. Evaristo had a funny comment about all of them. He gave them nicknames if

I hadn't already done so. It took us hours. I felt like a new woman when he finally left.

Evaristo came to see me often. He refused to treat me like a cripple. He took me out and around in his little cinquecento Fiat. He was a terrible driver, and I was petrified, but it was better than being bored. It was boredom that had been making me feel so old.

After Christmas he came to get me at Vanessa's and took me down to Sperlonga. Everything was just as I'd left it when I took off for London. There was sand all over the floor, and beach towels were hanging out to dry. I had expected to be back there in September, so had put none of my summer things away.

"What shall I do with this Chinese kite?" he asked as we began tidying things up.

"We'd better give it away. I'll never be able to run along the beach with it again. Maybe I'll never be able to get down to the beach at all—there are too many steps."

"Anne, don't let me ever hear you make a negative remark like that again. Whenever things are difficult for you, psychologically or otherwise, I'll be there to help you."

And he always has been. Evaristo is not only a rainbow, he's also a pot of gold.

At the end of January, Vanessa had her baby— another little boy. She called him Mark, hoping to have two more and call them Luke and John. She was, however, quite ill after Mark's birth, and had to stay on in the hospital. Suddenly I found myself looking after Matthew for two months when I was barely able to look after myself.

The struggle of dealing with a five-year-old child of extraordinary vivacity and unusual naughtiness would have tried the patience of a saint and worn out an Olympic champion. I'd heard that an athlete was once asked to follow and copy every movement of a small child throughout its day; the athlete fell exhausted to the ground by early afternoon. There were times when I did the same, but I had to carry on. Probably the effort of will saved my life and sanity. Although I often shed tears of fatigue and lay prostrate beside him in the spare room without strength even to stagger to my own bed, Matthew and I survived the ordeal. My daughter recovered, and, with the resilience and ebullience of youth, went back to her home in the country with a child under each arm. It was already spring. The winter of my discontent was over.

I went to my Rome doctor for a checkup. My feet and hands were slowly making progress. I had been told it would be a year before I could expect the motor nerves to grow back again; now six months had passed, and there was distinct improvement. It was unlikely at my age that all the nerves would renew themselves. However, I could type again, even though my hands had little strength, and I could walk quite a distance on my wooden feet, although I was easily thrown off balance. I couldn't yet go out without my cane.

"I think you must make an effort to get back to

work," my Rome doctor said.

"Oh, but I can't, I can't!" I heard myself cry. "You've no idea what a strain my job is. I have to do a lot of running around."

"Then do something else," he said.

Although physically improving, I was still suffering from the traumatic shock of serious illness. There is something biblical about it. You have been overwhelmed by fate, scourged by plague, suddenly struck down. It takes a good deal of courage and sustained effort to get back into life.

I asked a friend for some translation work, and my morale improved as I sat at my typewriter. My feet tingled and were numb, but I forced myself to walk everywhere, even though it took much longer; and I denied myself the luxury of taxis. I was determined to look like a normal woman, even if I didn't feel like one.

By summer I was feeling quite spry and eager to get out and about. Although I found it difficult to drag myself up the steep steps of the buses, I got around quite well, and the tempo of my life was back to normal. My world had been restricted to the four walls of my home, but now I felt conscious of the world outside again.

At this point, an Italo-Franco-German production company proposed that I go to Barcelona on a film about a handsome murderer who could only go to bed with virgins in their wedding gowns. He systematically kidnapped, raped and killed them before their new husbands could consummate the marriages. It was a horror movie, concocted of white satin and bridal veils dripping with blood, a challenge to any publicist, who would have a hard time making it sound like a grade A movie in any language. It sounded like just the sort of thing I needed to really get me back on my feet.

On a hot sunny day in late June 1972, I set off for Barcelona by Iberia Airlines. I had gotten used to ordering a wheelchair when I traveled by plane. It was a marvelous form of subsidiary VIP transport. One swept through the police and customs, whizzed down those endless airport corridors, carrying all your overweight in-flight bags on your knees. It was an ideal way to travel, and I had decided never to abandon it. This time, however, I had to prove myself in front of an entire film crew. If I was able to do a job again, I must be able to get there to do it. I felt honor bound to walk onto the plane.

I still walked with the silver-topped cane that Rudi had given me, my feet stiff wooden blocks with permanent pins and needles, and I had difficulty negotiating stairs. I was carrying a typewriter, an overnight bag, my camp stool, a camera and a summer raincoat.

"Would you mind if I leaned on your arm?" I asked the handsome Italian star of the picture, a young man I had helped to launch a couple of years ago.

"Of course, *cara*. Now it's your turn to lean on *me*."

A basically sweet, simple boy, he had not yet forgotten his modest origins or acquired the real panache of star quality—that dash of ruthless determination and driving ambition that lifted one out of the grade B movie into the big time. He was probably too nice to ever get there, but this was his big chance. He had been the lover of a famous female star who had moved on to better things, leaving him with his beautiful face, the wrong reputation, and little talent. I liked him, and regretted that I no longer had the strength to undertake an on-location romance. I felt like an elderly star in retirement myself as far as sex was concerned.

We arrived in Barcelona on a sultry summer afternoon, and were put at a second-class hotel off Las Ramblas. I set up my office, contacted the local press, and tried to think up a publicity stunt to celebrate our arrival. I hadn't been in Barcelona since running away just after the war in a jeep with Charles, the man who became my second husband. Both Barcelona and myself had changed a great deal since then.

"Come on, darling, let's go for a ramble in Las Ramblas!"

It was Bruno. The best thing about this film was the fact that I had been able to get my busy-bee, bearded ex-lover the job of still photographer. He might even have time to rush in and out of my bedroom between other rush jobs and get me into working order again. Bruno could fit more things into one day and more women into one night than anyone I knew.

"All right, Bruno. Just let me find my cane."

"You've got to learn to walk without it. Come on, now. Use my arm."

So I went out for the first time without my silver-topped cane, which had become my moral support.

Starting a new job is always nerve-racking; one feels insecure and inefficient and tends to over-prove one's work. I tried too hard in Barcelona and got nowhere. It was the middle of the summer, everyone was intent on going to the beach, taking long afternoon siestas, and eating outside until all hours of the night. Nobody even said *mañana*, they all said "next week" or "next month." I was forced to relax and take it easy too.

We were working in the rather ugly summer palace that Franco never used and which was sensibly hired out for public occasions. Our opening shot was a huge wedding reception and this palace was the ideal setting. The wedding guests wandered through the marble halls and out on the lawns among the flowering camellia bushes. The only trouble was that the Spanish extras looked too Spanish for an international film, and a call was sent out for some foreigners. I was called in to play the bride's mother!

"All right, but I insist on having a wide picture hat and long gloves," I said when I accepted the role.

The costume designer combed the city for a big straw hat but could only find a rather lugubrious black one made for a Spanish funeral. I picked some white camellias from the garden and pinned them on the brim. From time to time, Bruno renewed them for me as they wilted in the heat.

"The blood! We've lost the blood!" went up the cry on the third day's shooting.

As the bride went upstairs to change, our hero was to abduct her, carry her into an attic, rape her on an old iron bedstead, and leave her stabbed to the heart in a pool of blood, while he joined the guests again downstairs as if nothing had happened. Nice family entertainment: a U-certificate movie.

The makeup man from Rome had forgotten to bring his artificial blood, and it was suggested that someone go to the local butcher's and get some real blood. The Spanish starlet playing the bride-of-the-day promptly had hysterics, refusing to be covered in real blood. The scene had to be postponed.

"You'd think a race brought up on bullfights, civil wars and Garcia Lorca would be less squeamish," Bruno whispered to me. "Silly little bitch! She needs a good fuck."

"Now, Bruno, lay off. She's the girl friend of one of the Spanish producers. We don't want you being dismissed and sent back to Rome."

We broke early and went to eat shrimps washed down with amontillado on Las Ramblas at an open-air café near the flower stalls, where birds and small mammals were sold in little wicker cages.

"Would you like a canary from the Canary Islands?" Bruno asked me. "Or a parrot from Peru?"

"No, I'd much rather have roast chicken," I replied.

We wandered off into the hinterland behind the port to find the restaurant where chickens were grilled outside in the street while good-looking Catalan whores paraded in front, and sailors darted in to suspicious-looking chemists to buy contraceptives. It was very late by the time we got back to the hotel, but Bruno insisted on coming into my room. He was always a rapid worker, and I was left at the starting post—but it didn't matter. I was obliging an old friend, rather than seeking new orgasms, and at least I had come out of my sexual retirement.

The next day we started the wedding scene all over again, with artificial blood flown in specially from Madrid. Barcelona, it seemed, only had real blood, and the actors couldn't face it. The new blood looked like old blood, but it made the little Spanish actress quite happy, and she lay back in her white satin and veils and allowed herself to be killed and liberally sprayed with it while we were all drinking fake champagne on the lawn. As soon as the hero-villain had killed the bride, he had to join the reception to establish his alibi. Then came *my* little scene—I went into the house to look for my daughter, found her in a pool of blood, and fainted dead away.

"Now, Señora Anne, don't forget to reach the chalk mark before you keel over," the Spanish cameraman reminded me. "You don't want to be out of frame for your big moment."

It was surprisingly difficult to make myself fall down when for months I had been learning to stand up. My balance was still affected by my paralyzed feet, and I normally fell over very easily. Now, I couldn't make myself do it convincingly, and I needed twelve takes before I got it right. Then, with a sigh of relief, I took off my hat and gloves and went back to my usual job. My part was over, and the film went on to the next bride.

An Italian starlet was flown in for the next sequence. On arrival, she caught influenza.

"Spanish flu, I suppose," Bruno commented to me that evening as we took the cable car up to Tibidabo on the hill behind Barcelona. We had gone there to escape the heat of the city, wander around the fun fair, and eat at one of the open-air restaurants. I was using my cane again to get around, but I felt much better and could walk quite far. Production gave me a car for running around during the day, and I went over to Cadaques with the production manager to set up the next location shots.

Following the sequence with the Italian starlet, we had a German starlet arriving to play a tourist on holiday who marries a local sardine fisherman. This had been written in to secure the German market—a typical co-production tactic. At the very end of the picture, we were to fly to Paris to work in the French sequence. Quite a comprehensive common-market movie. I had to see that all the stars got write-ups in their own as well as other countries.

"We'll have to jump ahead to the next sequence if our flu victim doesn't get better quickly," the production manager confided to me. "We can't waste time."

"It means we'll have all three starlets here together," I worried. "I hope they won't try to upstage one another and tear each other's hair out in the hotel."

"You'll have to keep them all busy with press conferences and photo sessions."

"Sure ... and our hero or some of the bride-grooms can take care of their nights."

In the end, Bruno took them all on single-handed, and I was happy for his help. We now enjoyed friendship with only intermittent love-making. We have long since passed the stage of jealousy, and it amused me to see him buzz around the bedrooms like a busy mosquito.

Cadaques is a beautiful white fishing village, but it was quite difficult to find angles not yet ruined by tourism or the artists'-colony touch. I found the only genuine thing there—a boy just starting his career in the Spanish militia, with the shiny black patent leather tricorn hat of the Guardia Civil.

I had moved into our hotel in Cadaques two days before the rest of the crew to get things organized. It was the weekend, and I took time off to bask in the sun and swim, which was the best thing I could do for my legs. I also brushed up on my Spanish by sitting on the seawall in the evenings reading Garcia Lorca aloud in the semidarkness.

"Señora, excuse me for interrupting you," said a voice on my second night there, just as I was say-ing *"tengo un cavallo y una flor!"* with a flourish of my hand into the warm night air. "Señora, are you all right?"

I looked up to see a dark young Murillo face un-der a tricorn hat. He might have stepped out of a picture from the Prado.

"Excuse me, Señora," he said again. "I don't think you should be sitting here alone, at this time of the evening, calling out in a loud voice. Who were you calling to? There's nobody around." He looked puzzled.

"I was reading aloud. I got carried away." Thinking I would impress him, I added, "It's Garcia Lorca."

"Aha! Garcia Lorca?" The Murillo face turned into a more somber Zurbaran. "Why would a beautiful lady be reading that red revolutionary politician?"

"He's a poet, not a politician," I protested. "Poetry goes above and beyond politics. You're not a fascist, surely? At your age?"

"The Generalissimo has done a lot for my country."

I looked at him in amazement. It was 1972 and Franco was not yet dead, but the boy looked young and vital and free-thinking.

"Sit down and take off that ridiculous hat. I'll read you a poem."

His face clouded over, and he looked angry. "This is a fine uniform, and I'm not allowed to take off any part of it when I'm on duty."

I realized I was up against Spanish pride and political intolerance in the shape of a handsome young man. My own political feelings were considerably mitigated by his good looks, the warm evening, and the fact that I hadn't had a new young man since my illness. Little Bruno and my recurrent truck driver didn't count. They were old friends who had been keeping me in touch with life—which is not quite the same as a new adventure.

"Well, sit down anyway. It's your duty to guard

your country against subversive foreigners. I'm a nonviolent anarchist, but I might just turn violent at any minute."

He looked even more puzzled and glowering under that black patent leather brim, and I could see that a sense of humor was not going to be one of his attributes. However, he sat down.

"You are not like a Spanish woman," he said. "A Spanish woman would be afraid to sit alone with a man."

"Really? Well, now, I'm afraid to sit alone *without* a man," I exclaimed with feigned innocence.

There was still no hint of a smile, but he moved a little nearer, picking up the book that was on the wall between us.

"You have no husband?" he asked.

"Not here. Not even a lover," I replied sadly.

He put the book down on the far side of him and moved a bit closer still. Things were shaping up nicely, I thought.

"It's really a very handsome uniform," I said, touching the thick stuff on his thigh. I could feel the muscle tighten underneath. "I just don't like men in hats." I ran my finger up the coarse wool, but stopped before the groin.

He glanced quickly around him, but there was no one in sight, and we were beyond the range of the street lighting. He took off his hat and laid it on top of my book. He looked very young and defenseless without it.

"It is a bit hot to wear a hat," he said, wiping his forehead on his sleeve.

I remembered that I had a handkerchief in my

pocket, so I took it out and leaned forward to dab
at the thin line of sweat around his thick, dark
hairline. His hands went around my waist as I
leaned over him.

"Your pistol is getting in the way," I said after
he had kissed me. "Could you take that off too?"

The heavy revolver was laid beside the hat and
the book. I was wearing a thin pink sweatshirt,
and his hands now went underneath it. I took a
deep breath, and my nipples tingled as his rough
hands closed over them. His tongue went between
my teeth this time.

"Shall we take a little walk?" he said thickly
when we came up for air.

There was a path that led along the cliff to the
next cove; I had taken it that morning to go for a
swim. The going was not easy, and I still limped
badly. I hadn't brought my cane with me either.

"I've had an accident and can't walk far," I said,
afraid the word "illness" would put him off. "Shall
we go straight back to my hotel?"

He looked worried. "I can't be seen going in
with you to your hotel."

"Don't worry, there's a side door. I used it this
morning. The back stairs lead straight up to my
room."

"There might be a maid around or something,"
he said hesitantly. He might have been young and
hesitant, but he couldn't keep his hands off me. I
could tell he hadn't had a woman for a long time.
His hands had left my breasts, and one of them
pushed down inside the waistband of my skirt.
I sucked in my stomach to make room for it, but

he was having difficulty with the elastic of my panties.

"Wait a minute," I murmured, and swiftly slipped my panties off under cover of the skirt and stuffed them into my pocket.

His hand found the soft labia instantly, and his middle finger slipped straight into my vagina. I was just about to unzip his fly when we heard footsteps. It was dark, but not that dark.

I quickly brushed away his hand and smoothed my skirt. An elderly couple walked by. I realized they were not much older than I was, but it was not a moment when I wanted to think about my age.

"Look, I'll tell you what we'll do. I'll go back to my hotel, pick up the key at the desk, and go up to my room. If the coast is clear, I'll hang my beach towel out of the window. Then you can come up the back stairs."

"Which hotel is it?"

"The Hotel Playa. Walk back into the village behind me, and I'll go in by the side door so you'll see where it is. The stairs are on the right as you come in. I'm on the third floor—room 35."

We walked slowly back to the hotel, first of all side by side, then, when the houses started, a few yards apart, but still talking to each other. He told me he was twenty years old, his father had been in the Guardia Civil before him, and had only just retired. His parents lived in Salamanca.

"Why have you come so far away from home?"

"They always send us to a part of the country where we have no connections. It's easier to keep law and order when you don't know anybody. How could I penalize my own people?"

The whole setup sounded alien and unpleasant, but one's political principles and beliefs melt like butter in a warm bed. Not that I take butter to bed with me—I use baby oil instead.

That night there was no need for any lubricant. I had to get up and get my beach towel from the windowsill and put it under me to save the sheets. After the third time, I got up and washed myself, thinking I might have a rest—but I was wrong. He made love to me another three times before ten o'clock, then he put on his uniform again.

"I have to report to the police station at ten o'clock," he said. "I'll say I've been on special investigations until now."

"It's true in a way," I sighed, wondering if I had the strength to get up and go down for a late-night paella.

"Will you hang out the towel again tomorrow?" he asked.

"Yes. At about the same time?"

"Please. I'm on night duty all this week. I don't get up till afternoon."

"Just as well! I have work to do during the day. You'd exhaust me if I saw too much of you!"

He clicked his heels and saluted and allowed himself a little smile. I heard his boots clatter down the uncarpeted back stairs. I decided against dinner; I was too tired to move.

Bruno had turned up in Cadaques with the rest of the crew and the German starlet. The Italian starlet was to follow when her influenza was better.

"Can you go on keeping them both happy?" I asked.

"They're not as spoiled as you are," he replied. "They don't expect it six times a night!"

"Six times in three hours, Bruno, and he was not faking it."

Bruno agreed it was some kind of record, and, although Manuel didn't keep it up all week, his Kinsey average was well above par. As soon as I put out my beach towel in the evenings, he was up the back stairs in a flash and into my bed. I can't say his love-making was inspired or imaginative, but what it lacked in quality, it made up for in quantity. It was just what I needed to get my circulation going again, both physically and mentally. I had been sexually in the doldrums since Grant's death, which was doing me no good, nor would Grant have wanted it. His last message to me had been to keep running through life in spite of my legs. Up until now, I had been mainly limping.

I had a letter from Rudi, who was spending a lonely holiday in Austria with his father. He had also been in sexual retirement and was a little dispossessed since Tom's marriage. My postcard in answer to him showed a young girl behind the iron grille of a typical Spanish window, with a young man passing a rose through the bars.

I wrote: "I don't know whether centuries of keeping women out of reach has anything to do with it—but the pent-up sex drive of the Spaniards is almost alarming."

During the day I was mainly out on the set, sitting beside Bruno on my little camp stool. In the long waits between takes, while the electricians and grips got things organized, we gossiped and exchanged sexual recipes like two cooks preparing nightly banquets, although actually we were only having sexual snacks to keep ourselves going. Our affairs on the side were not as important to us as our friendship.

"How's the German starlet?" I asked Bruno. "Is she giving you an insight into Germany today? Don't forget that fornication is communication!"

"The only thing she's communicated to me so far is her own driving ambition—but she's good in bed."

"What do you mean by good in bed, Bruno?"

"No holds barred. She doesn't mind what she does, and she enjoys doing it. What do *you* mean by it?"

"I mean somebody who really wants me. It's the strength of the desire that matters. You can work out the details later."

Our conversation was interrupted by an accident. We were sitting on the beach watching the fishermen pull in the nets. The bridegroom in this scene—the sardine fisherman—was played by a dashing young Spanish actor who had obviously never seen a sardine except in a tin. He was helping the "extras," all the real local fishermen, pull in the nets. He was just being shot in close-up when he let out a scream, lifted up a bare leg with trousers rolled up to the knees, and looked at his foot.

A crowd gathered around him, and someone

helped him limp up to the dry sand. He had been paddling up to his knees and had stepped on a stinging ray, one of those dangerous little fish embedded in the sand of the Mediterranean. His foot was already swelling.

"Bruno, get me a photo of this," I said ruthlessly. "It's just the kind of thing that makes good copy."

I then offered to take the actor to the doctor, ordered a production car, and was genuinely sympathetic. It's a very painful thing and can mean staying in bed for a day or two unless you can get a Fargan injection. It's like a snake bite, so I bent down and sucked his foot before helping him up the beach. I still have Bruno's photo of me doing it—which appeared in all the local papers at the time. I managed to get it printed on the front page.

This was our second interruption in the shooting schedule, but this one only lasted twenty-four hours. The young actor was back on the beach to finish pulling in the nets the next day, hobbling with his foot bound up—but the show had to go on. In the meantime, the production manager had quickly sent for the German starlet, and the lost twenty-four hours had been spent shooting her scene on the seawall—where she waited for her lover to come back from the sea.

We then broke for the weekend, and the village prepared for the wedding sequence. All the local populace was to be used as extras, the streets were to be strewn with flowers, and my Manuel was warned that he'd have to work both day and night shifts in order to help keep back the crowds.

"You're going to have a busy weekend, Bruno,"

I said before dinner that night. "The Italian starlet has turned up from Barcelona, much rested after her flu. You've got the two girls on your hands again."

"Don't worry. I can always tell the one I'm not with that I'm in the darkroom at the local photographers, printing up her pictures. That always keeps them happy. Never underestimate the vanity of women. Now get upstairs and hang out your own beach towel!"

Manuel joined me as punctually as usual. He hung his black patent leather hat on the bedpost, his uniform dropped carelessly to the floor, but he put his pistol carefully on the night table. It was a repeating pistol.

"Manuel, if you've got Sunday off, let's go swimming together," I suggested.

"I don't think I should be seen with you. We're not supposed to get involved with female tourists."

"Nonsense! What else are the police for?"

In the end we agreed to spend Sunday just along the coast, where Salvador Dali has his villa. I went by bus, and Manuel joined me on his bicycle. He was out of uniform for the first time, in a smart white *guaya vera* shirt with little white pleats down the front. He was very handsome, I was very lucky, and we were both happy. I invited him to lunch in the big hotel there, which I knew would impress him much more than the little restaurant by the beach. We parked his bicycle in their car park, swam in their pool, and made love in one of the dressing rooms. Then we went back out again and fell asleep in the sun by the blue-tiled pool under the Mediterranean sky. When the sun began to set, we walked along the coast and found a secluded place under a pine tree. I unzipped his fly and admired that view, as well as the sea view. He was uncircumcised, like most Latins, and had a wonderful throb when he came. I went down on him in front of the orange sunset, and then he spent a long time stroking my pubic hair, refusing to go further until he himself was ready for another round. Then he ran his finger down, excited me to the crying-out point, and jumped on top of me at the last moment. We rolled over several times, and his white shirt got covered with grass stains before we had finished.

I fell asleep in the bus on the way back to Cadaques, and went up to my room exhausted. Manuel followed me up there, insisting on making love again, and I began to wonder if I had bitten off more than I could chew.

"Thank God you're on day *and* night duty next week, Manuel," I murmured into his neck.

Bruno and I compared notes on Monday in a spirit of friendly rivalry. He had had a busy weekend too. In fact, the whole village had had a busy weekend. They had paved the streets with flowers, as if for their local fiesta, and everyone had ironed his best dress to appear in our new wedding scene. Our handsome Spanish bridegroom of the day, with the German starlet in her white wedding dress on his arm, was to come out of the church, walk through the crowd across a carpet of flowers, and see his bride abducted before he could join her in the waiting car. Our Italian hero-murderer was disguised as the chauffeur, and had to start up the car with the bride inside and pull away from the curb before the bridegroom could get inside with her. After this, there was a wild car chase, but the murderer got away with the bride, took her to an abandoned farmhouse, raped her in the hayloft, and left her hanging from a beam.

The director was taking his job very seriously, but I was still afraid the film was going to turn out comic. I said so to the Spanish co-producers, who had come down from Madrid in a festive mood and had given us a big party on the Wednesday night before they went back to Madrid. The hotel complained that they hadn't paid the bill for the party before leaving.

"Bruno, I have a feeling this is one of those films where we're going to get stranded in a foreign country without being paid our last week's salary and with no plane tickets home."

We were sitting in the hayloft waiting for the German starlet to be hung. After this scene, she would be flown back to Germany, and we would continue with the Italian starlet, who was to be married in the same church, but to a different bridegroom, and then raped and murdered in a railway sleeping car as she left on her honeymoon. Our Italian hero, dressed as a sleeping car attendant this time, was to lock the bridegroom into his little service compartment while he went along the train corridor to commit the murder. The train sequence would be shot back in Barcelona again, so this would be our last weekend in Cadaques.

I had planned a quiet last weekend with Manuel, whom I now saw mainly on the set, as he and the other Guardia Civil were keeping back the real visiting tourists who were *not* in the scene. Manuel was longing to be in the film himself in his swashbuckling uniform, so I suggested to the director that he should be seen in long shot, directing the traffic as wedding guests arrived at the church. He was as pleased as Punch, and I got Bruno to take photos of him with the Italian starlet as well. That night he dashed up the back stairs between shifts and during his dinner hour to thank me. That was on Thursday night. On Friday, I got a telegram from Rudi: "Arriving Friday night to join you."

I asked hotel management for a single room for Rudi. They replied that there wasn't a bed to be had in the whole of Cadaques that midsummer weekend. I hoped perhaps Rudi meant the next Friday, but when I got back from work, there he was—lying on my bed.

I hurried to the window and took in the beach towel, now permanently hanging there, to give me time to talk with Rudi.

"Rudi, darling, why this sudden decision to join me?"

"I was bored and lonely. I thought you wouldn't mind. Don't you enjoy my company?"

"Yes, Rudi, I do. But it's an inconvenient moment."

"My treasure!" he exclaimed. "So now I've become 'an inconvenient moment' to you? Is it possible our relationship has come to that?"

"Rudi ... *You* chose to leave me, so now I reserve the right to choose when you're to come back!"

He looked crestfallen. I felt sorry, but Rudi has a habit of moving in on people. He likes *them* to rent the apartment, organize the holiday, plan the journey—and once *they* have taken the responsibility, he moves in on it. However, I still loved him, he was lonely without Tom, and I forgave him as usual.

"All right, Rudi, you can stay, since there's no other bed in the whole of Cadaques, but I'm sharing this one with a dashing carabineer. You'll have to take a long walk occasionally and leave us to it."

"You mean I can't share your lover?"

"No, Rudi. This time, definitely no."

I went downstairs and out onto the street to see if I could find Manuel and explain the situation. He was nowhere in sight, so I went to the little restaurant where he usually had his meals. Perhaps he was having an early dinner before coming to see me. Sometimes I ate there myself, at another table so no one would guess we knew each other. But Manuel was nowhere to be seen. I went out and walked around the town a little. The beach towel was not out on the windowsill, so it was unlikely that Manuel would go up and find Rudi resting on my bed.

I was wrong. Manuel now felt so sure of himself and our time together was so short that he had gone up to see if I was in my room.

"Come in," Rudi had answered in English when he heard a knock. The dialogue had ended there, as Rudi spoke no Spanish. Manuel had opened the door, seen Rudi on my bed, and asked where I was. This much Rudi understood, as my name was involved. He did the best he could under the circumstances. He explained to Manuel in elaborate gestures that I had gone out, but would be coming back to bed again. He ended by patting the bed beside him and then his own chest, finally pointing at Manuel. What he meant was that Manuel was to take his place in the bed and he, Rudi, would go out. Manuel misunderstood the signals and thought he was being given his marching orders because Rudi had taken his place. He took out his revolver and shot into the air through the open window.

When I got back, I found Rudi under the bed.

"Thank God you've come. Your lover's a madman! He tried to shoot me."

He told me the complete story. I couldn't help laughing.

"What's so funny, I'd like to know?" Rudi asked, seriously offended. "I might have been killed!"

"It's just that Manuel has no sense of humor—only Spanish pride. And you've got to admit that it's funny at fifty-five to be the heroine of a *crime passionnel*."

"You're too busy writing your own personal publicity," Rudi grumbled, brushing his trousers. It had been very dusty under the bed. "I'm getting out of here at once."

"Well, it might be a good idea. I'll phone the hotel in Barcelona. Go on and wait for me there . . . but separate rooms, Rudi. Separate rooms!"

I helped Rudi with his packing and put him into

a taxi to take him to the station, which was several miles away. Then I went to look for Manuel.

I couldn't find him anywhere. I even went to the police station, expecting to find him on duty. I could have invented a story about a lost passport or something, in order to speak to him privately. No sign. Finally I started walking about the village again. I usually bumped into him, wheeling his bicycle.

"Manuel!" I shouted when I saw him at last. He was sitting on the seawall where I had first met him, his bicycle beside him.

He turned his head to look at me, but didn't speak. He looked just as glowering under his black hat as he had when I had first seen him. Why didn't he answer me?

"Manuel," I said, going up to him rather bravely—after all, he might shoot at me too. "What's the matter? I can explain everything."

It sounded like a bad film script. He still didn't speak.

"Manuel, Rudi's just an old friend. He hasn't been my lover for years. He doesn't go to bed with women anymore, either."

"You mean he's a *maricon*?"

"Yes, he's a homosexual, although I don't usually like to label people."

"You think I'll believe that? *He's* no homosexual—and you're just a whore!"

I could see I was fighting a losing battle. Manuel did not have the light touch and never would. He meant what he was saying. In his eyes, I was a whore.

There was no reason to try to work it out. I
didn't feel guilty. We had served each other's purpose, and now the romance was over.

I spent the weekend packing; we were leaving
for Barcelona on Sunday night. I put my beach
towel back on the windowsill, but I didn't hear the
clatter of boots on the stairs. The tricorn hat was
not to hang on my bedpost again. I left a little note
at the restaurant where Manuel ate:

Dear Manuel,

Don't think all foreigners are whores. When
you're older, you may be more tolerant toward me.
Thank you for bringing me back to life, and I'm
sorry if you feel I brought you lust without love.
It's not strictly true. Lust doesn't make you cry. I
shall shed a tear when I leave Cadaques. You have
my eternal gratitude and affection.

Anne

Back in Barcelona, everything was bedlam.
There were unpaid bills, and our salaries were not
forthcoming. Telegrams to Italy, telephone calls to
Madrid, a strike among the Spanish crew—but we
foreigners were trapped. Shooting went on just
the same; it had to. We borrowed a train that was
sidetracked, and thanked God for nationalized railways. The Spanish government gave anything it
could gratis to encourage films being shot in
Spain, and the railway personnel loved being in on
the deal. The Italian starlet was given flowers by
the stationmaster, and we had our lunches free at

the station refreshment counter, but it looked as if the film would fold.

"I think I've arrived just in time to take you on a holiday," Rudi said. "Let's go to Sitges."

Sitges was a "gay" resort, but I felt I'd had all that and Spain too. If I was going to pay for a holiday, I wanted it elsewhere. To add to our troubles, Bruno had the clap.

"Bruno, did you get it before or after going to bed with me?" I asked.

"Don't worry, Anne. I must have got it recently. There was a moment when the German fräulein left and the Italian signorina had her period. I thought I'd better just slip in a Spanish señorita before we were run out of the country for bad debts."

"Bruno, you're incorrigible. How do you do it?"

"People in glass houses . . ."

"Oh, dear, I see what you mean. Do you think there's a lot of clap around?"

"I don't know, but you'd better come with me to the clinic."

I had my blood test and my swab test and waited nervously for the results. The doctor in the clinic asked me when I'd last had a period. I realized for the first time that I didn't menstruate anymore. I hadn't even noticed or missed it since my illness. My sex drive was just the same, and perhaps fucking would be all the better, now that the last lingering fears of pregnancy were gone forever. I didn't have the clap, either. That was a big relief! I began to look forward to a new affair and a new job.

The film folded quietly. We got the last shots in

the can, paid the hotel bills out of our own money, and were given IOUs promising us refunds and back salary in Rome. They were going to cut the sequence in Paris and rewrite it to be filmed in the studios at Cinecittà. They wouldn't need me, and I didn't mind. I felt fine. I wasn't using my cane anymore. I'd had a Spanish interlude as good as any holiday, and I could go straight back to Rome and get on with life.

"So you won't come to Sitges with me?" Rudi asked. "You don't want a holiday with me?" He was a little hurt, and a little offended to have discovered through the clap scare that I still went to bed with Bruno sometimes, while refusing him.

"Thank you, Rudi darling, but I won't come to Sitges. I've got over a serious illness, and I've got over my love for you. Now I just want to be on my own for a bit."

"Can't we have a little honeymoon first? Like you do with Bruno? Sometimes in bed together, sometimes in bed with other people?"

"Rudi, you and my husbands were my great loves. Bruno was in another category right from the start—friendship with fucking. It's a whole other trip. If I ever went to bed with you again, it would be for marriage. But I don't want to get married again just yet, and probably never will."

Rudi took it very well. He obviously wanted to try heterosexuality again on the rebound from Tom, but this time I couldn't help him; I had to protect myself. So I limped back to Rome with Bruno, both of us resting from sex for a different reason—his reason being more contagious than mine!

There is a story of Colette's in which she says that the months between love affairs are valuable for personal reassessment and for consolidating friendships. I agree with her. When you're in love, it's all-absorbing. If the relationship is a happy one, you move through life in a glowing halo that protects you from the outside world. An unhappy affair has the same effect: you are again isolated, but by despair. I now looked forward to those peaceful moments when I could become aware again of the other things and other people who make up my own personal world.

"I think it's time I visited my brother again," I said to Bruno, back in Rome. He had come in to tell me how the film was doing at Cinecittà.

"A good idea. It's too hot for you to stay in Rome. There's no point either, unless you're getting paid for it."

"By the way, is there any hope of our getting our back salary? I don't mind being laid off, but I would like what's owed me. It seems they've got some money from somewhere—the shooting is still going on."

"The finances of the film industry are very devious, aren't they?" Bruno commented, and then added, "Why don't you come out to the studios Friday and see the *ragioniere*?"

So I went out to Cinecittà to see the accountant on payday. It is significant that the Italian word *ragioniere* means "the one who reasons." Money is, alas, the reason for most things.

Everyone was glad to see me back on the set except the *ragioniere*. He was having trouble balancing the books for the day-to-day payments without going into back debts, so I left unpaid. It wouldn't be the first time I'd had to wait for months and eventually sue, the Italian film world being what it is. But films do get made, and that's something. I had my health back, and some savings, and another job in the offing, so I left to have a holiday with my brother Max in Paris.

Bruno came to say good-bye. "I'm dying to go to bed with somebody," he said. "I must be the safest man in the industry with all that penicillin inside me. How about it, Anne?"

I was a little reluctant. "I'm on a diet, Bruno. I'm giving up sex for six weeks."

"Why six weeks, for God's sake?"

"That's the length of my holiday. One must learn discipline in all things. Six weeks is a good length for a diet."

"But it's too long for a fast. You'll fade away, Anne. Come on, not the full meal, maybe. Give me just a snack!"

"Bruno, I really don't feel like it. One of the basic rules for a successful sex life is to be able to say no as easily as you say yes—and vice versa. The important thing in fucking is to really want it."

"You make me feel like a leper!"

"The clap *is* modern leprosy."

I kissed him on the mouth to make him feel better, but I kept him at arm's length all the same. I really needed that six-week period of abstinence.

Diary entry. Late August, 1972.

Thinking of Colette's words, I am leaving to consolidate my friendship with my brother. In spite of the usual brother/sister problems, he's been one of the few really constant relationships in my life, although I probably see less of him than anyone. He was there when I needed him during my illness, and however many lovers and husbands come and go, he will always be there.

It's been nearly a year since my brother took me to the hospital semi-paralyzed. Now, months later, I find that seven out of ten of the motor nerves have grown back, and I can walk quite well, although the doctors say I shall never be able to run again—but I don't want to run. Life may cease, but you can also come back to life, and that's enough for me. Grant can never come back—but then he chose to go. In a strange way, his death has given me a certain serenity. I wish I could write him a letter and tell him so:

"Dearest Grant, Thank you. I shall continue to run through life metaphorically, but every now and then, I'll stop to think. I'll be thinking of you too, but not with regret. You wouldn't want that. Love, Anne"

I think I will write him a letter and file it away in the shoe box as if I expected an answer.

8 ✍ From Jewish Prince to Irish Poet

I love a big metropolis in midsummer when everyone else has gone away. Max hates it, so I went to Paris to see him that year—August 1973. He was having a financial crisis and couldn't afford to go away himself. He was glad to see me, grateful to have me cook for him, as most of the restaurants were closed, and happy that I was almost well again. I could now walk quite normally and quite far. My balance was poor, as my feet still had some numbness, but I had learned not to let it show. I would live for the rest of my life with slight pins and needles in my feet, but I could forget it most of the time, only feeling it when I thought of it. For once, my reluctance to think was paying off.

"I wonder whether Françoise is back in Paris?" I asked Max toward the end of my stay.

Françoise and I had written to each other occasionally, and recently Joseph had begun to write postscripts to her letters. He had told me about some left-wing girl who was madly in love with him. He didn't sound madly in love with her, though—but then Joseph was only in love with himself.

"Perhaps I should try to see Joseph again. It was all so long ago. I always try to keep in touch with my ex-lovers. I mustn't spoil the record."

Max shrugged his shoulders. "You have a tendency to court disaster. I wonder why?"

Max was right. I decided I would just ring Françoise to say hello and pretend I was passing through. I did, in fact, only have one night left. We had a pleasant conversation, and I must have mentioned the name of the cheap hotel near Max where I was staying. I asked her to explain to Joseph that I hoped to see him on my next visit, by which time he would be safely married. Françoise had told me that he was now officially engaged.

I had a pleasant last dinner with Max. We went to an expensive tourist restaurant because only those restaurants were open. We walked back along the quais and said our good-bye on the Pont Marie. I felt sad at the parting. When the chips are down and my sex life is over, perhaps Max will turn out to be my only true love. Certainly our relationship has lasted longer than any other in my life.

When I got back to my hotel, I found Joseph sitting patiently in the hall. My heart sank before it rose. Then it became as numb as my feet, as if it were closing up in self-defense.

"Aren't you going to drop your handbag on the stairs and kiss me?" he asked. "I've never forgotten that day."

It all came rushing back. Little bastard—he

knew how to open old wounds. I should have thrown him straight out of the hotel. Instead, I took him upstairs.

My night with Joseph in Paris unnerved me. It was not quite like old times, and yet it was. Our rhythms were still very compatible. It was like a nostalgic quick waltz in a *bal musette*. When I left the next day, I even heard background music in my heart like an anguished Edith Piaf refrain. It had been a mistake to see him again so soon. Yet it had ended two years ago. How long does it really take to get over the disease called love?

"Will you take me with you to Rome?" he asked after we had made love and were lying in each other's arms. "I don't want to get married at all."

"I'll never take you anywhere to get away from another woman. If we ever see each other again, it will be because you seek me out for myself alone. But don't do it before you're twenty-five. You're aging so fast, you'll be middle-aged by then—you'll have caught up with me. I'm getting younger all the time myself."

I threw him out the next morning. He left the watch his fiancée had given him for Christmas on the night table. I had to mail it to Françoise from the airport.

Fortunately, Vanessa and the children were back from the sea when I returned to Rome. It was mid-September. They all came into Rome to see me. Matthew, now age six, settled back in as if he

had never left since the winter of our discontent.
He remembered where everything was, took over
the house as if he owned it, and bossed me around
more than any grown man had ever dared to do.
His year-old brother constantly struggled to crawl
after him, frustrated by his incapacity to move
around yet. Mark's little eyes were full of admiration for his big brother, and my heart was full of
love for both of them. I allowed them liberties that
none of my lovers would have been permitted.
They manipulated me more than any man.

"You spoil them terribly," Vanessa complained.
"I can do nothing with them."

She whisked them away to the country again
just in time. I felt the void. I needed a new job, and
I needed a new man.

As always in the film industry, there are periods
when there are no offers of work; when, like actors, you are "resting." Now that I was back on
my feet, the last thing I wanted to do was rest, but
I couldn't seem to find a job. I tried for a film with
Pasolini, but he preferred working with men.
Then I was actually chosen for a job, but another
woman publicist who had worked on their previous film threatened to commit suicide if they
didn't rehire her. I bowed out gracefully. I probably needed the job more than she did, but I
wouldn't fight another woman for it, particularly
a suicidal one. The general economic situation in
Italy was deteriorating, and this had provoked a
crisis within the film industry. Perhaps I would
have to consider another career.

I had done many things in my long working life.

I had trained for the theater, but there was not always work in the theater so I had worked as a model and then in an office. When war broke out, I had been drafted into the British Intelligence Service. After the war, I had worked for the British government in other fields more allied to the arts. When my second marriage broke up, I needed a change of scenery. I left London to take a teaching job in Italy, where I met Rudi. Through Rudi, I had come into contact with show business again, and I realized I had missed it. With my theatrical training, it was easy to get into the movie business through a side door. Most people in the Italian movie business were talented amateurs, particularly the actors. I began by teaching them English and acting. I occasionally got small parts myself, but there were not many parts for a woman in her forties. Now, it seemed there were no jobs at all for a woman in her fifties.

"Perhaps you could get into dubbing," a girl friend of mine said one day. "You have such a beautiful English voice."

"That might be held against me. The biggest market for dubbed films is in America."

Strangely enough, although the film industry was on the rocks, the dubbing business was booming. Big co-production movies were on their way out, and small local Italian films were on their way in. After the success of the spaghetti Westerns, there was suddenly a vogue for Italian comedies, Italian domestic dramas, and Italian mini-spectaculars such as the Pasolini film for which I had just been turned down. I decided to give dubbing a try.

I did try hard. My problem wasn't so much the accent as it was the synchronization. I found it nerve-racking; like ping-pong, it went too fast. You heard the original text over headphones, you saw a little red line wiggling across the screen when you were supposed to speak, you tried to follow the lip movements of the actors, and, worst of all, you had to act with your voice alone. No use making gestures or relying on facial expressions; those were already up there on the screen. You were a disembodied voice, a ghost speaker, but you had to make it sound real. I was just no good at it; and I hated being shut up in a darkened studio all day. I grew nervous and depressed.

"Hello, who are *you*?" a cultured American voice greeted me one autumn day. "What are you doing sitting all alone in the dark?"

I was at one of the dubbing studios to be tested for the role of a middle-aged mother whose daughter had gone astray. I had arrived early and was sitting alone in the empty studio, not bothering to turn on the lights. Someone had opened the door, and I could see a tall man silhouetted against the light from outside.

"I'm Anne Cumming. I got here a bit early because I was afraid of being late."

"That's very English of you, as if your accent hadn't told me that already."

"Is it going to matter? I have difficulty doing the mid-Atlantic drawl."

He laughed. "You make it sound like a new dance."

He crossed the room and switched on the little

reading lamp on the dubber's desk, and I could now see that he was that fortune teller's cliché—a tall, dark, handsome and mysterious stranger. His hair was graying at the temples, and he looked like a man in his early forties, though he turned out to be nearly fifty.

"I'm Martin Greenbaum. I'm your dubbing director for the day." He came over and shook my hand. "How come I've never seen you before?"

"I'm new to the job. I'm a leftover public relations person, and, as I specialize on location pictures, I'm usually out of town."

We smiled at each other. Some kind of inner recognition was beginning to hatch, although we had never seen each other before. I think we both knew that it was the beginning of something, although we were very circumspect. At our age, it was normal to expect the other person to already be attached to someone.

"Well, since we're both here, shall we begin?"

He handed me the script, then picked up the telephone and told the projectionist to run the film. I was extremely nervous, and it was particularly difficult. An Italian matron was talking nineteen to the dozen in dialect. What kind of an accent was I to use, and how could I fit the English into that flow of Latin hysteria?

"My God!" I exclaimed. "This is no mid-Atlantic drawl; it's a wild dervish dance with Mediterranean overtones. What am I to do?"

"It needs a Brooklyn accent. Can you do a Brooklyn accent?"

"Certainly not. Cockney, yes. Liverpool, maybe.

But I think I should just give up right now before the other actors get here."

"I'm sorry. E.L.D.A. shouldn't have sent you out on this one. They should have waited till we needed a British ambassadress or a Boston hostess."

We looked at each other ruefully, sorry that it was over before it had even begun. He switched off the little reading light, and we were in semidarkness. There was a glow from the Exit signs and a faint reflection from the projection room across the floor, then the house lights went on. But in that moment of darkness something had happened, and as the lights went up, we instinctively reached out to touch each other. I put my hand on his shoulder and said, "I'm sorry, too. I would have liked working with you."

He took my other hand in both of his and said, "I'll call you when something more suitable comes up. I can always find you through E.L.D.A., can't I?"

E.L.D.A. was the dubbers' union and an agency all in one. It had recently been founded by English-speaking actors who specialized in this type of work. I had only recently joined it.

"Yes, of course, although E.L.D.A. hardly knows me. But you'll find me in the phone book if you can remember my name."

"I can remember your name. It's Anne Cumming. My ex-wife's name was Anne too, but that was a long time ago."

It was as if he were telling me something and asking a question at the same time.

"I have two ex-husbands, and they were a long time ago too," I replied. I realized that this didn't give us all the information we needed, so I took the plunge and asked, "Are you living with anyone now?"

"Only vaguely," he said. "And you?"

At this point the door opened, and two American actresses came in—tough, hard-drinking women, either of whom would be perfect for the part I had just lost. My answer to Martin's question got a bit lost with their arrival. In fact, when I found myself on the street, I realized that I hadn't spoken a word. I had just put both of my hands trustingly into his, squeezed hard, smiled wistfully, and left.

"Darling, I think I've just met Mr. Right, but I doubt that I'll ever see him again!" I was talking to Vanessa on the phone.

"Why not? What have you done wrong, mum?" Vanessa always calls me "mum" when she's feeling fond of me.

"Nothing. I just don't think I did and said the right things. And I can't even remember his name."

"Can't you ask the person who introduced you?"

"We weren't introduced. We found each other in a dubbing studio."

"Well, go back there. Can you think of a reason to call around casually until you run into him again?"

"I can think of countless reasons, but none of them will do. You can't go cruising around like a sex-starved spinster at my age."

"You always have, mother. And what's all this

about age? I've never heard you mention it before."

"I'm rather conscious of the fact that he's probably younger than I am."

My daughter laughed. "But that's never worried you before, has it?"

"It does now, because he's so *nearly* my own age."

"What a nice change! He really does sound suitable. Now think up a reason right away to go back over there before someone else gets him."

"They have. He has a vague relationship, whatever that means. He told me so."

"What did you tell *him*?"

"Nothing. He doesn't know who I am, or where I live, or that I live alone, or anything else about me."

"Probably just as well! He'll find out soon enough. Everyone in Rome knows *you*—and everything about you. Relax, mum, you're sure to run into him again soon."

But I didn't. Several weeks passed before I met him again. Then my friend Esmeralda brought him to my house.

Esmeralda was known as the Red Princess. She was a liberal left-wing lady from one of Italy's most exclusive titled families. I had known her even before I married Charles, and when I ran away with him, we went to stay with her. When Charles and I split up years later, she consoled me by lending me her own husband as a lover. After Charles, I had brokenheartedly gone to live alone in Rome, where Esmeralda was having an affair with a duke from Florence at the time. Her husband was complaisant but at loose ends, so Esmeralda loaned him to me. It was very consoling, but when the duke went back to Florence, Esmeralda's husband had gone back to her, and we had all lost touch. We ran into each other from time to time, and I knew she still had lovers, but I didn't know that Martin Greenbaum was one of them.

I had decided to give a big party on my fifty-sixth birthday. I was planning to go to England and spend Christmas with Fiona, so I decided now would be a good time to reunite all my old friends. I wouldn't mention that it was my birthday. I've never lied about my age, but I do sometimes gloss over it.

I had called Esmeralda. "Esmeralda, I haven't seen you for years. Will you come to a party I'm giving on December 14? Bring your husband, of course. I haven't seen him for years either."

"My husband's away, but I'll bring someone else if I may. You're sure to like him. We've always had the same taste in men."

Esmeralda arrived wearing a beautiful Turkish dress and some barbaric jewelry. Walking behind her was Martin Greenbaum, looking very sober in a Brooks Brothers suit.

"Hello," he said as we shook hands. "How's the mid-Atlantic drawl?" I was, of course, delighted to see him. I allowed myself to hope he felt the same way; after all, he had come to the party knowing I was the hostess.

"I've given up the drawl. I'm doing a slow waltz instead. I'm writing a book."

He and Esmeralda got lost in the crowd. There were too many people there. I always intend to give small, select parties, but they usually end up as huge free-for-alls where everyone brings someone else, and I don't know all the guests myself. Vanessa and the children were there, and little Mark slept peacefully through it all in his portable crib. Matthew ran around among the guests, getting in the way and getting underfoot, and even getting under the furniture. Eventually he too fell asleep, under a coffee table. I was trying to extricate him when Martin Greenbaum came over to help me.

"I think I'd better put him into bed before someone steps on him," I said. "Aren't children incredible, the way they can sleep through anything?"

"I haven't had much experience with them. I was married very young, and it didn't last long. We never had children."

"And you've never remarried?"

"No, I haven't. It hasn't seemed necessary."

We looked at each other inquiringly, as if trying to fathom the depths of each other's past, or even of each other's present. I wondered just how important his relationship with Esmeralda was, and whether once again she was prepared to lend me a man.

Vanessa came over then and helped me pick up Matthew and put him to bed. We managed to do it without waking him, but when I went back into the drawing room, I had lost sight of Martin Greenbaum. Other guests occupied most of my time and attention, but my eyes kept searching the room for him. Finally I caught a glimpse of him, and he seemed to be looking at me. Then Esmeralda decided to leave and went into the bedroom to get her coat. Martin was beside me in a moment.

"Can we meet again soon?" he asked.

"I'm going to England for Christmas to see my other daughter. I'll be back at the beginning of January."

"I'll call you then. It'll be a nice way to start off the New Year."

Christmas was clamorous rather than glamorous. Vanessa and her children had accompanied me to Fiona's, and four small children under one roof was too much. The little cousins fought tooth and nail, and sibling rivalry was rife. My Sicilian son-in-law had decided he would someday be a great composer, and played the piano incessantly and tunelessly. Charles and his wife had sensibly decided not to join us and had gone skiing in Klosters. I was very glad to escape from England and get back to Rome in the New Year, but once there, I felt dispossessed. Bruno had temporarily fallen in love with a lady pharmacist, Evaristo was in America, my diplomat had been transferred to Bonn, Germany, my truck driver was on a long-distance haul to Belgium, and Charles and his wife were still away skiing. I began looking around for a new movie assignment.

I was offered two jobs: one I refused because I couldn't face the thought of working with drunken actors, and the star was an alcoholic; the other fell through for lack of funds. January is a slow month for movie-making anyway. My life in gen-

eral seemed to be slowing down, but perhaps that
is what middle age is all about. I was fifty-six years
old and I had to face the fact that jobs and men
were hard to come by. I tried to concentrate on
writing my book, but it was difficult to sit alone
with nothing but a typewriter and one's thoughts
after such a crowded, hectic life in the cinema. I
can't say I was lonely; I had a busy social life and
many friends. I even came to enjoy the hours of
solitude—it was a new experience. But somehow I
wanted to share even that feeling of solitude with
someone. Then a voice came out of the blue, and
light came back into my life.

"Hello? I'm looking for someone who can do the
mid-Atlantic drawl. I want to go dancing tonight."
It was Martin Greenbaum.

"I haven't been dancing for a long time" was all
I could think of to say.

"You do like to dance, don't you?"

"Yes, of course I do. And I like you too. It
sounds like a good combination."

It was, in fact, the perfect combination. Martin
was a beautiful dancer, an excellent host, and a caring and loving man. We celebrated his fiftieth
birthday that night.

"I'd like to give myself a present. Will you be my
self-selected present? They're usually the ones that
give the most pleasure and last the longest."

I smiled at the idea, remembering my own fiftieth birthday and the young man I had been given
by my fat friend. He had not lasted long, nor had
Jean-Louis, although we were still in touch. However, now the boot was on the other foot. I was giving *myself* away.

I gave myself to Martin that night with a great sense of commitment. This was no light indulgence of my love habit. This was a suitable suitor at last, a man for all reasons. He seemed to feel the same way about me.

"You're the woman I've always had in the back of my mind," he said. "I'm glad you've moved up to the front."

I began calling him my Man for All Reasons, and he called me his Woman up Front. We settled into an almost-domestic relationship. Although neither of us wanted to get married again, our relationship became more like marriage than we had intended. Martin was just moving into a new apartment, and I helped him to furnish it. When spring came, he bought me some roses for my terrace and helped me to plant them. We divided our time equally between the two apartments, although we weren't together every night. We didn't want to be; both of us were used to our independence.

It was interesting to have such a fulfilling relationship again with a man of my own generation and cultural background. Martin came from a good American Jewish family. After studying at Berkeley, California, he had planned to pursue a university career. He had married a fellow student, but it had been a short-lived marriage. He took a government position when he graduated, but he didn't take his wife with him to Washington. They got a divorce, and he was transferred to Europe. He had worked in several European countries. We spoke the same languages; we had been in the same places—both literally and metaphorical-

ly. We were compatible, in bed and out. He was a
tender and understanding lover. His hands had a
sensitive touch. My sex drive was stronger than
his, but I played it down for him. We seldom made
love except at night in bed. He was not fond of
oral sex, but his caressing hands were as good as
any tongue. Yet I sometimes missed the frenzy and
the fervor of my younger lovers.

"Be your age, Anne," he would say with a smile
when I sometimes expected him to behave like one
of the impulsive boys I had grown used to, and
make love at odd times and in odd places.

"We don't grow old down there," I lamented.
"A woman's sexual dynamics are not always affected by age."

"Well, a man's usually are. We must learn to be
compatible in bed, or else we'll be unhappy out of
bed."

So I learned to enjoy a more restrained rhythm
of love-making. It was the first time I had consciously worked on the physical side of love. Previously, I had just let it take its course—taken the
ups with the downs, so to speak.

Our friends approved of our relationship. We
were a well-matched pair, and we seemed to fit
into everybody else's lives as well as we fitted into
each other's. There were only a few things we
couldn't share. Martin had a great interest in
Krishnamurti, who was living in Rome at that
time. He took me with him on several occasions,
but I didn't find answers to anything I was asking,
so Martin continued to go alone. We liked the feeling of independent interests as much as we enjoyed our shared pleasures.

Another of Martin's independent interests was skiing. "Do you like skiing?" he had asked early in our relationship.

"Yes," I replied wistfully, "but my illness has made it impossible for me."

"Of course. I always forget. You handle your slight disability so well that one never notices it."

"Thank God at my age nobody expects me to hop, skip and jump, so I can cover up my physical shortcomings with dynamic conversation instead!"

Actually, I still had reduced strength in my hands and a slight paralysis of my feet. My balance was bad, but I had learned not to do anything too demanding. Skiing would definitely be out.

"Do go skiing whenever you wish," I had urged him. "I like to go down to Sperlonga even in winter. And I enjoy having Vanessa and the children for weekends in Rome."

So sometimes Martin took off alone for the slopes, and sometimes we spent our weekends together in Rome or Sperlonga. He had no children of his own, but he enjoyed my grandchildren when they came to stay. That was one pleasure we shared. Little by little, feelings of solidarity and security were building up inside me. Unfortunately, they didn't last long.

"Do you mind if I go skiing for a week or two at Easter?" Martin asked. "There's a place in France I'd like to try."

We had been together in the Biblical sense for three months, but it seemed much longer, probably because it had been nearly six months since we first met in the dubbing studio.

I noticed there was no suggestion that I should

go too. I'd been looking forward to a long Easter weekend in Sperlonga with him, with perhaps a little trip farther on down south in the car. Neither of us knew Calabria and had discussed exploring it together. However, I played it cool.

"Yes, do go, darling. I shouldn't take two weeks off anyway."

It was a lie. I could easily have done so, and Martin knew it. Perhaps our togetherness was weighing on him more than it was on me. Had I been deluding myself that this was the perfect romance? Was I slipping back into that fairy tale fantasy life of Prince Charmings and Living Happily Ever After on which I was brought up? How wrong we are to bring up children with that illusion. Children should be prepared for the difficulties ahead and the impossibility of a one-hundred-percent happy relationship. Prince Charmings are not where you find them, but what you make of them. Was I making my Man for All Reasons into something he was not? And, above all, what was he making of me?

"Martin, if you had to give me marks for being the perfect mistress, what would you give me?"

He answered immediately, "Nine out of ten."

"What's missing? What do I do wrong?"

"Nothing's missing. There's just too much of it."

"What do you mean?"

We were lying in bed together. I had chosen my moment carefully. We had just made love and were very relaxed and happy. He looked at me affectionately but quizzically.

"You're strong meat, Woman up Front. You're vibrant, dynamic, magnetic—sometimes it's hard to live up to you."

"But is anything wrong? Actually wrong?"

He smiled, but looked embarrassed at the same time. He hated personal discussions, as I knew. Perhaps I was being too direct.

"Of course nothing's wrong. Now turn off the light and go to sleep. I'm very happy with you. Isn't that enough for you?"

I didn't answer. I just hugged him tightly to me and eventually fell asleep with my nose against his neck. He hugged me too, but not quite so tightly— but there's always a difference in the intensity between two people.

When Martin came back after Easter, he was as affectionate as ever—perhaps more so—but our relationship had changed. At the time, I thought it was because *I* was the one playing it cool; I was deliberately trying to tone down my vital energies to match his.

"Am I on a better wave length now?" I asked one day. "Do I seem less demanding?"

He laughed. "What are you trying to do? Program yourself like a computer? Relax; be a human being. What I've loved most about you is that you're so human."

I ignored the past tense. Women are full of wishful thinking, and I wanted to be happy—so I was happy. Martin came and went with the same frequency as before, and if the quality of our relationship had changed, I put it down to his age and temperament. The honeymoon was over, so I mustn't expect continual fireworks.

Still, I couldn't get over the feeling that something wasn't quite right. "Martin, are you getting bored with me sexually?" I asked him one evening.

"But we've just made love! What a stupid question!" He actually seemed quite annoyed.

"Yes, but you seldom stay the night now."

"I'm busy. I'm preoccupied. The new film I'm working on is a bastard. Be patient, darling. Don't always take things so personally. I need a little space around me."

Middle age was supposed to be like this, I reassured myself: you were companionable rather than passionate.

"It's a period of adjustment, mum," Vanessa said when I talked it over with her. My daughters are so much more mature than I am; they know how to think.

A couple of months went by happily enough. I was working on a new film at the Palatino studios behind the Coliseum. It was on the way to a couple of the biggest dubbing studios, so Martin often called for me after work. It was getting warm enough to eat out at the many trattorias where tables are put out on the Roman cobbles and fenced in with box hedges and big umbrellas. Summer was in the air. We began to discuss a possible holiday in Greece. Friends had offered to lend us their house on Hydra for August. Our relationship seemed to be settling down.

Then, sometime in June, Martin made a quick, mysterious trip to Paris.

"I want to see some French dubbers about doing a movie for them in the fall," Martin explained.

"You never mentioned you were in touch with anyone in Paris. Maybe Max could help you—he knows everyone. I'll call him."

"No, don't bother. It all seems to be under control."

"You will go and see Max, won't you? I want you to meet so much. The two men I love best in the world will surely get on together."

"Don't be too sure. I might be jealous!"

We both laughed, and Martin kissed me. He did not, however, go to see Max. He seemed distracted when he returned from Paris, but I thought perhaps his business hopes had been dashed. He didn't seem to want to talk about his trip at all, so I let it drop. Max wrote to me that Martin had telephoned but had been polite rather than friendly, so Max had not pressed for a meeting. "Your new boyfriend seems a bit evasive" was Max's comment. I didn't show the letter to Martin.

We began to discuss our summer plans again in early July. I had to let our friends know if we wanted their house.

"Why don't *you* go?" Martin said. "I think I'd like to take off alone in August and go camping—perhaps discover the Camargue and then drive on up to the Krishnamurti seminar in Switzerland."

It was a big shock. I had planned on spending the month of August with him. I would be between jobs, and Martin's work never lasted more than two or three weeks at a time. We had worked it out so carefully.

"Are you having a mystic crisis?" I asked.

He smiled and kissed me. "Don't try to understand everything about your Man for All Reasons.
Just have faith."

I had faith. He was being particularly sweet to
me around that time, so it was easier to tell myself
that everything would turn out all right.

One night toward the end of July, Martin told
me that his dubbing friends from Paris had arrived
for a short visit. He was very taken up with them
for a few days.

"Why don't you bring them over for a drink on
my terrace one evening?"

"No. They are such bores, I wouldn't want to
wish them on you."

At that point Vanessa and the children arrived,
on their way to Sicily for their summer holidays
by the sea. It seemed natural not to get involved
with Martin's business when I was so busy with
my family. Vanessa was leaving on Friday, and I
looked forward to spending Saturday night with
Martin.

When Saturday came, Martin explained to me
that his friends were leaving too, and that this was
their last night in Rome. They had opera tickets,
with an extra one for him.

"You really don't like opera, do you?" Martin
asked consolingly.

It was true that I didn't like opera, but this was
something Rudi had designed, and I wanted to see
it. At the last minute, I decided to go with my

friend Franca. We went out to the Terme di Cara-
calla by bus. I didn't have time to tell Martin I was
going.

The open-air opera in Rome is in the old Roman
baths. It's in a vast auditorium divided into several
parts. I didn't expect to see Martin, since it would
have been quite possible to sit through the whole
opera and never run into him.

Franca and I were glad to be together. I don't
have many girl friends, but those I have are very
dear to me. Franca was as interested as I was to see
Rudi's sets, which had been sent down from Vero-
na, where they had been in repertory at the Arena.

"Look, there's Martin," she said at intermission.
We had gone out for a stroll. "What a pretty girl
he's with!"

Martin was at the open-air bar with a blond girl.
He was handing her a drink; they seemed to be
alone. She was laughing up into his face as they
clinked glasses. He bent forward and kissed her. I
felt all the cliché reactions. My heart sank, my
stomach turned over. But I was determined not to
show it.

Martin never knew I had seen him at the opera.
He told me the next day that his friends had left
Rome, so I presumed the girl had gone. I decided
to say nothing. Our life together went on, although sex was minimal.

Several evenings later I was tidying up his study
when I found some skiing pictures he had taken at
Easter when he was on holiday in France. There,
waving from a ski lift, was the blond girl. It was
not only jealousy but sadness over the hypocrisy of

it all that hit me. I had no doubt that the girl lived in Paris, and Martin's mysterious visit in June had been to see her. If only he had told me! I had been open with him about my own sex life.

I had a sudden wish to see Esmeralda, so, out of the blue, I called her. I had no guilt feelings about having taken Martin away from her, because he had told me so often that their affair was really over by the time he met me.

"Martin is two-timing me," I said to her over coffee in the Café Greco. "Did he do it to you, too?"

"Of course—with you."

"You mean your affair wasn't over when you brought him to my house? He's always told me that you were practically giving him away."

"And you still believe men when they tell you things like that?"

"Well, I did this time. Particularly because you and I knew each other so well that I thought you'd call me and complain if you didn't want to dump him. After all, you must remember how you loaned me your husband all those years ago, when I had just left Charles." We both laughed at the memory. Given time, you can laugh at anything.

This time I didn't feel like laughing. I felt hurt, betrayed. I really loved Martin. It was not only the present hurt that undermined me, but the pain from the past as well. All the buried feelings from when Charles had left me and Rudi had run away reached out across the years. I began to cry. There, in the Café Greco, tears ran down my cheeks.

Esmeralda put her arms around me. "It'll pass," she said. "Remember how it always passes?"

"It takes at least two years to get over a real love affair," I wailed.

"I've never noticed you take that long," Esmeralda commented wryly.

"Well, I begin sleeping around again sooner," I admitted between sobs, "but the ache of betrayal is still there—sometimes forever."

"Think how lucky we are to have had so many men to betray us," Esmeralda said with a slight smile. "Some women don't meet so many bastards. Wouldn't life have been boring with only one long monogamous marriage to look back on?"

I looked over at Esmeralda and began to smile too, although my cheeks were still wet with tears.

"Thank you, Esmeralda," I said, and hugged her warmly. "Women are so much nicer than men—I wish I could be a lesbian."

"Why not try?"

"My behavior pattern is too set. I'm fifty-six years old."

"Then be glad you've still got a man to be unfaithful to you," she said firmly. "We're old ladies, Anne."

"Oh," I demurred, "I never think of that. The only way to stay young is to never think of your age."

"Don't split your infinitives!"

We burst out laughing. I hugged her again. "Don't you think girl friends are much nicer than lovers, Esmeralda?"

"No, I don't," Esmeralda replied. "But they do last longer."

I went through a bad time, though I never cried again. I hid my pain, even from Martin. There was no point in saying anything. Martin was obviously not good at confrontation and was doing everything to avoid it. Although I personally prefer a clean break and a clear decision, you can't expect everyone to live by your rules. Martin was no doubt suffering from guilt, and I couldn't hope for his sudden transformation into a clean-cut white Anglo-Saxon Protestant. There would be no clean cut—we would just decorously drift apart.

And that's how it happened. It had all been too reasonable and continued to be so. Perhaps that was the trouble. It had been so right, so easy, so compatible. Great love needs obstacles.

My Man for All Reasons packed up and slipped away on his camping trip to the Camargue. I have no doubt that his pretty young blonde joined him there in his sleeping bag—all very rejuvenating for a middle-aged man.

My friend Kurt once said to me, "There's no good way to end an affair." This time I felt I had not done it too badly. We didn't end it; we just knew it was over. We said good-bye as though we would meet again in September, both of us knowing it would probably be longer and on a different basis when we did.

Actually, we were not in Rome again at the same time until the following spring. It turned out to be easy to meet again after a lapse of six months and feel only affectionate friendship; everything was reasonable to the last. Martin was engaged to be married to the French blonde by then, and she had moved to Rome. We got on quite well, although I found her rather hard and had my fears for Martin. I only felt maternal toward him now—something I seldom felt for my younger lovers. Circumstance and temperament are probably stronger than age difference.

Another year had gone by, another August had come around, and again I was alone. It was time to change countries, I decided. I needed my yearly checkup at the hospital in London, and I had an offer to stay there and superintend an Italian film about a runaway girl whose mother comes to London to look for her. I was sure a new lover would come along—and he did. A nail to knock out a nail, as the Italians so aptly put it. He was rather a rusty nail, but he served the purpose. He was young—very young. I don't think I would ever have gone back to teen-agers if an older man had not just let me down; but history repeats itself, and we make the same mistakes again and again. My love habit was becoming an addiction.

It was nice to be back in good old England. Nothing had changed this time. It was raining, it was September 1973, there was another sensational murder case, and the Irish were still giving trouble. There were notices in the underground reading: "If you see an unattended package or bag in this car, don't touch it. Pull the emergency handle when the train has stopped at the next station. Tell

the other passengers to leave the car." London had
stopped swinging and was beginning to stand still.

Caspian and Kate were married, Bad Gregory
was living happily with a new girl friend, Good
Gregory was still unattached, and I was still not
quite sure which was Peter and which was Paul. I
could hardly even recognize my English grandchildren, they had grown so much. Caroline was
already into the gym-tunic stage and Malcolm was
in long trousers and a school cap. They were eight
and ten respectively, and I was nearly fifty-seven.
It was the first time I had been back in London
since Grant's death. I decided to call his father.

"Hello, Dad. It's Anne Cumming."

" 'Ullo, Lady Anne. 'Ow's things?"

"Fine, Dad, fine. I'm in London for three
months on a job. Like to come and see me sometime? I've taken a little flat near Oxford Circus."

"You come 'ere, girl. I'll bake you one of me
cakes, and you can see Grant's 'ome. I keep 'is
room just as it was, although maybe I'll take in a
lodger soon. It's a bit lonely like sometimes, but
life goes on, don't it?"

Dad sounded cheerful and glad to hear from
me—not a hint of blame or regret. He invited me
to Sunday tea in Hackney and I took the 22 bus
through parts of London I had never visited. I was
interested to see the council flat where I had once
been invited to stay, and which Grant, in his
imagination, had filled with beautiful antiques.

Dad welcomed me at the door with a hug and a
smile. It was a bleak, modern block of municipal
housing, but a few people had window boxes, and

Dad was growing a new health-giving herb called comfrey in his.

"Come in, luv. I've baked you one of me special cakes."

As I entered the narrow hall, it was like going into a stately home. Grant had not been fantasizing; it *was* full of beautiful antiques. Dad opened the door to Grant's room. There was a four-poster bed in it.

"Where on earth did you get such lovely furniture?" I couldn't help exclaiming.

"I'm a first-class cabinetmaker, girl. I often gets given bits an' pieces other people think are not worth mending. I do 'em up and puts 'em 'ere."

"You're a marvelous restorer, Dad!"

"One of the best in London, so they say," he replied proudly. "See them chairs? In fifty pieces, they was. Took me an 'ell of a long time to put 'em together again, bit by bit, but worth it, mind you."

I could see how Grant had put his fantasy life together, bit by bit, in the same painstaking way his father had achieved reality. He had lain in the four-poster bed and changed his name, matching his image to his surroundings—but then the rest of his life hadn't matched up to it. I always did the opposite. I traveled around making my surroundings match my image—an easier and more realistic approach. Whenever I went on location, I always took my Georgian carriage clock, photos in silver frames, and two little antique Battersea boxes. They were on a table of the anonymous, modern, furnished apartment I had taken now, beside some books of poetry.

We ate a rather heavy cake of whole-wheat flour and dates—very nourishing. Dad was good solid value all around. I persuaded him to rent Grant's room to another student so he could have someone to fuss over and maybe teach his trade to. It was quite dark by the time I got up to go, and Dad walked me to the bus stop. I had enjoyed my visit; Dad was wonderful. He hadn't allowed me to feel guilty or nostalgic about Grant, although I sometimes wonder whether seeing Dad again didn't make me wistfully pick up the next teen-ager I saw who reminded me of Grant.

I was walking home late one night after the theater when I saw a scarecrow propped up against a lamppost. This rural effigy in a wasteland of urban night seemed so strangely out of place that I crossed Oxford Street to take a closer look. It was one of those nights only the English can invent, on which cold wind and rain combine to chill the marrow of one's bones and provoke rheumatism even in the very young. I was walking only because when it rains there are never any taxis.

The scarecrow was a real live young man, standing with outstretched arms in a sodden black overcoat and a dripping felt hat. Even his long black lashes were fringed with raindrops, and the harsh light revealed the bluest eyes I had ever seen. He was staring into the sky, his face gleaming with moisture.

"What are you doing?" I asked almost involuntarily.

His gaze shifted down to me, although his arms remained outstretched.

"I was wondering what it was like to be crucified," he replied with a slight Irish accent.

"This hardly seems the night for such an experiment," I said, surprised but intrigued. "People weren't usually crucified in a hat and overcoat, either. They were generally naked."

"It was too cold," he said logically enough. "And besides, the hat and overcoat were the only things my father left me. He died last week."

He paused, evidently expecting some reaction I didn't yet feel. Then he went on, "I have no home. I was waiting for the last Green Line bus to nowhere, but I think it's gone."

The lamppost was, in fact, also a long-distance bus stop. We looked at the timetable together. It was a good half hour after the last bus. Maternal instinct vied with good sense. The young man looked pathetic and harmless and appealingly poetic.

"You'd better come home and sleep on the couch in my sitting room."

He lowered his arms, shaking himself like a wet dog, and a pair of cycle clips emerged from under his sleeve on his left wrist, worn like a bracelet. He said, "Thank you," and moved under my umbrella.

"Have you got a bicycle?" I asked, looking at the clips.

"I sold it," he replied, "to pay for the flowers at my father's funeral. You can't have a funeral without flowers, can you?"

"I suppose not," I replied, at a loss for what to say next.

I needn't have worried. He seemed quite at ease.

"I like the yellow of your umbrella," he said, taking my arm. "It's like a ray of hope on Oxford Street. A woman who can find a yellow umbrella in a gray world is worth knowing. My name's Desmond O'Reilly. What's yours?"

Diary entry. September 20, 1973.

He is *not* on the couch in the sitting room!

He seems even taller lying down, and is lying diagonally across the bed, arms outstretched again in what appears to be his favorite crucifixion position. This time he *is* naked . . . aside from the cycle clips, which are still around his wrist and which he is reluctant to take off. He's also fast asleep, and I shall eventually go back and snuggle in beside him. He smells of soap and sex, because before we got into bed, I gave him a hot drink, a hot bath, and dried him like a child in front of the gas fire. It awakened memories in both of us. It also awakened his long, thin cock, which was bent slightly on erection. I was sitting on a chair in the bathroom rubbing his legs with a turkish towel when it popped up just level with my mouth. After a few minutes he said, "I don't want to come like that; I want the warmth of you around me." We ended up in bed, and he fell asleep while he was still inside me. Eventually I slipped out and came in here to turn out the gas fire. Now my front is as frozen as my back, and I have to get into bed again to keep warm.

"Where are you? You belonged to me, and now you've left me," the scarecrow called from the other room.

I went back into the bedroom. He was still lying there with outstretched arms, with the covers thrown back and with another erection. He certainly needed warmth and love. With every word and every gesture, he was crying out for it. He was too thin, too long, an overgrown child; his ribs even stuck out. Only that cock of his was grown up, moving by itself with adult pride. I climbed onto him and slipped it in. He reached up and held my breasts. He did not play with them; he just held on. When it was over, I fell forward and then asleep.

It was not yet daylight when I woke up and heard him moving around in the sitting room. He struck a match and lit a cigarette. As he had undressed in the bathroom off the hall, he had obviously gone back there to get a cigarette out of his jacket pocket, have a pee and a smoke. I could hear him roaming around the sitting room, probably not wanting to wake me up or to smoke in the bedroom. I snuggled down again, content in the warm anticipation of his return to my bed, but fell asleep immediately.

When I awoke again, it was quite light, but he had not come back to bed. I called out to him, repeating his own words:

"Where are you? You belonged to me, and now you've left me."

There was no reply. The scarecrow had flown.

Diary entry. London. September 21, 1973.
Today is my granddaughter's birthday. I've just been robbed of some jewelry, a clock, two Batter-

sea boxes, and a book of poetry. I was right about
the young man being poetic, but he was also a
thief. Should I call the police?

Later the same day.

I thought a long time about calling the police. I
would have to tell the truth, and I could imagine
their response. What could they think but that a
middle-aged nymphomaniac had desperately
picked up a juvenile delinquent and got what she
deserved. "You might have been murdered,
ma'am," I could almost hear them say. Their version would probably be as near the truth as mine;
seeing is in the eye of the beholder, after all. I had
seen bright blue Irish eyes through a mist of soft
rain; the police would have seen a suspicious character loitering with intent. There's no point in
calling them. I'm the one who should be punished,
and I got what I deserved.

Apart from this unfortunate start, it was a happy
family day. I went down to the country for Caroline's birthday party. She was a bubbly nine-year-
old now; she sparkled and bounced and exhausted
us all. She was much more like her aunt Vanessa,
my second daughter, than her own mother, Fiona,
who is a quiet, shy girl. I still thought of Fiona as a
girl, although she was already a serene and capable
young woman in her thirties, a much better mother than I had ever been. My ex-husband Robert
was also there. He was now in his sixties—a witty,

sophisticated man and a wonderful raconteur. We danced the Charleston for the grandchildren to a recording of Sandy Wilson's *The Boy Friend*, an old family favorite. Granny and grandpa's dance was the high spot of the party, and the children thought it much more fun than hide-and-seek. They tumbled over with laughter, and my grandson said he could see granny's knickers when she kicked her legs up. My ex-husband said I hadn't changed at all and had always been prone to kicking my legs up—only he could remember when I wore bloomers. This was entirely untrue, as we were married in the late thirties, and I had not worn bloomers since boarding school. My trousseau undies were pink rayon locknit briefs with ecru lace trim, worn with pink Kestos crossover bras.

Gorged with cake and jelly, deafened with firecrackers popping and balloons bursting and children screaming, Robert and I were driven to the station at last, where we kissed good-bye on the platform rather formally, like the old friends we still are, and took separate trains back to our separate lives.

"Is this Mrs. Anne Cumming?"

"Yes it is. Who are you?" The unknown voice on the telephone sounded nice.

"This is the CID, Savile Row."

"Don't be silly! Who are you, really? I hate this kind of joke."

A slight pause.

"It isn't a joke, ma'am. This *is* the CID. Have

you recently lost a book of W. H. Auden's poetry?"

"Yes, I have. But how did you know?"

"It was found in Ireland, in a BEA airbag with some pawn tickets and other articles belonging to a young man called Patrick O'Grady. Do you know him?"

"No . . . well, perhaps I do, only he called himself Desmond O'Reilly. But I still don't see how you found me. Did he tell you he had taken it from me?"

"No. He left his bag in a Belfast café by mistake. Because of the bomb scares, the café owner phoned the police, who called in the Army Bomb Disposal Squad. There was an envelope tucked inside the book with your name and address on it. The pawn tickets made us suspicious, and when the young man came back to look for his bag, he was held for questioning. Did you lose anything else?"

"Yes, some jewelry, a Georgian carriage clock, and two little antique Battersea boxes."

"Did you report this to the police, ma'am?"

"No, I didn't. He seemed like a nice young man. I didn't want to get him into trouble."

"Had you known him long?"

"No, I'd only met him the night before." Another pause.

"I think you'd better come in and make a statement, ma'am."

"Yes, I suppose I should. I'll come straight over."

It all seemed unreal. The young man had been brought back to London and was to appear at Bow

Street, as this was the district in which the robbery occurred. I was called in again to identify him. He was looking very neat in his dry clothes. I had only seen him wringing wet or naked. We looked at each other with new eyes. His were still bright blue and very appealing. In a way, I found I liked him better. He had a sense of humor and was quite at ease. As I came in, he held out his arms in the scarecrow position and smiled. "Recognize me?" he said. He looked so young. Nineteen, they said, and with two other minor robberies to his credit, which had sent him to Borstal at the age of sixteen. And he *was* an orphan. He had been staying with his sister when he was picked up, and he had given the Battersea boxes to her. "I didn't know they were so valuable," he said calmly. "Otherwise, I would have pawned them with the rest of the stuff!"

I was given back my jewelry, after first describing it. The police had retrieved it from a pawnshop. Then I was given the clock and the book. I said his sister could keep the Battersea boxes.

"That's very nice of you, Anne," Desmond-Patrick said, surprised. It was strange to hear him use my Christian name. The formality of the surroundings had made me forget that, technically, we were lovers. For the first time I felt shocked at myself, and even the police looked disapproving. Up till then, they had believed my story: a young man, stranded, innocently taken home to sleep on my couch.

"Are you sure you wish to press charges, ma'am?" one of the policemen asked.

"I don't really want to, but I suppose it's my social duty," I replied.

"Don't worry, Anne, I won't get long. You can come and see me in jail."

"Come along, lad. That's enough," they said, and he was roughly taken away.

He was given three months' preventive detention.

Letter to Wormwood Scrubs Prison. September 30, 1973.

Dear Desmond-Patrick,

I didn't get a chance to tell you that I didn't mean to be the cause of your going to prison again. I didn't go to the police myself; they came to me. I was caught up in a court case, so to speak. They wanted to prosecute you, and they did. I wanted to help you, and I still do. I want you to look on me as a friend, not a victim. I shall come and see you in jail. I believe you are allowed one visitor a week. I don't want to take anyone else's place, so let me know if you have other people who want to visit you. I remember you with affection, not resentment.

> Yours,
> Anne

Letter from Wormwood Scrubs. October 8, 1973.

Dear Anne,

I got your letter today—a week late. They read them here first, you see. I suppose I should say I'm sorry, or something like that. I can't, because I'm not sorry. I needed the cash to go and see my sister. You seemed fairly flush and had a nice flat, and I suppose I could have asked you for money, but somehow I didn't want to—not after you'd given me love. It was easier to take what I needed and leave while you were asleep.

I wish you were here now. You're a lovely woman. When you come to see me, could you bring the Auden poems? I didn't get a chance to read them. I've always wanted to be a poet, and I'll have plenty of time now to try my hand at it. Will you help me? You remind me of my English teacher. The first thing I ever stole was a book to give her.

Love,
The Scarecrow

I went to see him in Wormwood Scrubs, a huge complex of bare, nineteenth-century buildings in forbidding gray brick. The high wall and the big black wooden door struck a somber note in the middle of the busy residential streets of Hammersmith. It was not a district of London I knew well, and I got lost twice going there.

"Could you tell me the way to Wormwood Scrubs?"

People looked at me strangely when I asked, but directed me politely. Soon I saw it looming up before me. There was a line of people waiting to get in, all respectable citizens, relatives and friends of those who had fallen from grace. They were rather silent—didn't chat much among themselves as most people would while waiting in line.

"Are we allowed to take in packages?" I asked a girl standing next to me.

"Yuss," she replied with a heavy Cockney accent, "but most of us 'ands 'em in before, or sends 'em by post. You'll 'ave to 'ave it searched. They won't let you give it 'im yourself."

"No, I suppose not." I smiled at her, but she wasn't very friendly. She could see I was new to prison visiting, while she was obviously a habitué.

We were allowed to go through a smaller door within the big door, which only swung open for cars and prison vans. As we walked across the yard toward one of the buildings, some prisoners passed with a prison officer. They looked at us curiously but stealthily. I thought that if they had been soldiers in a barracks, they would have been more open and would probably have whistled at us. The girl I was with was very pretty.

We were shown into a room, after being searched and my package taken away from me. I had brought the Auden poetry, some other books, cigarettes and food. We all sat at individual tables with a lone chair on the opposite side. Two prison guards sat at one end of the room and surveyed the scene.

The prisoners were brought in one by one, dressed in shapeless gray suits. Desmond-Patrick looked even taller and thinner than I remembered. They had taken away his bicycle-clip bracelet, and his wrists looked bare and skinny. They had also cut his hair, and he looked less like a scarecrow and more like some tall gray bird in his prison uniform. I told him so.

"You look like a thin gray bird I once saw in a cage at the zoo—a secretary bird I think it was called."

"I wish I were one. I'd break out and fly to freedom."

"Don't try to make me feel guilty. The reason you're 'inside' is inside *you*."

"I suppose you're right. I promise I'll try to go straight when I come out. Will you still be here?"

"Yes, I'm starting a new film on Monday. The shooting schedule's only three months, but it'll probably run overtime. The leading role's being played by a new French actress, and she has been delayed. She's still making another film."

"Who is she?"

"A new girl. Her first film's just about to be released, and they think it's going to be a wow. I met her in Paris on the way here."

"What's she like?"

"Pretty—but I think she's on drugs. She's going to be hard to handle, and if she's got no discipline, she won't last."

I was right. She had to be replaced after two weeks' shooting. Once she was too hung over with dope to act, and her dressing room was always full of marijuana smoke. Production was afraid she'd get busted, and it was better to replace her before too much film was in the can. The new girl looked too old for the part, but she was a quiet, well-disciplined little English actress. They are the ones who last.

I was allowed back once a week to see the Scarecrow, now known as the Secretary Bird. We wrote

to each other as often as was permitted. Never underestimate the power of letters. They can turn a
one-night stand into an intimate friendship. Desmond-Patrick had plenty of time to write, and he
wrote well. He returned the Auden book of poetry, together with some poems he had written himself. They were rather good, and I filed them away
with his letters to take back to Rome. They were
going to fill quite a space in the shoe box.

"I may have to start a new filing cabinet," I told
him. "Another box marked 'Letters from Young
Jailbirds.' "

The film progressed, with the usual ups and
downs. I had got the whole film company into the
Chelsea Cloisters, and it was strange to go back
there and visit them, because it evoked memories
of my time there with Bad Gregory and Rudi. Bad
Gregory and his new girl friend came to dinner
with me sometimes, and Rudi wrote from New
York:

Dearest Treasure,
A year has passed without seeing you, and that
leaves more of a void in my life than even Tom's
departure. I miss you more than I miss him. Please
plan another visit to New York soon. You can stay
with me this time. My apartment is quite big
enough for us to lead "separate lives in separate
beds," as you always put it. I don't foresee a trip to
Europe myself, because my whole year ahead is
mapped out with a musical on Broadway and various opera work at Lincoln Center, San Francisco
and Washington. I am even going to try my hand

at directing an opera! Designing is not enough; I
want the ultimate ego trip. I want to play God
with the whole cast! Hurry over and help me.

Love and a little kiss,
Rudi

I wrote back, promising to go and see him. I
missed him too. But by the time I got there, it was
a year later, and Rudi had unexpectedly gone back
to Europe to design a film in Rome and a new opera for German television. It was to be the longest
separation we had ever had.

Christmas came and went.

It was a quiet Christmas. Vanessa and Company
were having their festivities at home in Italy, and
Charles and his wife were going to her parents'.
But good old Robert came down from Wales as
usual, and his bronchitis seemed better that winter. Fiona gave us all a lovely time. Caroline had a
new, dark blue velvet party dress and looked as
pretty as a nineteenth-century picture. Malcolm
was becoming less angelic and more aggressive—
which was just as well for the time we were living
in.

The film was going well except for weather
problems. The Italian production company had
not reckoned on the unpredictable English rain.
On the days when we were to shoot outdoors and
needed it, there wasn't any. So we would start
without it, get caught in a sudden downpour, and
all the matching shots would go haywire. People
would step out of doorways into pale sunshine,

only to find themselves in driving rain on the street a few seconds later, film time, because we had shot that sequence the following day. Eventually we had to have a rain-making crew plus the fire department with their hoses standing by at all times. Then the fake rain looked more real than the real rain in the rushes, and we had to shoot all over again. Once we flooded somebody's basement apartment while spattering rain on an upstairs window. I became a public pacifier as well as a PR person.

In the meantime Desmond-Patrick's letters fell regularly through my letter box. They let him use a typewriter in jail, and he was doing a lot of writing. I started typing my diary with a carbon copy, which I sent him. It was strange to have such a concentrated relationship without actual physical contact, but our intellectual exchange was very satisfying. I was continually surprised by his youthful wisdom and intelligence. I wrote and told him so:

Dear Secretary Bird,

You would think by now that I would be used to the fact that teen-agers assimilate knowledge faster than older people and are therefore exceptionally bright. All they lack is life experience, and I have quite enough of that for two! My feelings are verging on those I once had for a young man in Paris called Joseph. The sharpness of his mind and the clearness of his ideals were very tempting, and I considered a long-term relationship with him. I would certainly never suggest such a thing again

with anyone so young, but I would like to know
you better. I feel perhaps that if you had a mother-
figure in your life, it might help you "go straight."
You also physically resemble a young man, now
dead, with whom I had an intensely sexual affair.
That side might work out well between us, too—
we didn't get much time to try! All this is leading
up to the suggestion that you might like a little
holiday when you get out of jail. I shall be going to
New York immediately after your release. Would
you like to come with me for a month? The fact
that you type quite well would be put to good use,
and you would really become my Secretary Bird. I
often need one. If this works out, it could even become a part-time job while you continue your
studies. We'll talk about it on Sunday.

Love,
Anne

It was a happy visiting day. He was to be released on the following Saturday. I promised to be
waiting outside the gates in the role of welcoming
mother and potential mistress rolled into one.

My life often resembles a rather trite movie.
This time I saw myself as Jeanne Moreau, full of
drama and sentiment mixed with sex—something
she does so well. I waited outside the gates in the
rain with my yellow umbrella. I was glad it was
raining because it gave me the chance to use it and
so re-create the mood of our first encounter. He
came through the little door within a door, wearing the same clothes I had first seen him in, but
without the hat. He was carrying a flight bag,

which I realized must have been the one he had left in the Belfast café. The police had returned my clock and my book, but naturally the rest had been returned to him.

"Hello!" I said casually. "You look as if you'd been crucified."

"I have," he said, coming up to me and standing under the umbrella with me.

He smiled, lifting up his left wrist. The clips hung strangely. They had been given back to him as he left prison.

"I like the yellow of your umbrella," he said as he leaned down to kiss me. "It's like a ray of hope outside Wormwood Scrubs. A woman who can find a yellow umbrella in a gray world is worth knowing. My name's Patrick O'Grady. What's yours?"

I laughed. He had a better memory than I. I couldn't have remembered our original conversation verbatim.

I looked up at him. "You've got raindrops on your eyelashes again. I remember that. You've also told me your real name this time. That's a better start!"

We linked arms and walked toward the Underground.

Diary entry. London. January 8, 1974.

This is where I came in! I've just been robbed of my Georgian clock, two silver photo frames, my remaining jewelry, and another book of poetry. This time he has taken my T. S. Eliot for a change.

What do I do now? Go to the police? At least this

time we know who he is, and they can pick him up at once. But what's the point? Prison doesn't help. Love and sex didn't help. We had plenty of that last night. He was raring to go after three months of masturbation in Wormwood Scrubs. He hugged me to him time after time, longing for human contact. I gave as much as I could—and not only sexually. All to no avail. He must have some need to take material objects as well. Why? I was offering him so much more—a trip to New York, understanding and love. Perhaps he didn't want possession—but if he wanted freedom, why clutter himself up with guilt? I must remember to ask Kurt when I get to New York.

No, there's no point in telling the police. I'll just chalk it up to experience. We all make the same mistakes twice.

9 ∽ Happiness Is for Free, Right?

Diary entry. Rudi's apartment. New York. February 20, 1974.

After a few days in a new place, I feel I have never lived anywhere else. I forget the past, I am right *there*. I fall into the pattern of *that* place. I buy *The Village Voice* instead of *The London Times*, or *Le Monde*, or *Paese Sera*. I shop at the A & P, or the Jefferson Market, or Smilers, which is open day and night. I cook American dishes and drink California wine. I say elevator instead of lift, but I preserve my British pronunciation for the pleasure of hearing "I just l-o-o-o-o-ve your English accent" a dozen times a day.

I am here to arrange the publicity for the New York première of a film shot in Italy. The female star is Italian; the male star is American. The usual co-production. Rudi is back in Rome; we have swapped apartments. He is designing the costumes for a big Italian film, then will go on to do something for German television. He will have left for Berlin before I return. Separate apartments, separate lives. This is the first time I have stayed in his New York home. Now that Tom has left him and got married, the apartment feels empty. I wonder whether Rudi has ulterior motives in lending me his home? Is he planning our happy reunion? I hope not. Freedom is all!

As I stepped out on that cold February day in 1974, New York was like a ski resort. Everyone was slipping around in the fresh snow. The air tingled, the sun shone, and everything crackled with static. I smiled with happiness and good health as I teetered down the street. A boy was coming toward me. He was smiling too, only his smile was bigger and brighter and whiter than mine because he was black. His woolly Afro stood out against the snow like a dark halo. Coupled with his radiant smile, it made him look like a shining black angel. His smile was a smile of recognition. Perhaps I knew him? In this day of blue-jeans regimentation and old leather jackets, you can't tell who's who. He could have served me at the supermarket or met me at a chic uptown cocktail party.

We passed each other smiling, hesitating to speak. I turned to look back, and he was also looking back. We had stopped about five yards apart.

"Do I know you?"

"I don't think so."

"Excuse me. You smiled at me as if we knew each other."

"I smiled because you looked a happy lady."

"I am a happy lady."

"You don't often see a happy face in this city."

We didn't move nearer. Our voices carried to each other with ease across the snow in the deserted street. There was no traffic. Nobody passed by at that moment.

"Where are you from?"

"Santo Domingo."

"Is that a happy place?"

"Not for me it wasn't."

"But you look happy now."

"Why not? Happiness is for free, right?"

"Right."

We smiled at each other once more, then we both turned and went on our way. It didn't seem necessary to say good-bye. As I turned the corner, I saw him at the far end of the street, smiling back at me as he also turned. Even at that distance his face glowed with warmth between the walls of banked-up snow. It stood out like a small black pearl in a white satin case. I dived down into the subway, and the moment was gone.

I came out of the subway again at Fifty-ninth Street. I was wearing a pair of borrowed snow boots two sizes too large and a long scarf wound first around my head and then around my neck. I looked like Mother Courage in a third-rate road company. No wonder the black boy had smiled. I would have to unwind myself before entering the Plaza Hotel, and use all my Stanislavsky-method stage training to make an elegant entrance. I was going to check the suite booked for Miss Superstar. It had to be filled with flowers from the producers and champagne from the director, and there must be plenty of gilt chairs in the sitting room for the press conference. I had already arranged for the press to be at the airport the next day, although we would brush them aside and say she was too tired to speak. She would be allowed a good night's rest, then she would have to face them all again the next day, reinforced by some fearsome ladies from the glossy magazines ready to criticize every false eyelash and every drooping hemline. Fortunately, the Italian producers were sending over her hairdresser and her makeup man with her. We would all be there to wake her up the next day, hours before the press conference, and, while she was put in order physically, I would put her in order mentally by telling her what to say. Fortunately, she was a bright girl; otherwise, she would not have come this far. Stars are *not* born; nor are they often found in drugstores. They've usually been around a long time working their way up by stages. They can't relax when they get to the top, either. There's no peace for the famous.

Conversation in the V.I.P. lounge of Kennedy airport.

The plane was late. My job was to keep the press amused so that they wouldn't go away and get drunk. The photographers were upset because it was snowing again, and they couldn't take a classic shot of the star stepping out of the airplane into the sunlight with her hand raised in greeting on the top step of the gangway.

"But you don't step out onto the runway anymore," I protested. "You crawl out into a tunnel shaped like a plastic caterpillar pushed up to the plane exit. What kind of a shot is that? You'll have to wait until she takes out her Italian passport at the immigration desk or sits on her Gucci luggage in the customs hall."

"Goddammit, I hope she's wearing a skirt," said one of the photographers. "You can't get no cheesecake anymore, now they're all in blue jeans."

"I'm sure Valentino's thought of that. He designs all her clothes."

"Is it true she was a whore?"

"No, but she was a film extra. If she'd been a whore, she'd still be a mere extra. A would-be star has to be very careful who she sleeps with."

At this point the arrival of the flight from Rome was announced, and the pressmen and I rushed to our action stations. I wanted to be the first to meet her so that she didn't say the wrong thing.

"*Carissima!*" she greeted me warmly, and we kissed on both cheeks.

"*Bellezza!*" I said. "How was the flight?"

"Boring. They showed one of my old movies. It was embarrassing, sitting there looking at myself with everyone looking at me."

I could tell she'd really loved it, but I pretended to sympathize. Then I stepped back so the photographers could get at her. She was looking divine, and I complimented her makeup man, who was emerging from the economy class with her hairdresser.

"Well, darling, it was *terribly* difficult," said the makeup man. "That *mean* production company put us both in tourist class so we could hardly get *near* her. Can you *imagine?* We *always* go first class with her, don't we, Isabella?"

"Yes, dear," murmured the little hairdresser, who always talked as if her mouth were full of hairpins.

"Don't worry, dears. You have lovely rooms in the Plaza Hotel right on the same floor. They wanted to put you in a cheaper hotel around the corner, but I told them that for everyone's peace of mind, you must both be near her."

Under a mountain of hand baggage and two extra fur coats, Suzanne now emerged from the plane. Suzanne was Miss Superstar's French secretary. She spoke several languages, dressed beautifully, behaved perfectly, never grumbled, and coped with everything. I adored Suzanne.

"Darling! Give me the furs. I've always had a yen for that snow leopard. Where's the white fox?"

"We decided it was corny, so we left it in Rome."

"I think that was a mistake. Now that the thirties are back, white fox would have been just right."

"We thought it might make her look too vulgar."

"That's not a bad fault. Valentino is getting too elegant. A little vulgarity shows up better in a crowd."

I hurried forward to catch up with the star. The newsmen were asking her what she thought about her new film.

"I don't think. I just do what the director says and hope the public will like it." She turned on her ravishing smile.

"You mean you don't read your own scripts, signorina?"

"Of course I read. I read and then I do. I am—how you say?—a poor working girl. I read, and then I do my best."

It was a good line, but we mustn't let her overdo it.

"I think the signorina is tired after her flight," I said quickly. "You are all invited to the Plaza at twelve tomorrow. Mr. Pollitzer, the director, will be there too."

We swept through Immigration and Customs. I refused to let her be photographed sitting on her luggage.

"She's a star, not a starlet," I protested.

Instead, I suggested they photograph her smiling at a red-capped black porter. Good for race relations. He handed her the smallest Gucci bag as she got into the rented Rolls limousine. She smiled her most radiant smile. The cameras flashed. Her secretary, Suzanne, handed out the tip. I got into the car beside the Italo-American chauffeur, who had been very busy stowing luggage and tucking in the star under real fur rugs. As he got in beside me, I realized how big he was—a real tough bodyguard type. Probably the production had decided to bring the Mafia in on the deal. It's a good move; we often did it on location in Italy, too. The local Mafia give better protection than the police, who are fine at keeping back crowds, but not much good at preventing theft, accidents, rape and kidnapping. A certain amount of this occurs during the making of most films.

The car moved away. I felt relief that this nice big protective thug was going to be looking after us for the duration of our visit. I took a second look at him as we drove along. Not bad. Could have been the stand-in for Sonny in *The Godfather*. Probably a very good lover. I knew the type. He reminded me of my truck driver. He would be tough when out with the boys, but tender in bed with the girls, and he might well solve the problem of my sex life in New York.

I like to get regular sex efficiently lined up while away on an assignment. No emotional hang-ups, just affection and a good working relationship. There was enough of the gangster in this one to give me the sense of adventure I liked. I have a secret weakness for gangsters, and, unlike most women, I don't nurse my sexual fantasies, I act them out right away.

"What's your name? Mine's Anne. We might as well get to know each other. We're going to spend a lot of time waiting around together on this job."

"Antonio. Call me Tony." He smiled at me, glad to find that I was human. "Waddaya do in this outfit, Miss Anne?"

"I'm the press agent. I get the news into the papers, sit around with the stars, hold their hands, cope with their hysteria, let them cry on my shoulder, and then get their names in the newspapers."

"Sounds like a great kinda job."

"Not really. I write a lot of crap and spend the rest of the time licking people's asses."

He smiled at me again, more observantly this time.

"You're quite a gal, Miss Anne."

"Drop the 'Miss,' Tony."

"Okay, doll."

It's very cozy up front in a Rolls Royce limousine. I looked back through the glass partition. Both the travelers had fallen fast asleep. They had learned how to take cat naps between performances.

"Do you have to hurry home to a wife and six children, Tony, or could you run me back to Greenwich Village after we've dropped them off at the Plaza?" I asked.

I was right about Tony. Tender as a lamb. After I had settled Miss Superstar into her gilded cage overlooking Central Park, he drove me home. I asked him up for a drink. He was a bit embarrassed at first, like a bull in a china shop. It's rather an unusual apartment, mainly furnished with delicate art nouveau furniture Rudi had found at a Salvation Army depot and had painted interesting colors. There was no chair big enough for Tony to sit in with any comfort, but I had to install him somewhere till I could successfully get him into the king-sized bed in the next room.

"Do take your jacket off," I said, to put him at ease. "Sit down; I'll fix you a drink."

He took off his jacket and eased his tie. He had chosen a rather spindly Gothic chair with wooden arms, and sank into it. He looked up at me like a big hunting dog waiting for instructions. He was summing up the situation. He looked even bigger with his jacket off; huge muscles bulged under his shirtsleeves.

"You look like an athlete, Tony," I said, going over to him.

"I was a heavyweight boxer once. I still work out in a gym sometimes. Wanna feel them?"

I stood in front of his chair while he flexed his biceps. I moved in between his knees to lean over and feel his muscles. My breasts brushed his lips. It was all he needed. Thank God for uncomplicated men. No more talk. No more doubts. He knew why he was there. He went straight to the point. His big arms dropped down to pick up my skirt and pull down my panties. I stepped out of them and stood with my legs apart as his big head zoomed in and his tongue hit my clitoris bang on. He made me come almost at once, then he leaned back with his crotch bulging and unzipped his fly. He pulled me down between his knees.

"Blow me, baby. Blow me good."

I knelt down and took it into my mouth. He spread himself back over the delicate armchair and writhed in ecstasy until I thought he would break the chair. He groaned constantly. I love that. I went on sucking furiously till he came with a huge heave of his pelvis. The sperm spurted into my mouth as the chair collapsed completely. We lay on the floor in the ruins. Rudi was not going to be pleased!

Diary entry. New York. February 28, 1974.

The trouble with sex is that you always get too

much or too little! I have set up an ideal working
relationship with Tony. He lives well below the
Village in Little Italy, with a wife and four kids,
and passes my door to get there. It suits us both for
him to stop off on his way home and come upstairs
with me daily for half an hour's extramarital bliss.
The classic continental 5-7, New York style. When
you're working hard, there is nothing better than
an affair with a fellow worker. You get through at
the same time, you're tired or not for the same reasons, and you know just where the other is at any
given moment. In this case, I'm also getting a ride
home in a Rolls Royce as part of the bargain.

It should have been enough, but more was to follow, and I soon began leading a double life.

Everyone in New York has his "shrink," but I
was totally unshrunk. I hadn't even found time to
go and see my old friend Kurt for our usual nostalgic chat, but I finally got around to it. I arranged
to go over and cook dinner for him in his West
Side apartment.

"Anne, dear, do come in," he greeted me. "But
forgive me if I keep you waiting a few minutes. I
have an unexpected patient in my study."

"Don't worry," I replied, embracing him warmly. "I'll go into the kitchen and get on with my
cooking."

"Shall I ask my patient to stay for dinner?" Kurt
asked. "I think you'll like him."

"For God's sake, Kurt," I protested, "I spend my

days with hopeless neurotics. Can't we just be alone?"

"You may change your mind when you see him."

"What do you mean by that?"

Kurt looked at me quizzically and smiled.

"He's a beautiful boy of nineteen. I think you'd do him good. You might even take him home with you."

"I see. Instant sex therapy. Masters and Johnson and me. You get the patient's money; I cure him."

"There's no money involved. It's part of my voluntary work as a 'gay' counselor."

"Really, Kurt, why should I want to take on another homosexual?"

"Because you once told me that most of your best lovers were gay."

It was true up to a point. They're always anxious to please and want to learn what a woman likes—unlike certain male chauvinists who think they know it all and usually get it wrong.

"This boy has had women before," Kurt added. "It's just that he's now being kept by a man and feels guilty about it."

"How old-fashioned! He's probably far less of a whore than anyone I work with."

"Exactly. Just say a few things like that, and he'll feel better immediately. Come on, Anne. You'll like him."

"But I'm tired of teen-agers."

"One more won't do you any harm."

"But I've got a perfect lover at the moment."

"You can't have too much of a good thing."

"Yes Kurt, you *can*."

Kurt had installed me in his sitting room and was heading for the study before I could stop him. As he opened the sitting room door, he said casually, "Oh, by the way, our teen-ager is black."

I'll never forget Kurt's face as he came into the room with his young patient and saw us walk straight into each other's arms. It was like one of those unreal television programs—"This Is Your Life" or "It Can't Happen Here."

The young man was the Black Pearl, the boy with the radiant smile from the snowy street. His smile reached out to me again, and the room was suddenly full of warmth and laughter. We were doubled up with surprise and pleasure and hilarious mirth.

"What's going on?" Kurt asked.

I suppose it was a strange sight: two people who could not have met before, kissing on sight; a shy, awkward black boy holding out his hands in friendship rather than formal greeting to a middle-aged stranger from another world, who took his proffered hands and stood on her toes to kiss him on the lips.

"I am Juan Esposito."

"I am Anne Cumming," I said through the laughter, and we moved spontaneously into a close embrace, our whole bodies touching. I laid my head on his shoulder as our laughter died down, and he held me closer still as our laughter ceased altogether. We stayed there quietly, silently enjoying the physical moment of contact. Something moved against my stomach. His penis was hardening, but his jeans were too tight for it to become erect. He was embarrassed and, without letting me go, moved an inch or two backwards so it didn't touch me. I took my hands off his shoulders and put them on his neat, firm, beautifully rounded buttocks, pulling his hips back toward me as I stood on my toes again so that his hard-on fitted into my pelvic hollow. The message was clear; it was instant sex therapy all right.

It was then that I saw Kurt's face—battling with confusion, astonishment, relief, incomprehension, comprehension, a whole gamut of surprise-reaction. He understood what was happening, but not why. Some trick of time and fate was making a *fait accompli* out of something not yet accomplished. Only one thing was clear: the two participants must be left alone to catch up with time and to straighten things out in space.

"I think I'll just slip down to the grocery store," Kurt said tactfully. "I've forgotten the salad dressing."

As the front door clicked and we heard Kurt go down the stairs, Juan eased his jeans so that his erection popped up like a jack-in-the-box inside them. He was wearing a tight belt with a big buckle that I had to undo before I could run my hand down inside. I didn't have to go far; the big purple knob was practically peeping over the edge. Its eye looked at me as if to say "I want you."

"It wants me," I echoed.

It still surprises and delights me that my aging body can spark off instant desire, so I seize every opportunity. I seized this big, black, throbbing opportunity with the fingers of my right hand, while pulling down the zipper of Juan's fly with my left. I don't suppose it was any bigger than Tony's, which I had seen and felt and handled only a couple of hours before, when he had run me home from work as usual. Tony and I had made love and then had taken a shower together. He had got another hard-on in the shower, but I had told him to take it home to his wife. Just as well I did!

Now I was holding another hard-on, different only in color, but it seemed more exotic. As Simone de Beauvoir says, "It's the 'otherness' that attracts."

I led Juan into Kurt's bedroom. He was a little doubtful, but I assured him that Kurt wouldn't mind; it was part of the therapy.

"You mean you know all about me?"

"Yes, I know all about you." I was already taking off my panties. "None of it matters. Only here and now matters. We'll talk later."

I lifted my skirt. He stepped out of his jeans. I threw myself face down over the edge of the bed, my legs still on the floor. I knew my white buttocks would turn him on, especially with the rest of me fully clothed. I arched my buttocks and guided him in as he came down on top of me. I was afraid he would come too fast, so I touched my own clitoris, but he went on a long time. We came almost simultaneously as Kurt opened the front door. He found us on the bedroom floor laughing again. We had fallen off the bed in our excitement. Kurt blinked at us through his spectacles.

During dinner, we explained the whole strange set of circumstances to Kurt. I was bubbling over with the joys of youthful encounter, which had nothing to do with the solid weight of my affections for Tony.

"Don't let Freud tell you my predilection for teen-agers brings out the mother in me," I said to Kurt. "Young boys make me feel young. That's all there is to it."

I had stayed behind to apologize to Kurt for my outrageous behavior while Juan hurried home after dinner. The White Queen, as I had already maliciously nicknamed Juan's rich protector, had a business dinner, but would be back early to check on Juan's movements. It was his jealous possessiveness and the financial dependence that was slowly killing Juan's affection for him.

"I was surprised at the speed with which the boy responded to you," Kurt said to me. "Perhaps he's not homosexual at all."

"Possibly mildly bisexual. It was more the situation and the strange coincidence that shocked him into it. He didn't have time to think."

"Yes, I could see that!"

"Forgive me if I embarrassed you by letting it happen. After all, you did ask me to do it."

"Of course, of course. It was very interesting, my dear. Clinically interesting. You seldom see heterosexual relationships skipping even a token courtship period. There is usually at least a short verbal exchange, although my homosexual patients tell me they often get down to it without a word being spoken."

"We *did* introduce ourselves. I distinctly remember saying my name."

"Yes, you did. I was amused at the formal social overture to such an immediate physical coupling."

"Do you forgive me?"

"My dear Anne, even Masters and Johnson would forgive you!"

The next day I waited on my doorstep in the morning sunshine for Tony to pick me up as usual. I was nearly always downstairs waiting for him, to prevent parking problems. I didn't feel remotely guilty or unfaithful as I slid in beside Tony and kissed him warmly on the cheek.

"Did your wife enjoy it last night?"

He looked at me, and his ugly, friendly face reddened slightly. *He* felt guilty and unfaithful. I burst out laughing, but I didn't tell him why, because he might never have touched me again for having been with a black, or even just for being unfaithful. There's not much tolerance in Tony's circle.

We were on our way to get my charge and then take her to the Metropolitan Museum to be photographed in the new Hollywood costume section. I thought the costumes themselves looked lifeless and tawdry on the mannequins, like dead people's clothes. Even the intricate workmanship and expensive materials looked cheap when divorced from flesh and blood.

By way of contrast, our golden girl looked vibrant and alive as she moved through the costume

display. It was as if she were putting the other
stars in the shade. Her subtly simple Valentino
suit and cape made their sequins look garish and
their laces phony. She radiated elegance and sex
appeal. As she moved around, we took off first her
cape, then her jacket, and finally unbuttoned the
plain white silk shirt to a deeper décolleté. Her
famous breasts could "inadvertently" be seen as
she leaned over a velvet dress once worn by Greta
Garbo.

The photographer was very quick and clever,
keeping ahead of her, hardly asking her to pause,
so it would look like a natural stroll through the
museum. She could have been any intelligent girl
on her afternoon off who just couldn't help looking sexy. I was extremely pleased with my own
stage-managing, and carefully selected the back-
grounds and poses as if I were directing a film sequence. I avoided Marilyn Monroe's evening gown
or Elizabeth Taylor's Cleopatra costume. These
were too much competition, since one could still
remember the succulent flesh that once had filled
them. All three women abundantly possess the
sensual quality that makes a star, I thought. It has
nothing to do with classic beauty and everything
to do with animal magnetism.

Tony was good at keeping back the crowd. Although the exhibition was roped off for half an
hour, people naturally wanted to get in. I stood beside Tony for a few minutes to give him moral
support and also to explain to the crowd what was
going on so we could win their cooperation. Suzanne took a child's autograph book up to Miss Superstar, who came over and gave it back to the

little girl herself with a few well-chosen words the child would never forget.

Finally it was all over. We took our leave of the museum officials, thanking them warmly—although they should have thanked us, as we were giving them as much publicity as we were getting ourselves. I herded everyone into the car—Nino and Isabella, the makeup man and the hairdresser, as usual on the little put-up seats, the star and Suzanne draped with the fur rug in the back and me up front with Tony.

"Let's take her back to the Plaza for lunch so we can have a quick pizza around the corner and then a nap in the back of the car," I whispered to Tony.

"Okay, doll," Tony replied, taking his right hand off the steering wheel to pinch my left thigh. Perhaps a nap in the car with him was not going to be such a good idea—but you couldn't do too much parked on Fifty-ninth Street in broad daylight, could you?

I was wrong; you could. We sat on opposite sides of the car pretending to sleep, but under the fur rug, our hands reached out to each other. His big fingers went up into my panties, my hand down into his fly. We went on pretending to sleep while our hands moved frenetically under the fur covering. Later we made use of the Kleenex Suzanne so conveniently kept on the back windowsill.

At around four o'clock, I went up to the suite in the Plaza. I washed my hands in the comfortable ladies room of the Palm Court on my way up. I wondered what the hell I was doing at my age with two illicit lovers at once, even though neither of them could spend much time with me. Tony had his wife waiting and Juan had the White Queen. It was an unnecessary complication. But then, I'm adventure-prone. It's a state of mind, like being accident-prone. You feel a certain way, so certain things happen. You grasp opportunities as they flash by that others wouldn't dare to grasp, or wouldn't even notice.

When I got upstairs, I found Miss Superstar in a panic because the valet service had scorched the hem of the very delicate silk dress she would wear to the première. Actually, the scorch mark blended into the pattern around the hem and was hardly visible, but everyone was in hysterics. I suggested embroidering it with sequins, but the problem was to find an embroideress at once. Valentino was called in Rome, and he said that some of his dresses were at Bendel's around the corner, off Fifth Avenue, but would they fit? Suzanne was to be sent dashing to Bendel's to bring them all back to the Plaza on approval, when I remembered that Bendel's had fitters there ready to do alterations. I went down to find Tony, whom I had left still asleep, as we couldn't expect our star to walk two blocks in the cold. Tony and the Rolls were missing, and he hadn't left a message with the doorman as he was supposed to do if he went to get gas. As there is nowhere in the world windier or colder than Fifth Avenue in winter, we called a cab.

In Bendel's model room, a middle-aged French saleslady said, "I think mademoiselle would look wonderful in white."

"But I haven't got the jewelry for white!" Miss Superstar moaned. "You need diamonds for white!"

"I'm sure Harry Winston will lend them to us," Suzanne suggested.

"I wouldn't be seen *dead* in borrowed diamonds. Elizabeth Taylor has her own."

"We could have covered the lack of them with the white fox, only you forgot to bring it," I added.

We were plunged into depression, as nothing else seemed suitable. At this point Tony arrived, having been told by the Plaza doorman where we were, ready to take us back empty-handed.

"Don't worry, doll," he said optimistically when I explained the situation to him. "My wife will know how to get it out. I'll bring her up with me tomorrow morning."

I was intrigued by the idea of meeting Tony's wife.

That evening our male co-star arrived from Los Angeles, and the dazzling pair were to be duly photographed in the right restaurant, to create the myth that they were having an affair. He was an American tough guy with a soft center, a huge, handsome man who couldn't hurt a fly, although with a carefully built-up tough macho image for the unsuspecting female public. I knew he was really a weak masochistic homosexual, forever getting himself beaten up by truck drivers, marines, and small-time prizefighters even bigger than himself. The studio went to a lot of trouble to keep these escapades out of the gossip columns by inventing romances for him. Consequently, the public thought of him as the Casanova of the Silver Screen, screwing his female co-stars right, left and center. He was given a new fiancée with every film.

On the way home, I wanted to leave a note for Juan, whom I hadn't been able to get on the phone. I didn't want him to think I had dropped him after a one-night stand. He had begged to see me again as he left Kurt's, where he had told me a lot about himself over dinner. I realized I now had a social responsibility as well as a new sexual partner. It was all a bit heavy.

Juan lived in Gramercy Park with the White Queen, who referred to him as "my *au pair* boy" when business friends came to dinner. The term "my houseboy" would not have entitled Juan to sit at the table with them. Juan accepted this. He knew what he was doing and why he was doing it. He was putting himself through school at the expense of a white father-figure. "So I screw him occasionally and he pays my school fees. How else could someone like me go to a university?" Juan had said unhappily.

Tony unsuspectingly delivered the note I'd written to Juan.

"Did you tell the doorman he was to give it *personally* to Juan Esposito? And not if he was with someone else?"

"Yeah, I did. But who is this guy? You're not two-timing me, are you, doll?"

"Tony, darling, how would I ever have the time, the energy or the inclination?" I said as I snuggled up to him.

"This Juan Esposito sounds like he's a spick," Tony said suspiciously.

"He's a black model, and I need him for some photos to catch the black public. I'm going to have him escort Miss Superstar to the Cotton Club show at LaMama."

It was a quickly devised excuse that might even turn into a good idea. I was surprised at my own inventiveness and perfidy.

"Yeah, but why the hell does this Juan have to get your note when he's alone?"

"Because he lives with an old faggot who wouldn't give him any pocket money if he thought the boy could earn his board and keep."

"Poor kid!" Tony meant it. He took a dim view of old faggots. Now I could probably count on Tony's sympathy if he and Juan ever met. Tony was a great big sentimental lovely hunk of man, and I was delighted to have him in my life.

I was sitting in the back of the car with Tony's wife. When they had picked me up, she was sitting beside Tony. She got out to be introduced to me, and it was quite easy and natural to suggest she get in the back with me.

"How did you meet Tony?" I asked her.

"In school," she replied.

She was a tiny woman, about half his size. I had expected a big, bosomy Italian woman, vulgar but lovable. Maria was a neat, refined little Italian dressmaker, almost spinsterish. I couldn't imagine her in bed with Tony.

"How did you come to get married?" I asked rather untactfully. "He doesn't seem to be your type." She could have said the same to me, with more reason!

"Tony always needed me, even in grade school. I was sorry for him because he always got his homework wrong. He was such a big boy, two years older than me, but he couldn't read or write very well. He needed me. We lived on the same block, so even when he dropped out of school, he still came in to get me to write things for him. Application forms, driver's licenses, anything. He was a good boy, and he used to fix things around the house for my mother and me. I never had a father."

"Where's your mother now?"

"She lives with us. Tony wanted her to. I was only sixteen when I married him, and we both needed Mother to look after us. Now we look after her."

"So you were with him all the time he was a boxer?"

"Yes. I was very proud of him. But I'm glad he gave it up. It took him away too much."

I began to understand this unlikely marriage. He was her man—a big strong protective figure. She was his woman—a demure, delicate little schoolteacher type whom he loved and respected and looked up to as his Madonna and the mother of his children. I was just an easy lay, maybe a bit more classy than usual, but not anyone to matter. I rather enjoyed the thought. I looked at the back of Tony's bull neck as I sat beside his little wife, and I wanted him. I enjoyed being treated like a whore, a woman you could do anything with, to whom you said all the dirty words you thought your wife didn't even know. I could hardly wait to get my hands on him again.

We had a strange day; all of us united as a team to prepare the star for her big night: little Maria, big Tony, Isabella the hairdresser, and Nino the makeup man.

I stayed close to Maria because I *felt* close to her. I was grateful to her for unknowingly lending me her husband. We both loved him in our own way. Our roles were perfectly clear. I wasn't usurping her rights in any way. *She* wouldn't want to be his whore, as I didn't want to be his devoted little wife. He was a big man and had room for both of us.

Tony was enjoying the situation. He hung around with us while we worked, towering over us proudly and protectively while we spread Miss Superstar's dress out on the floor to assess the damage.

"Tony, go away; you're getting in the light," I scolded affectionately.

"*Si, caro*, the signora's right. This is woman's work," Maria added. She felt the solidarity between us. We were two women working on a rush job.

"Okay, okay. I'll be outside in the car if anyone needs me." Tony shambled off like a big hurt dog.

Maria was busy with pins, trying to see if she could take a dart in the hem to eliminate the worst of the big scorch mark.

"If only we had a bit of the stuff! I could fit a patch over this pattern so you'd never see it."

"Suppose we embroider a motif with sequins?"

"If the material was on the straight, it would look good and weight it down, but with these full skirts on the cross it wouldn't hang right."

Maria held the dress up. She was so tiny that it brushed the ground.

"Give it to me," I said, taking it from her, and I held it against me to show her the effect.

"You'd look lovely in it, signora."

"Who wouldn't look well in a Valentino! And for heaven's sake call me Anne, Maria."

We smiled at each other in a moment of friendship, then concentrated on the dress again.

I moved my body so the dress floated around me as I pressed its soft folds against me. It swung a little heavily where the darts had been taken in the hem. Maria knelt at my feet and took out the pins, clucking like a little hen. "Ttt ... Ttt ... Ttt ... I'll try rubbing it with silver or gold."

We placed the dress on the ironing board provided by the guilty valet service, and searched for something silver.

"A silver coin is best, but a gold wedding ring will do."

I had never heard of this old-fashioned remedy.

"What a pity we're not in England, where there are still real silver coins."

"Don't worry, Signora Anne; we'll make do with my wedding ring." Maria slipped off the wide gold band.

Our heads were bent together over the board. She smelled of some old-fashioned Eau de Cologne.

I had a near-jealous flash as I imagined this delicate little woman crushed under Tony's huge weight.

She rubbed hard, but the brown patch remained. She shook her head.

"The material is too thin. It only works well on wool, where you can rub off the nap."

We looked at each other sadly, at a loss to know what to do next. Suzanne came in to see how we were getting on.

"If the signorina would just slip the dress on," Maria said. "I'll try again to take out a piece so it doesn't show. But I have to see it on somebody."

Suzanne went back to relay this information to Miss Superstar, who was sitting under a portable dryer in the bedroom. She obligingly got up and came in, wearing a hairnet and rollers. She never pulls the star act with people who are working with her. She's a great girl.

"Good morning. How nice of you to help us." She held out her hand to Maria.

"Good morning, signorina," Maria said, gasping with awe. "Good morning. It's a pleasure."

She hardly dared shake hands. It was as if the Madonna had stepped down from her pedestal.

"This is Tony's wife, Maria," I explained. "She's Italian too."

Soon they were chatting away happily in Italian while Maria pulled the dress over that gorgeous body and knelt at the feet of her idol with pins in her mouth. They managed to come to some compromise with the mark, making a little row of flaring tucks radiating out from the central seam. It was a very clever job.

"I'll have to take you back to work for Valentino," the star said gratefully.

"I could never leave Tony and the children," Maria sighed wistfully. "But one day I'd like to see Italy."

"You mean you've never been there?"

"No, I was born here. I'm a real American."

She was obviously as proud of that as she was of Tony.

"Now signorina, I must do the sewing. It's going to take a bit of time to do it all by hand."

"Good; come and talk to me while you work. I'm having my hair and face done because the *Vogue* photographer is coming soon."

They disappeared into the other room, two Italian women who probably had the same background, but who were now poles apart. Maria has probably never forgotten that morning. I can imagine her still telling her children about it to this day.

There seemed nothing more for me to do. We all needed to get to bed early, in order to be rested for the première the next day. I could fit in some shopping on the way home and make some last-minute calls to see that the press were properly covering every angle of tomorrow's opening, and then I could spend the afternoon making my own simple preparations for tomorrow's big night: wash my hair, do my nails, press my dress, and blissfully go to bed early and *alone*.

But it was not to be. My telephone rang as I walked in.

"Hello, Anne? It's Juan. I'm calling from a telephone on the street. I must come over and see you."

I hesitated. The last thing I wanted just then was sex.

"Juan, darling, I told you in my note I was terribly busy."

"But this is important. Really."

"Could it wait till the day after tomorrow—when the première's over and I can concentrate on other things?"

"No, it's really urgent."

"All right, come over," I reluctantly agreed.

"I'll be right over."

As I hung up, I thought of Napoleon's famous words: "If something is marked urgent, it means it's urgent to the sender." Well, I'd asked for it. I'd taken on a sexual liability—a social problem with racial overtones. Juan was going to be an unnecessary responsibility. I must learn to resist the love habit.

I phoned Kurt while I waited.

"What's wrong with Juan?" I asked. "He's on his way over to me with a problem."

"I don't know. I haven't seen him since you took over!"

"Oh hell! Don't let anyone ever tell you it's all fun sleeping around. I sometimes wish I'd given it up!"

I sighed and put down the receiver, then I went into the bathroom. Did I have time to wash my hair before he arrived? I began taking out the hairpins, and it fell around my shoulders. I looked at myself in the mirror. Was I still young enough to wear it down? I longed to change my image and be somebody else. I took off my clothes and put on a robe.

The entry phone rang just as I dipped my head into the basin. "Come up; I'll leave the door on the latch. I'm washing my hair," I said, and went back and plunged my head into the basin again.

Juan came into the room and put his arms around my waist as I bent over the water. He laid his woolly head on my back. I went on with my shampooing. Juan hugged me to him, pressing his pelvic bulge into my backside.

"I love you, I love you, I love you," he said.

I squinted around at him, soap in my eyes.

"You're mad. You hardly know me."

"You don't take me seriously."

"I'm hardly in a position to."

"I like this position."

He took his hands off my waist and lifted my robe, continuing to press his penis against me while I rinsed my hair. I began to relax against him. Perhaps his problem was just that he was sex-starved. Perhaps the White Queen was old and impotent. I began to enjoy the situation.

"Just wait till I finish the rinsing," I begged.

But he didn't wait. He had to bend his knees and I had to stand on my toes, leaning over the basin. He was a tall boy, which made it difficult to fuck standing up.

When he had finished and had withdrawn his long, purplish cock, I said, "Let me wash it."

We stood side by side at the basin. I took his

black penis in my hand and washed it with baby
shampoo.

"It would make a good commercial: 'Cannot
hurt the most delicate skin.' Shall we sell the idea
to the producers?"

He giggled. "I can hardly see it on television."

I picked up a bath towel, and we went into the
sitting room. He zipped up his fly, I wrapped my
hair in the towel, and we sat down facing each
other.

"Now what's the matter, Juan?"

"I can't go to bed with my lover anymore."

"Why not?"

"It revolts me. It makes me sick to my stomach. I
want a woman. I want you."

"Juan, this is serious. He's your life. He's your
fortune. He's putting you through the university.
He's feeding and clothing you. I can't do any of
those things for you. I don't even want to."

"I don't care. But I don't want to be a kept boy
anymore."

"There's nothing wrong with being a kept boy if
you know why you're doing it, and you do it hon-
estly. Women are kept. Why shouldn't men be?
Some people just like to look after others. The
White Queen wants to look after you. You're not
blackmailing him into it."

"No, of course not. He *begs* me to stay with him.
He doesn't care what I do or don't do as long as I
stay with him. But I can't take everything and give
nothing back, can I?"

"I don't know why not. There are lots of middle-
aged homosexuals who go on keeping boys long

after the affair is over. In Italy the boys get married, and the father-figure very often goes on helping him and the wife and taking care of their children too. Usually the wife knows what the score is. She's quite happy with a rich protector for her family."

"I just can't do it. I want to live with a woman. I want to live with *you*. Why can't I move in here?"

"Juan, I don't live here. This isn't my apartment. Anyway, I'm leaving very soon."

"I see. I didn't know that."

"I told you that you knew nothing about me. Even if I lived here, I couldn't take on that kind of obligation."

Juan looked embarrassed and downcast. He was a simple outgoing boy who lived by instinct and had never given much thought to what he was doing.

"You don't despise me for living off a man then?"

"Not at your age. When you've finished your studies, and you're earning your own money, then you can think of living with a woman."

"But I'll never get someone like you. I'll always be a poor black boy from the wrong side of the tracks."

I went over to him and put my arms around him.

"You're a beautiful boy, Juan, and a nice loving boy. The right woman will one day lose her head over you. It's just that I personally have no intention of falling in love ever again."

"Why not?"

"Because love has brought me more suffering than joy. I've had two husbands and several live-in lovers. It was nice while it lasted, but from now on, I just want the fun and none of the responsibility."

I took the towel off my head, rubbed my hair, then shook out the damp strands. Juan stroked my hair. "You look funny with your hair wet," he said, but it didn't deflect me from my main theme.

"I guess I'm not very good wife material, nor a good mother either, for that matter," I continued.

Juan went on playing with the wet strands of my long hair, twiddling them around his brown fingers. The palms of his hands were pink and the tips of his fingers quite pale on the inside.

"Could I spend the night with you?"

"Would that be sensible? What about the White Queen?"

"He's at the opera. I told him I was going home to see my mother in the South Bronx."

I was tempted, but I made a firm decision.

"I want to be alone tonight, Juan dear. There's no poing in getting used to something you can't have, either. It makes it worse later. Am I being very cruel?"

"No. You've taught me a lot tonight. I've never looked at things from a woman's point of view before. I wish you weren't going away. You'd help me to grow up."

He smiled at me, that wonderful, warm, outgoing smile. I put my arms around him. I suddenly wanted him to spend the night, but I knew I mustn't give in.

I saw him to the front door. He went quietly, thank God, and I said, "Be happy, Juan, that's all that matters. Go back to that poor man and make him happy too. If he's happy, there's nothing wrong about what you're doing. Relax and you'll enjoy it yourself too. Happiness is for free, right?"

He went out the door and pressed the elevator button. I waited till it came. He gave me a last look.

"You're a different person with your hair wet," he said.

We both smiled, and he was gone.

It was snowing again on the Big Day. I arrived at the Plaza to find the producers pacing up and down their suite.

"Nobody will come out in this snow," they were saying alternately to one another. Now they said it simultaneously to me.

"An invited audience always comes," I said reassuringly, turning on my public relations optimism.

"You're right. You're so damn right," said Bob. "Anne always cheers me up."

"That's what you pay me for, boys—to cheer you up, and to spread good news and hush up the bad. That's what publicity is all about."

"You're worth your weight in gold, Anne."

"Okay. Weigh me! I'll take it. Twenty-two carat, please!"

We all laughed, and I looked out of the window at the pond; a few skaters were circling around under the bare black trees of Central Park despite the snow. I turned back to the producers.

"Now, boys, get your tuxedos pressed. I'm planning plenty of pictures. I'll go up and see if Randy's polished his platinum S and M chains for tonight."

"Anne, you don't think . . . ?"

"No, I don't. He's wearing wine-red velvet with only an identity bracelet. And if I can, I'll take that off him at the last minute."

I joined Suzanne in the star's suite. She was answering the fan mail. I was happy to see that my advance publicity was working. Dozens of youngsters had written in for photographs. Suzanne and I sometimes amused ourselves by trying to guess what the male fans were like.

"Let's ask them to send us *their* photographs in return," I suggested this time. "We might discover some new talent."

"Can't you keep your hands off teen-agers yet?" Suzanne teased me. "Most of the fans are under sixteen."

"A pity. I usually draw the line at seventeen!"

"Tony's a bit old for you then?"

"He's in another category. Heavyweight class. But even Maria admits he's got the mind of a child."

"Don't you ever want someone your own size?"

"I guess not. I suppose I want to be the dominant factor between the sheets. But most of my *friends* are my age, Suzanne."

"That's certainly not true of your lovers! How many have you got now, Anne?"

"Only two in New York, and I think I've sent one of those home to Big Daddy."

"And you look so quiet and ladylike!"

"That's what my husbands thought, but when they found out I was neither quiet nor a lady, they left me."

"But they both still adore you. And everyone else thinks of you as a great lady, whatever you do."

"That's the trouble. I spend my life trying to live down that lady image. It's getting to be a bore."

Miss Superstar came in wearing her wrapper. She had no makeup on and her hair was in rollers.

"What are you two talking about?" she asked. "You're always gossiping."

"Secrets!" I replied.

"How lucky you are to be free to have secrets," she said enviously. "I can't have any."

We'd all been given the afternoon to rest, so Tony took me home. We had lunch on the way at an Italian restaurant run by some friends of his near Broadway. They refused to let us pay.

"I kinda feel like a quick siesta," Tony whispered to me as we left. I could never refuse Tony anything.

We parked the Rolls on Sixth Avenue in front of the liquor store and walked to my apartment, arm in arm.

"Your hair's turning white," Tony said in the elevator, brushing the snow off it. He kissed me solidly from the first to the eighth floor. I was out of breath on arrival.

We took off our coats in the hall. Tony still had a hard-on from the elevator, and he took my hand and made me feel it.

"C'mon, doll. Let's get movin'! I wanna get some sleep afterwards. Who knows what time I'll hit the sack tonight. They'll be celebrating till dawn if the film's a success."

"Let's hope so." I went into the bedroom and turned the covers back. "What I like about you, Tony, is that you don't waste any time getting going. And once you're there, your timing's perfect."

He was already undressing, not listening. I sat down on the bed and watched him. Tony, naked, turned me on. Other more intellectual men might have to turn me on verbally first. It would not be enough for them just to get undressed. Tony wouldn't think of a thing like that. He didn't have to.

"What'sa matter, doll? Take off your clothes."

He was still wearing his socks. He seldom took them off when we made love.

"I like watching you, Tony."

"C'mon, you're gonna feel me too."

He pushed me back and ripped off my panties, pushing my skirt up over my head to do it. I had on my French tights with the open crotch, so he didn't need to take them off. He left me fully dressed, went down on me for a few seconds, but then quickly put it in. From then on he took it very slowly. He knew how my motor worked. If the piston went in slowly, then the clutch would clutch it. I have quite good pelvic muscles.

"You know how to take a man, baby! You really take it all!" He gasped, but held back.

He began to rotate very gently. When he felt me reaching climax, he changed the movement for his own satisfaction and shoved in and out so fast, it was like a pneumatic drill. He even made a noise like one, "Grrrr ... Grrrr ..." and then a roaring groan. He came a minute too soon for me, but kept moving till I climaxed.

"Oh, Tony, I love it, I love it! Ah, Tony!"

Sheer peace and happiness afterwards. There were no problems with Tony, no responsibility, no complications, not even any guilt. I don't think Maria would even have minded had she known. A great big husband like hers should have a few mistresses. It went with the full-blooded nature she loved him for.

"I'd better leave you, baby. I'll go home and sleep it off, and we'll see each other later." He lifted his 200 pounds off me and got out of bed. He was still wearing his socks.

I had set my alarm for six o'clock to give me plenty of time to dress. At 7:30 our producers, Bob and Bill, were giving us all champagne and caviar in their suite on the top floor. There was the usual element of hierarchy and one-upmanship in the fact that Miss Superstar and Randy were booked on slightly lower floors. It always had to be made quite clear who was putting up the money and who was earning it.

I called for Miss S and Suzanne on the way up.

Isabella and Nino were putting their finishing touches to her hair and face, having spent two hours only to make her look perfectly natural. Now they were all standing back looking at her in the mirror.

"I'm going to rechristen you Miss Divine," I said as I stood looking at her in the mirror too. "There are too many Superstars anyway."

"You can't," Suzanne interrupted. "Some man over here is calling himself Divine—a transvestite star in Underground movies."

"Wouldn't you know? As soon as we try to eliminate the star system in commercial movies, the Underground brings it back."

With this, we gathered ourselves together to go up to the producers' penthouse suite. Nino helped Miss S into her floor-length snow leopard, which covered the hem of her dress so that no one would ever have noticed the slight repair so carefully done by Maria. She and Tony were missing.

"Where are Tony and Maria?" I asked. I had insisted on them being given tickets for the opening, and they were supposed to be at the Plaza early, because Maria had offered to help Miss S get dressed.

"They were here, but they went downstairs again to the car," Suzanne replied. "They were too shy to stick around."

"I'll go and get them," I said. "You all go on up."

I dragged them out of the Rolls. Maria was wearing a neat, long black skirt and a mink jacket.

"I borrowed the jacket," she whispered to me. "Does it look all right?"

"Perfect," I assured her. "You look as if you always wore it."

I pushed them into the penthouse suite and introduced them to Bob and Bill, who were surrounded by their minions from the New York production office, all of whom had seen Tony around, but none of whom had ever seen Maria. She was being as dignified as Tony was awkward, and stood holding her champagne glass in her tiny dainty hand with the same care as if it were a box full of pins.

Everyone was drinking toasts to each other. Randy was looking immaculate in his velvet, not a chain in sight, not even his identity bracelet. He kissed his co-star, who in turn kissed the producers, and then everyone raised his glass and kissed someone. Tony kissed Maria and then looked at me.

"May I kiss your husband?" I asked her.

"Don't let her," Nino interrupted teasingly.

Maria drew herself up. "It'll do him good to be kissed by a real English lady," she said with dignity.

I wondered how much she knew. It was as if she were protecting us.

The opening went with the same champagne sparkle. It had stopped snowing, and everyone was there. The critics had seen the film at a private morning viewing, but the reporters and photographers were there for the social occasion. Our stars scintillated in the foyer and again from the silver screen. Miss S got live applause after her big scene, as if it were a stage show. The audience loved her. She had made the transatlantic crossing, that roughest, toughest sea in show business.

Everyone was euphoric by the time we went on to celebrate at "21." Randy was getting drunk, Miss S was as excited as a birthday child, and I was tired. I wished I had slipped away after the show in the taxi with Maria. She had to get back to her children, while Tony waited for the stars.

After half an hour, I left the restaurant and went to see if Tony could drive me home and then come back later for the others.

Tony was asleep at the wheel of the Rolls. Instead of waking him, I crunched on in the fresh snow in my unsuitable slippers. It had been stupid of me not to get the doorman to call me a cab, as an icy wind was blowing down Fifth Avenue straight from Alaska. The sparkle of success seemed a long way off and very artificial. I shivered till a taxi came. All I wanted was to get home and take off my wet shoes.

I was awakened the next morning by Kurt on the telephone. He reported that Juan had come to see him quite relaxed and happy. "He said he was going to stay with the White Queen forever, and that there's nothing wrong with being kept."

"That's what you told me to do, wasn't it? Persuade him his life was all right?"

"Yes, but I never thought your private form of sex therapy would work so quickly. I can see I'd better start sleeping with my patients myself! You're a great girl, Anne."

"So everyone keeps telling me. It doesn't help my own feelings of futility though. I was thinking of coming to you as a patient. Have you a cure for boredom?"

"The day you ask me that seriously, I'm giving up my practice! You have the least boring life I know. Now when are you coming out to dinner with me to cheer me up?"

"In two days' time. Today we're sleeping off the sweet smell of success. Tomorrow Miss Superstar flies back to Italy, and when I've seen her off, I'll devote myself to my friends."

"Good. I'll be waiting. And thank you for helping me with Juan. If you stick around, I might lose all my patients!"

"Don't worry. I won't take the rich ones," I promised, and went back to sleep.

At lunch time I was just surfacing again when the entry phone buzzed. It was Juan. His voice came up the wires as if from under water.

"Can I come up, please?"

What could I say? I had only wanted the flash of a smile, but I'd taken on a whole responsibility. I couldn't back out now.

I let Juan in. "Have you had lunch?" I asked.

"No, I just came from the New School." Then he hesitated, and finally said, "The White Queen wants to meet you."

"Good God! Did you tell him about me?"

"Of course. He makes me tell him everything."

"He must be a masochist, poor man. I don't want to hurt him."

"But that's what a masochist wants, isn't it?"

"Maybe, but I'm not a sadist. What am I supposed to do, invite him for dinner? Or does he want to watch us in bed together?"

"I don't know. I hadn't thought about it."

"Well, let's forget it. Now go out and buy me all the papers while I get brunch ready. I've got to read the critics. Here, take some money."

We were in the kitchen eating bacon and eggs and reading the papers when the entry phone went again. It was Tony. I had forgotten he was coming to get me. What would I do now? It was getting like a French farce.

"Tony, you'd better come up. I'm still having my coffee."

I went back to the kitchen.

"Listen, Juan, it's the production chauffeur. I've told him I need a black model for some photographs. That's you. Now don't let me down."

Before I could explain any further, Tony rang the bell. I took him into the kitchen where we were eating.

"Tony, this is Juan. He's doing some photos for me. Sit down and have some coffee with us."

Tony didn't seem suspicious. He accepted the fact that I had a life he knew nothing about. He didn't want to move into my world; he was quite happy where he was.

I went out and finished dressing, leaving them together. I wondered what they'd talk about—not me, I hoped.

I came back and found them talking boxing. Relieved, I sat down and took another cup of coffee. Juan said he must go, and treated me with the right amount of formality.

"You must come and have a drink with me and my friend before you leave," he said. "We're giving a small party the day after tomorrow. Will you come? You can bring anyone you like."

He began walking toward the front door. I went with him into the hall, where Tony couldn't see us. I gave Juan a warm kiss good-bye.

"Yes, I'll come," I whispered.

Packing was the key word at the Plaza, and Suzanne had a checklist of garments in her hand. I took the list from her.

"Here, I'll read out the list while you check the clothes."

Miss Superstar's couture dresses, handmade shoes, Gucci handbags and hand-embroidered Florentine underwear were lined up on the bed beside some American tights, costume jewelry and gadgets and gifts she had bought to take home. Her real jewels were downstairs in the hotel safe.

Our beaming producers arrived with two incredible call girls. It was relaxation time all around, I could see.

The girls were introduced. They must have been summoned after Bob and Bill got home from "21" and obviously wouldn't go until they had met the stars.

"Shall I call Randy down now?" I asked. "The photographers will soon be here."

The telephone rang to say a well-known gossip columnist was downstairs. "Send her up," I said. Then I telephoned Randy. He was not there.

"Randy's disappeared," I announced.

"Didn't you tell him last night that we had the press coming today?" Bob snapped. His call girl must have worn him out, and his California charm was slipping.

"Of course I told him," I replied, trying to keep my tone pleasant and understanding. He was paying me, so he was entitled to snap at me.

At that moment there was a knock at the door, and Randy walked in with his arm in a sling.

"Fell off the back of a truck?" I asked mischievously.

Randy raised his good arm to take a swipe at me.

"I may get beaten up by the boys, but I can still hit a woman," he quipped.

The phone rang to announce more journalists, and there was a knock on the door from the one who had already arrived.

"We'll say Randy was accidentally pushed over by fans crowding around for an autograph, right?"

"Right!" Randy replied with a wink.

I let in a militant feminist journalist who looked as if she meant trouble. She strode straight over to Miss Superstar, who had stood up graciously to receive her, but now seemed in danger of being knocked down.

"What does the Italian woman think about Women's Liberation? Don't you find it demeaning to be a sex symbol?"

Miss Superstar looked at me for help.

"I think she doesn't understand the word *demeaning*," I cut in quickly, and gave her a rapid suggestion in Italian as if I were interpreting the question.

Miss S smiled modestly. "No work is 'demeaning,' as you call it; if you do well what you are paid to do, that is always a satisfaction, no? I am paid to be a sex symbol; to me it is a job, and I try hard. Is that wrong in America?"

Bob and Bill beamed gratefully at her. In spite of their own vulgarity, they were shrewd enough businessmen to realize that they had bought into a commodity with class and dignity as well as sex appeal—which was why she stood head and shoulders above the pretty call girls who sat like identical dolls on the Louis Quinze–type sofa, completely overshadowed by her.

The other members of the press arrived, and the questions became more general. I handed out the potted biographies I had prepared, together with photostats of the best reviews from the morning papers while Randy explained about his arm.

"It's nothing really; got it caught in a revolving door getting away from some teen-agers last night."

The farce went on. At last I intervened.

"I think, gentlemen, our stars have been through enough ordeals in the past few days. We must let them go now and enjoy their last day in New York."

"Where are they going?" asked Miss Militant Feminist. "Are they making another picture together?"

Bob and Bill answered this one. "We hope to team them up again in the near future. Right now they have other commitments."

I pushed both stars out of the suite, holding

hands. We had carefully planned that little scene. They were only going up to Randy's suite until I called to say the coast was clear, then Miss Superstar could come down and get on with her own schedule.

Our producers answered a few more questions about future plans, and then gathered up their living dolls from the sofa and disappeared too. I could see I'd have to get my check from them before the call girls began asking for snow leopard coats like Miss Superstar's. I had noticed they both already had mutation minks.

Finally Suzanne and I were left alone.

We kissed each other good night and I left, determined to go to bed really early. As I went out the door, I said, "I'm going to hang a notice outside my door tonight. 'Do not disturb.' "

"I think 'House Full' would be more appropriate," Suzanne called after me.

I awoke to a cold, mauve dawn and planned my last few days.

My job would end at the airport as I put Miss Superstar on the evening plane back to Europe. I would kiss her good-bye, kiss Tony good-bye, and start my brief holiday next day by going to the White Queen's cocktail party to kiss Juan good-bye. Kiss all the boys good-bye and take a brief holiday from sex. I could then concentrate on other things, like shopping in the snow, seeing as many plays as possible, calling all those old friends I hadn't had time to see yet, and for a few days I would be myself. Then I'd fly back to England and play granny. A modern granny arriving in a Jumbo Jet with little packages from Macy's and Gimbel's and the Fifth Avenue Woolworth's. I shut my eyes at the thought and fell asleep again.

When I woke up again, the sun was shining in across the snowy roofs. It was ten o'clock. I got up and went to the Plaza to collect my check from Bob and Bill. They were leaving at midday for the Coast.

I savored the old-fashioned luxury of the Plaza for the last time. When my daughters were little and we stayed in a hotel, I used to say to them, "Breathe it in, it's costing me $5.00 a day." Now I said to myself, "Breathe it in, it's costing $50.00 a day." Once, for $5.00 at the Plaza, you got your room and a full meal in the main dining room with Hildegarde singing "Smoke Gets in Your Eyes." Now you wouldn't even get a sandwich.

The elevator boy let me off at the top floor. Bob let me into the penthouse and immediately dashed back into the bedroom, where he was talking on the telephone to California, cooking up deals that would come to a boil as he stepped off the plane in a few hours' time. It gave me time to look out again at the skaters on the pond. That hadn't changed in all the years I'd been coming to New York. There were always skaters circling around and around in Central Park.

"Sorry, Anne! Busy tying up a new star. Now where's Bill with the checkbook?"

Bill was in another bedroom with the two call girls. They were sitting on his suitcase, trying to close it over the presents he was taking home to his wife. Bob was fresh and rested and on the ball. Bill, on the other hand, looked particularly worn out. Perhaps *both* girls had been sitting on him all night.

"Anne, you've done a great job. You must work for us again."

They handed me my check and a Tiffany lighter. I don't smoke, but I kissed them warmly for the thought. For good measure, I kissed the two call girls as well. They smelled identical—of too much expensive French perfume.

"Good-bye, everyone. See you at the next première."

I went downstairs to see Suzanne. She had finished the packing. Miss Superstar decided to have a quick lunch in the Palm Court and go last-minute shopping. We went with her.

When we got back to the hotel, Tony was already there to help load up the luggage and intimidate the doorman. It was snowing again when we left. Romantic but unnerving. Miss Superstar was worried about takeoff. I consoled her.

"You'll fly well above the weather, close to the other stars."

There was only one photographer at the airport. Success was two days old, and the press were looking for new prey. More kisses. I waved my last wave from the barrier, and they were gone. I went back to find Tony. He had been given a big tip; Suzanne always saw to that. I gave him my Tiffany lighter. He was overcome and wanted to give it back.

"But I ain't got nuttin' for you, doll."

"You've given me all I ever want, Tony. Come on home and give it to me again for the last time."

"Okay, baby. I'll take you home, and I'm gonna fuck the fuckin' life out of you. You'll never forget me."

And I never have.

10 ∽ The Hippie Hustlers

A rather dull year passed, except for Martin Greenbaum's wedding. After our breakup, Martin and I had fallen into an easy friendship, and I liked his youthful French fiancée, Solange, very much. She had come to live with Martin in Rome by this time. Quite often we all went out together with whomever else I had in tow. The previous summer, after my return from America, Martin and Solange had taken an apartment in Sperlonga for their holidays. It was here that they decided it was time to get married. We were all lying on the beach together at the time.

"I don't want to get married in Paris," Solange said. "My parents' home is small, and their life is restricted. I'd much rather get married in Rome."

"It's rather unusual to get married from the bridegroom's house," Martin replied laughingly. "Your parents are very bourgeois; they might not like the idea."

"Then why not get married from my house?" I suggested. "As Martin's parents are dead, I can play the part of the 'other mother' and gracefully give Martin away!"

So the ceremony took place in my house. There was even something Biblical about it: Martin was a Jew, Solange was a Catholic, and I was a Protestant; and there was no just cause or impediment. It was quite in line with the new ecumenical council's preachings for religious and moral understanding. We all understood the situation; only God is eternal love, and we mere mortals change partners from time to time.

The wedding reception was held in my large green drawing room, and the guests spilled over onto the terraces. It was a warm autumn day. I felt no pangs and had no trouble with the role reversal from mistress to mother-in-law. It rather tickled my sense of humor. I had played the part twice at my daughters' weddings, and at fifty-seven I still looked the part. I even wore a large hat with a rose on it.

Evaristo was among the guests. He said, "I see the Peace rose continues to bloom. You're a remarkable woman, Anne."

"No . . . I'm a fading flower. I sometimes feel my age now—when I have time to think about it. Fortunately I'm not much of a thinker."

"Then don't start thinking now. Just keep on doing."

I smiled. His remark reminded me of Grant's "keep on running through life." My boys evidently didn't want me to stand still and be introspective, although Evaristo was hardly a boy now. He was a young man of twenty-six and was already getting a little stout and bald. His dynamism and charm had, however, increased with the years.

The rest of the year jogged along. I had a boring job with a boring film, which prevented me from flying over to spend Christmas with Fiona. Vanessa was going and I saw her off with her little boys, then spent a quiet three days alone in Sperlonga. Some friends who live there the year round invited me to Christmas dinner in front of a roaring fire. I had previously helped to gather driftwood for it along the wind-swept beach. I took many long, cold walks alone to places where I had spent long, hot, passionate hours during the long, hot summer days of my past. Surprisingly, I was not unhappy. I was resigning myself to solitude.

Spring eventually came, and with it the return of some of the old lovers and the advent of a minor and short-lived new romance. When that was over, I really didn't crave sexual excitement or the "high" of falling in love. Perhaps I was beginning to kick the habit. Then during the summer, I got the following letter:

St. Tropez. August 30, 1975.
Dear Anne,

What are your summer plans this year? Are you coming to St. Tropez? I know you only like it out of season, as we all do, so perhaps we could tempt you here in September. We've kept our little apartment in the village for guests, since we moved into the villa. Won't you come and use it? Rome must be unbearably hot just now.

We're planning to make a little film—a silent surrealist fantasy in color. There's a part in it just for you. Wouldn't it amuse you to be on the other side of the camera for a change?

The part calls for a lovely middle-aged woman who always arrives too late for everything, who misses the action every time. Your only companion is a big black dog who follows you everywhere, and finally dies in your arms. As you hold his dead body and shed a tear, the audience thinks that life has ended for you. But no! The image of the dog fades, and in your arms is a handsome prince.

How about it?

Love,
Bart

Bart is a rich industrialist from the Midwest who lives in Europe and is full of cultural projects to help him get rid of his guilt complex about being rich. He would do better to underwrite some worthy and needy going concern, but then he couldn't strut about his barnyard and play cock of the roost, surrounded by pretty disciples in beautiful settings. He has fitted up spacious villas, duplex apartments, Georgian townhouses, Arab palaces and antique farmhouses all over the world, complete with swimming pools, saunas, Japanese living rooms, Moorish-tiled patios, marble bathrooms and modern kitchens, to suit the time and place. The St. Tropez house is a converted mill, halfway up the hill to Gassin, with a sunken pool hanging over the red roofs of the town. You can't see the view, however, because the whole place is surrounded by a high wall.

Bart's present wife is a young lady half his age, with frizzy hair and barbaric jewelry, who paints and makes enamel boxes in a studio at the bottom of the garden. I like them both, because they have become what they intended to be: she was a poor, arty girl who wanted money, and he was a poor, rich boy who wanted Art.

I answered:

Your proposition amuses me. I don't like holidays unless they are adventures or honeymoons, and maybe this could be both. Who's to play Prince Charming?

Love,
Anne

Bart replied:

Delighted you can do it, and we'll arrange the shooting schedule to fit your dates. We have a henna-haired hippie here whom Fellini might have created for the Prince. The ingénue looks like the girl in *Emmanuelle* only she acts better. So you must admit we are giving you a good supporting cast.

Bring every white garment you own, as we see you dressed always in white. If you feel like a nude scene, you can take it all off at the end. I know your figure can stand it.

Awaiting you with open arms and turning cameras.

Love,
Bart

Dear Bart,

Arriving September 19 with a red suitcase full of white clothes. I am not too sure about doing a strip tease; my thighs are beginning to sag. However, my French tights with the open crotch will cover my legs, and I can wear a white rose in my pubic hair.

See you soonest,
Anne

I was just finishing a boring Italian gangster picture. I was glad it was nearly over so I could take a holiday. Bart's invitation was just what I needed. I renewed my passport, bought a new white *maillot de bain* suitable for an aging superstar, and took the night train to the South of France.

St. Tropez. September 19, 1975.
Dear Bart,

I've arrived laden with white garments, from lace negligées to full evening gowns. Do you want to come over for a drink this evening and choose my costumes? I'm ready to shoot tomorrow if you are.

Anne

I sent my note up to Bart's elaborate villa overlooking the town. The little guest apartment had no phone. A neighbor's child had obligingly let me in and took my message up the hill.

Bart and his wife came at seven, wearing identical kaftans. They had brought my Prince Charming with them. He was obviously a member of that

new floating population—the hippie hustlers—
who are invading Southern Europe and the East.
They are mainly from cold, northern countries,
and often from the States. They sit around piazzas
and beaches and discothèques hoping someone
will offer them a meal and possibly a bed. This one
was obviously Scandinavian and was called Buf,
after a Swedish troll. His lank brown hair had
been dyed a violent purplish red and cut into wis-
py bangs over long green eyes. He was wearing a
mauve satin shirt, jeans, a red boot on his left leg
and a green one on his right. He had charm and intelligence—all requisites of the game. I liked him
immediately, although I have become wary of the
type. An unattached middle-aged woman with a
comfortable home is a sitting target for the New-
Look hustler. Moreover, I had decided to give up
new adventures and stick to my few remaining
part-time lovers. Sex was getting to be too much
trouble.

The next day we began early, shooting near a
ruined tower supposed to be my home. This was
an amateur movie, but they were professional
enough to shoot the end before anything else. According to cinematic theory, sets and actors have a
tendency to disintegrate or disappear, so the beginning and the end must be got in the can right
away. So I began by doing my death scene before I
knew what else I was supposed to be doing. It was
all quite hallucinating. I was dying before I had
even lived! No wonder actors took to drink or
drugs and continuity girls went mad!

I had always avoided offers of small parts, unless

the movie I was working on ran into trouble and the production begged me to step in and fill the gap. I don't know what possessed me to get involved in St. Tropez just then, except the idea of a free holiday and fun with friends, in a place I loved and near a man I liked—although I had not yet seen Emile, my fisherman.

So there I was, dying over and over again on a premarked spot, as the cameraman needed several "takes" to get it right. He was Bart's fifteen-year-old son by a previous marriage. His arty stepmother had chosen the costumes, and I was dying in a large white straw hat that kept falling off at the wrong moment. I seemed fated to make films wearing difficult hats. In the end, the dog ran off with this one, so I died hatless just before we broke for lunch.

My hippie Prince Charming conveniently appeared at the prospect of eating at Bart's expense, although he was not on call yet. He was wearing a sequined sweatshirt and two matching red boots that day. He announced that he was tired of living off bread and cheese and cheap wine, and was getting rheumatism from sleeping on the beach or in a vacant stable. I resolved then and there to keep him at arm's length. Our love scene was scheduled for the last day of shooting, so it shouldn't be difficult. I didn't expect to see much of him off the set. I knew plenty of other people in St. Tropez.

That night after dinner at a friend's house, I walked home via the port and discovered the henna-haired Buf at his café table. He was now in an emerald green jacket and was surrounded by other young people, among whom was our ingénue, Blanchette. She was ravishingly pretty, and if all the hungry young men in town would have let me get a bite too, I could have eaten her up.

Although I lack active lesbian tendencies, I sometimes have vague fantasies about sex with very beautiful girls—although a man's attraction for me has nothing to do with beauty. Sex is often best with the ugly ones; a purely beautiful man seldom turns me on.

Henna-haired Buf was almost plain, but he had beautiful green eyes which he immediately sunk into mine. He knew his job as a professional charmer, and said outright for everyone to hear, "Shouldn't we have an undress rehearsal tonight?" I replied that I had a secret lover waiting for me, which was true.

Emile, my local lover, had once been a handsome young fisherman and had caught my eye years ago when I first went to St. Tropez. He now ran a small fish restaurant on the beach, where he kept his wife firmly tied to the kitchen range till after midnight while he played "boule" with his friends in the evenings. He was always ready to go to bed with me whenever I turned up in St. Tropez—which was usually after the Film Festival at Cannes. I used to pass casually by on arrival in St. Tropez, and nodded distantly if I was going to be alone that holiday. If I shook my head slowly or shrugged my shoulders, he knew that I was down for a short stay with somebody else. He accepted this with bad grace, however, and took it out on me in bed the next holiday we were alone. It never occurred to him to give me up entirely. His possessive jealousy throughout the years had made an otherwise routine romance intermittently more colorful.

It was Sunday, and we had a day off. Buf came to lie beside me on the beach. His bathing suit was a 1920s one-piece in black-and-white stripes. He borrowed my suntan lotion and asked if I had already had lunch, and was obviously disappointed that I had already eaten. I suddenly felt sorry for him and asked him for dinner that night in a local brasserie. Then I fell asleep under my hat. The dog had thoughtfully brought it back to me the day before. He was a remarkable dog, half Labrador, half Boxer, with a negroid look to his big flat face and an Oriental shine to his thick black fur. The next day he had to die in my arms. I shuddered to think what Bart would do to him to make this possible.

When I woke up, Buf was gone. I could see him at the far end of the beach, running in and out of the sea with the dog. The dog was also a nomad, and attached himself to any summer visitor who would have him. I would have to be very careful that evening or I might have them *both* in my bed.

"Thank you for a delicious dinner. It was kind of you to invite me," Buf had said on the quai as we walked home late that night.

"I *am* kind, but I've also enjoyed your company," I replied.

"Then shall we go and make coffee at your place? I'm very good at making coffee."

"I don't doubt it, but I never drink coffee."

"There are other ways of enjoying my company."

"I don't doubt that either, but I'm expecting other company later."

"Who is this secret lover of yours?"

"A fisherman."

"And are you in love with your fisherman?"

"Not at all. Some people have marriages of convenience. I have lovers of convenience."

"What about your marriages?"

"I married for love. Marriage is never convenient. Good night."

The next day we sat around waiting for the dog to die. Buf was still not officially working, but had been brought along as dog tamer, wearing a purple-and-yellow football sweater for the occasion. He was very sweet and patient with the dog, getting him to lie down and sleep in the hot sunlight by stroking him soothingly. The only trouble was that the flies made him twitch, and he had a tendency to wake up and lick my nose. Buf stroked both of us in turn. It occurred to me that he would make a very tender young lover, but I put the thought out of my mind. I was determined to break the love habit.

In the end, the dog died in my arms, and I shed a tear. Buf took me in his arms and kissed the tears away. This was not in the script, and Bart was very annoyed because his son went on filming it.

"But you didn't say 'cut,' Daddy. How was I to know where the shot ended?"

"You know perfectly well that Anne has never seen the Prince before. The next shot is a dissolve. The dog's dead face fades away, and the focus comes back in on the unknown face of the Sleeping Prince. You can hardly expect Anne to look at him in surprise if they have been necking for hours beforehand."

We retired, rebuked, to the side lines, and all three of us sat on a wall while they were getting ready to shoot the dissolve. This required a lot of technical discussion between Bart and his cameraman son.

I was eventually called back on the set for the dog's close-up, although only my right hand was going to show as I clutched the dying dog to me. I tried not to laugh. It was all so amateurish and early Cocteau. The dog opened one eye as I picked up his head, but promptly went back to sleep. He was the only professional on the set. It was a pity he couldn't actually *be* my Sleeping Prince—or perhaps he would! Maybe the dog *was* to be my lover, and they hadn't dared tell me! That's why my love scene was being kept to the last. I was not going to get Buf after all!

Buf, however, was determined to get *me*. I found a note under my door when I got home.

Dear Lady in White,

You are as much in demand as a smash hit on Broadway, and it appears one must book well ahead to see you. Maybe tickets are even changing hands on the black market. Would it be possible to have a front seat in the stalls tomorrow night? I will even dip into my meager savings and take you out to dinner. I have a little money from home for "cultural pursuits," as my mother puts it. You fit the bill perfectly.

Buf

I was amused by his technique: rank flattery and even willingness to part with some money. An old English proverb sprung to mind: "A sprat to catch a mackerel." Was I getting too cynical? Perhaps the poor young man really fancied me. He might be suffering from mother-privation and was not really on the make at all, but just wanted to crawl back into the womb, which is as much a part of the sexual drive as any other feeling. I decided to be kinder to him and accept his invitation.

The next day, I had to run through the sea in my white bathing suit and miss the boat, literally, seeing it sail off into the distance with the other actors in it, including Blanchette, the ingénue. On the way to the beach, I pushed a note under Buf's door, accepting his invitation for that night and suggesting I pick him up at the bar on the port. I was not asking him in for a drink before or afterwards! Rudi could not say this time that I was "acting available." I'd never played more hard to get!

It was a pleasant day on the beach. Blanchette, our ingénue, was wearing a topless bikini—and the bottom didn't cover her bottom, either. The cross she wore on a little chain between her tiny breasts made her an innocent but sexy virgin. If I hadn't already known that she'd been to bed with the whole of St. Tropez, I might have been fooled too. Her long, golden curls reminded me of Jean-Louis.

I wondered whether that was why I had fantasies about going to bed with her myself. Draguignan was not far away, and I was tempted to telephone the original. I had not seen Jean-Louis for some time. He had passed through Rome once or twice on holiday with a girl while he was at the university. Now he must be a lawyer like his father. He had studied law in order to go into the family firm. I had met him in Paris once, while visiting Max. He was warm and friendly, but not overly familiar—just an old friend. Aurélien, on the contrary, usually wrote very affectionate letters at Christmas, but now I had not heard from him for a couple of years. I put in a call to Draguignan.

"Hello? Is Jean-Louis Laroche there? Or his father, Monsieur Aurélien Laroche?"

An unknown woman's voice answered. I hadn't heard from any of them for such a long time; perhaps they had moved.

"I'm afraid the Laroches don't live here anymore, madame. Monsieur Laroche died of a heart attack last year. His widow moved to Paris. Would you like her address?"

For a moment I couldn't speak. So Aurélien was dead! The man who had taken my virginity no longer existed.

"You mean Monsieur Aurélien Laroche is dead?"

"Yes, madame."

"And his son—did he go to Paris too?"

"I'm not sure, madame. I believe he's married. I've only got Madame Laroche's address in Paris."

"Thank you . . . No . . . It doesn't matter. Thank you, madame."

I hung up. Of course it all mattered. Jean-Louis

must now be twenty-five years old and was married. And Aurélien was dead. The years were rolling by.

I pulled myself together and went to meet Buf at
the café on the port. Our conversation was fitted
in between mouthfuls of *croque-monsieur*.

"Don't you get bored, sitting in a café all day?"

"Yes, I do—but even that is part of the experience."

"Do you get enough to eat?"

"More or less. If I'm not asked to someone's
house, I generally get apples and cheese. My stepfather's a doctor, and I was brought up to understand the importance of diet."

"Do you make love enough?"

"Nearly every night."

"Good God! Where?"

"In the stable. On the beach. In *their* house."

"Who's 'they'?"

"Oh, any girl who's got left out or left behind."

"Don't you mind who?"

"It hardly matters, does it? I can always get
drunk first."

"Do you go to bed with boys too?"

"No, never. I'm an obsessive heterosexual."

"Have you been to bed with Blanchette?"

"Yes, several times, but her brains are as tiny as
her tits. I like conversation, big breasts, and soft
thighs—in that order."

"Just as I thought—you miss your mother."

He looked unusually startled, stopped eating,
and stared at me silently.

"And you're jealous of your stepfather," I added.

He suddenly had the greenish hue of a real red-head. I was surprised that such simple Freudian suppositions could upset a presumably cool, modern young man. I changed the subject to give him a chance to change color again.

"What are you going to do in the winter when the squares and piazzas are cold and windy and they take the tables inside?"

"Where should one go in the winter?"

"Ask the swallows."

"Will you take me to Rome?"

"Why should I?"

"For company—friendship. I'm good around the house. I'm tidy, and I cook and wash dishes."

"I don't need a wife."

"I'm very masculine in bed. Give me a try."

"I don't want any complications at this point in my life."

"I'm beginning to think you don't want sex, that your reputation is unfounded, and that your secret lover is nonexistent."

"You're cleverer than I thought, but I'm not going to be caught. You can't get me into bed by taunting me."

"How *can* I get you into bed?"

"Wait, I guess. Patience is sometimes rewarded."

The next day, we were shooting outside a ruined tower. Buf was hanging around, looking disconsolate. I was amused that he should be offended or puzzled because I wouldn't sleep with him. I flirted outrageously with Blanchette. I hadn't realized it could be so easy, as easy as it is to flirt with a man. In our scene, we met outside the tower and went in together. I turned it into a love scene. Bart was delighted, his wife was embarrassed, and the fifteen-year-old cameraman tried hard to be sophisticated, and talked of panning in on my hand opening Blanchette's blouse. Buf was furious. The tiny tits felt delicious, and they hardened to my touch. It was the first time I'd felt that on another woman. We gave each other a deep kiss and disappeared through the doorway together. We had to repeat it several times because the poor fifteen-year-old was so confused that he was getting his focusing all wrong. I noticed, too, that he'd developed a hard bulge in his jeans.

"One of us will have to go to bed with the cameraman tonight," I whispered to Blanchette as we went inside for the tenth time.

"Oh, yes," she said vaguely.

"Or perhaps both of us could go to bed with him."

"Oh, yes," she said again.

She was as stupid as Buf had said. I'd need someone more dynamic for my first real lesbian experience.

I didn't feel like seeing anyone that night. I was still too upset by Aurélien's death. I went for a long walk alone.

I returned very late, walking in the moonlight up the steep hill where fireflies dance over the grassy banks at night and cicadas sing in the olive trees. The sleeping village greeted me with silence, its bars shut, restaurant shutters closed. The only sound came from a discothèque in a cellar, throbbing softly underground.

I opened my front door to find a note from Buf:

Belle Dame sans Merci,

I have been haunting your doorway, hoping for your return. I am bored with life, bored with the local girls, bored with myself. The season is over. Do I go home and give in to the system? Shall I cut my hair, give up the theater, and exchange my green jacket for a white doctor's coat? I know I could find the answers in your experienced arms. But where are you?

Buf

I put his note away carefully. Back in Rome it would join the others in the shoe box just for the record. I climbed into bed, thankful to be on my own. I had the feeling that old age was learning to be alone. Solitude is part of freedom.

The next day I was "on call" until they finished shooting another scene. At around eleven, there was a knock on my door. Buf had been sent to get me. The door was on the latch, and he walked into my little apartment for the first time. I was lying on the bed reading.

"You're on in half an hour, so we just have time to make love," he said, taking off everything except his red and green boots. I was too surprised to interrupt him. He had one of those knobby cocks with visible veins, and it was pointing straight at me. I touched it gingerly; it bounced.

I was wearing a dressing gown, because I wasn't

sure what I was supposed to wear later. I presented a perfect target lying down. He hit my target
bang on. I relaxed and enjoyed it.

Later, he told me what I was supposed to wear,
and helped me dress. I walked through the gray village wearing my white dress in a rosy glow, leaning on his arm. He had won, but he was not
triumphant; on the contrary, he seemed rather
melancholy.

"What's the matter?"

"I was thinking of committing suicide."

"Good God! What a backhanded compliment!
You'll be the first man to commit suicide because I
have been to bed with him. How Swedish of you!"

He smiled involuntarily at that.

"I'll tell you about it tonight," he said morosely.

"Why should there be a tonight? I don't see that
rape at eleven in the morning justifies an encore in
the evening."

We had reached the set, and no further conversation was possible. By then all the actors had been
kept waiting.

That night there was a knock on my door. I
thought it was Emile, arriving early. We had a sign
that he was to come in only if the key was left in
the door; that way he could open it without knocking so as not to attract the neighbor's attention.
However, sometimes I would forget to leave it
there, and he had to knock. I opened the door tentatively. Buf was on the doorstep, looking like an
orphan. Even his clothes were more subdued than
usual—both his boots were green. I could hardly
send him away.

I had been laying out some cards, and he came in and sat down in front of them.

"Do you believe in them?" he asked, pointing to the cards.

"I neither believe nor disbelieve. Destiny usually just takes its course."

"And don't you believe *I'm* your destiny?"

"Certainly not. Why do you want to be?"

"Because you're the first person who's guessed that I've slept with my mother."

I tried not to show my surprise and shock. So that's why he'd looked so startled when I said my Freudian piece on the square.

"Why did you?" I asked coolly.

"To get even with my stepfather. He was furious with me when I dropped out of medical school and went on the stage. He threw me out of the house."

"Why did your mother do it?"

"She was a little drunk at the time."

"That doesn't seem sufficient explanation."

He was silent for a few seconds. "I guess we both needed each other very much at that moment, so it just happened. It wasn't something we went into deliberately."

"What about afterwards?"

"She just laughed. She seemed rather happy, actually."

"And you?"

"I felt I knew her better. We were closer than we had been for a long time."

"That's putting it mildly!" I turned it into a joke to try to lighten the atmosphere.

"Do you think it's so terrible?"

"No—only if the after-effects are destructive. In this case, they seem to have been quite positive." But I wasn't as sure as I made myself sound.

His long, green eyes were looking deep into mine.

"Has it ever occurred to you that your eyes are exactly the same color as mine?" he asked at last.

It was a melting remark.

"You can't throw me out now, can you?" he begged.

I couldn't. Our green eyes melted together as we moved in close, followed by our hands, our hips, our most personal parts. Afterwards I snuggled up against him with a sigh of maternal resignation. Once a mother, always a mother!

That night Bart gave us a dinner party at the most expensive restaurant in town. I dressed in basic white. Buf called for me, wearing purple corduroys and a patchwork shirt. Bart and his wife were in their His-and-Hers kaftans, and our cameraman was in jeans as usual. He was a very earnest boy and rather nice, I thought. In another year or two perhaps ... but no, I was giving all that up and planning to settle down with a suitable elderly suitor. But where was he when I needed him?

I looked around the restaurant. There were a lot of smooth, middle-aged gentlemen in short-sleeved sport shirts or navy blue blazers. They all seemed possible and yet impossible.

My eyes went on roving until they fell on a small table in the far corner, and then nearly popped out of my head! Two young men were just sitting down, one black and one white.

"What are you looking at?" Buf asked possessively.

"My God!" I exclaimed. "Someone has outclassed you!"

Our whole table turned around to look. The white one was a classic blond Adonis, well worthy of note, but the black one was simply unbelievable. He was the most exotic creature I had ever seen. His hair was neither the Afro bush nor in the newer little plaits. It was a wild mass of tiny black ringlets. Each frizzy hair had been coaxed into a little corkscrew, and they swung around his head like Medusa's snakes. Thin black legs shone through shocking pink organza Zouave pantaloons, tight at the ankle, where golden bells tinkled; a black silk shirt was covered by an embroidered wine-red waistcoat. The whole outfit was embellished with barbaric jewelry at neck and wrists.

"My Prince!" I gasped. "Of course—the black dog must turn into a Black Prince!"

Buf looked startled, but Bart's eyes lit up with enthusiasm.

"I can hardly go straight over and ask him to play my lover, can I?" I asked the table at large. "Buf, are you big enough to give up the part in the name of art and ask that gorgeous savage to come over and talk business?"

It was something I wouldn't have done, of course, if it had been a professional film. I would never dream of losing an actor his part unless he was undeserving or incompetent, but I thought Buf wouldn't care whether or not he were in a home movie.

Buf did care, but he knew how to lose like a gentleman. He went over to speak to the gorgeous savage, who agreed to join us when he had finished his dinner.

"We could even fit his companion in somewhere," I suggested. "Couldn't the Black Prince have a white slave? What a blow for integration!"

Bart thought it a marvelous idea. Buf was annoyed and sarcastic.

"That's just because she wants to go to bed with both of them," he said bitterly.

"Sour grapes," I said, reaching out and taking some, which I hung on his ear. He looked like a beautiful bacchante. I was being bitchy and I knew it, but it was partly in self-defense. I was afraid I wouldn't have the strength to leave Buf behind tomorrow when the film was over and I left St. Tropez.

An old phonograph record got stuck in the groove of my mind: "He wants a mother, and you don't want a son. He'll move in, and take over, and waste your time, and waste your money, and fuck all the other girls in town in your very bed if he gets a chance."

It was true. I had heard it all before, lived it all before, but the green eyes enhanced by the green grapes were very appealing. I leaned over and bit into one of the grapes still hanging from his ear.

The gorgeous savage was called Jimmy, which was a bit of a letdown, though he did pronounce it

"Jeemee." He came from Mauretania and spoke only French. He was terribly polite and reserved, bowing low and calling me madame. He was delighted at the idea of appearing in a film, honored to know us, touched to be invited. His beautiful blond friend bowed too, and they both sat down and drank a bottle of champagne at Bart's expense. Then they disappeared into the night as magically as they had appeared, having agreed to meet me on the square at ten the next morning so I could show them where we were shooting.

"That phony will never do anything. He's so uptight, he won't even take his shoes off," Buf said when they had gone.

"I don't think he had any shoes on," I snapped.

"Yes, he did—cheap Indian sandals."

Buf proceeded to get drunk and didn't even walk me home—which was just as well, because I needed a good night's sleep before my love scene. I also packed my red suitcase. I had decided to leave for Rome as soon as my Swan Song was over. The night train from Nice would take me away from temptation. It would be better to go back to Rome than back to young lovers.

The next day I awoke early, had a shower, and generously sprayed myself with Arpège. I was to accompany Jeemee and his white slave to Bart's house, where our big scene was to be shot. As the dog had died on the doorstep, the Black Prince was to wake up there in my arms and carry me over the threshold into the privacy of the walled garden.

Once inside, what we did was up to us. I was to explain all this to the Black Prince on our way up there.

I had remembered to leave off my bra so the marks wouldn't show, in case the Black Prince plucked up enough courage to take off my shirt—though I secretly agreed with Buf that he probably wouldn't go much further than that. However, I put on my crotchless tights just in case. We had purposely decided that I was to wear a skirt for this scene; there's no graceful way to strip a woman wearing trousers.

When I was ready, I wrote a farewell note to Buf. I doubted if he would turn up that morning, even as a dog tamer. I might never see him again.

Dear, dear Buf,

You are too intelligent for me to hand you out clichés like "It's been nice knowing you," or "It was fun while it lasted." If I have been unkind or inhospitable to you, it was to protect myself.

I'm tired of sons who are lovers and lovers who are sons. I want to be a free woman, and perhaps that means I no longer want a man at all.

I advise you to go to Sweden and start again. Just leave your real mother alone—that's not a mistake to make twice!

Good luck, good love, good-bye.

                                                Anne

I pushed it under Buf's door on my way to pick up the Black Prince.

Jeemee was wearing a daytime outfit nearly as exotic as the previous night's costume. I saw that Buf was right: his clothes *were* assembled from cheap Indian and Arab boutiques. They would have looked sleazy on anyone else, but they looked magnificently ethnic on him. The white slave, alas, was missing, and there was no time to go looking for him. We had to hurry because the sun had to be just as it was when the dog died. It might not be terribly important in an amateur film to have matching shots, but it would be difficult to photograph a black man in shadow when you were shooting without lights. I was tactful enough to omit this, but just hurried him along, talking about the naturalness and the inevitability of nude scenes in contemporary cinema.

He just replied "*Oui, madame*" after each of my statements. Finally I said, "The dog died without clothes, so of course you ought to wake up naked, don't you think?"

"*Oui, madame.*"

I couldn't tell if he had really understood what I was getting at. Anyway, he could keep his trousers on in the first scene, as the dissolve from dog to man was just to be on his sleeping face.

To my surprise, Buf was there to drag the dog away and help substitute the Prince. And to our pleased amazement, the Black Prince was perfectly willing to take off all his clothes, even on the doorstep. We had to stop him, as we were still in full view of the whole village. Once inside, it would be different.

Buf mumbled, changing his tune, "Of course

those savages are used to going about stark naked
in the jungle. But there are all kinds of sexual ta-
boos. You're never going to get a love scene out of
him."

The dog was wonderful. He closed his eyes and
allowed himself to be dragged away by Buf, who
hissed as he came near me, "You've got too much
Arpège on. They're not used to French perfume in
the jungle. That'll put him off, if nothing else
does."

The Black Prince lay in my arms with his eyes
shut. His body, from what I could see of it, was
quite hairless, and his skin was as soft as satin. He
smelled clean and sandalwoody. It really turned
me on.

"Now, open your eyes, look at Anne for a long
time, then begin to get up. Lift her up with you,
take her in your arms, and carry her over the doorstep." Bart was explaining.

"*Oui, monsieur,*" the Black Prince replied politely.

It went beautifully. He had a natural grace and
perfect timing. He carried me right across the garden to some cushions in the corner of the patio
without being told, and gently laid me down with
a kiss.

"*Excusez-moi, madame. C'est pour l'art,*" he apologized after the kiss.

Buf closed the street door with a bang when
Bart yelled "Cut!"

The Prince had, up to then, only been in frame
down to his waist, and was still wearing his trousers. Now we were to be taken in long shot as we

lay on the cushions, when the cameraman would zoom in as we started to make love. Jeemee took off his trousers and lay down beside me. I was pleased to see that at least he had pubic hair; it might have been a bit off-putting without. He was very well hung indeed.

"Now don't be shy," I said encouragingly. "Loosen my blouse, loosen my hair, do anything you feel like. We'll do our best to make it look real."

I hoped I had put him at ease. I lay back and waited for Bart to say "action," wondering what would happen.

I don't know whether Bart said "action" or not, but he certainly didn't say "cut." The next half hour must have been the longest master shot in film history. The Black Prince began by taking off my blouse and letting down my hair as directed. Then, with complete nonchalance and utter sophistication, he went through what seemed like the whole Kama Sutra for real. My skirt flew through the air like a bird, though my crotchless tights were left intact—they didn't get in the way, whatever position we assumed—and it all happened with a sureness, a grace and a rhythm that I have seldom experienced. The only drawback was that we were in the midday sun and were sweating like pigs. I've no doubt it was a very good special effect. We needed no makeup man to squirt glycerin on us.

As he reached orgasm, the Prince gave a primeval roar that echoed through the patio. Then he fell forward and rolled slowly over onto his back, his penis still glistening with moisture. I too lay back, looking at the blue sky and holding his hand. I felt a little stunned.

"Don't just lie there! Do something! This is a movie!" came Buf's roughened voice. "You're not supposed to lie there and relax!"

I raised myself on one elbow. The Black Prince was lying immobile, like an effigy on a black marble tomb, dewdrops of sweat and sperm sparkling like diamonds and pearls on his black satin skin. With my long blond hair, I gently wiped him clean, then I laid my tired head on his stomach and cradled his now limp penis in my equally limp arms. The tip was near my lips. I kissed it.

"Cut!" It was I who finally said it.

At some point, Bart had moved into the cameraman's seat and had taken over the camera. He was sweating almost as much as we were. His fifteen-year-old son had disappeared, possibly to masturbate in the bathroom. The arty stepmother was looking considerably less rarefied and more down to earth. She was probably considering some new positions to try with her husband that night. Buf and the dog were huddled together in a corner, like two naughty children banished from the classroom. The Black Prince was in total command of the situation. He drew himself up to his full height, helped me up, and shook my hand warmly, as if meeting me for the first time.

"*Merci, madame.* Thank you for a very pleasant morning."

His tone was formal and correct, and he still used the polite *vous*, as he had before our love scene.

"I think we may be allowed to break for a shower, no?" He looked at Bart.

"I think we can say we've completely finished shooting," Bart replied. "There's nothing more we need. The film had better end there—we couldn't have a happier ending!"

"Then may I accompany you to your home, madame?" Jeemee asked, picking up my silk blouse from the floor and holding it out, as if helping a lady into her coat at the end of a party. My skirt was similarly held out, after being retrieved from a tree, and my shoes were put on my feet for me, as in a Cinderella scene.

We walked through the village, exchanging polite banalities, like two strangers who have met by chance and feel obliged to enter into small talk. However, on arrival, he walked into my apartment as if he owned it, fixed himself a drink, had a shower, and generally settled in with an air of the divine right of kings and black princes. I asked where his blond friend was, but he told me that he hardly knew him—they were not really traveling together—and that everyone must fend for himself. I mentioned my own intention of getting my things together and going back to Rome on the night train.

"I'll come with you," he announced.

An old English proverb again sprang to my mind: "Out of the frying pan into the fire."

"But you've only just got here!" I protested.

"I can't do business in St. Tropez. The territory is too well covered already."

"What business?"

"Precious jewels from Pakistan."

I envisaged uncut emeralds and star sapphires sparkling in his brown hands. I am sometimes singularly naive. I even imagined one being dropped into my navel if I took him to Rome.

"I'm taking the bus into St. Raphael," I said. "There's a convenient night train that gets into Rome tomorrow morning."

"Good. I'll come with you then. I'll just go back to my room and collect *mes affaires*."

His *affaires* turned out to be very curious luggage indeed. There was a bundle of clothes that looked more garish than gorgeous in the light of day. He repacked them carefully on my bed, folding them away into one side of a large double African satchel that he told me was a camel bag. The second side seemed to be stuffed with paper.

"Where is your jewel case?" I asked.

He took out some of the paper, which seemed to be divided into lots of tiny packets.

"Do you need any?"

"No, not right now. I never wear jewels on a journey."

"You're right; it is rather dangerous. But they tell me the authorities don't bother to inspect the sleepers at the frontier."

He put the packets back into the satchel and slung the whole thing over his shoulder.

"Isn't that rather a casual way to carry around such valuable merchandise?"

"It looks less suspicious, as if I'm just out for the day. Now, shall we go and have lunch?"

He picked up my suitcase, and we walked down to the cheapest of the little restaurants at the port—which was just as well, as I had to pay for our lunch. He asked for the bill, but as it arrived, he jumped up and said, "There's someone I must see on that yacht."

He darted rapidly across the cobbled dockside and disappeared into the bowels of a boat, taking his bundles with him. He didn't reappear for some time, and the bus was about to leave. I paid the bill and carried my own heavy suitcase to the bus stop, slightly relieved that I had shaken him off. The vision of a thousand and one nights in Rome, dripping with jewels, was a mirage after all. It also began to strike me as rather strange that in all the time he had been in my house—having a shower, lolling on the bed with a drink, doing the packing—he had not once laid a finger on me. Not a caress, not a kiss. Perhaps he only raised his totem pole in public, as part of a tribal rite. All those Kama Sutra positions would not have been for my private delight. I settled back into my bus seat in peaceful resignation, and closed my eyes.

I didn't wake up until the bus reached St. Maxime; then I half-opened my eyes to check where we were. I opened them wider when I saw Medusa's snakes writhing two seats ahead of me, as the bus jogged Jeemee's elaborate hairdo. He must have jumped in at the last moment. I shut my eyes again in case he turned around. I was playing for time, and I was playing for my independence. He obviously planned to move in on me. I knew the type. If you didn't take them into your bed, they managed to invade the spare room. If there was no spare room, they were quite happy on the floor. Soon they had all their friends there too. I had only recently successfully eluded one of the most charming of the hippie hustlers, young Buf, only to be stuck with a more insidious kind.

When we arrived in St. Raphael, Jeemee claimed me and my suitcase and obligingly carried the suitcase across the road to the station. I was hoping that we would not be able to get sleepers in the same compartment, then perhaps I could get off the train quickly on arrival in Rome and vanish. If we should ever meet again, I could say I had looked for him everywhere. After all, I had not invited him to stay. The subject had not even come up.

At the ticket office, I resolutely asked for one ticket and one sleeper, intending to stand aside and let Jeemee buy his own. Instead, we were directed to the international ticket section, which was in a separate office. The pretty girl behind the long counter saw us arrive together.

I fumbled in my bag for my billfold.

"I wonder if you could advance me the money for the journey?" Jeemee asked. "I seem to have run out of francs. It's so difficult to exchange Mauretanian money."

I was lost. What do you reply when someone with whom you have just had sex only a few hours ago, by invitation and with all due encouragement, is actually standing beside you? I'd certainly asked for it this time. I paid for two tickets and handed one to him.

There were already two people in our compartment—an elderly French couple who looked at us disapprovingly. You could tell by their tightened lips that they didn't much like black men, especially in conjunction with white women.

When the luggage was stowed away, Jeemee took a little piece of paper out of his pocket.

"I saw Buf in the square when I went to get *mes affaires*. He asked me to give you this note."

It said simply: "Bon voyage. Every woman gets the Prince she deserves."

The train moved away. I looked out the window and smiled at the darkening sea. I was smiling at myself and my weaknesses.

From Nice to the frontier, the train runs right along the coast, with sudden views of that incredible blue framed by jagged red rock, views often obscured by the ubiquitous dirty white cubes of cheap modern architecture. I remembered the views of my childhood, across the terraces of spacious Belle Epoque villas guarded by tall palm trees. But then, only the elite came there to see them. I could remember sitting on the Croisette in Cannes so my governess could watch the Dolly sisters go into the casino. The summer I was eight, we stayed in Juan les Pins. I can remember my mother saying, "Look! Zelda Fitzgerald has had her hair bobbed just like mine!" as the Scott Fitzgeralds and the Gerald Murphys walked past us on the beach.

I had met the Murphys again during the second World War. But my mother and the Fitzgeralds had already died, along with their era. My mother, who'd always traveled on the Blue Train, seated on cut-velvet upholstery in the first-class sleeping cars with an Italian count, would have been surprised to see me in a second-class sleeper on plastic seats in a green train with a black "prince."

The nostalgic journey continued: Monte Carlo, Antibes, Juan les Pins, Menton, and then the Italian frontier of Ventimiglia. I had just taken off my skirt and settled into my sleeper when the French police came through the train, followed by the Italian customs inspectors. Jeemee seemed nervous and was pacing up and down the corridor. He had left his camel bag at the foot of my sleeper, drawing the blankets up over it. It was quite a rational thing to do, as he was moving about. We were in the middle berths, with the French couple down below. No one had yet claimed the upper berths.

"And which is your luggage, monsieur?" they were asking Jeemee in the corridor.

"I am traveling without luggage," he replied, to my astonishment.

They asked to see his ticket.

"You are going as far as Rome without luggage?"

"I can buy anything I need there, if I decide to stay."

"And which is your compartment?"

Again, to my surprise, he pointed vaguely to the compartment next to ours. The customs inspectors went in there, asked everyone to identify his luggage, were satisfied that none of it was Jeemee's, looked vaguely puzzled, but shrugged their shoulders and moved on to our compartment. The camel bag with its jewels suddenly weighed very heavily on my feet.

I showed my British passport and pointed out my big red suitcase. The customs men turned around to go out, but in such a confined space, there was not much room to turn, and one of them inadvertently brushed back my blanket.

"Is this yours, madame?" he asked politely, prodding the camel bag.

"No. Someone else must have put it there." I tried not to sound nervous.

"Does it belong to either of you?" he asked the elderly French couple.

They stared back at him from their berths, their thin lips getting even thinner. The man said, "I saw the black gentleman put it there."

The customs inspector picked it up and looked in both sides. He pulled out one of the little paper packets. He passed it to his companion, who opened it. There were no jewels inside—just some white powder. They opened another. It was the same. My enlightenment was sudden—and shocking. I knew it must be either heroin or cocaine—and there were dozens of little packets.

"Do you know the gentleman?" the man asked me.

Jeemee appeared in the doorway.

"The lady and I have never met," he replied, courteous to the last.

I couldn't think why he hadn't jumped off the train, until I saw more French policemen behind him. They had a quick consultation, and then asked me to open my red suitcase. I got out of bed clad only in my slip, fumbled for my keys, and lifted the lid. It was full of harmless white clothing, but they opened the envelope in which I had carefully preserved Buf's two little letters to me; his farewell note was still in my handbag. They found nothing suspicious. Then they looked at my passport again and noted my age. Evidently it seemed unlikely to them that I was connected with Jeemee. The elderly couple stared at me, but kept quiet.

"Come with us," the customs men said to Jeemee.

He looked at me from the doorway without recognition and with aristocratic cool. My heart went out to him for the first time since we'd met. He bowed politely to the whole compartment.

"Good night, messieurs-dames!" he said.

I watched them take him down the platform. There was nothing I could do.

When the train moved on again, it was quite dark. The moon was coming up over the sea as we slipped past the suburbs of Ventimiglia, now already in Italy. Out of the window, I saw the tall cypresses of the Hanbury Gardens in the moonlight, and remembered the famous English expatriate family who had spent so much time and love creating these elegant gardens between two wars.

Now it was a public park. Thank God they haven't built over them yet, I thought.

I drew the blind and lay back in my sleeper, relieved to have left trouble behind and to be alone. I closed my eyes and slipped into a peaceful sleep.

∽ Epilogue: Don't Look Now, but Sixty Is in Sight

Another year had passed, I was fine, but Italy was in a bad way. The cost of living had risen yet again. The Common Market was successfully driving prices up and getting people down. My Italian friends were predicting a Communist takeover, and my foreign friends were all asking "And where does one live next?" There was a general election in the offing.

"I shall vote Communist and then leave the country," my Sicilian son-in-law said when he came to call. "Communism is what Italy needs, but I myself don't need it. What are *you* going to do, Anne?"

"You should find yourself a nice American millionaire and settle down," my daughter Vanessa said sternly. "Sixty is in sight."

As usual, I was watering my flowers. There was no point in letting the geraniums die just because Communism was coming, although I might have to plant some red ones next year. Up to now, I had specialized in every shade of pink. Years ago, Norman Douglas had said to me on Capri, "Red geraniums are vulgar flowers, my dear. They don't belong in private gardens, only in public parks." I had accordingly eliminated red geraniums from my life, but since then my life had become a public park anyway.

"Granny! Granny! Look at the airplane!"

Vanessa's two little boys were dancing about, pointing at the sky, where an old-fashioned plane was trailing a banner reading: VOTE FOR THE DEMOCRATIC CHRISTIAN PARTY.

"What does it say, granny? What does it say?" asked Mark, who couldn't read yet.

"It says, 'Drink Coca-Cola,' " I replied.

"Why did you tell them that?" my daughter asked.

"Because I don't want to poison their innocent little minds with politics."

As if on cue, the airplane released a shower of election pamphlets, which drifted down to cover a city already knee-deep in garbage. Matthew and Mark were delighted, and leaped around snatching at the flying papers and collecting them from the ground. When they had several handfuls, they went to the edge of the terrace and threw them into the street one by one, shouting, "Drink Coca-Cola! Drink Coca-Cola!"

"Now look what you've done," said my daughter. "You've instilled commercial instincts into their dear little minds."

"You can't get it right, can you?" I replied, and went to answer the telephone.

It was Rudi. "I've just arrived, and I want to give you lunch at Ranieri's."

"But that's too expensive now. Prices are skyrocketing with inflation. Where are you staying anyway?"

"I'm at the Hassler."

"Good God, Rudi. Only American millionaires stay there!"

"I'm about to become one. Now, will you meet me in an hour's time at Ranieri's? I've got something very important to say to you."

"All right, fine. Vanessa's here with the children, so I'll give them a quick lunch first. She's trying to marry me off to a suitable suitor, as usual. I'll be glad to escape."

"But that's just what I want to talk to you about. *I* think you should get married too."

"Don't make me nervous, Rudi. I'm having a hard time just trying to give up sex. Don't deflect me from my course."

"Marriage may help you give it up."

"It often does, I'm afraid. But we'll discuss that over lunch."

On the terrace, the children were splashing in the puddles left by the hose, where the terra-cotta tiles were broken. I needed a rich husband to re-pave the terrace for me. My home had begun to look shabby.

"That was Rudi," I said.

Vanessa like Rudi because he was nearly my age and had been around so long that our relationship had become quite respectable.

"Rudi wants me to get married too," I moaned.

"Good. Why not marry Rudi? At least you know the worst; that's a good start to a marriage."

"But I want freedom, you cynical child!"

"What are you going to do with freedom when you're over sixty?"

"I'll cross that bridge when I come to it."

"You're nearly there, mother."

I ignored the remark.

"Come here, you little bastards," I shouted to the boys. "Either stop that or take your clothes off to keep them clean." They paid no attention. "Matthew! Mark!"

I seized one and my daughter seized the other. We undressed them, and they ran about happily, stark naked, leaving wet footprints on the tiles.

"I must say your boys are well hung. They'll make some woman happy," I observed.

"Is that where happiness lies?" my daughter asked.

"I wouldn't know. I've tried too hard to find out. When you know too much, you can't make up your mind."

"Granny! Mummy! There's that airplane again."

I looked up at the sky. It was a different plane. This one was exhorting the Italian populace to vote for the new fascist party, with a banner that read: VOTARE M.S.I. E VOTARE BENE.

"It's a different plane saying a different thing," Matthew exclaimed, showing off his reading.

"What does it say this time, granny?" Mark asked, ignoring his brother's superior knowledge.

"It says, 'Drink Pepsi-Cola,' " I replied firmly, as again the leaflets floated down.

"Drink Pepsi-Cola! Drink Pepsi-Cola!" the naked children shouted happily, throwing the leaflets around.

My daughter and I went inside to prepare lunch.

"I'll feed them, mummy. You go on and make Rudi propose marriage," Vanessa said encouragingly.

"Don't be silly! Rudi will never propose."

But Rudi did propose. Sitting in the corner of the red brocade room at Ranieri's, he told me that his father had died and that he was now the owner of a castle in the Dolomites, a large apartment in Vienna, as well as his own apartment in New York. The old Baron had left him everything.

"I need someone who can take care of all these houses!" Rudi said.

I felt rather put out by the implication. "What's wrong with a housekeeper?" I snapped. I was trying hard not to feel sentimental. Rudi's proposal had unnerved me.

"A housekeeper would be out of style," Rudi replied. "My life needs a baroness in it."

"It's been difficult enough for me to be a lady all my life. Now I have to be a baroness too?"

"Why not? You'll do it beautifully."

"And where are *you* going to live, Baron Von Hoffman?"

"Mainly in America. You can visit me there whenever you like. I've been offered a wonderful job as the artistic director of a new theater there. A wife would go well with that too."

"Rudi, marriage is *not* a question of interior decoration."

"Nonsense! It is. A successful marriage is having materials that match and putting everything in its right place."

"Maybe—but I've always married for love, Rudi, and a lovetime is not a lifetime. I've got used to changing my men with the season. How could I settle down with just you?"

Rudi reached for my hand across the pale pink damask tablecloth. It was my left hand, on which were my three wedding rings.

"Do you remember when I gave you that one?" he said, fingering the top one.

"Yes. The day you left me."

"Well, I've come back."

"I think you've waited too long, Rudi. I'm set in my ways. I'm hooked on the love habit."

"I'm not asking you to change anything or give anybody up," he pleaded. "*You* taught me not to try and change life; only to add to it, never subtract." He looked at me appealingly, then added, "Surely, Anne, at our age, young men are not going to keep knocking at our doors?"

I smiled, but didn't answer. Suddenly I felt more relaxed. A waiter was passing, and I said, "Shall we have champagne? Can you afford it?"

"Of course I can. My father left quite a lot of money, mainly in Switzerland. I want to enjoy it, and I want you to enjoy it with me."

"I enjoyed being poor with you, Rudi; I don't know if I want to be rich. I've always noticed that the rich are so terribly bored."

The waiter brought the champagne. We had often drunk champagne in company, but never alone. It was not like us at all. We were already becoming two different people.

Diary entry. Rome. June 21, 1976.

Is Rudi right? Will no young men ever knock on my door again? Why should they? I'm nearly sixty. Would I go to bed with someone my age?

It seems to me there are four reasons why a young man goes to bed with a much older woman. Here they are:

(1) Money. She pays for the things he needs, or at least has luxuries he can share—her own house, a car, a way of life that is probably more comfortable than his. It costs money to take out young girls—or to take them in.

(2) Propinquity. A young man finds himself in a propitious situation with an older lady. He has no one else to turn to, and his youthful sex drive urges him on to the point of no return. He enjoys it and finds her a convenient and problem-free sexual outlet, and soon comes back for more.

(3) Class or color. They don't see that you are old; they only see that you are a princess and/or white!

(4) He needs a mother-figure, either because he's afraid of failure with young girls, or simply because he always wanted to fuck his mother!

I got up next morning still not knowing whether to accept Rudi's proposal or not. He was coming for lunch to see Vanessa and the children, who had stayed overnight.

I opened my closet, trying to decide what to wear on this auspicious day. On the top shelf were my shoe boxes full of love letters. I took down the box labeled "Letters from My Boys" and looked

through it. There were postcards from Jean-Louis,
a poem from Gregory, Joseph's manifesto, letters
from Grant, Evaristo's *collage* of love, and many
others. Had it all been worthwhile?

I went out to do my shopping and met Rudi in
the market. He bought me some flowers from the
dark-haired woman who kept the corner flower
stall and looked like Anna Magnani, God rest her
Roman soul. When *she* died, the neorealistic era in
the Italian cinema died with her. The Rome I had
known for twenty years was dying too, torn by political strife and worn thin by inflation.

Rudi and I slowly wandered home through the
cobbled market street near the Piazza di Spagna,
basking in the hot sunshine and the smell of warm
fruit. I bought the last basket of tiny wild strawberries from Nemi. The strawberry season was
over.

The house was very quiet as we let ourselves in.
Vanessa was resting on her bed. She jumped up
and embraced Rudi.

"Where are the children?" he asked. "I'd like to
see them."

"Oh, they've been rummaging through granny's
closets, and now they're out on the terrace playing."

"They're too quiet," I said. "They must be up to
something."

"I'll go and look for them," Rudi said obligingly,
and went out to the terrace too. We heard them
chatting excitedly. I sat on the edge of Vanessa's
bed.

"I can't make up my mind," I told her. "I don't

know what to do about Rudi's proposal."

"Just relax. Fate will decide," she said wisely.

There were childish screams from the terrace. Rudi came running in. Another airplane was passing over again; perhaps a revolution was at hand.

"I don't know what these children are doing," Rudi said breathlessly. "But they seem to be throwing away all your letters. Matthew says it has something to do with the elections."

Vanessa and I ran out to the terrace. The little boys had found my shoe boxes marked "Letters from Lovers" and "Letters from My Boys," and they were throwing them all to the winds, like the election leaflets.

"Drink Coca-Cola!" shouted Matthew.

"Drink Pepsi-Cola!" shouted Mark.

The new plane had a banner reading: VOTE FOR THE RADICALS AND FIGHT COMMUNISM.

"It's a losing battle," I commented, as I saw my precious collection of love letters disappearing over the rooftops of Rome like big white butterflies.

"Just as long as we have peace," Rudi said.

The children had thrown away the last of the letters and were now looking around for more. Would there ever be any more? I wondered. Perhaps now was the time to give up young men before they gave me up.

I went back into the house, leaving everyone on the terrace. It was June 22, 1976, and I had just decided once more to give up sex.

As I went into the kitchen to make a cup of tea, the front doorbell rang. Who on earth could it be? I wasn't expecting anyone.

The bell rang again, insistently—a youthful, impatient, masculine ring.

I hurried into the outer hall and opened my front door.

A selection of books published by Penguin is listed on the following pages.

For a complete list of books available from Penguin in the United States, write to Dept. DG, Penguin Books, 299 Murray Hill Parkway, East Rutherford, New Jersey 07073.

For a complete list of books available from Penguin in Canada, write to Penguin Books Canada Limited, 2801 John Street, Markham, Ontario L3R 1B4.

NOSTALGIA ISN'T WHAT IT USED TO BE
Simone Signoret

Provocative, passionate, intelligent, and witty, Simone Signoret leads several lives. In private, she is the wife of the celebrated actor and singer Yves Montand. As a political activist, she has traveled widely, involving herself in important issues and encountering such leaders as Nikita Khrushchev and Marshal Tito. As an actress, she has created unforgettable characters in films like *Room at the Top* (for which she won an Oscar) and, most recently, *Madame Rosa*. Starting with her life in Paris before World War II and through the Nazi occupation, her debut in films, marriage, and international acting successes, Signoret tells a story studded with famous names, filled with courage and drama, a story she shares fully in this vital and warmly human memoir.

DEAR ME
Peter Ustinov

Peter Ustinov—actor, film and opera director, playwright, novelist, producer, short-story writer, and one of the most brilliant and well-known entertainers of our time—displays his much admired talent as a raconteur in these scintillating memoirs of his adventurous life, a story so droll and colorful that even Ustinov could not have invented it.

LOVE FOR LYDIA
H. E. Bates

Lydia is a beautiful English girl growing up in the 1920s. She is also wayward, passionate, and utterly unpredictable. "Don't ever stop loving me . . . even if I'm bad to you," she demands of her lover, Richardson, and Richardson swears that he will never stop. But how can he know that love for Lydia will be so dangerous? . . . *Love for Lydia* has been a recently acclaimed television dramatic series. "A compelling story . . . vital in its characterizations, and especially rich in its rendering of natural and seasonal detail"—*The New York Times Book Review*.

THE GLITTERING PRIZES
Frederic Raphael

This witty and sardonic novel is based on the highly praised television series. From their student years at Cambridge in the 1950s to the onset of middle age two decades later, a small and talented group of men and women pursue "the glittering prizes" that success in an acquisitive society can offer. Although they achieve varying degrees of material wealth and spiritual poverty, none of them will ever forget those heady, golden days at Cambridge spent unraveling the knots of friendship and in exploratory sex and badinage. "There are many stories here, and in all aspects of writing, this book goes beyond simple entertainment"—*Publishers Weekly*.

MURDER ON THE YELLOW BRICK ROAD
Stuart Kaminsky

The yellow brick road ran through the famous *Wizard of Oz* sound stage at M.G.M. studios. On November 1, 1940, a dead man lay upon it, blood from the knife wound in his chest flowing along the cracks of the bricks. Summoned by the young and frightened starlet Judy Garland, private detective Toby Peters tries to hold off the police and the reporters, protect M.G.M. from unpleasant notoriety, and make sense of the few slim clues. Before long, he realizes that he is confronting nothing less than a plot against the life of Miss Garland herself. Enlisting her help (as well as that of Clark Gable and Raymond Chandler), Peters uncovers further clues. He knows he is near to the shocking truth when shots are fired at him from a passing car and he is attacked in a motel, almost demolished by a muscle-man, and falls victim to an outrageous frame-up, with the police closing in. "Toby Peters is a tough guy, faced with some tough opponents. . . . It's a cute idea, if any murder can be described as cute, and Mr. Kaminsky has a high old time with his Hollywood characters"—*The New York Times Book Review.*